RACING HEARTS

RACING HEARTS

KEVIN ROBERT ALDRICH

For Holly, Jayda, and Taegon

CONTENTS

1

Lᴏɴᴅsᴀʏ Rʜᴏᴅᴇs ꜱᴛᴏᴏᴅ at her desk, fingers flying over her keyboard. Her desk was pushed up against a bay window that overlooked the San Francisco street from her third-floor walk-up apartment in the heart of the theater district. The afternoon late-winter sun was shining and the sky was deep blue and full of California promises. Throngs of workers, tourists, families, and residents made their way up and down the sidewalk looking for souvenirs, a bite to eat, or merely an uncomplicated commute back home.

If her windows had been open, Lindsay would have heard the buzz and bustle of the crowds and the traffic. She would have smelled the street food—fresh noodles and dumplings, sausages and hot dogs, even fried tofu. Her stomach might have growled, helping her to realize she hadn't eaten in a very long time.

But Lindsay's windows weren't open.

She didn't smell any food. Her stomach was growling, but she didn't notice it.

And she didn't hear anything beyond the voices of her two colleagues through the wireless noise-cancelling headphones that covered her ears.

And she couldn't see the blue sky or the shining sun because her vision was blocked by three massive 42-inch computer screens arrayed two feet in front of her face in a configuration that mirrored the shape of the bay window. Code-filled windows in black and white covered the monitors in well-ordered chaos.

Lindsay Rhodes didn't care about tourists, street food, or blue sky.

When she was working she was focused on the job at hand.

And she was almost always working.

"Raj, have you got that second node online yet?" said Lindsay.

"Coming up in two seconds, boss," said Raj.

From the corner of her eye, Lindsay could see Raj's bearded face move in the video call on her leftmost screen. His voice came through her high-definition, noise-cancelling, wireless over-ear headphones. It felt like the voice was nestled in a corner of her brain, back by her left auditory area, though Lindsay was sure that was only a cognitive artifact caused by her using the left monitor for her video feed.

Lindsay made a few more keystrokes.

"Marina, how's that now?" she said. "Can you see the changes?"

Lindsay waited for a few seconds, listening to the clack of Marina's keyboard keys through her headphones.

"Yep, I can see it now," replied Marina. "Looks good."

Lindsay nodded to herself.

"It's been more than two seconds, Raj," she said.

"Forgive the imprecision, Linds," Raj replied. "Probably a rounding error. I'll be sure to use eight significant figures next time."

Lindsay snorted at the joke.

"Try it now," Raj said.

Lindsay touched the arrow keys on her keyboard, scrolling through her last few commands on a window in the corner of her center screen. When she found the one she wanted, she hit the Enter key with a bang.

After an agonizing few seconds as the white cursor winked deviously at her from its black background, Lindsay's monitor filled with information, scrolling vertically.

"Got it," she said. "Data is flowing now. Nice work, Raj."

"Anything for you, Linds," Raj said. "You know that."

Lindsay did not respond, focusing instead on another window where she was kicking off her library of data processing functions, setting them to work on the data pipeline that Raj had just gotten moving.

"Alright," she said, once satisfied with the progress, "the libs are cranking. How much data in there, Raj?"

"I'm seeing about 1.4 terabytes," said Raj.

"Okay," replied Lindsay with a sigh.

This setup was taking forever.

Lindsay tapped a few more keystrokes in a third window. A progress bar appeared on her monitor. She pulled it to her right-most screen and settled it in the upper-right corner.

"It's going to be a few more hours while this processes," she said, reading the number below the progress bar that represented the estimate of time remaining. Usually wrong, since so much depended on network traffic, bandwidth congestion, and simple CPU load, but useful as a general approximation, nonetheless. "Everything set on your side to pull the data in once it's ready, Marina?"

"It'll be there," replied Marina. "Just let me know when it's done and I'll refresh the staging tables."

"Just write a listener," said Raj. "Then it'll pick up as soon as it's ready."

"My rig is a finely-tuned instrument, Raj," said Marina. "I'll not be introducing useless processes just to satisfy your need for instant gratification."

"I don't *need* instant gratification," retorted Raj. "I just *want* instant gratification. Right now."

"And the prod environment is all ready to go, Marina?" said Lindsay.

"Yes, Lindsay," said Marina slowly, pushing her face closer to her webcam and opening her eyes wide for the camera. "For the tenth time, it's ready. We just need the data."

Lindsay sighed. She could spend hours—days, even—lost in the intricacies of writing code or analyzing data, but no matter how much optimization she did, she still ran into the inevitable limitations of physics and the current state of computer hardware.

And with the large amount of data her small startup handled for each new client, that meant lots of waiting.

Lindsay twisted her torso from side to side and rolled her neck on her shoulders. She was pretty sure the loud popping sounds she heard were not normal.

"Was that your neck?" said Marina.

"Yeah," said Lindsay.

"That can't be good," said Raj.

"You might need a doctor," said Marina. "Seriously."

"Or a good back rub," said Raj. "I can be there in six to ten hours, depending on traffic and flight schedules." He folded his fingers together and turned them inside-out toward the camera, stretching them, then rolled his neck and shoulders. "These muscles aren't just for show, you know," he said. "I give a mean massage."

"Maybe just a nap," said Lindsay. Her stomach growled loudly. "And maybe some dinner."

"Midnight snack for me," said Marina. "AKA lunchtime."

"You sure you're not a vampire, Marina?" said Raj. "It rains a lot in London. Perfect place for a vamp to hide out. No risk of sparkling in the sun that way."

With Marina's various piercings and her wild haircut, shaved on one side, long on the other, with blue streaks through jet-black hair, she did look like the vampires in some movies.

"Vampires don't actually sparkle, Raj," said Marina. "The sparkling effect is just an optical illusion that comes as they suck the last few pints of blood from your twitching body. Kinda like seeing stars before you pass out."

"You're the expert," said Raj.

"Just remember that, Raj, and we'll always be good."

"Roger roger, 'Rina."

Lindsay shared the window with the progress bar with the other two on the video call.

"There's the countdown timer," she said. "Let's be back by 95%."

"Peace out," said Raj.

"Never say that again, Raj," said Marina.

"Got it. Peace out, 'Rina."

"Lindsay, we've talked about this. You have no choice. The man has to be fired. Immediately."

Lindsay smiled, a distant, wan effort, her exhaustion finally catching up with her.

With a few more keystrokes, she set an alarm for herself to chime when the progress bar hit 90%. Then she muted her microphone and wandered to the kitchen.

She glanced at the clock on the wall.

It was the first time she'd left her desk in seventeen hours.

Sleep. Coffee. Food.

Not necessarily in that order.

Lindsay looked inside the refrigerator. A metal-and-white emptiness looked back at her. A box of energy drinks stood torn and abused on the top shelf, half-empty. On the middle shelf was a brown cardboard take-out carton from last night's food delivery.

The rest of the refrigerator was completely barren, a yawning accusation of neglect.

Lindsay opened last night's take-out carton.

Okay, maybe it was from two nights ago.

Or three.

The noodles were dry in places, stuck into interesting curls and gravity-defying shapes. The chicken looked a little brown around the edges, its meat dry and split. The entire dish had the appearance of an Instagram photo with a vintage filter applied.

Lindsay folded the carton closed and put it back on the refrigerator shelf.

She pulled open the cupboards. In one was a box of Kashi cereal with the top open. In another was one plate, one bowl, and one mug. In a third was a box of fruit leather and two protein bars.

The rest of the cupboards were as bare as the day Lindsay had moved in three years earlier.

Three-day-old take-out, stale Kashi, and protein bars.

Maybe she would sleep first.

Her stomach growled its opinion.

Lindsay sighed, closed the cupboard, and slid open a drawer filled with compostable potato-based utensils wrapped in equally-compostable plastic baggies. The contents rustled as the drawer slid open, a soft chitter of sad anticipation. She grabbed a baggie and the take-out carton from the fridge and flopped on the couch.

When she awoke, alarm blaring in her headphones, it was dark outside her windows, the yellow glow from the streetlamps gilding the blue glow from her computer screens. Lindsay had slid sideways on the couch, her face mashed against the couch cushions, her eyeglasses askew on her nose, her headphones canted over one ear. She still held her fork in one hand, arm extended awkwardly beneath her body, but the take-out carton had slid onto the floor, spilling over the thin grey carpet. When she sat up, a slender line of drool extended like spider silk from her lip to the couch, tugging gently as if urging her back to sleep.

Lindsay removed her glasses and rubbed her face hard to pull some blood back into it. Her mouth tasted like the underside of a muddy Labradoodle. She must have managed at least a few bites of the leftovers before she'd passed out.

Maybe it was the leftovers themselves that had caused her to lose consciousness.

She scraped the noodles and chicken off the floor and back into the cardboard box, reminding herself to clean the carpet stains later, then dumped the box into the garbage, grabbed an energy drink, and cracked it open. Lindsay wasn't super fond of the taste, but it was cold and fizzy and it gave her the jolt she needed to get her work done. She preferred coffee, but her standards were high and it took too long to make good espresso at home. So, as unhealthy as she knew they were, energy drinks were her go-to source of caffeine when she didn't have time to run to the coffee shop down the street.

Which was most of the time, these days.

"Holy mother of—" said Marina when Lindsay came in view of the webcam. "Did you fall down the garbage chute at a funeral parlor or something?"

Lindsay toggled on the selfie view of her camera. Her eyes were sunken, deep black circles underneath. Her blond hair was a tangled mess. And she had something shiny and wet on her cheek. She wiped it with her hand.

Butter sauce from the pasta.

Lovely.

"Be right back," she mumbled.

"That's a little better," said Marina when Lindsay returned, face wiped and hair at least moderately brushed. "Now you just look like a customer at a funeral parlor, not a dumpster diver." She tilted her head sideways in the camera. "And I don't mean the customers with the tears in their eyes, either," she said. "You look like the ones laid out in the basement. When's the last time you slept?"

"I just did," grumbled Lindsay.

"No, I mean *slept*. Like a proper eight hours. In a bed."

"I don't know," said Lindsay. "High school?" She thought for a moment. "No, middle school?"

"Woman, you need to start taking care of yourself."

"I do take care of myself," she snapped.

That was a lie. Lindsay knew it. And from the look on her face in the webcam, Marina knew it, too.

"I don't have time to take care of myself," Lindsay mumbled. "I've got too many more important things to do."

"Listen," said Marina, an uncharacteristic softness entering her tone, "I know you're busy. Hell, I admire the fuck out of you for everything you've done and everything you're doing. You're a badass, Lindsay. No doubt."

The energy drink finally worked into Lindsay's bloodstream. She quickly scanned her email, the usual mix of newsletters, shipping notices.

"But you're also a workaholic," Marina continued. "You've gotta take care of yourself."

Another in a series of scam emails from 'a law firm in London'. At least they'd moved on from the Nigerian prince.

"Not your business. Not your code packages. Not your analytics methodologies." Marina leaned closer to the camera. "Your. Self."

"Mmm hmm," said Lindsay, now reviewing the output from her code. Everything seemed to have processed without a hitch, thank goodness.

"Hey," Marina said, tapping at her microphone, "you listening to me?"

"Yes, yes, of course," murmured Lindsay, focusing on the output details. "Get some sleep. Take care of my code."

"Well, I'm glad to see my message of love and respect is resonating with you, at least."

"Is the prod environment ready to go, Marina?" asked Lindsay. "The data processing is at 93% now."

Marina sighed.

"Yes, Lindsay. It's ready."

"Okay, we'll need to refresh staging to test that everything's working before we cut over to prod."

"Just let me know when."

"Morning, ladies," said Raj, sipping a cup of coffee and grinning into the webcam.

Lindsay didn't say anything, focused instead on parsing the performance metrics from her processing run. Marina was silent, as well.

Raj's grin slowly faded.

"Or whatever greeting is time-zone appropriate for you," he said.

"That greeting isn't even time-zone appropriate for you," said Marina. "What time is it in Texas right now, eight PM?"

"It's always morning in Texas, 'Rina," said Raj, his broad grin returning to life. "And afternoon and evening and nighttime. The sun never sets on the Lone Star state."

"Good thing," Marina retorted. "Your electrical grid wouldn't hold out if it did."

"Spoken like a true Londoner."

"I'm from New York."

"That explains a lot," said Raj.

"You're from Mumbai."

"A quirk of my birth. My heart was born right here in Austin."

"So you were born without a heart? When do you think you'll get it—"

"Okay, okay," said Lindsay. If she didn't intervene, those two would go on all night. "We're at 97%. CPU history looks good on my side. Raj, how does it look on your end?"

"Smooth as glass, Linds. Low skew, low impact. Looking good."

"Okay, I'm going to share my screen." Lindsay tapped a few buttons and pulled up a browser window, sharing her screen so the others could see it, too. "Logging in to the client portal now."

She tapped in some login credentials that allowed Lindsay to see exactly what the client would experience when they accessed their new data portal. While the portal loaded, a vector graphic showing the head of a blonde woman wearing glasses and striking a thoughtful pose, chin cupped between thumb and forefinger, appeared on the screen above a progress bar.

"I still love that," muttered Marina. "I did one hell of a job, if I do say so myself. It's a perfect likeness of you, Lindsay."

Lindsay said nothing. The graphic did look like her, which made her mildly uncomfortable, but it was just a splash screen. It appeared for two or three seconds, at most, while the system loaded. Hardly anything to get uncomfortable about.

And Lindsay didn't want to rob Marina of her fun. Marina worked her ass off and was fully dedicated to the startup. On top of that, she was a genius front-end web developer.

"Even got the brown on the eyes just right," said Marina.

"Almost," said Raj.

"What do you mean 'almost'?" Marina said. "It's perfect."

"No," said Raj. "Lindsay's eyes are more chocolately than that."

"Chocolatey? Save the ad copy for your wank sessions, Raj." Raj's face blushed. Lindsay tried her best to tune them out. She hated it when their banter moved in this direction. "I sampled that eye color from a series of screenshots, okay? Blended it on color, luminosity, brightness, etcetera. It's spot on."

The graphic disappeared, replaced by a series of charts and tables, all of which were currently empty.

A bell dinged in Lindsay's headphones.

"Okay, processing is complete," she said, glad for a reason to pull the conversation back to a work topic. "Go ahead and refresh the staging environment, Marina."

"Already on it." After a few seconds, Marina said, "go ahead and refresh now."

Lindsay refreshed the browser screen. The charts and tables flashed through an animation Marina had made where they all seemed to fill with data, like someone was pouring water into them. It was useless, really, but Marina had insisted that it added a touch of whimsy and humanity to an otherwise dry data dashboard. Since Marina had cleverly written the animations in such a way that they didn't add much overhead to the code, and since the animation used time when the user would be waiting for the data to load anyway, Lindsay had no real objection.

"Look at those beautiful animations," cooed Marina. "Buttery smooth. Get me some popcorn. Like watching a Pixar movie."

"Yeah, Loco," said Raj, barking a laugh.

Marina and Lindsay were silent.

"Come on," Raj said. "Loco? Like Coco?"

No response. Lindsay and Marina were deadpan.

"That was a good one. You guys wouldn't know humor if it punched you in the face."

"With a little luck, it'll punch you in the face for that lame-ass joke," said Marina.

"Okay, data is loaded," said Lindsay. She played with a few of the charts, changing settings, hovering over them to see the tool tips, little pop-up windows with detail on the data. She adjusted date ranges and filters to check for response times. "Looks good," she said. "You ran the full QA suite, Marina?"

"Of course. 100% green."

"Okay, switching to prod." Lindsay changed a part of the web address and refreshed the page. The vector graphic came up again, followed by the animation of the charts and tables loading.

"Loco," muttered Marina. "Ought to have WALL-E turn you Inside Out for that joke."

"Okay, Dad," said Raj. "And you think my Coco reference was lame?"

The data loaded, Lindsay clicked through everything again, checking for responsiveness. She set a few filters and parameters, checking the results on the display against her own calculations to verify the accuracy of the information.

A notification popped up in the upper right corner of her screen, alerting Lindsay that an email had just arrived. More spam from the London law firm. Even for a spammer, they were annoyingly persistent.

"Data looks good," she said. "Response times look good. Raj, how's the server?"

"What did that email just say?" asked Marina.

"Cool as the other side of the pillow," Raj said. "Should have no trouble with the anticipated server load."

"Did that say Marinelli, Loufer, and Hayes?"

"Okay, good," said Lindsay, feeling the edge come off her tension for the first time in over a week. They'd been grinding to get this new client up and running, despite several spec shifts and a whole new dataset added on at the last minute. Lindsay had doubled their fee to cover the scope creep and make sure it was worth their while, but it had been a slog for the whole team. "I think we're ready to open it up to UAT."

User Acceptance Testing, or UAT, was the last stage before final handoff, when the job was done and Lindsay could collect the rest of her much-needed payment. Lindsay dreaded UAT the most, since it was the stage when actual users from the client team, users who often had no idea what they were talking about, would ask all kinds of stupid questions and make tons of stupid requests that would often require a complete rewrite to implement.

In the UAT stage, Lindsay had to put on her founder and CEO hat, act diplomatic, address each concern as if it weren't completely asinine, and generally make everyone go away as quickly and as happily as possible. Then she'd get her money and could pay her company's bills. And her own.

All, somehow, without completely losing her mind.

"Marinelli, Loufer, and Hayes, like the London law firm?" said Marina.

"What are you on about now, Rina?" said Raj.

"Lindsay," said Marina.

Lindsay was still thinking about UAT, steeling herself for the ordeal.

"Lindsay?"

She would start tomorrow. She could wait until then to let the client know the portal was ready.

"Hey, Lindsay!" Marina snapped her fingers into the microphone.

"What, Marina?"

"Damn, woman, you really need to get some sleep. You're barely even here half the time."

"I know, I know, Marina. Take care of myself. I get it."

"Forget that," Marina said. "I mean, don't forget that. Do it. But forget it for the moment. Why are you getting emails from the most prestigious law firm in London?"

"What are you talking about?"

"Marinelli, Loufer, and Hayes."

Raj and Lindsay gave her blank looks.

"MLH? They're in the magic circle."

Raj spluttered a laugh. "Magic circle? Is that some kind of Old English cult, like Druids or Stonehenge or something?"

"No, Raj, it's what they call the top law firms in the UK. MLH is the law firm that repped Tommy Danforth in that defamation trial that ended last month."

"Tommy Danforth the actor?" said Raj. "Like"—he used a deep movie-trailer voice—"Agent Will Sharp has one chance to save the world. That Tommy Danforth?"

"Yeah, that one," said Marina. "It was all over the papers over here. He hired the best law firm in the country—hell, maybe in all of Europe—and they mopped the courtroom with his ex. Made her and her lawyers look like total idiots."

"Dang," said Raj. "You suing somebody, Lindsay?"

"What?" said Lindsay. "No, it's just spam or something. Some kind of scam."

"Hmm, maybe, but I doubt MLH would let spammers get away with using their name for long. Did you check the headers on the email?" asked Marina.

"Why would I do that?"

"Look, if MLH was emailing me," said Marina, "I'd want to reply. Those guys are fucking rock stars."

"Pull up the source, Linds," said Raj. "Let's take a look."

Lindsay pulled up the raw source code, showing the code behind the email itself, including the path it had taken to get to her inbox. If the email were fake, there would often be clues in the source code. A really good spammer could hide their tracks, but most didn't bother. They weren't interested in snaring the recipients who would comb through an email's source code to prove its authenticity. They were looking to fool the people who barely knew how to turn on their computers.

"Addresses all match," said Raj.

"And the return path is legit," said Marina. "I think this is real. What do the emails say, Lindsay?"

"I don't know," Lindsay replied. "I never read them. I just delete them right away."

Marina shook her head and sighed.

"I'm... not even going to comment on that," she said. "Just open this one, okay? Let's see what it says."

Lindsay double-clicked on the email.

From: Marinelli, Loufer, and Hayes
Subject: Estate settlement
To: Lindsay Rhodes

Dear Ms. Rhodes,

We have repeatedly attempted to contact you regarding the settlement of your late father's estate. We will continue to attempt contact until we succeed, per the very specific instructions in your late father's last will and testament.

Upon receipt of this message, please contact us at your earliest convenience using the contact information provided below. Please note that, while we will not proceed without your participation, this is a matter of some urgency. Your immediate attention in this delicate matter will be greatly appreciated.

Once again, we are very sorry for your loss. We look forward to speaking with you soon.

Sincerely,
Margaret Hayes, Partner
Marinelli, Loufer, and Hayes

"Damn, Lindsay," said Raj in a whisper. "I didn't know your father died. I'm so sorry."

"I didn't know, either," said Lindsay.

Lindsay's mind whirled.

How could this be real? In her whole life, she'd never met her father, had never even spoken with him. Her mother had always described him as an irresponsible, irrational free spirit who wanted nothing to do with Lindsay or her mother. She said he lived in England, far away from where Lindsay and her mom lived in upstate New York. Lindsay's mom had written him off, refused to waste any tears or energy on him. Barely even spoke of him.

So, Lindsay had learned to do the same.

The last time Lindsay thought about her father was when she was maybe thirteen years old, when a persistent, youthful curiosity had prompted her mother to finally share the full story with her.

Lindsay's father had written her off, so she'd written him off, too.

And now some lawyer was contacting her because her father, for some reason, had put her in his will.

"I didn't think you and your father were close," said Marina.

"We weren't," said Lindsay. "I never knew him."

They were all silent for a long moment.

"Well," whispered Marina, "it looks like he knew you."

2

LINDSAY STOOD beside her bed and checked her black carry-on bag for the fifth time, making sure she had everything she would need for the trip to England. Three pairs of high-waisted dark grey jeans, four light-grey t-shirts and two black sweaters, all rolled into tight cylinders and slotted carefully into the suitcase. Plenty of underwear and socks. Hairbrush, toothbrush, toothpaste, floss.

With the outfit she was wearing on the plane—dark grey jeans, light-grey t-shirt, black-on-black low-top Vans, and a black wool blazer—she figured she'd have enough to get her through however long it took to get this over with. She had no idea what to expect, but had always heard that probate proceedings could take a long time. She hoped she'd be back in San Francisco by the weekend, five days from now, but figured it could take as much as a week. Worst case would be ten days. She had plenty of clothing to make it that long.

Maybe even too much. She was considering removing one pair of jeans, one t-shirt, and one sweater when her phone began to chime. Lindsay slid on her wireless headphones and tapped a button on the earpiece.

"You ready?" said Marina.

"I think so," replied Lindsay, staring down at her bag again. "I think I overpacked."

"Show me," said Marina.

Lindsay held her phone over the bag, camera on.

"That's all you're bringing?"

"Too much?" asked Lindsay.

Marina smacked her lips and said nothing for a moment.

"So when do you leave?" she asked.

Lindsay checked her watch and flipped the camera around so she and Marina could see each other's faces while they talked.

"The car should be here in twenty minutes to take me to the airport."

"Right on," said Marina. "Then non-stop to Heathrow."

"Yes, ten hours and twenty-eight minutes flight time, then four hours and thirty minutes drive to Skipsea."

Marina clapped her hands excitedly.

"Wow, Lindsay, so cool. Marinelli, Loufer, and Hayes are swanking you out from San Fran to London. First-class on British Airways. Your father must have had some money. What was his name again?"

Lindsay shrugged.

"I don't know," she said. "My mother never told me and I never bothered to ask."

Marina just nodded silently.

Lindsay could tell Marina wanted to say something. And Lindsay knew most people would find it weird that she knew so little about her father. It wasn't like he was some vagrant or some one-night stand. Her parents had had a relationship. Her mother had known her father's name, had known he lived in England. For all Lindsay knew, her mother might have had his address and phone number.

But Lindsay was certain that her mother had had no contact with Lindsay's father during Lindsay's life. And she could tell by the way her mother's face hardened whenever the subject of her father came up that there was no love lost between the two. She didn't know exactly why, but she knew enough.

According to her mother on the one time they'd discussed the topic when Lindsay was thirteen years old, Lindsay's father had been impulsive, passionate, irrational, and immature.

And he'd been incredibly dashing and handsome, too.

While studying abroad in England during graduate school, her mother had been taken in by his charm and his good looks. That summer, they'd had a whirlwind affair before her mother had regained her senses and returned home to America. When she had told him weeks later about her pregnancy, Lindsay's father had wanted nothing to do with it.

And that was all Lindsay needed to know.

He'd made his decision twenty-six years ago.

Lindsay's father didn't want her.

And, aside from a brief exploration when she was thirteen and filled with the initial rush of pubescent hormones, Lindsay didn't want him, either.

"I wonder what your mother would say about all this," said Marina.

Lindsay sighed.

"She'd probably tell me to do what needed to be done and move on with my life. Sign the papers. Sell the estate or whatever. Tie up all the loose ends."

Her mother had died three years earlier, just after Lindsay had gotten her first big client for her startup.

You have to control your own life, Lindsay, she would say. *If you don't, someone else will pull all your strings. You'll be a puppet forever.*

She'd been Lindsay's champion her whole life, encouraging her to leave the big tech firm that had been her first employer after college and strike out on her own.

"She'd tell me to make it go away, then put it all behind me forever and forget it ever happened."

Lindsay zipped her suitcase shut, corner to corner to corner. Zip. Zip. Zip.

Always the little corners left over at the beginning and at the end, loose ends that interrupted the satisfying certainty of zipping shut the other three sides.

"And that's what I intend to do," said Lindsay, pulling her suitcase off the bed and onto the hardwood floor, wheels down.

Marina pursed her lips upward and shrugged.

"Okay, there you go," said Marina. "You've got a plan."

Lindsay wheeled her bag into the living room and checked her watch.

Fifteen minutes until the car would be there.

"You gonna have time to meet me in London?" asked Marina. "First time face-to-face. A rare opportunity to meet the whole package." She leaned back and gestured up and down her body with her hands.

Lindsay could only see her head and torso, all she'd ever seen of Marina. She'd hired Marina via video conference, based on the portfolio on her website, and had worked with Marina remotely for the last three years. Same with Raj.

"I don't know," said Lindsay. "The schedule will be pretty tight."

Marina's face fell into an expression of disbelief.

"Lindsay, come on," she said. "I live in London. You live in San Francisco. You're on an all-expenses paid trip to England. If you don't meet up with me then, when will it ever happen?"

"No, no, I know," said Lindsay. "It's just, I'm sure there's a lot they'll need me to do and I want to get back here as soon as possible to start on the Brinksley setup."

"We all work remotely, Lindsay. You can work on the Brinksley job from literally anywhere in the world."

That was technically true, but Lindsay had tried working in places other than her apartment. Coffee shops were too loud. Green spaces were too itchy. Hourly office rentals were too uncomfortable, and a waste of money, besides. Lindsay liked her setup at home, with everything arranged just the way she wanted it.

"When's the last time you left the house, Lindsay?"

Lindsay sighed.

"Why would I need to leave the house, Marina? I've got too much to do."

"Oh, I don't know," said Marina. "For food?"

"Doordash."

"I mean real food. Groceries."

"Instacart."

"Okay, how about shopping, then. Retail therapy?"

"Waste of money," said Lindsay. "And, also, Amazon."

"Of course. The mighty Zon." Marina's tone grew softer. "What about exercise?"

"Peloton."

Lindsay glanced at the machine in the corner, gathering dust.

"Recreation? Fun? Maybe see a movie?"

"Netflix. Hulu. HBO Max. Amazon Prime."

Marina stared into the camera for a beat.

"What about friends, Lindsay?" she said quietly. "Or a boyfriend?"

Lindsay liked Marina. A lot. Since her mother's passing, Marina was the closest thing to a best friend in Lindsay's life.

But she also liked the ability to switch the camera off when she wanted to, or to ignore an incoming call. To interact on her own time and on her own terms.

With friends in real life, they had a tendency to interrupt at very inconvenient times, times that were good for them, with no concern as to whether they were inconveniencing others.

And boyfriends?

They had a tendency to create all kinds of inconvenient problems.

"I've got too much to do," muttered Lindsay. "Besides," she added, "I've got you, Marina. You're my friend."

Marina smiled into the camera, but there was something off, some wistful distance in the eyes, perhaps, that made the smile a little less bright. Lindsay could feel the disquiet in Marina's expression, but couldn't quite identify the source of the feeling.

And that fact made Lindsay very uncomfortable. She liked to be able to identify things, to measure and analyze them, to understand how they worked in every possible detail.

"I am definitely your friend, Lindsay," said Marina firmly. "You can count on that."

Marina clapped her hands and leaned forward, making her face comically huge and warped, nose-first, in the camera.

"Which means you're definitely going to come and see me in London before you leave, right?" she said.

Between the combination of the comic image on her screen and the desperate optimism in Marina's voice, Lindsay couldn't help but laugh.

It felt good to laugh.

She couldn't remember the last time she'd laughed.

Maybe she should watch some comedy movies on the plane.

"I'll try, Marina," she said. "That's all I can promise."

"I know that's all I'm gonna get," said Marina, "so that's good enough for me."

Out her window, on the street three floors below, Lindsay saw an elegant black Cadillac sedan pull up to the curb.

"Gotta go, Marina. Looks like my ride is here."

As Lindsay clicked off the call, a large, muscular man with a shaved head got out of the driver's side of the car. He wore a black suit with a white shirt and a black tie. As he turned inside the nook of the car door and smoothly buttoned his suit coat, his eyes scanned the street and the sidewalks in both directions.

He looked incredibly calm and incredibly competent, like one of those drivers in movies who can handle any situation, from picking up the dry cleaning to killing the crazed assassin with their pinky finger while holding the door open for their employer.

As she watched him, the driver looked up, looked right at Lindsay's window.

Looked right at Lindsay.

Lindsay stepped back and shivered involuntarily.

What on earth was she getting herself into?

The next seventeen hours were a haze of travel-induced anxiety, boredom, and discomfort. The ride to the airport proceeded silently and efficiently, with the driver polite and professional, working through traffic with the speed and skill of a race car driver, while somehow making the ride so smooth that Lindsay could have closed her eyes and imagined she were sleeping in her bed at home the whole time.

The driver did not take her to the international terminal, as Lindsay was expecting, but dropped her off at a small building on the outskirts of the airport, near the employee parking lot, where a beautiful dark-haired woman in a neat black pantsuit and a British Airways scarf greeted her with a bright white American smile and a soft, soothing British accent. A man took Lindsay's bag from the driver while the woman led Lindsay through the building to a car waiting on the tarmac. It drove Lindsay directly to the massive airplane. It towered above her, gleaming white metal in the afternoon sun, as she climbed the stairs of a rolling jetway directly into the first-class cabin.

No waiting in line like cattle at security. No dehumanizing need to undress and be scrutinized, to stand in the airport in your socks, holding your pants up by the waistband so they wouldn't fall, beltless, around your knees. No wandering through the terminal looking for something remotely edible or idly wasting time waiting for the plane to board.

The driver had taken Lindsay to the building, and ten minutes later, she was seated on the airplane in a wide oval seating area, a mix between a high-class office cubicle and one of those egg-shaped nap pods that companies like Google had to distract their employees from realizing how much of their lives were being spent in service of someone else's wealth creation.

This must be how the other 0.1 percent lives.

Over the next eleven hours, more elegant, scarved women and the occasional trim, black-vested man catered to Lindsay's every need. They offered her champagne, cognac, orange juice, and water. They fed her pan-fried stone bass with grilled fennel and saffron beurre blanc for dinner with warm apricot sponge pudding and a cheese platter for dessert, then fresh-baked fruit scones with clotted cream and strawberry preserve for breakfast before landing.

During that time, Lindsay very intentionally avoided making eye contact with the tech bro wearing the $400 blue hoodie in the cubicle beside her. When it looked like he was giving up on subtlety and was going to come over to try actually talking to her, Lindsay donned her wireless headphones, stared straight at the very large television screen in front of her, and tried to watch a comedy movie. Something with Rosalind Carter and Pete Raglund where he hits his head and forgets who he is while she tries to convince him that he's her husband and has to wait on her hand and foot.

The movie was vapid and completely nonsensical, but it shut tech bro down enough for Lindsay to eat her dinner in peace. After the cheese plate and the tiny glass of port they handed her as a digestif, she must have fallen asleep, because the next thing she knew she was being tapped ever so respectfully on the shoulder by a flight attendant bearing breakfast scones.

Before the seat belt sign had even been turned off, Lindsay

had been escorted from the plane to another car waiting on the tarmac, her luggage already stowed in the back, and whisked away by yet another über-competent driver on the long journey to Skipsea.

"Straight to the office, miss," said the driver in a warm, rural British accent, "or would you prefer to stop at the residence to rest for a bit?"

Lindsay leaned her head back against the seat. The cool leather soothed her neck, aching from hours on the plane. Even in first-class, with a cubicle as big as a bedroom, she had still woken up stiff and sore. She wanted nothing more than to go to the residence and sleep for a few hours.

"Straight to the office, please," she told the driver.

Better to get things moving. The sooner they started, the sooner she could get back home and get to work.

Her throat was dry and ragged from disuse. She smacked her dry lips and swallowed hard.

"Beverages in the center console, if you like, miss," said the driver. Lindsay could see his kind eyes in the rear-view mirror, watching her. "Still and sparkling water, cold tea, juice. Please help yourself."

Lindsay opened a well-hidden flap in the wide console between the front seats and found a compact mini-fridge stocked with a dozen small plastic bottles. "Thank you," she rasped as she opened a bottle of still water and took a long pull.

She checked her watch

The battery was dead.

"I don't suppose you've got a watch charger in here, do you?" muttered Lindsay.

"Wireless charging pad on top of the refrigerator, miss," replied the driver. His eyes crinkled when he saw her surprised expression.

Lindsay set her watch on the pad and watched the screen come to life, glowing gratefully as it fed off the car's power.

She pulled her phone—still charged to fifty percent—from her pocket and checked the local time.

Two-thirty in the afternoon. That meant six-thirty in the morning in San Francisco.

No wonder Lindsay felt like she'd been hit by a truck, despite the long sleep on the plane.

She checked their route on her phone. They'd be in Skipsea around six-thirty in the evening.

Despite her fatigue and the disorientation that comes with jetlag, Lindsay spent the car ride on her laptop answering emails from her latest client, the usual UAT questions that needed to be fended off. She figured they'd be ready to sign off by early next week.

Then she got started on the Brinksley job.

According to her website, Lindsay's company, Datasure, Inc., provided "business insights through advanced data science capabilities, delivered in an intuitive, fully-customizable interface with seamless responsiveness across all sizes of data repositories, from single-user databases to enterprise-scale installations". However, despite the customizability mentioned in the ad copy, they rolled the same basic package out to everyone, then tweaked things from there.

Raj handled the data engineering. He did it all from Austin, only having to go onsite with the client in the rarest of cases, mostly for very old companies who, for whatever reason, hadn't kept up with the latest data technology.

Marina had designed and built the web interface from the ground up. She would customize it with the company colors and logos and set up the user groups and access privileges on the back end. She would also design and code any custom charts or tables needed for a specific client.

Lindsay was responsible for the data-processing algorithms and code packages. Every client used the base packages, which Lindsay had written at home in the evenings during her last two years as a data scientist at her big tech job. The base package gave her clients ninety-five percent of what they would use.

But every client had a few quirks and special requests that required some additional coding. Maybe they needed a particular kind of machine-learned ranker or some kind of specific natural-language processing or an image detection system. Whatever it was, Lindsay would build it to spec for them, quickly, efficiently, and accurately.

That was what she loved to do.

That was what she was good at.

No, that was what she was great at.

She could do it more quickly, more efficiently, and more accurately than anyone else.

And that was why they paid Lindsay three times more than her nearest competitor.

When she could find someone willing to give her the job. Turns out finding clients was harder than the work itself, and a surprising number of companies, even big, wealthy ones, were looking for the cheapest offer they could find. They called it "good corporate stewardship", but really it was just good old-fashioned penny-pinching.

Absorbed in her work, Lindsay didn't notice the light fading around her as they drove, the sun dropping lower in the sky, reaching fingers of darkened gold through the tinted windows of the car. She didn't notice the car slowing as it pulled off the highway onto a small side street in the countryside. She didn't notice anything until, thinking about how many parameters the Brinksley team would really need to tweak in the random forest classifier she was coding, she happened to look up from her laptop and caught sight of the building growing larger ahead of them.

The grounds were pastoral, wide fields interspersed with thick copses of lush green trees. Coming from drought-stricken

California, Lindsay had not seen such an abundance of green in a long time.

The road they traveled described gentle arcs through the scene, winding lazily along, bringing Lindsay a sense of peace that settled into her subconscious like the heat of a warm fire and a hot cup of cocoa on a snowy night.

As they wound through the fields and trees, the wide, flat building ahead drew slowly closer. It, too, was built with gentle curves. The building was roughly kidney-shaped, with no angles on its facade at all. It occupied half of a massive round lake bordered with a low stone wall. The kidney shape of the building inside the circle of the lake formed a yang, of sorts, to the lake's yin. In the fading sun, the lights of the building filled the sky, an inviting cool white light that reflected off of the still water.

The walls of the building were fully glass, hundreds of windows joined by a lattice of supports barely visible to the eye, making the structure seem like two wafers of metal, the roof and the floor, floating above one another, suspended in air like two magnets of opposite polarity, pulled together by gravity, but held apart by the force of their own resistance.

Inside the glass windows, on the first floor of the two-story building, brightly lit by the blue glow of the cool lighting, were dozens of what looked like cars. Was this just the parking structure? If so, it was the most elaborate parking structure Lindsay had ever seen. Marinelli, Loufer, and Hayes must have more dollars than sense if they were willing to waste money on such an elaborate building just to park their cars.

As they drew closer, though, Lindsay saw an outdoor lot, a traditional parking lot filled with cars, situated behind the building itself. And she could see now that the cars inside the building were painted in various shades of blue and purple, the paint jobs too similar to be caused by random human selection, even considering the ways in which people were so easily influenced by fads and peer pressure and the need to be loved and accepted by those around them.

The driver pulled around the front of the building, giving Lindsay a clear view through the windows. The cars were race cars, polished and gleaming, covered in corporate logos, spanning construction styles that seemed to range from very old to very modern. Some cars looked more like the Wright Flyer than a race car, with wings as wide as the wheelbase set at the front and back on poles that reached three feet up over the cockpit of the car, presumably to provide a downforce as the car sped around the track. Other cars looked like something from a low-budget Batman movie from the sixties, with wide, fin-like chassis and wedge-like silhouettes, also undoubtedly optimized for aerodynamics. Anything to avoid wind drag.

At the other end of the lineup were the more familiar modern race car designs, which looked like prototypes for a new kind of ice scraper that some rich recently-minted millionaire IPO idiot would try to sell into the venture capital market as the next big-tech disruption. Revolutionizing the ice scraper market with an ice scraper on wheels, probably Wi-Fi enabled, possible autonomous. Just put it on your windshield when you got home at night and it would have your car cleared of snow when you were ready to head to work in the morning.

Why on earth Marinelli, Loufer, and Hayes would have so many race cars at their headquarters was beyond her. But, having such an elaborate headquarters in the first place seemed a waste of money to Lindsay, as was flying her all the way to England just to settle the estate of a man Lindsay had never known.

But if they wanted to waste their money, who was Lindsay to stop them? She would find out what they wanted, sign whatever documents were necessary, and head home to get back to work.

The driver pulled to a stop at the far end of the kidney-shaped building, under an overhanging roof. He held the back door open.

When she stood from the car, Lindsay was greeted promptly by a tall, lean woman in a charcoal grey pantsuit with a wide-collared white shirt opened elegantly at the neck. The woman's greying blonde hair was pulled back along the sides of her head and gathered in a pony-tail that draped down to her shoulder blades. Somehow, the style was neither severe nor childish on her, but instead lended her an air of both approachability and immense dignity.

She approached, hand held out. Her hazel eyes twinkled, as if they held a wisdom Lindsay could not yet fathom. Despite the greying hair, the woman's skin was smooth and unwrinkled. Her age could have been anywhere from forty to a well-preserved seventy, for all Lindsay could tell.

But as she took the woman's hand and shook it slowly, Lindsay felt light-headed. She could see the woman's mouth moving, but the sound of her voice was muffled in Lindsay's ears. Her thoughts spun through her mind, struggling to connect with each other, struggling to form a coherent whole.

Lindsay's daze wasn't from the jetlag or the demands of the long journey she had just completed.

It was from something far more jarring.

"Lindsay Rhodes?" said the woman, the sound finally reaching Lindsay's brain.

The woman's voice both soft and incisive, her accent the most refined Britain could possibly have to offer.

"I'm Margaret Hayes, of Marinelli, Loufer, and Hayes."

Margaret Hayes looked exactly like Lindsay's late mother.

3

Lᴉɴᴅsᴀʏ ʙᴀʀᴇʟʏ ʜᴇᴀʀᴅ a word as Margaret Hayes gave her a quick tour of the facility.

They crossed the first floor of the building, Ms. Hayes discussing landscape design while pointing out the lake and the grounds still visible in the early dusk outside the panoramic windows. She provided the history of the company as they walked past a series of blue-and-purple race cars in the long showroom which occupied fully half of the first floor of the building. She relayed the conception of the structure while pointing out features of the architecture of the building itself, the curved walls, the segmented glass, the slate and metal aesthetic.

Lindsay was sure whatever Ms. Hayes was saying was fascinating, but she could barely wrangle her own thoughts, let alone process new information.

If Marina were there, she would say her mother had come to England to haunt her, and had taken the form of Margaret Hayes of Marinelli, Loufer, and Hayes.

But Marina wasn't there, and Lindsay did not believe in ghosts.

But she could barely believe the uncanny resemblance between this woman and her late mother.

And she could barely believe how long it was taking her to process this information. It had to have been the jetlag, the fatigue of travel. Lindsay had never traveled so far in her life. She must be a bad traveler, one of those people unduly affected by the disruption to their daily routine.

Lindsay didn't usually struggle to concentrate. No matter how late the time, no matter how long the hours, no matter how disruptive the new data, Lindsay prided herself on her ability to focus, to crank through the information, reduce the problem to its core elements, cut through the noise, and strike at the heart of the issue. At her big tech job, that's what had helped her solve so quickly problems that had plagued her data science colleagues for months.

But she'd been walking with Ms. Hayes for ten minutes and still could barely bring herself to hear the words coming from her mouth. Her mind was drifting in a fog of confusion.

She looked like Lindsay's mother. Big deal. Doppelgängers exist. It was simple coincidence. The odds were low, but non-zero.

Get over it.

As Ms. Hayes swiped a badge against a reader on the wall and led Lindsay through a set of wide doors into a row of conference rooms and offices at the far end of the building, Lindsay tried to shake herself back to reality. A long hallway with the same slate tile floors as the rest of the building curved gently into the distance. The walls were a gleaming, glassy white, with gunmetal grey accents from the fixtures on the doors and walls and the pendulum lights hanging from the high ceiling.

"I'm sorry, Ms. Hayes," said Lindsay, "but could you please direct me to a restroom?"

She needed to splash some cool water on her face, something to wake her up and bring her to her senses.

Plus, she hadn't peed in twelve hours.

"Of course, Ms. Rhodes," said Ms. Hayes, "I'm terribly sorry. I should have thought to show you that straight away." Ms. Hayes picked up her pace immediately, walking briskly down the hall toward the end of the building, her heels clicking against the slate tile floors. "The restrooms are back here near the showroom garage."

"There's a garage in here?" said Lindsay.

Ms. Hayes smiled.

"This venue is used to reveal the new cars to the press each season," she said. "Good for pictures, good for publicity."

Lindsay nodded.

"The garage is used for any last-minute tweaks, mechanical or cosmetic, that the cars may require."

"You keep a full garage to use only one day each year?" asked Lindsay.

Ms. Hayes tilted her head at Lindsay, a long, thoughtful look, a slight smile playing at the corner of her mouth.

An expression Lindsay had often seen from her mother.

A chill swept over her. She shivered for just a moment.

Her mother's incorporeal ghost passing through her body.

Lindsay spent way too much time on video calls with Marina late at night.

"When it's not being used for press reveals," said Ms. Hayes, "it's used as a regular garage, a sort of private workspace in addition to the production centre next door."

"Private for who?"

"Our team principal often uses the space for various purposes. Experimental designs, exploratory ideas, that kind of thing. He likes to stay separate from the team in the production centre so as not to disrupt their work."

"Production center?" said Lindsay. "So you manufacture the cars here on-site?"

"Yes, the cars are assembled here," nodded Ms. Hayes.

"Roughly ninety-five percent of the parts are manufactured here, as well. The remaining five percent come from a Japanese manufacturer."

Lindsay raised her eyebrows. Impressive to have that capability in one site. Makes for a much leaner, more efficient operation.

"That is the idea," said Ms. Hayes when Lindsay shared her thoughts. "Your late father wanted to bring one-hundred percent of manufacturing, assembly, and administration into this location, but was unable to achieve that goal before he died."

Lindsay shook her head, her mind again reeling into that annoying fog.

Her father?

Something suddenly occurred to her, something obvious that she should have seen right away. That she would have seen right away if not for her fatigue and disorientation.

Ms. Hayes was talking about a race car company, not a law office.

This wasn't the offices of Marinelli, Loufer, and Hayes at all.

This was something completely different.

Something to do with her father.

Had her father built this company?

"Here you are," said Ms. Hayes, gesturing toward a short hallway leading to the restrooms. "Shall I wait for you here?"

"Um, no," said Lindsay, her mind still dazed. "No, thank you. I'm sure I can find my way back."

Ms. Hayes nodded. "I'll be in conference room five, then," she said, gesturing back down the hall, "just down here on the left." The clicking of her heels grew quieter as she strode back from the direction they had come.

∼

Lindsay entered the women's restroom, a large space at least forty feet long and twenty feet wide, with a row of toilet stalls on her right, a long, tall mirror along the wall on her left, and another door at the far end. It had the same slate floors and glassy white walls as the rest of the building, but in this more enclosed space, it gave Lindsay an otherworldly feeling. With the soft blue-white glow of the overhead lights, she felt like she were in a spaceship, or floating in a cloud.

That image certainly matched the haze still lingering in her mind.

When she emerged from a stall, her body felt more comfortable, but her mind was still foggy. She pushed up the sleeves of her blazer and splashed cold water on her face, trying to wake up, trying to force herself to focus. But when she stared in the mirror, she couldn't recognize the face she saw there. Same face as always, long and square and pale. Same straggly blond hair, though a bit more unkempt and uneven than usual. Same weird orange-brown cat eyes.

But the face staring back at her didn't seem like her own. The mouth seemed slacker, the skin more pallid.

And the eyes. There was an emptiness in the eyes that she did not recognize.

Alone in a corporate bathroom, not recognizing her own face in the mirror?

This was like a scene from a psychological horror movie. She'd push her fingers through her cheeks and start tearing her face off next.

Lindsay shook her head and ripped a paper towel from the dispenser.

She was going nuts.

Had to be the jetlag.

Enough of this nonsense. She was going to pull herself together, ignore Ms. Hayes' uncanny—and purely coincidental

—resemblance to Lindsay's mother, dispatch her father's estate and head back to California to move on with her life.

Her perfectly normal, uncrazy life.

She tossed the paper towel in the trash and strode through the door.

Into a completely different room than she expected.

This wasn't the hallway she'd come from.

Instead, she was standing in a wide room lit blindingly bright by fluorescent lights overhead. The floors were concrete, white and slick and so clean Lindsay could see a shadowed version of her own reflection in the glossy floor sealant.

Ahead of her, against the far wall, was a white desk with a bank of computer monitors, a keyboard, and a mouse. To her right was a pair of thick black poles, eight feet high, spaced about six feet apart, standing straight up. From near the top of each pole, a thick metal arm extended perpendicularly for about ten feet, about seven feet above the floor, holding remarkably stable, considering their length and apparent weight. They must be lighter than they seem. Or counterbalanced in some clever way Lindsay could not discern from a distance.

To Lindsay's left stood two U-shaped bays formed by low, grey desks, a set of six monitors hung on the wall above each of them. Underneath the desks, Lindsay could see a variety of cabinets and drawers, even a few screens. Some kind of diagnostic workstation, she presumed.

What caught her eye, though, was the race car parked in the center of the closest bay, its chassis gleaming brilliant blue and dark purple in the fluorescent overhead lights. Some part of the car—a thin rounded shape that looked like a hood or some other part of the carapace—rested on the floor in front of the bay. Two men were bent over the car. Lindsay could see the back of one, his torso tucked deep inside the car's innards. The other, facing Lindsay, was watching his colleague from above. They both wore what looked like full-body coveralls, colored the same blue and purple as the car.

When Lindsay entered, the man facing her looked up. He startled at seeing her, his brow crinkling in confusion.

"Uh, boss," he said, quietly. "Someone's here."

Lindsay felt her cheeks grow hot. Disoriented though she was, she knew she had stumbled into someplace she shouldn't be.

"That you, Maggie?" called a deep voice from within the guts of the car, muffled by the layers of machine and metal. "I thought you were just going to text. Is it showtime already?"

"Not Maggie, boss," whispered the other man. "Don't know who it is."

Lindsay felt her heart beat in her ears. She knew she should just turn and go back through the bathroom, out the other door and back where she'd come from, but her body seemed to be frozen in place.

The man extricated himself from the car with some difficulty and turned toward Lindsay.

His face was pale, his jaw strong and angular. A streak of black grease sliced across one cheek. Sweat beaded on his forehead and streamed down his temples into his dark beard. His thick, unruly black hair stood high on his head, tangled and stiffened by the sweat and what had undoubtedly been a cramped space inside the car engine.

The man wiped his forehead with the back of his forearm, his coveralls leaving another streak of grease that mixed with his sweat and slowly slid down toward his brow.

"Who the hell are you?" he said.

His voice was deep, and he spoke with a sultry British—no, Scottish?—accent, soft and rhythmic, like Lindsay imagined the hills and valleys of Scotland to be.

Or like laying before a warm fire on a soft fur rug, with him running his hands over her own hills and valleys.

Lindsay shook her head quickly.

Where the hell did that come from?

"You're not supposed to be here," said the man. "I'll ask you to leave, please. Right now." He waved toward the door.

As appealing as the sound of the man's voice was to Lindsay—and it definitely was, bringing sensations to places in her body that only deepened her mental confusion—the abruptness in his tone rankled her. Lindsay had made an honest mistake, taken a wrong turn in a very confusing bathroom and wound up in this workspace quite by accident.

And weren't the English supposed to be unfailingly polite?

"There's no need to be rude," said Lindsay.

The man's jaw set. "Oh, well, I'm terribly sorry, miss," he said with a tone that implied he was anything but sorry, "but I wouldn't need to be rude if you hadn't just barged in here while we were working."

The confusing sensations deep in her body disappeared in an instant.

This guy was just another asshole.

Lindsay crossed her arms over her chest. At least she'd gained that much control over her body, but her hot cheeks and racing heart were now joined by a heavy tightness in her stomach, like she'd swallowed one of those greasy engine parts.

"Well, I'm sorry," said Lindsay, her voice much harsher than it needed to be. Her jetlag was really getting the best of her. "But that bathroom is very poorly labeled. There should be signs on the doors that clearly indicate where they lead."

"Oh, so now it's the bathroom's fault, is it?" said the man. He pulled a rag out of his back pocket and came around the corner of the bay, approaching Lindsay, wiping his hands.

As he came closer, Lindsay could see that he was tall.

Very tall.

And his shoulders were broad.

Very, very broad.

He wiped his forehead with the rag, removing the streaming grease just before it reached his thick, dark eyebrows, then put the rag in his back pocket and unzipped his coveralls.

"What are you doing?" asked Lindsay, taking a step backward, back toward the exit, suddenly aware of just how empty the room was, of the fact that she'd seen no other people in the entire building since she'd entered.

"I'm trying to fix this damn car," he said shrugging his arms out of the coveralls and tying them around his waist. With his coveralls around his waist, Lindsay could see just a white t-shirt, gleaming and pristine, untouched by any grease.

"And I'm trying to figure out why some woman has wandered into a restricted area and interrupted my work."

Soaked with sweat, the t-shirt clung tight to the man's muscular arms and chest, various tattoos peeking out on his right pectoral, both of his corded biceps, the inside of his left forearm.

Lindsay felt herself getting hot, as if someone had just cranked up the thermostat.

"That 'some woman'," she said, "is just trying to get where she's going and made an innocent mistake. You don't have to chew her head off about it."

"Oh, dear," said the man, running his hands through his thick hair, smoothing it into a curl on his head that made Lindsay's stomach do somersaults.

What was wrong with her? Maybe she should have gone to the residence to sleep for a while.

"Tut, tut, tut," continued the man. "Call 9-9-9, Gerald," he said over his shoulder to the other man, "she's referring to herself in third-person now." He shook his head with mocking sadness and stepped closer to Lindsay. "First signs of madness. And in someone so young, too. Such a shame."

He was close enough now that Lindsay could smell faint cologne mixed with his sweat, a spicy, musky, earthy smell that sent a flush of heat through the core of her body. It mingled with her anger, sending a confusing mix of fire throughout her entire body. Her mind was aflame with anger at the way he was treating her. The rest of her body was aflame with... something different.

Lindsay clenched her fists, both in anger and in an attempt to control her body.

He stepped even closer to her, now just a few feet away, so close that Lindsay could feel the heat coming off of his skin in waves. She could reach out and touch him, put her hands on those firm biceps, place her palm against his pecs to feel if his heart was racing as fast as hers, run her fingertips over his shirt where the sweat clung to the ridges of his abdominal muscles.

She looked up at his eyes. Lindsay was nearly six feet tall herself, and accustomed to looking down on the men around her. She couldn't remember the last time she'd met a man tall enough that she had to look up to meet his eyes.

And this man's eyes were an arresting, electric blue, a blue that shocked Lindsay, speared her and held her frozen, speechless.

Her body and her brain were glitching in very odd and very disturbing ways.

"Hello," said the man, waving his hands in front of Lindsay's face. "You there? You okay?"

But she knew what to do. In situations like this, she did what her mother had taught her.

Don't get distracted. Just get to work.

She clenched her fists even tighter, closed her eyes, and took a deep breath.

"Oh, Gerald, now she's gone to sleep," said the man.

The breath pulled in another whiff of the man's dizzying scent. She could smell a hint of citrus, now, mingled with the musk and the spice.

Glitch.

And the heat.

He radiated heat like a sun.

Glitch.

Don't get distracted, Lindsay.

"Thank you, sir," Lindsay bit down on the word, filling it with as much venom as she could, "I'll be going now."

"Oh, okay, you'll be going now," he said. "That's wonderful. Would you like me to show you out, or should I print some signs to lead you along?"

Lindsay opened her eyes and stared at the man, stared hard at those blue eyes, those tattooed muscles, that tall, broad body, that thick, dark hair.

She memorized it all.

Then filed it in her brain under 'asshole'.

Her body finally back under her full control, she turned and left the way she had come.

4

"THERE YOU ARE," said Ms. Hayes, standing as Lindsay strode into the conference room and shut the door behind her. "I was beginning to worry."

The conference room, like the rest of the building, was ultramodern in design, with the same slate tile floors, glassy white walls, and metal accents. One entire wall was covered in windows that looked out over the lake. Lights arrayed along a walking path that curved past the water dotted the grassy fields with splashes of gold. It wound near what looked like a helipad on the opposite side. A gentle evening breeze ridged the water and a series of cleverly placed lights gave the lake an otherworldly blue glow that contrasted beautifully with the golden pools of light on the fields.

In the center of the room, filling most of the space, was a long conference table, stained and polished to show off the grain of the dark walnut wood in the light from the overhead fluorescents. It was like all of the conference rooms at the big tech job Lindsay had worked at before she left to start her own company. Sleek, modern, expensive.

Soulless.

Lindsay counted fourteen leather chairs around the long table, but only one was occupied, near the end.

Ms. Hayes gestured to the chair opposite her and sat back down. Several stacks of papers and folders were arranged on the table in front of her. Her cell phone lay face down beside them.

"Can I get you anything?" asked Ms. Hayes. "Tea, coffee, bottled water?"

A nap, an espresso, a ride to the airport so she could get on the next flight home.

"No, thank you," Lindsay said as she sat down. "I'm fine. Will it just be the two of us?"

She had expected an army of lawyers, or maybe a roomful of angry, jilted family members, resentful that this American interloper had even been invited to the reading of their father's will.

She had probably seen too many bad movies.

"I have a colleague who should be joining us soon," Ms. Hayes said, "but I'll just get you orientated in the meantime." She opened a folder and drew out some papers.

"Okay, sure," said Lindsay, suddenly feeling more tired than she'd ever felt, like a thousand-pound elephant was sitting on her chest, pressing her into sandy ground, and all she wanted to do was sink and slip away. With the long journey, the lack of sleep, and that confrontation just now—her nerves still jangling, her irritation still pumping in her blood—Lindsay was nearing the end of her rope.

"I think we can make this quick," Lindsay said. "I really didn't know my father, had no contact with him at all. I'm not sure why he put me in his will or why I had to come all the way out here for it. I really don't want anything he has to give me, so if you have something you need me to sign so you can move on to the next person on the list, I'll just sign it and be on my way."

Ms. Hayes tilted her head at Lindsay, a quizzical expression on her face.

"You can just give his possessions to charity or whatever," said Lindsay. "Or keep them for yourself, if you like."

Ms. Hayes slid the papers back into the folder, tidied it with a tap on the table, laid it down carefully and folded her hands together on top of the folder, as if she were praying. She took a deep breath.

"Ms. Rhodes," she began, "do you know who your father was?"

That seemed to Lindsay to be an odd question from such a supposedly smart lawyer. Lindsay had already answered it.

"As I said, I really didn't know my father at all."

"No, I'm sorry. I understand that you didn't have any personal relationship with your late father," said Ms. Hayes, "but did you know who he was, in general? Did you know of him?"

Lindsay shook her head slowly. What was Ms. Hayes getting at?

"I don't even know his name, Ms. Hayes," said Lindsay, "but I really don't see how any of this matters. He didn't want a relationship with me or my mother, and we're fine with that." Lindsay corrected herself. "I'm fine with that. I've been fine with that for a long time. My mother and I got by just fine on our own."

Ms. Hayes eyes widened a touch, then filled with a wistful sadness.

"Your father's name was Kellen Hart," she said.

She tilted her head again, eyebrows raised, as if looking for a sign of recognition. Lindsay shrugged and shook her head. Ms. Hayes nodded slowly, sadly.

"He built this company," she gestured toward the room, "from nothing. From a dream and a passion he had." She paused for a moment. "Your father was a very passionate man," she said quietly.

Great. Did Lindsay really come all the way across the world

to listen to the ramblings of one of her father's former lovers? One of many, from the sounds of it.

"Not in the way you might be thinking," said Ms. Hayes, looking up at Lindsay as if reading her thoughts. "His passion was for his life and the people in it. He loved racing. And he loved this company. He knew each and every employee by first and last name. Knew their children, their spouses, even their latest boyfriends or girlfriends. This company," she sighed, "is a family."

Lindsay's body was betraying her. She tried to stay calm, to remain stoic. She stared hard at Ms. Hayes, not seeing her, just willing the sabotage within her to abate.

But, she hurt.

Ms. Hayes' words physically hurt her. Her chest was constricting like a snake had coiled around it, squeezing the blood from her body. Her fingers felt thick, like they might pop.

Her father had rejected his real family, his own flesh and blood, and gone off to build a new one filled with strangers.

That hurt.

But, I guess it's true what they say. You can't pick your family. You have to take what life gives you, in that regard.

Only her father had found a loophole. He had sent his family far away and built a new one, person by person. Hand-selected, hired one-by-one.

Lindsay reeled her pain in, willing herself back to her senses. This wasn't her. She didn't get emotional like this.

Had to be the jetlag. She checked her watch, doing the time zone conversions in her head. She hadn't slept in nearly a day, not counting the fitful doze on the plane. Between that and the rush to finish the last job at work, her body needed rest. Her brain needed rest.

Focus. Don't get distracted. Just do the work and move on.

"He sounds like a wonderful man, Ms. Hayes," said Lindsay, her voice steady and cool. "But if this company is such a close-knit family, and if it meant so much to him, there must be someone here who knew my father well. Better than me, certainly. Someone who might be more deserving of whatever my father has left behind."

Ms. Hayes smiled softly.

Lindsay heard a soft knock and the door opened behind her. Ms. Hayes stood.

"Hi, Mac," she said. "Please come in."

"Sorry I'm late," said a deep voice with a sultry Scottish accent that immediately set Lindsay's blood pumping into her ears again, her jaw clenching.

"Have a seat, Mac," said Ms. Hayes, gesturing to the empty chair at the head of the table, beside Lindsay. "We're just getting started."

Lindsay didn't stand, didn't even bother to look up.

"Lindsay Rhodes," said Ms. Hayes, "this is Cormac McEwan."

"We've met," said the man as he sat at the head of the table.

Typical asshole man, taking the seat at the head of the table as if it's his right purely by virtue of his gender.

Lindsay shook her head in frustration. He was definitely an asshole, but Ms. Hayes had told him to sit there, had pointed to the chair. Why was Lindsay acting so irrationally?

"Have you?" said Ms. Hayes, her eyes moving back and forth between Lindsay's face and the man's face. It was clear from her expression that she was wondering about the story there. And the tension in the room had become thick as mud, the atmosphere ice cold. But, to her credit, she didn't ask. She just moved on with her work.

A true professional, Ms. Hayes. Lindsay appreciated that much.

"Let's begin, then," Ms. Hayes said with a quick look at her watch. She opened a folder and picked up the first sheet of paper from a thin stack within it. "My firm, Marinelli, Loufer, and Hayes, has been tasked with the disposition of the last will and testament of Sir Kellen Hart, MBE. I, Margaret Anne Hayes, have been named as executor of this will. Our purpose here today is to attest the reading of that will and to agree to the disposition of Sir Hart's assets in accordance with its provisions."

The man shifted in his seat. Lindsay cast him a sidelong glance. He'd cleaned up since she'd last seen him. He was wearing a grey sport coat over a deep blue button-down shirt that set off his blue eyes, charcoal slacks and black leather shoes. His hair was still wet—from the shower, most likely, given the way his skin was glistening and slightly red from scrubbing—and swept back off his face. His beard was neatly brushed and combed.

He looked good.

Really good.

Lindsay drew a deep breath, as slowly as she could so as not to attract attention. She closed her eyes, savoring the man's musky, spicy, citrus scent. It was heaven.

No, heaven was too demure a place to bring that kind of heat to her body.

The man was trouble. Lindsay didn't go for bad boys. Didn't go for any boys, usually. No time for that nonsense. But this guy pushed all of her buttons, the best buttons, in all the worst ways.

Too bad he was such an asshole.

Or, maybe it was a good thing. Lindsay couldn't afford to be distracted. Her business was in a precarious place, teetering on that edge between taking off or going completely bust. She needed to be focused one-hundred percent on her work to make sure it didn't go under. For her sake, and for Raj and Marina. She didn't want to let them down.

She pulled in one more breath of that heady scent, letting herself taste it once more before she forced herself back to reality.

When she opened her eyes again, Ms. Hayes was staring at

her quietly, her hands folded on the table in front of her, that same quizzical look on her face again.

Lindsay's eyes popped wide as a cold tingle swept up her spine. She glanced at the man beside her. He was leaned back in his chair, his arm on the chair back, looking at Lindsay with one eyebrow arched.

"I'm sorry," said Lindsay, feeling her face flush hot, "what was that?"

"I said," began Ms. Hayes with calm and patience, ever the true professional, "are you willing to abide by the provisions of Sir Hart's last will and testament as presented in this document?"

That snapped Lindsay back to the present moment.

"Is that a legal question?" she asked. "Is my response expected to be legally binding? I haven't even heard the will yet. Why would I bind myself to do what it says?"

"Oh, for fuck's sake," muttered the man.

Lindsay glared at him.

Asshole.

"A fair question, Ms. Rhodes," said Ms. Hayes. "Your response here is not legally binding. It's just a good-faith commitment to hear the full text of the document and discuss with the present parties the best way to fulfill its spirit." She smiled that sad, wistful smile again. "This document represents the dying wish of your late father. The question is merely seeking agreement among the three of us to hear that wish completely and objectively and work together to the best of our abilities to find a way to honor both the wish and your late father's memory as best we can."

Ms. Hayes held her emotion behind a wall of professional detachment, but Lindsay could hear it in her words, in her voice. It was clear that Ms. Hayes had been very close to Lindsay's father. In what capacity, she didn't know. Or care, really.

Nor did Lindsay particularly care about honoring her

father's memory. She bore no ill will toward the man. He had made his choice and Lindsay and her mother had moved on with their lives. But she had no memory of him to honor.

But it was clear that Ms. Hayes did. And even the asshole in the chair beside her seemed to be invested in the process. Maybe her father had been important to him, too, somehow.

And Lindsay knew that social convention demanded that the dead be honored, whether they were saints, strangers, or total shitheads.

She considered the statement. In the States, she would have had to be informed if the session were being recorded. But she didn't know if the laws were the same in the UK, so she thought through the words carefully, looking for any legal gotchas. She didn't see any.

"Okay," she said. "I agree."

"Well, blessed day," said the man. "We got through the first fucking question."

Ms. Hayes smiled that sweet, soft, patient smile again. She may look like Lindsay's mother, but Lindsay had never seen a smile like that on her mother's face. Lindsay's mother was a wonderful woman, but 'sweet', 'soft', and 'patient' were not words that anyone would have used to describe her.

"Ms. Rhodes is well within her rights to ask these questions, Mac," said Ms. Hayes, "as are you, should you have them." She looked at Lindsay, her smile widening. Something about it made Lindsay feel safe, accepted. Welcome, even. "And I encourage Ms. Rhodes to continue asking these questions throughout these proceedings. I want you to be absolutely clear about what is happening every step of the way."

"Good lord, Maggie," the man said, "don't encourage her. You'll be reading *my* will before we get through this."

"Promises, promises," muttered Lindsay.

Lindsay saw a sparkle in Ms. Hayes eyes as they flicked back and forth between Lindsay and the man.

"Shall we continue?" said Ms. Hayes.

She set the paper in her hand upside-down, starting a new stack beside the first, and picked up the next sheet.

"I, Sir Kellen Hart," she read, "resident of 21 Cliff Road, Skipsea, East Riding of Yorkshire, England, being of sound mind and body..."

As Lindsay listened to the stilted, formal words coming from Ms. Hayes' mouth, her eyes drifted to the windows behind her, to the blue glow of the lake and the yellow-painted fields beyond, the tall, wispy grasses swaying in the breeze that was picking up as the night grew colder. The grasses seemed so soft, so comforting. Lindsay wanted nothing more than to walk out there, running her palms over the tufted tops of the grass, then lay down in a warm spot and drift off to sleep.

Lindsay took a deep breath, forcing oxygen into her system, into her brain, to help her focus.

"I nominate and appoint Mrs. Margaret Hayes, resident of..."

How did Lindsay wind up here? She stared at her hands, moved them back and forth against the glossy, smooth surface of the conference table, feeling a tickle in her fingertips. The last few days had been a blur. She should be at home, in her apartment. Her fingertips should be tickling her keyboard, cranking out code for the Brinksley project. Doing what she did best.

Instead she was in a foreign country in a room full of strangers discussing the estate of a man Lindsay had never met, had never known. She didn't even know him well enough to know if the text Ms. Hayes was reading sounded like her father or not. Was he formal? Was he laid back? Was he warm and gregarious or was he reserved and aloof?

It seemed completely ridiculous to Lindsay to even be here right now. She had her own life to live, her own company to care for. As far as Lindsay was concerned, her father was just a sperm donor. Why on earth should she be forced to disrupt all of that to tie off some crazy legal loose end related to some guy whose DNA she just happened to share?

"Now we come to the section on the disposition of property," said Ms. Hayes.

"That means it's time for you to stop daydreaming and pay attention, Barbie," said the man.

Barbie?

Had he just called her Barbie?

Lindsay had never been called that in her entire life. Aside from the obvious difference in Lindsay's intelligence and the implied intelligence of the vapid, materialistic doll, Lindsay didn't even look like Barbie. Blonde hair, sure, but Barbie's eyes were California blue. Lindsay's were Cleveland orange-brown. She and Barbie were both white, both tall, both slender, but Lindsay wouldn't be caught dead in a convertible with her friends in Malibu.

Lindsay was no Barbie. The man was just an asshole.

She considered a Ken-related retort, but the man didn't look like a Ken doll. He was too muscular, too broad, too brooding. Ken, like Barbie, was plastic and shallow. This man was anything but that. There was a simmering, almost frightening, depth to his blue eyes, and an edge that could cut your skin with just a glance.

Lindsay went for the high road, a dignified silence.

She had been daydreaming, after all.

Ms. Hayes raised her eyebrows at Lindsay. Lindsay nodded.

"I devise and bequeath my property," Ms. Hayes read, "both real and personal and wherever situated, as follows:

"To Ms. Lindsay Rhodes, currently of 974 Franklin Street, Apt 3D, San Francisco, California, USA, I leave all of my personal possessions, both tangible and intangible, both physical and electronic, including but not limited to my real estate holdings, automobiles, investment accounts and their contents, and cash balances, with the exception of the following bequest.

"To Mr. Cormac McEwan, currently of 19 Cliff Road, Skipsea, East Riding of Yorkshire, England, I leave fifty-percent of my ownership stake in Hart Racing, Inc., with all rights and privileges contained therein, with the governance structure of said corporation to be altered as outlined below."

Lindsay sat back. Her father had left her everything. What 'everything' meant, she didn't know, but it sounded like he had at least a house and a car, as well as some investments. She sighed. That mean more time away from home, as she would now need to find a broker to sell the house, find a buyer for the car, and liquidate or transfer whatever stocks he held. Then deal with the taxes for two countries, probably, and who knew how much else.

What a hassle.

And he'd left her half of his company, half of the company that owned this building. Hart Racing, Inc., whatever that was. More stuff that Lindsay would have to deal with before her life could return to normal. And more time it would take to do it.

Lindsay glanced at the man. His expression was blank, composed, but his skin was a shade whiter than it had been and his facial muscles had gone slack. He was leaned back in his chair, his hands in his lap, not moving. He seemed like he might be in shock.

Plus, he wasn't making any snide comments.

That was a dead giveaway. He was definitely in shock.

Maybe he had been expecting Lindsay's father to leave everything to him. That would make more sense than leaving it to Lindsay. Whatever their relationship had been, at least the man had known Lindsay's father.

Maybe he was already devising a scheme to steal the other half of the business from Lindsay, to take everything as his own. Well, if that was his plan, he didn't need a scheme. Lindsay would be happy to give it to him, just to be rid of the burden of selling everything herself. She didn't know how a racing company was run, but she assumed it wasn't cheap. Building all those cars, paying all those engineers. And this swanky building out here in a seaside town, that must have cost a pretty penny, too. The company was probably drowning in debt. If the asshole wanted to go down with the ship, Lindsay was more than happy to smash the champagne bottle on the prow and sing Anchors Aweigh from the dock as he sank.

"Are you ready to continue?" asked Ms. Hayes, staring at both Lindsay and the man.

They both nodded.

"Resolved," she read, "that Hart's Racing, Inc. shall be henceforth owned by two shareholders, each holding 500,000 shares, or fifty percent of total shares issued, and that these shareholders shall be the aforenamed parties, Ms. Lindsay Rhodes and Mr. Cormac McEwan.

"Resolved that Ms. Rhodes and Mr. McEwan shall henceforth be named to the board of directors for the company, and named as corporate directors, assuming all rights and responsibilities of this position, including responsibility for the management of the company's business, for which purpose they may exercise all the powers of the company.

"Resolved that Ms. Rhodes be named Chairperson of the Board of Directors and Chief Financial Officer, with all rights and responsibilities as previously outlined in the filings of Hart Racing, Inc.

"Resolved that Mr. McEwan be named Chief Executive Officer and Secretary, with all rights and responsibilities as previously outlined in the filings of Hart Racing, Inc.

"Resolved that no sale of Hart Racing, Inc. nor transfer of ownership interest shall occur without the unanimous agreement of all board members.

"Resolved that no sale of Hart Racing, Inc. nor transfer of ownership interest shall occur during an active racing season, nor during scheduled or unscheduled breaks from an active racing season.

"All other articles and bylaws shall stand as previously outlined and presently constituted in the filings of Hart Racing, Inc.

After discussion, the current directors of Hart Racing, Inc. shall approve these resolutions by unanimous consent, to take effect immediately upon the presentation of this document to the parties listed above."

Ms. Hayes, a satisfied smile on her lips, turned the page over onto the stack, folded her hands on the table in front of her, and stared pleasantly and patiently at Lindsay and the man.

"Um..." said Lindsay, struggling to make her jetlagged brain sift through all of the legalese she'd just heard.

She glanced at the man beside her. He was still leaned back in his chair, hands still in his lap, but now he was frowning down at them, his brow furrowed.

"Shall I review these stipulations for you?" said Ms. Hayes.

"Yes, please," said Lindsay quickly, the man nodding vigorously by her side.

Ms. Hayes smiled. Despite her fatigue, despite her confusion, somehow that smile again brought a tiny sliver of peace to Lindsay's mind.

"Your father," she said to Lindsay, "has left all of his possessions to you, including his houses—"

Houses. Plural.

Great.

"—his car collection—"

A whole collection?

Groan.

"—his bank accounts and portfolios—"

More plurals.

Lindsay was going to be stuck in England for weeks.

"—and half of his company. The other half," she said to the man, "he left to you, Mac."

The man nodded.

"I'm with you that far," he said, his voice a low growl that teased something very deep and very discomfiting within Lindsay. She squirmed in her chair. He turned his head and arched an eyebrow at her.

"That means that as of right now, you two," Ms. Hayes pointed at them both, "are the co-owners of Hart Racing, Inc., with exactly equal ownership stake and controlling interest."

So now Lindsay not only needed to sell a bunch of her late father's stuff, but now she needed to unload half of his company, too.

"What if I don't want to be co-owner of Hart Racing, Inc.?" Lindsay said.

"You mean you want to own the entire company?" asked Ms. Hayes.

"Over my dead body," muttered the asshole.

"More promises," said Lindsay under her breath. "No, what if I don't want to own it at all? Any of it?"

Ms. Hayes frowned slightly and sat back in her chair.

"Do you mean you wish to refuse that part of your bequest?" she said.

"I'd like to refuse the whole damn thing," she said. "I didn't know my father and I don't want any of his stuff. I just want to get back home and get back to work."

The man snorted beside her. Lindsay didn't bother to respond.

Ms. Hayes' eyes flashed and her mouth twisted in a professionally amused way.

"How's about I buy it from you," said the man. "I'll give you twenty quid and make all the hassle go away. I'll even buy you a plane ticket home."

Lindsay turned to face him. His eyebrows raised at her stare and he nodded to her, encouraging her to say yes.

Which immediately made Lindsay suspicious.

"I would encourage you to think about this decision, Ms. Rhodes," Ms. Hayes said. "Sleep on it. Perhaps evaluate what it is you now own before you do anything..." She glanced at the man. "...rash."

The man looked at Ms. Hayes, eyes wide, and spread his arms to the side. Ms. Hayes smiled kindly and shook her head.

Ms. Hayes was probably right. Maybe Lindsay was going about this all wrong. She was jetlagged, after all, and shouldn't be making any legal decisions in her present state. Instead of just trying to make it all go away, she should approach the problem systematically. She should collect the data, analyze it, and come up with the most efficient and effective solution.

Starting tomorrow, after she'd gotten some sleep.

"Okay," Lindsay said, "but, just hypothetically, can I refuse all of this stuff if I want to?"

"Beneficiaries can disclaim their bequests," nodded Ms. Hayes, "in which case the bequests would go to any alternative beneficiaries named in the will. However, no such alternative beneficiaries are so named."

"What about me?" said the man. "I'm in there. Doesn't that make me an alternative beneficiary?"

"Sorry, Mac," said Ms. Hayes. "Alternative beneficiaries have to be specifically named as such. We can't just choose another name from the beneficiaries that are in the will."

Lindsay smirked at the man. He wasn't just an asshole. He was a greedy asshole.

"Okay, so if I..." What had Ms. Hayes called it? "...disclaim my bequest and there's no alternate, what happens then?"

"Then it falls to intestate law, which is what is used in the case of an improper will or no will at all. Under that law, the property goes to next of kin."

"Next of kin," said Lindsay, swallowing hard.

"I'm afraid so," said Ms. Hayes.

"And my father has no other kids? No wives or siblings or parents?"

Ms. Hayes shook her head.

Lindsay blew out a long breath. Okay, so she was stuck with it. So what? What could happen if she just didn't deal with it at all? Just walked away and went back home?

"In that case," said Ms. Hayes when Lindsay asked the question, "you would still be liable for any inheritance tax on your late father's estate. And if you failed to maintain the procedures of the corporation, such as regular meetings, fiduciary duties, and the like, your creditors could take you to court and claim that the corporate veil had been pierced."

"What the hell does that mean?" said the man.

"That means that both of you would be personally responsible for the debts and obligations of the corporation," said Ms. Hayes. "Your personal possessions—homes, cars, investments, other companies—" Ms. Hayes looked pointedly at Lindsay. "—could be seized by the court and sold to pay any outstanding debts held by Hart Racing, Inc."

Lindsay fell back in her chair.

Now she was the one in shock.

She was completely trapped.

If she stayed here to deal with all of this bullshit, she'd be stuck in England for weeks, maybe longer. She could lose her business. The Brinksley job was the biggest client she'd gotten yet. They'd given her a small job, but Brinksley was a huge corporation. If she did the small job well, it could lead to a huge contract down the road. And Lindsay needed that. She was barely paying the bills as it was. If she couldn't make something happen in the next six months, she might have to shut the company down, fire Marina and Raj, and beg for her old job back.

But, if she just went back home to do her work, all of her father's stuff in England would come back to bite her in the butt. It could ruin everything she'd built, everything she'd worked for.

She was stuck.

"The will said something about selling the company," Lindsay said. "Can't we just do that? Sell it to someone else?"

"I told you," said the man, grinning, "I'll buy you out for twenty quid, right here and now. Hell, I'll even sweeten the deal. Twenty quid and a ride to the airport."

Ms. Hayes shot the man a warning glance.

"You can sell either your ownership stake or the entire company, if you wish," said Ms. Hayes, "but either decision can only be made by unanimous consent of all active members of the board of directors." She looked between Lindsay and the man. "That means you both have to agree."

Lindsay's mouth fell open. She stared at the man. He just grinned back at her.

"That's the bad news, I suppose," said Ms. Hayes.

"What's the good news?" asked Lindsay.

"The good news is that you've got time to think it over. The will stipulates that you can't sell during the racing season, anyway," said Ms. Hayes.

"And the season started last week," said the man, his grin widening. "That means you've got nine months to make me an offer I can't refuse."

Lindsay's mouth fell open again.

Nine months? This can't be happening.

She looked at Ms. Hayes, who just shrugged back at her.

This was happening.

Now more than ever, Lindsay really needed to get some sleep.

5

LINDSAY WOKE up the next morning to the sunlight streaming through the window, turning the inside of her eyelids a bright orange. Her neck was stiff and sore and she groaned as she lifted her head. Cracking her eyes open, momentarily blinded by the bright natural light filling the room, she could see she was still fully clothed, shoes on, sprawled face-down atop the bed.

She barely remembered coming home. She'd come straight from the conference room to her father's house—her house now. The driver had said it was only a five minute ride, but she'd fallen asleep in the back seat before they'd even made it back to the main road. She vaguely remembered her driver helping her inside with her luggage and kindly pointing the way to the bedroom.

Too many turns, too many long hallways, her mind shutting her body down too quickly. She'd spotted a bed through a doorway and collapsed in it.

Now, she sat up, her mouth tasting like a family of squirrels had used it for a bathroom. Her glasses were bent and skewed underneath her, leaving her vision fuzzy and soft-edged in the sunlight. She pushed herself upright, her head pounding, her throat dry and scratchy. Probably still dehydrated from the travel.

She needed a glass of water, a shower, a change of clothes, and caffeine.

Not necessarily in that order.

She smacked her mouth open and closed. The squirrels chittered angrily at her.

She needed to brush her teeth. Immediately.

She pushed her hair out of her face and pulled on her glasses.

The bedroom she was in was large, but not extravagant. The bed was queen-sized, with a pile of blue and white pillows pushed up against a tufted leather headboard. The rumpled duvet underneath her was thick and comfortable. Beside the bed was a simple wooden nightstand and a wide window, blinds open to the view of a couple of wide-leafed trees through which the sunlight blazed, dappling the room with spots of orange and yellow. Inside, the room was chilly, the sunlight warm where it touched Lindsay's face.

Aside from that, there wasn't much else in the room.

Lindsay stood up, searching for her luggage before remembering she'd left it by the front door last night. The squirrel infestation would have to wait. Right then, a more urgent need jumped to the top of her to-do list. She walked through the doorway to the bathroom.

And discovered she was in a closet.

A closet that was twice as big as her bathroom back home.

She turned around and tried another door, this time winding up in the right place, a spacious bathroom with a large shower, a wide mirror above two elegant sinks set into a long wooden vanity, a shelf full of neatly folded white bath towels, and a slatted wooden door to Lindsay's right behind which she could see the toilet.

That item checked off her list, she stripped down and stood

in the shower for a long time, letting the hot water soak the fatigue from her bones, the grime of travel from her skin, the fog of jetlag and overwhelm from her mind. Tilting her head into the stream, she let the hot water fill in her mouth, swishing it around to evict the squirrels. She might have preferred a long soak in a steaming hot bath, but the shower was big, the water was hot, and the house was empty. It was enough for Lindsay to relax a little.

Finally feeling human again, she stepped out of the shower and grabbed a towel from the shelf. Most normal-sized towels looked like skanky miniskirts on Lindsay, but this one was enormous, more like a tasteful pencil dress. After squeezing most of the water from her hair with another towel, she went in search of her luggage, letting her wet hair hang loose down her back.

Toothbrush, toothpaste, deodorant, clothes. In that order.

She padded barefoot down the hallway. The floors were covered with a thick, cushy carpet that massaged her toes as she walked. She could feel the tension shaving off bit by bit, a tiny slice with each step. She tried to retrace her steps from the night before, but the house was massive, a maze of hallways and turns, and Lindsay quickly got lost.

Lindsay's mind started to awaken as she wandered. Even in a town nearly five hours from London, a house this big had to be worth a fortune. But how much did her late father owe on it? She still had to find a buyer, pay off the mortgage, pay any taxes. Appearances could be deceiving, and most people who seemed wealthy were really just in debt up to their eyeballs.

Lindsay finally emerged into a massive kitchen. The floor was slate tile, cool but not cold under her bare feet. The counters were a sparkling white marble, the cupboards a white-washed driftwood. A ten-burner gas range, a double-oven and microwave, an enormous farmhouse sink, and two islands with sinks and prep stations, one with several bar stools situated behind it. This was a gourmet kitchen. Lindsay wondered if her late father actually knew how to cook or if it was just for show.

The whole room opened onto an elegant dining area, with a long wooden dining table that stood before a wall that was one giant window facing the ocean. The sea was grey, the wind whipping white-caps onto the waves. But the sky was clear and brilliant blue, and the sunlight filled the room with warmth and light.

Lindsay's heart skipped a beat as she spotted an espresso machine on one of the side counters and made a beeline for it. Whether the kitchen was for show or not, her father had purchased quality equipment. The espresso machine was a La Marzocco, from Italy, with a matching grinder. A row of espresso cups was arrayed on top of the machine. She pulled the lid off the grinder's hopper and smelled the beans. The coffee scent lit up her senses, as fresh as if the beans had just been poured into the hopper that morning.

She heated the portafilter, filled it, tamped it, and pulled herself a double shot. The machine hummed and buzzed. The noise was loud, but it was music to Lindsay's ears. She hadn't had a decent cup of coffee in days.

Holding the tiny espresso cup up to her nose, she breathed deep, the intense coffee smell sending shivers through her body. She took a sip of the hot espresso and was immediately in heaven. Rich and heady, just bitter enough to bite, but still leaving a silky finish on Lindsay's tongue.

She'd unload the house, the car, and the company, but Lindsay might have to keep the espresso machine.

She finished the cup and pulled another, indulging herself just a bit longer. Not for too long. She had a lot of work to do, and the sooner she got to it, the sooner she got through it. Still, one more cup wouldn't hurt.

As the machine buzzed away, the music of her filling cup in

her ears, Lindsay couldn't help swaying back and forth, almost dancing with eager anticipation.

"Coffee in a bath towel," growled a voice behind her. "And a dancer to boot. I didn't peg you for the type, Barbie."

Lindsay whirled, her heart immediately racing as a surge of adrenaline coursed through her body. The buzz of the machine stopped dead, the last dribbles of coffee slipping into the cup.

The man stood behind one of the islands, a smirk on his face. He dropped his keys on the counter and sat down on a barstool.

"I figured you more for a pink frilly pajama set kind of girl, really," he said. "You're just full of surprises, aren't you?"

Lindsay felt her face flush hot.

"I do not wear pink," she said through clenched teeth, "and I've never worn a frill in my life."

The man chuckled.

"Good to know," he said.

He was wearing a navy blue V-neck sweater and a charcoal-grey beanie that slouched against the back of his head. As he crossed his arms, leaning on the counter, Lindsay could see the bulge of his biceps against the slim cut of his sweater.

She felt a flush of heat elsewhere in her body at the sight.

Lindsay clenched her fists. Why was this man always bothering her so much?

"What are you doing here?" she said. "You can't just walk into my house."

"Oh, It's your house now, is it?"

"Yes, actually," said Lindsay, lifting her chin slightly. "It is."

"Well, that's true enough, I suppose," said the man softly, "though yesterday you couldn't seem to be quit of it fast enough."

Lindsay didn't respond. She just raised her eyebrows.

"The front door was unlocked," said the man, laughing. "I called out for you, but no one answered, so I just came in to see where you were. To make sure you were alright." He grinned at her, his broad smile and white teeth glinting in the light.

Weren't the English all supposed to have crooked, yellow teeth or something? This man's teeth were movie-star perfect.

"It's Danny's day off," he said. "I'm here to give you a ride into the office."

"I thought my father owned a car," said Lindsay.

"Aye, he does," the man nodded. "He does at that. He owns more than one, in fact. But do you know how to drive any of them?"

Lindsay's heartbeat rushed in her ears, her fists tightening by her side. This guy had some nerve. First he came in calling her Barbie, and now he was accusing her of not even knowing how to drive a car? She wasn't some blonde bimbo, and she wasn't about to let some arrogant asshole intimidate her.

And she sure as hell was not going to give him the satisfaction of seeing her get flustered.

She took a deep breath through her nose, silently, slowly. She forced her hands to unclench.

"I'm sure I can handle it," said Lindsay, turning to pick up her espresso from the counter behind her. She smiled sweetly as she brought it to her lips. "Who's Danny?"

"Who's Danny?" said the man, his eyes popping wide. "Danny? You know, the guy you spent five hours in the car with on the way from bloody Heathrow yesterday? The guy who carried you into the house last night while you were practically sleeping in his arms? Danny Withrow?"

"Ah," said Lindsay. Her driver. "I didn't catch his name."

"Is that right?" The man shook his head. "You're a real people person, aren't you?"

Lindsay threw back her espresso, the caffeine now coursing through her veins. Her mind felt awake, alert, buzzing along at her usual hundred-miles-an-hour.

She checked the clock on the microwave. It was already

almost ten AM. Lindsay must have slept for more than twelve hours.

"Well, thanks for the offer, but I won't be needing your services," said Lindsay. "How about I meet you at the office at noon?"

"Noon?" said the man, checking his watch. "Still need to do your makeup and hair and such?"

Lindsay smiled sweetly again.

Asshole.

"I've got a few calls I need to make this morning," she said.

"Uh huh," he said, furrowing his brow. "You sure you can find your way to the office?"

Lindsay smiled sweetly once more. The expression was starting to burn a hole in her face.

"I'll manage," she said, walking toward him, gesturing toward what she hoped was the front door.

"I can just wait here for you," he said. "I promise I'll stay out of your way." As Lindsay approached, he stood up from the stool and grabbed his keys, backing away. "Maybe I should give you my number, just in case."

"I'm sure that won't be necessary," said Lindsay, doing her best to bore a hole into the asshole's head with her stare, keeping that damn sweet smile plastered on her lips, "but thank you anyway."

She moved forward. He backed away.

"But, you might not—"

"Thank you," said Lindsay, herding him out of the kitchen. She could see the front door at the end of a long hallway. The man stumbled backwards toward it.

"I'm happy to wait if—"

"Not necessary," said Lindsay, pressing forward.

"Are you sure—"

"Listen, ass—" Lindsay caught herself. "Mr... I'm sorry," she said, pinching the bridge of her nose, her head suddenly throbbing, "what was your name again?"

The man rolled his eyes.

Actually rolled his eyes at her.

That wiped the smile from her face.

Ass. Hole.

"Mac," he said. "Mac McEwan."

"Thank you for your help, Mr. McEwan, but, despite what you may have been led to believe, women are perfectly capable of driving cars, navigating roadways, and adhering to schedules."

He looked taken aback, his eyes flashing with anger. "I never said you couldn't—"

"And," continued Lindsay, striding forward as he stepped back down the hall, "despite what you may think, we don't need anyone to hold our hand while we live our lives."

"Don't put me in—"

"So I'll thank you very much to leave my house now," she said, pushing forward, "and don't come in uninvited ever again."

"I'm just trying to—"

"Ever again," said Lindsay, flames shooting from her eyes. "Is that clear," she said as the asshole bumped into the front door, "or would you like me to hold your hand and help you to your car?"

She smiled sweetly.

That same anger flashed again in the asshole's eyes before his expression fell flat and neutral.

"Very well, Ms. Rhodes," he said, emphasizing her name as he opened the front door. His voice was low and smooth and professional, but his eyes were still aflame. "I look forward to seeing you at the office at noon."

Lindsay nodded.

He stepped out onto the front porch. "If you find yourself in need of assistance before then," he turned back to her, shrugging, "well, go fuck yourself, I guess."

"Spoken like a true gentleman," she said, and slammed the door in his face.

What a dick.

Lindsay could hear the man cursing through the door, his voice fading as he stomped off to his car, calling her any number of ungentlemanly names. Some of them, she didn't even recognize. Must be local curse words or Scottish terms. But she could tell from the context and the venom in his voice what they meant.

Fine with her. If she never saw that asshole again, it would be too soon. She'd have to call Ms. Hayes about it. Maybe they could coordinate schedules to avoid each other in the future.

She pulled in a deep, deep breath, closed her eyes, and blew it out slowly, resetting herself. Coffee on board, mind clocking at top speed, it was time for Lindsay to get to work. She opened her eyes again and noticed her luggage beside her.

Perfect.

Twenty minutes later, fully dressed and ready, hair dried and pulled back in a pony tail, Lindsay was sitting at the table in the kitchen staring out the huge window at the sea, Marina's face on the laptop screen in front of her.

"Kellen Hart?" Marina said. "Like the race car guy? That Kellen Hart?"

"Yeah," nodded Lindsay. "Have you heard of him?"

Marina laughed, blinking rapidly. "Yeah, I've heard of him. So has half of Europe. He's a big deal over here."

"Really? Why?"

"Well, he's got that racing team," she said. "I don't follow car racing, but I see the billboards and the headlines everywhere. England is crazy for car racing. They just hired some famous old driver, an English guy. Stole him away from some Italian team, I think. Coming back to his roots, his home country. That kind of thing. They're eating it up over here."

"Uh huh," said Lindsay, opening her email. There were several messages from Brinksley.

"But mostly he's known for his philanthropy. He does a lot of charity work."

"Who?" said Lindsay, opening the first email. "The driver guy?" Shit. The VP at Brinksley who was managing the job wanted to know when she would be starting. Lindsay had no idea.

"No," said Marina, "your father. Late father." Marina cringed. "He's involved with a whole bunch of stuff. Mostly to do with kids. Cancer, adoption, that kind of thing."

"Okay," said Lindsay. "Have you been able to scope the front-end work for the Brinksley job yet?"

Marina frowned. "Um... yeah, it looks fine. Just the usual. They're asking for lots of users, though, with tons of different roles, so that will take longer to set up."

"Got it," said Lindsay, starting to compose a reply to the VP. "Have you spoken to Raj about it?"

"No," said Marina, drawing out the word. "I thought we were talking about your father."

"Right," said Lindsay, nodding. "Right, yes, we were. Big deal, charity, old driver."

Marina sighed, then smiled.

"Actually, the real big deal is the guy who runs their team. He is smoking hot."

"Mmm?" said Lindsay, typing. "Who's that?"

"I don't remember his name," said Marina, "but I know his face, I'll tell you that. I see it every night in my dreams."

"Right," said Lindsay. "Would you say four weeks for the front-end work, plus two more for the role setups?"

"His face, his hair, his smile, his chest..."

"Maybe I'll say eight weeks, just to give a buffer."

"I'd give my left tit to see that guy with his shirt off."

"Okay, Marina," said Lindsay, "focus now. Eight weeks sound reasonable?"

"Mac something. MacGyver? MacGregor? No, that's the Obi Wan actor. Ewan..."

A chill ran down Lindsay's spine.

"Mac McEwan?" she said.

"Yes," said Marina, snapping her fingers. "Cormac McEwan. Whoo. That guy is fucking fire." She leered at the camera. "If you see him anywhere, give him my number."

Lindsay shook her head quickly, fighting against the intense pain that had started in the center of her forehead. Time to focus. Focus on the Brinksley job.

Marina narrowed her eyes. "Have you met him?"

Lindsay pressed her lips together and didn't answer, trying to focus on the email she was composing. She'd read the same line three times already.

Marina's eyes popped wide.

"You have met him," she said, her voice a hushed whisper. "What's he like? Is he as hot in person as he is in the pictures?"

Lindsay blew out a breath she hadn't realized she'd been holding. "Mac McEwan is a total fucking asshole," she said.

Marina sat back in her chair. "Woah," she said. "Never heard you talk like that about someone before. You're usually so... diplomatic."

"Yeah, well," said Lindsay, her chest tightening, "I've never met anyone who was such a complete dick before." Her jaw was clenched so tight she felt like her molars would crumble to dust any second.

Marina leaned forward, her head on the heel of her palm. "What happened?"

"Nothing happened," said Lindsay, her words snapping much more sharply than she had intended. She closed her eyes and took a deep breath. "Nothing happened," she said again, softly. "I met him once, by accident. Through no fault of my own, I walked into a restricted area." She tightened her fists at the memory. "And he chewed my head off for it."

"Okay," said Marina. "Then what—"

"And then I had to sit through the will reading with him."

"Wait. He's in the wi—"

"And now we each own half the fucking company and neither one of us can sell or do anything without the approval of the other. It's a total pain in the ass." Lindsay fell back in her chair, running her fingers over her hair and pulling on her pony tail. "And," she said, her voice reaching a crescendo of fury, "he called me a goddamn Barbie." Lindsay leaned forward into the camera. "I am not a fucking Barbie, Marina."

Marina's grin filled the screen.

What the hell was she smiling at? There was nothing funny about this at all.

Marina sat back in her chair, holding both palms up toward the screen. She closed her eyes and nodded, her face somber.

"No, you are definitely not a Barbie, Lindsay," she said, her voice calm and soothing. "You are one-hundred percent correct about that."

"And then he showed up here," Lindsay continued, gesturing to the space around her, "in my house—"

Marina leaned forward again. "He came to your house?"

"—while I'm in a towel—"

"In a... you were naked?"

"—making coffee—"

"He saw you naked?"

"—and called me Barbie again."

Lindsay's chest was heaving, her breath blowing in and out of her nose like a bull before a matador.

"Hoooo," cooed Marina, spinning once around on her swivel chair. "Lindsay Rhodes. You are truly my hero." She clapped her hands quickly. "I mean, you were my hero before, but now you are my numero uno hero." She clapped again.

Lindsay sighed, a deep, chest-wracking sigh. She honestly didn't know why she was so worked up about all of this. So what if some asshole called her a stupid name? It wasn't the first time. The world is full of assholes, and Lindsay had met a thousand of them in Silicon Valley. Why all of a sudden was this particular asshole getting under her skin?

"I think I'm still jetlagged, or stressed from the trip or something," she said, rubbing her palm over her face.

"Yeah," said Marina, nodding vigorously, "yeah, maybe so. Or maybe," she said, leaning into the camera again, her face filling the screen, her voice sing-song, "maybe you like him."

"Ugh," said Lindsay. She pretended to retch, making the vomit sounds, but she honestly didn't need to pretend too much. The thought of being with Mac McEwan really did make her want to puke. "Don't even joke about that."

"You like him," sang Marina.

"Okay, that's enough."

"You looove him." Marina spun slowly on her chair, arms and legs pumping in a little dance.

"Marina," said Lindsay, laughing in spite of herself. No one could make Lindsay laugh like Marina, no matter how dark her mood or frazzled her mindset. "Listen, I know you've got a crush on this guy," she said, "and I get that. He is," Lindsay hesitated, "better looking than average."

"Better than average? Calling Cormac McEwan better than average is like calling the Mona Lisa a finger painting."

"But, if you knew him—"

"It's like calling Pride and Prejudice an okay love story."

"—like I know him—"

"It's like calling stracciatella gelato a chocolate-chip ice cream."

"—you wouldn't feel that way anymore," finished Lindsay

with a laugh, practically shouting to be heard over Marina. "I am not going to be with Cormac McEwan," she said. "Ever. Never, ever, ever. Sorry, Marina. You're just going to have to live your fantasy through someone else."

Marina's face fell, a mock pout on her lips.

Lindsay laughed again at the sight.

"Besides," she said, "I don't have time to date anyone. I've got too much to do. The Brinksley VP has already sent me three emails. Now with this estate thing and the stupid company..." She threw her hands up, her shoulders slumping as the weight of her workload fell down upon them. "The last thing I want right now is some needy man getting in the way."

Marina nodded slowly, giving Lindsay a thoughtful, appraising stare.

"Okay," she said. "Okay, fair enough. How can I help?"

Lindsay blew out a long breath, the tightness in her chest finally loosening. She hadn't realized how much she had needed to hear someone ask that very question.

But the only way out is through. That's what her mother had always taught her. Most people shy away from a heavy workload, she would say. That's why most people don't succeed. When you've got the workload, you've got an opportunity. And the only way to dig out of the workload is to dig through it, come out the other side, and look for the next opportunity.

Time to get to work.

6

AN HOUR LATER, after adding Raj to the video call—at an ungodly hour, even for him. Lindsay would need to work on her time zone etiquette—working out the scoping and the preliminary schedule on the Brinksley job, and replying to the Brinksley VP's emails, Lindsay was ready to head to Hart Racing headquarters.

She'd wandered through the house for a while, looking for the door to the garage. Now she stood, dumbfounded, in the largest garage she'd ever seen. Anywhere, let alone inside someone's house. There had to be at least twenty cars in there, spaced evenly before her in two columns of ten cars each. Except for one extra car parked in the middle of the aisle, each car was parked at the same angle, nose turned forty-five degrees toward a wide garage door at the far end. Each car was polished and gleaming under its own overhead lamp, making it seem like some kind of game show giveaway, with the lights putting each car on its own stage. The only things missing were little round stages spinning each car in a slow circle. That and the bikini models draped over the hoods.

A small box with a glass front hung on the wall beside Lindsay. She could see keys hung on hooks inside, just like at a valet stand.

Her father had really liked cars, apparently.

None of the cars really suited Lindsay's taste. They were all too flashy, too shiny. They were all sports cars. None of them were remotely practical. Lindsay was more of a Toyota Prius kind of girl. Or maybe a Tesla, for the environment's sake. Model 3, though. Not the stupid expensive ones. A car was just a way to get from Point A to Point B, after all. Why would anyone spend a hundred grand on a personal conveyor belt?

She walked up and down the rows, peering inside the windows. None of the cars were practical, and none of them were automatics. They all had stick shifts.

Despite Lindsay's impassioned defense earlier, the asshole, Mac, hadn't been too far off base, in reality. Lindsay did have a valid and current driver's license, but she hadn't driven a car since she'd taken her driver's test years earlier. Cars in San Francisco were more of a nuisance than a help. Lindsay lived most of her life within a five block radius, anyway.

When she actually left her apartment.

And on those rare occasions when she did need to go far away, like to the airport or across town, she called an Uber or used public transportation.

So, Lindsay had a license. She knew how to drive. But she was a little out of practice.

And she'd never driven a stick shift in her life.

But, how hard could it be? She pulled up a video on YouTube on her phone. Five minutes later, she had the basics in mind. Clutch on the left, gas on the right. Inverse relationship between the two. As you ease off on the clutch, ease down on the gas. Shift through the gears with your right hand. Shift up at 2500 RPM, down at 1500 RPM.

Simple.

She decided to take the car in the middle of the aisle. It was blocking the exit anyway, and it was already pointed straight toward the garage door.

The car was a tiny red thing with a flattish, roundish front. It was a two-door, two-seater car that sat so low to the ground that Lindsay practically had to crawl into the front seat. She recognized the logo in the center of the steering wheel, a little prancing pony of some kind, though she couldn't recall the brand name it represented. One of those fancy car brands. But this was an old car, with a wide thin leather steering wheel with three metal spokes, a metal gear shift on a long metal stalk, and a slew of old-school analog gauges on the dash, most of which Lindsay could not see a use for. Oil. Water. Something called Benzina. Why would anyone need to see all of those metrics while they were driving? And looking down to check them all the time was inefficient and dangerous. The metrics should project on the screen in front of the driver. Or, given the age of the car, sit on top of the dash so the eye had less distance to travel to read the number.

But the car was old. The design was old. Lindsay had decades of innovation to inform her thinking. Whoever had built this car was just following the conventions of the time.

Large in the center of the dashboard was the only gauge with any claim to usefulness, the speedometer. In the center of it, Lindsay saw the brand name she'd been trying to remember earlier: Ferrari.

Yep. Impractical and fancy.

Okay, Ferrari. Time to go to work.

She pulled up the route to the office on her phone, leaned it on the dash in front of her, against the gauges, pushed the button on the overhead visor to open the garage door, and twisted the key in the ignition. The tiny car roared to life like an angry lion, the sound much bigger than the car itself, then lowered its voice to a purring, chortling rumble that Lindsay could feel in her butt.

Felt kind of nice, really. Like a gentle massage.

The car was already pointed toward the door. Through the windshield, Lindsay could see the driveway extending straight out in front of her, grassy fields all around it on either side.

Remembering the steps in the video, Lindsay pushed down the clutch, put the car into first gear, and set her foot on the accelerator.

Inverse relationship. Ease off the clutch, ease on the gas.

The engine roared, deafening. The tires screeched, echoing in the garage like a thousand startled bats. Jerking Lindsay against the seat back, the car lurched forward.

Then died, rattling to silence.

Odd. She pulled up the video again. She'd done everything right. Maybe the car was just too old. Maybe it didn't respond quite like the newer car in the video.

She restarted the car, feeling that rumble again through the seat.

Ease off the clutch, ease on the gas.

The engine roared again. Lindsay lifted off the clutch more slowly. The car slid forward maybe ten feet this time, out of the garage and onto the driveway, the engine screaming, before it lurched to a stop like it had hit a wall and rattled quiet once more.

Progress.

Trial and error. Hypothesis, experimentation, observation. The scientific method.

Lindsay had this. No problem.

Lindsay's phone had said it would take five minutes to drive the three miles to the office. Thirty minutes later, the office building arose on the horizon in front of her.

The old car had been surprisingly difficult to drive, even

though Lindsay had followed the video's instructions to the word. Old car, less precise manufacturing, and none of the benefit of modern AI undoubtedly made the car more unwieldy. Lindsay wondered how on earth anyone had managed to get anywhere at all back in the sixties.

The progress was slow and uneven, with the car sometimes taking off at alarming speeds, other times creeping forward maddeningly slowly, with frequent stalls in between that were making Lindsay's neck hurt. And there was a nasty burning smell that filled the inside of the car. Halfway to the office, despite the chilly air, Lindsay cranked both windows down trying to clear that smell out.

And while she fought the car all the way to the office, she fought herself, as well. A nagging feeling plagued her, sat in the back of her brain telling her she was doing this all wrong, that cars weren't supposed to smell so bad that you had to roll down the windows while you drove them. Lindsay did her best to ignore that feeling. It wasn't helpful.

Ms. Hayes and the asshole were waiting out front as she pulled into the parking lot. Ms. Hayes's eyebrows were raised, probably irritated at Lindsay being twenty minutes late, but she was otherwise perfectly composed in an elegant cream pantsuit with matching heels, a brown leather folio tucked under her arm. Mac's beanie was flopping out of the back pocket of his jeans. He had one hand on his hip, the other pulling against his hair, eyes wide open.

Lindsay aimed for a parking spot right in front of him, revving the engine once more to pull in. The car leapt forward. It scraped against the concrete block on the ground at the front of the parking spot, jerked to a halt, then died one last time, centered between the lines.

Perfectly parked.

Mac looked furious. He must have thought Lindsay was going to hit him with the car.

Lindsay smiled to herself at that thought.

"What the bloody hell are you doing?" he spluttered as Lindsay levered herself up and out of the front seat of the impossibly low car.

"Don't worry," said Lindsay, patting him on the shoulder as she passed, "I wasn't going to hit you."

"But, why..." More spluttering. He gestured with both hands at the vehicle. "The car... You can't..."

"Hello, Ms. Hayes," smiled Lindsay, reaching out to shake Ms. Hayes' hand. "It's nice to see you again." She leaned in close and lowered her voice. "If we get a moment later, I'd like to talk to you about some scheduling concerns."

Ms. Hayes furrowed her brow, but nodded.

Ever the professional.

Ms. Hayes looked at Mac, eyebrows raised.

Mac had his phone up to his ear. He waved at her.

"Go ahead, Maggie," he said, irritation in his voice. "I'll be there in a sec. I've got to get Sam on this." He tilted his head, looking at the front of the car. "And maybe Gerald, too." He shook his head and glared at Lindsay.

Lindsay had no idea what he was suddenly so upset about. She really hadn't even come close to hitting him. But, he was an asshole, and assholes had all sorts of stupid reasons for being assholes. Not her problem.

And it would give Lindsay a chance to talk to Ms. Hayes about the scheduling.

Ms. Hayes held open the glass front door to the building. They strode together through the showroom, the history of Hart Racing cars around them, Ms. Hayes' heels clicking against the floor, echoing in the vast room as she walked. Lindsay was tall and walked quickly thanks to her long legs, but even though Ms. Hayes was at least a few inches shorter, Lindsay had to rush to keep up with her.

"Ms. Hayes," said Lindsay, "Mr. McEwan and I don't quite see eye-to-eye on most things." That was a vast understatement, but Lindsay was trying to be diplomatic. "I think it would be best if we made an effort to stay away from one another while we decide how to manage my father's bequests. Is there a way we can arrange our schedules to minimize our contact with each other?"

Ms. Hayes smiled that smile of hers, looking straight ahead as she did so. Lindsay had always thought of it as a kind smile, and it was, but now it seemed more enigmatic. What the hell was going on in Ms. Hayes' mind? She was so close-lipped, so professional.

Even so, Lindsay still felt like she could trust her with anything. Maybe it was just the uncanny resemblance to Lindsay's mother, but there was something there, some feeling deep inside that set Lindsay at ease when she was with Ms. Hayes.

It was disturbing, in a way. Normally, Lindsay would ignore any feeling that wasn't grounded in observable truth. Emotions and feelings were unreliable, too easily swayed by brain chemistry, blood chemistry, fatigue, fluctuations in body temperature, even the weather. But Lindsay clung to this particular feeling. Maybe it was her mother, maybe it was the professionalism, maybe it was simply seeing a friendly, competent face in the whirlwind of chaos Lindsay had fallen into. Whatever it was, for better or for worse, Lindsay trusted Ms. Hayes.

Ms. Hayes looked at Lindsay, her eyes twinkling.

Her eyes were always twinkling.

"Ms. Rhodes," she said, "I understand your concern. Mac can be..." She tilted her head from one side to the other, thinking. "He can seem a little rough around the edges sometimes, before you get to know him. But, I promise you, he's a good man. An honest man."

Okay, maybe Lindsay didn't trust Ms. Hayes completely after all. Even the best person can have a horrible lack of judgment from time to time.

Lindsay believed the honest part, at least. Mac seemed to have no filter whatsoever.

As to the good part, well, agree to disagree.

"I appreciate that, Ms. Hayes, but I still feel it would be more efficient for the disposition of the estate's assets if Mr. McEwan and I stayed away from one another. We can each perform our own analysis, share our results via email, then convene to sign the paperwork once the final sale is arranged."

"Sale?" said Ms. Hayes.

"Of the company."

Ms. Hayes stopped at the door to the office area, one hand on the door handle.

"You've decided to sell the company?" she asked.

"Well, yes," said Lindsay. She thought that much would have been obvious. Lindsay had her own company to worry about. What the hell would she do with a racing firm in England while she built a data science startup in San Francisco?

"Hmm," said Ms. Hayes. She swiped her badge against the reader on the wall and held the door open for Lindsay, then led Lindsay into a conference room down the hall from the one they had used the night before. It was similar in configuration, with the conference table in the center and the wall of windows facing the lake, now glittering in the noon sun. But it was smaller, the table only big enough for six people, and there was a large whiteboard on the wall beside the door.

They both sat down on opposite sides of the table. Ms. Hayes set down her leather folio and folded her hands on it, staring out the window over Lindsay's shoulder for a long moment.

"If you wish to sell your share of this company," she said at last, "that is certainly within your rights. You must honor the stipulations of the will, of course, which means you cannot sell until the end of the racing season."

"When will that be, exactly?"

"The final race is in Abu Dhabi on November 20th of this

year," she said. "Beginning the following day and until the next season begins with testing in Spain on February..." She checked a paper in her folio. "February 24th, you and Mac will be able to make changes to the ownership structure of the company, should you wish."

Lindsay nodded. Nine interminable months until she could do something about this damn ownership stake, but at least there was a specific end date. Between now and then, she would assess the company's assets, determine the fair market value of the company and her stake in it, then look for someone willing to buy it.

Oh, and deal with the massive house, the twenty race cars, and whatever else her late father had left her to deal with.

Oh, yeah, and run her own company, too.

"In the meantime," continued Ms. Hayes, "I'm afraid it would be inadvisable to separate yourself from Mac in the way you've suggested."

Lindsay's mood immediately darkened.

"Why is that?"

Ms. Hayes took a deep breath, then leaned forward in her chair, bending over the conference table toward Lindsay.

"Officially," she said, "my law firm is employed by Hart Racing as a legal consultant. We would provide legal advice to your father, answer questions for him, help him vet business ideas and decisions, that sort of thing."

"Okay."

"I have worked with this company and your father from the very start. In fact," she shrugged, "it's not unfair to say that my work with this company is what helped me become a partner at my law firm. It made my career, as it were."

Why was Ms. Hayes telling Lindsay all of this? It didn't seem relevant to the discussion.

"This company, your father, my career, they all grew together. Started small and grew to become what they are today."

"Ms. Hayes, while I appreciate the background, I don't see how this impacts the question I posed."

"Mac was here the whole time, as well," said Ms. Hayes. "From the very beginning. I can advise you very well on any legal issues, including transfer of ownership, shifts in corporate leadership, even exploring the market for buyers. But, if you want to sell your ownership stake, you will want to do your own due diligence in establishing a valuation for this company. I cannot advise that strongly enough."

"What do you mean, Ms. Hayes?" Lindsay had started a company, but that had been as easy as filling out a few forms online and paying a few hundred dollars. She'd never bought or sold a company before. Still, wasn't it just as simple as summing up the value of the property and equipment, then maybe adding a scaling factor to account for future growth?

"Everyone at this company is completely trustworthy. I attest to that with all my heart. But everyone has their own point of view, their own opinion, which may differ from yours. Mac offered you twenty pounds for your stake in the company." Ms. Hayes smiled. "That was obviously ridiculous, but offers from potential buyers will come in that are equally ridiculous, but not quite so obvious." She tilted her head at Lindsay. "Do you have any idea what this company is worth in today's market?"

Lindsay blinked. She hadn't really even thought about an actual dollar value for the company. More than anything, she just wanted to be rid of it. She knew it was worth more than twenty pounds, but she almost might have agreed if it meant she could go back home and get on with her life.

"If you were offered," Ms. Hayes shrugged, "a hundred million pounds for your stake in this company, would you take it? Would that be fair market value for half of Hart Racing?"

A hundred million pounds? Lindsay's mouth fell open. That was around 125 million US dollars. A fortune. Lindsay would be set for life with that kind of money. She could do whatever she wanted, live however she wanted. Was this company really worth that much?

Ms. Hayes smiled.

"I can't advise you on corporate valuation," she said. "Not in an official capacity, at least." She gave Lindsay a long, compassionate stare. "But I can advise this. In the time you have, learn as much as you can about what your father has left to you. Understand what it is you now own, if for no other reason than simply to understand what it's worth before you sell it into a market that will gladly steal it from you for a fraction of its worth."

Lindsay blew out a long breath. Her hopes for a quick, easy resolution to this mess were fading quickly. It was becoming clear that she needed to treat this estate with thought and consideration. If her half of the company could be worth a hundred million pounds, how much was everything else worth? The house? The cars? Lindsay needed to work carefully, to figure this out slowly and methodically.

But how on earth did she do that? She didn't even know where to begin.

Ms. Hayes smiled again when Lindsay asked, that damn twinkle back in her eyes.

"You're not going to like my answer," she said.

Lindsay's stomach sank.

There was a quick knock on the door.

"Sorry about that," said Mac as he slipped into the room. "Had to undo this morning's damage." He dropped into the seat beside Lindsay and glared hard at her. Lindsay felt her cheeks flush hot, her muscles tensed. "From now on," he said to her, "consider your driving privileges revoked."

Lindsay sat back in her seat, arms folded across her chest, looking at Ms. Hayes. Ms. Hayes just shrugged and smiled that damn smile again.

Lindsay was definitely not going to like it at all.

7

Lindsay glared at Mac, her legs crossed at the knee as she sat in the conference room chair, arms folded so tight across her chest her knuckles were digging into her sides. But the physical pain was nothing to the tempest raging in her mind.

Asshole was not nearly a strong enough word to describe the man sitting beside her.

Devil was too generic.

Satan himself, maybe?

Satan seemed like a dress-wearing hand-maiden compared to Cormac McEwan.

"Not in a million years, Barbie. Not in a hundred million years will I sell this company."

Ms. Hayes had left the conference room a few minutes earlier, after explaining what she wanted them to do. Mac was to show Lindsay the ropes, explain the company to her from the ground up so she could understand what she was dealing with before finalizing her decisions.

As soon as Ms. Hayes left, Lindsay had asked Mac what he thought a fair market value for the company would be. Seemed an innocent enough question.

Satan would have answered it easily enough.

Lindsay swiveled in her chair, putting her back to the uber-demon. She looked out the window over the gentle chop of the lake surface, winking silver in the sunlight, and forced herself to breathe. Once again, she was letting this man get under her skin. What was it about him? Lindsay didn't overreact with anyone else this way. With everyone else, she could easily keep her emotions in check, stay logical, and calmly point out the fallacies in their thinking. With this man, though, the fallacies were so complex, so deeply-rooted, and so numerous, it made Lindsay crazy just thinking about trying to untangle them all.

But she didn't need to do that. She had to keep reminding herself of that fact. She didn't need him to sell his stake in the company. She just needed him to agree to let her sell her own stake in the company. And surely he wouldn't object to that.

But, as Ms. Hayes had counseled, Lindsay needed to figure out for herself what that stake was really worth. A hundred million pounds was a fortune, but if Lindsay's stake was actually worth two hundred million or five hundred million, Lindsay wanted to know. She may be new to the corporate game, but she would not allow herself to be taken advantage of, especially if a little legwork and a quick analysis would prevent it.

She took one more deep breath through her nose, then swiveled in her chair to face the asshole once more.

"Mr. McEwan," she said, "let's table that discussion for now."

"Table it?" he snarled, folding his own arms across his chest. "You can bloody well chuck it out the window. It's not gonna happen."

Lindsay closed her eyes, willing the flare of anger inside her to cool. It took nearly every ounce of self-control she possessed, but she was able to keep her voice calm and even.

"Let's start where Ms. Hayes suggested, okay?" she said. "I've been named Chief Financial Officer of this company." Mac grunted. Lindsay ignored the sound. "Who was in that role prior to me?"

"Your father."

Right. Of course he was. Otherwise the CFO would be in the room right now.

"Who were the other officers of the company?"

"There were no other officers," Mac said. "It's a privately held company. Your father was the owner, sole shareholder, and sole member of the board. He was the president, CEO, CFO, CMO, CTO, C-bloody-XO and whatever other fucking letters you want to throw between the C and the O. Your father was this company, period."

"He couldn't have done everything himself," said Lindsay, furrowing her brow. That was impossible. She had no idea how many people worked at this company. She'd only seen a handful in the two days she'd been here. But surely her father hadn't built or bought this huge building if he didn't have employees.

"No, of course not," said Mac, "but he ran everything himself. He was aware of and involved in every single detail. Not making all the decisions, necessarily. He trusted his people to do that. But he was aware of everything."

"What about the bookkeeping? The finances?"

"We have accountants and finance people to handle all of that," said Mac. "But your father was the CFO. He kept an eye on all the financials."

"Okay," said Lindsay, "good. Let's start there, then. Can you introduce me to the finance team?"

Mac stared at Lindsay for a long moment. It wasn't an angry stare or an accusing stare or a stare of disbelief. It was just a long, appraising stare that brought a slow tingle creeping across Lindsay's neck. She forced herself to stare back, forced herself not to fidget with her hands. Just returned his gaze with as much calm and cool as she could muster.

Finally, he closed his eyes and sighed, a deep, sad sigh that almost made Lindsay feel sorry for him.

Almost.

"Today's Sunday," said Mac. "The finance team won't be in until tomorrow. But maybe we should start somewhere else, anyway."

He stood, giving her another long stare.

"Come on," he said at last, waving her forward, his voice heavy with what sounded like resignation. "I'll give you the bloody tour."

He led her out the conference room, down the long hallway, and through a series of doors that led them outside. Lindsay squinted against the sudden brightness of the sun. Despite the blue sky and bright sunshine, the air was cold, a bone-soaking late-winter coastal cold. Hugging her arms against the added chill of a quiet breeze, Lindsay could smell the salt from the sea on the wind.

"Shouldn't you be showing me the inside of the building?" she asked Mac, who strode ahead of her down a concrete path. "I don't really care about the grounds."

"You should care about the grounds," said Mac. "They were your father's idea, and they're brilliant." He stalked forward down the path. "But I'm not taking you to see the grounds."

They walked over the top of a small rise. Below them, Lindsay could see a second building, one story, set low to the ground, as if it had burrowed itself into the earth. Because of the small rise and the low profile, it had been completely invisible from the main building, despite the fact that it was only a few hundred yards away.

Mac stopped, letting Lindsay catch up to stand beside him.

"I'm taking you to the very beginning, where this whole company started." He gestured toward the low building ahead of them. "This is where we build our cars."

Mac held the front door for Lindsay as she entered the building, then led her through a maze of hallways.

"The company didn't start in this building," Mac said as they walked. "We only built this a few years ago. But the company started with the first car your father ever built."

The main building they had come from was a visual feast, with the high ceilings in its showroom, the glass walls all around, the view of the beautiful lake. It was clearly meant to impress. This building, while equally beautiful and impressive in its design and detail, had the feel of pure business to it. This building was made for work.

"Everything starts in the machine shop," said Mac, opening the door to a massive space.

Just like the garage Lindsay had stumbled into the day earlier, this room had a smooth concrete floor painted a gleaming white. Throughout the room in neat, widely-spaced rows, were a variety of machines of all sizes. There were huge machines for grinding or turning or hole-punching, Mac explained. There were newer, more sophisticated machines that cut materials with lasers or plasma cutters. Along the wall, on a long table set into the wall itself, were a series of smaller tools, some small enough that Lindsay could hold them in her arms, if she could lift them. These were for precision manufacturing of the smaller engine components and interior parts. Manufacturing tolerances were tight, Mac told her, and there was little room for error. A defect could cost the driver or crew their lives, so quality and precision were of the utmost importance.

"Aside from some of the telemetry equipment, every single part is designed right here in this building," said Mac. "Every one." There was a quiet pride in his voice that Lindsay hadn't heard from him before, a sense of satisfaction, solid and firm. And running through it like the veins in his arm, a deep passion.

"How many parts are there in a car like this?" Lindsay asked.

"Almost fifteen thousand," he said. "All designed here, made by hand, assembled by hand. We don't make cars here, you see. We call them that, but that's not really what they are." He strolled through the room, running his hands lovingly over the smooth metal surfaces of the machines as he walked. His features bore a soft solemnity Lindsay hadn't seen before. "They're works of art," he said. "They're expressions of the ideas and care and skill of the hundreds of people who make them." They came to a set of doors at one end of the room. Mac paused. His mouth twisted into a boyish grin that made Lindsay smile back, in spite of herself. "And they just happen to drive at 370 kilometers per hour," he said.

Lindsay did some quick math. That was about 230 mph.

Boys and their toys.

"Why aren't the telemetry parts made here, too?" asked Lindsay. It seemed to her that data collection for a car with that many parts would be critical. How else would you know what was working and what was failing?

The muscles in Mac's jaw flexed and his face darkened.

"Your father was pushing to move those parts in-house when he died. His goal was for us to be one hundred percent in-house, fully self-reliant." He pushed through the doors into a small vestibule, with another set of doors on the other side. "We got burned a few times in the past when orders weren't fulfilled on time or parts weren't up to spec. The third-party manufacturers just weren't nimble enough to make the changes we wanted before the next race. Or," he growled, "they sold them to our competitors first for a higher price."

"He got everything else in-house. Why not the telemetry equipment?"

Mac shook his head.

"We have the tools to make them. We just haven't found someone with the know-how to design them yet. They're complicated parts, requiring not just the chips themselves, but wireless antennas, data protocols, data storage and processing."

Mac shrugged. "We understand the manufacturing. To be honest, it's the data side where we're missing. We just haven't gotten there yet."

It didn't seem complicated to Lindsay. She didn't know specifically what systems these cars used, but telemetry was telemetry. The silicon was basic. A chip talks to a system, like a machine or a program. The code measures whatever that system is doing that needs to be measured. Then the results are sent wirelessly to a receiver where the data are stored for analysis. Real-time analysis can be tricky, especially if there's a lot of information coming through, but that was just a bandwidth issue. Those kinds of problems had already been solved by others. The manufacturing was the hard part. If they already had that worked out, Lindsay couldn't see why they were still outsourcing their telemetry chips.

Mac showed her the pattern shop, where designers invented new ways to build the materials for the car parts, which were mostly made of composite materials. Beyond that was the clean room, which they couldn't enter without dressing up in special clean suits and booties. That was where the composite building materials were actually made from carbon fiber coated in resin and stored in huge freezers Lindsay could see in the back of the room. The doors looked like the freezers in a commercial kitchen.

"Tightly controlled environments," explained Mac, "with the air pressure, the humidity, the temperature all closely monitored. If any impurities get into that composite, with all the stress these cars are under on the track, it could cause a crash."

He showed Lindsay the design labs, which looked similar to the tech offices she had worked in for years. Lots of collaborative open spaces, with TVs on the walls for presentations, whiteboards for brainstorming, and rows and rows of workstations with wide monitors and tablets on the desks for drawing with styluses.

"We've got hundreds of people designing and refining every single part in the car," said Mac, "usually with multiple people working on each part. They design them, then test them in computer simulations. From there, we make scaled-down versions of the parts and test them in the real world."

The tone of Mac's voice had changed. Where before it had been soft, reverent, passionate, now it was more business-like, a bit more strained. And his movements seemed a little more strained, too, a little more stiff. Unlike the ease with which he'd moved through the machine shop earlier.

They moved on to another room filled with pedestals topped with complicated setups of plates and rods and wires. "This is our small-scale testing lab. Every part is examined and tested under real-world conditions. These testing stations put stress on the parts across any axis, any dimension, any plane. Shear, tensile or compression stress, everything."

Other setups tested the integrity of the manufacturing, using a variety of techniques to look for cracks or weak joints. They put the parts through longevity tests, too, to see how long they could withstand the stress and strain of normal racing conditions.

They pushed into another room, similar to the first, but with just one large testing station, about ten times bigger than the others. A long, clear cylinder surrounded the platform.

"The last testing stage before final build is here," Mac explained. "We make a large-scale model of the car, fully assembled, about sixty-percent of the actual size, and put it in the wind tunnel to test for aerodynamics and performance."

By the time they got to the end of the tour, Lindsay's mind was whirling. The process of building a race car was a lot more complex than Lindsay had thought. Granted, she'd never really thought about it before, but car racing had always seemed to her to be nothing more than back-alley street racing with corporate marketing sponsorships. Instead, there really was an art to all of this.

But more than that, there was a science to it. The attention to detail, the creativity of design and manufacturing, the rigor of the testing. Lindsay was impressed, and intrigued. She loved a good process, and her mind immediately looked for ways to improve it.

Mac turned a corner and led her down a short hallway. "That's all the design, manufacturing, and testing. Here," he said, pushing through another doorway, "is where the final assembly happens."

The room was tall, but smaller than Lindsay expected. She had pictured a long room with high ceilings and long tracks along which the car would travel as it was built.

"Those are assembly lines," said Mac. "They're for factories that are pumping out hundreds of thousands of cars a year, where the workers do one thing over and over, screwing in a door handle or bolting a tie rod. For us," he said, gesturing to the room, "we only build two cars at a time, iterating on the design over and over throughout the year."

As he said it, Lindsay could see it. The room was essentially divided in half, with each side being a duplicate of the other. Room for two cars, side by side, and all the teams, all the tools and parts needed to assemble them. At the far end were two identical garage doors that went from the floor to the ceiling high above them.

And she saw Mac's body language shift again, too. Once again, he seemed at ease, in his element, moving with smooth stealth, almost like a jungle cat. In this room and in the machine shop, he gave off a sense of total command, total control. In the design and testing labs, he had seemed less sure of himself.

They exited the building into the chill air and the bright sun again, walking slowly back up the hill, side-by-side.

"We start maybe a year in advance," said Mac, "designing the car for the season after next. So right now, for example, half of the design team is iterating on this season's car while the other half have started working on next season's designs. Slowly, over time, more and more designers and testers will shift over. Then the manufacturing team will shift. Then the body work, finishing, and assembly teams and so on."

Lindsay glanced at Mac, walking beside her. Gone was the irritation, the anger on his face. There was no hint of the asshole now, aside from the same angular jaw, the same dark beard dotted with bits of grey, the same muscular torso...

Despite the cool air, Lindsay felt her forehead break out in a sweat.

"Where are the cars right now?" she asked, swallowing hard, her mouth suddenly dry.

"They're in Sakhir, Bahrain."

"Bahrain?" said Lindsay, incredulous. "Like, Saudi Arabia?"

He chuckled, a lilting sound that made Lindsay smile. "Don't let the Bahrainis hear you say that," he said. "They'd be very upset to hear that their country had been taken over by the Saudis."

Lindsay furrowed her brow.

"But, yes," he said, giving her a sidelong look, "Bahrain, the *country* that's in the Persian Gulf, near Saudi Arabia."

Lindsay's cheeks reddened. She was not up on her Middle Eastern geography.

"What are the cars doing there?"

"Testing," said Mac. "They were in Spain two weeks ago, now Bahrain. The first race of the season is in Sakhir next weekend."

"I thought you said the season had already started," said Lindsay, her voice sharp. Was this guy trying to trick her into waiting too long to sell this company? If she could get that taken care of quickly, she could get back home and focus on her own issues. The Brinksley people were not going to wait forever.

His face hardened, his eyes flashing at her. "It has already started," he said through gritted teeth. "As far as most racing companies are concerned, the season starts when that season's cars are revealed. That happened a few weeks ago, before Spain." He faced forward again, his strides lengthening, his pace quickening up the gentle hill. "Sorry, Barbie," he said, "you're just going to have to wait to get your hands on your father's money."

Lindsay stopped on the path, clenching her fists.

He acted like she was just some ungrateful, money-grubbing relative who cared about nothing but getting rich. Getting rich was the furthest thing from Lindsay's mind. She just wanted to get home, to get back to her own life.

And what business did he have acting like she was in this for herself, anyway? She hadn't even wanted to come. She didn't want a damn thing from her father. But now she had to take time away from her own life to deal with all the shit her father had left behind.

Lindsay felt her pulse pounding in her temples. She hated men who jumped to illogical conclusions based on false assumptions, then assumed they were always right.

And she hated being called Barbie.

But, she swore she wasn't going to let this man get to her again. She closed her eyes and pulled a long breath in through her nose, felt the cool air come in, tasted the saltiness on the back of her tongue. She blew it out slowly, her lips pursed, willing calm over herself with the outbreath.

She released her fists and hurried to catch up to Mac, who had already disappeared over the top of the rise. Lindsay reached the top of the hill just in time to see him entering a windowless metal door in the side of the building. It closed before Lindsay could catch up. She tried the handle.

Locked.

A badge reader hung on the wall beside the door. But, of course, Lindsay didn't have a badge.

She tried the handle again. Naturally, it didn't budge.

She knocked on the door, quietly at first, then louder, then banged the side of her fist against the door, loud, heavy metallic thunks resounding with each strike.

Lindsay felt her pulse thudding heavier in her temples with each pound of her fist, fought down the urge to scream. Her face flushed hot and she felt a tingling heat in her neck and shoulders.

What the fuck was this man's problem? Why was he so goddamn rude to her?

And what the fuck was Lindsay doing here in the middle of nowhere, thousands of miles away from home, banging on a fucking metal door on the side of a building?

She grabbed the door handle and rattled it, put one foot against the door and pulled. She knew it was pointless. She knew the door wouldn't open. But she had to do something, something to vent the heat now in her cheeks, the sweat now on her brow and chest. The scream?

The scream she could no longer suppress. It swelled from her throat, long and high-pitched and rising in volume as she poured her frustration into it.

Fuck this door.

Fuck this company.

Fuck this whole goddamn country.

Her scream became a roar, deeper, both filling her chest and emptying it at the same time. She put both feet up against the door, hanging off of the handle, riding it like a pogo stick, rattling the handle and banging with both feet against the door.

Fuck her fucking father.

Fuck her fucking clients.

Fuck her goddamn, fucking life.

The roar filled her body and her mind. She closed her eyes and let that sound, the physical force of the screaming, draw every last bit of anger from her.

And fuck the goddamn, motherfucking asshole who locked her out of this fucking building.

She pressed both feet against the door, locked her knees, held hard to the handle and arched her back, screaming up at the cold, empty sky.

And she was spent.

Lindsay dropped her feet back down to the ground. Released the door handle. Stood slumped in the path, chest heaving.

Nothing had changed. She still had all the same problems as she had a moment before. But she felt a little better for the exertion, for the release. Her chest was a little less tight, her muscles a little looser.

The door opened.

Mac stood there, one arm swinging the door toward her.

Lindsay straightened, all the tension flooding back into her. Mac stared at her for a long moment, his eyes intense, but his face blank, inscrutable.

"Keep up," he said, turning away.

Lindsay leapt forward to catch the door before it locked her out again.

Asshole.

8

THE METAL DOOR opened to a short hallway, beyond which was the garage Lindsay had stumbled into by accident the day before.

Had it only been a day? It felt like a week.

They entered from the opposite side of the room. Lindsay could see the door to the treacherous bathroom set into the far wall. On her left was a tall garage door that ran from floor to high ceiling.

The same mechanic that had been with Mac yesterday was there again, wearing the same blue-and-purple coveralls, cleaning a tool with a rag. He was tall and wire-thin, with a wispy, scraggly brown attempt at a beard that looked more like dirt on his chin than anything else. His hair was light brown and lay in short, tight curls on his head.

The same car was there, too, the race car that Mac had been working on. Only now there was another car in the bay beside it.

"Is that my car?" she said.

"No, actually," said Mac. "It isn't."

"It's the car I drove here this morning, isn't it?"

"Yes, that's the one."

"Then it's my car."

"No," Mac shook his head, "sorry, it isn't."

Lindsay blew out a deep breath. This whole petulant man-child routine was really getting on her nerves.

"Look," she said, "I get that you and my father were close, and I understand that you would resent him giving his possessions to me instead of to you. I mean, I've never even met the guy."

Mac put his hands on his hips and rolled his eyes toward the mechanic.

"But I didn't ask for any of it," Lindsay continued, her voice rising in pitch. She had sworn she wouldn't let this man get to her any more, but she couldn't help it. Something about this asshole just rubbed her in all the wrong ways. "It was my father's choice to leave his stuff to me. Not mine. So stop acting like this is all my fault." She pushed her hands through her hair, wanting to pull it all out. "It's been a really long day already, and it's not even three o'clock yet. So just... get over it, okay?" she spluttered. "The car and everything else he mentioned in the will is mine, for better or for worse."

Mac laughed, a quick bark, and shook his head, staring at the ground, his hands on his hips.

"First of all, Barbie," Mac began.

"Don't call me that," said Lindsay, forcing her voice to be soft.

"I'm not jealous of you for what your father left you," Mac said. "I don't care about that kind of stuff, and I've got plenty of stuff of my own, anyway, thank you very much."

"Right, okay," said Lindsay, rolling her own eyes. "Good for you."

"Second, I'm sorry if your sudden wealth is such an inconvenience to you. It must be very hard to have to deal with so much good fortune all at once. My heart bleeds for you. Truly."

This guy was an idiot and an asshole. What wealth? She hadn't looked into her father's finances yet, but most of the rich people Lindsay had heard of were in debt up to their eyeballs and then some. Keeping up appearances. Behind that big house was probably an even bigger mortgage. Behind the big company, a pile of debts.

"And third, I'm sorry to tell you that this particular vehicle," he stabbed a finger toward Lindsay's car, "is not included in the stipulations of your father's will."

"Oh, it isn't, huh?"

"No, it isn't."

"This car that was in my father's garage—my garage—this very morning?"

"Not included."

"This car that I drove to work not three hours ago?"

"I don't think any reasonable person would call that driving."

"And why would this car not be included?"

This ought to be good. Another mansplaining job, with this asshole trying to gaslight poor, little, ignorant Lindsay into letting him take the fancy old sports car from her.

"Because your father had already donated it to the company for its collection of historical race cars."

"Right," said Lindsay. "And is that collection stored in your garage at home, by chance?"

"No," said Mac, "it's stored right here in this building." He smiled sweetly at her. "You walked right by it this morning without a care or a clue in that pretty little plastic head of yours."

The showroom at the front entrance. Lindsay had thought all the cars were from Hart Racing, but she hadn't really paid much attention. She scowled at Mac.

"Then why was the car in my garage?"

"Your father had just made the donation."

Lindsay scoffed. "That's convenient."

"Maggie can show you the paperwork," said Mac. "We were about to come to the house to pick up the car when..." A cloud fell over Mac's features. "When your father passed."

A pang of pain stabbed through Lindsay's heart when she

saw the change in Mac's demeanor at the mention of her father's death. Maybe he really had been close to him.

And maybe he was telling the truth about the car. That would explain why it was sitting in the middle of the garage facing the door, blocking all the other cars from exiting.

But she didn't even care any more. She didn't want the car. She didn't want any of the cars. She just wanted to be done with this whole mess.

"Whatever," she said, throwing her hands up.

"'Whatever', she says," said Mac to the mechanic, clapping his hands. "Gerald, she says, 'whatever'." He bowed to Lindsay. "We thank you for your graciousness, your highness."

Heat crept up Lindsay's neck again. She was sure her palms would start bleeding from all the fist-clenching she had done that day.

"Is that the end of the tour?" she asked.

"Er, no," said Mac. "Not quite." He gestured to the mechanic. "This is Gerald, one of our lead mechanics. Sam should be around somewhere." He turned in a circle, searching.

"Parts room," said Gerald. "Surprised you didn't run into each other over there."

"Not part of the tour," said Mac. To Lindsay, he said, "You'll meet Sam later."

"Who's Sam?" asked Lindsay.

"Sam is our head mechanic," said Mac. "But let's press on with the tour," he said moving past Lindsay toward the door. Mac stopped, gesturing toward the bathroom door. "Would you like to use the loo before we move on?"

Asshole.

"You didn't tell me what this garage is for," said Lindsay.

"Ah, right, sorry. This is the old assembly room," said Mac. "This is where we built the cars before the new building came to be. Now it's my personal test garage." He grinned. "My little playroom."

"What are you testing?"

"New designs. Alternate assemblies."

"Wild hairs," said Gerald.

Mac grinned again. "I've been known to have a wild hair from time to time," he said. "Let's move on now."

He led Lindsay through a set of double doors back into the hallway with the conference rooms. Instead of going ahead, though, Mac took a sharp right, up a curling flight of stairs that opened onto a massive open seating area. The floor was covered in thin carpet. The walls were made of windows, tinted against the sun. Throughout the space were an array of tables, soft chairs, low glass-walled cubicles, and the occasional rolling whiteboard, all arranged in a series of groups down the length of the room. The arrangement seemed to occupy the entire top floor of the building.

"You wanted to know where the finance team was," said Mac. "Here you go. This is where all the admin teams work."

They strolled along an aisle that ran down the center of the room. It was a familiar setup to Lindsay. Typical corporate office environment, with the open seating meant to provide a sense of space, the soft chairs meant to provide a sense of comfort, the gathering areas with tables and whiteboards meant to provide a sense of community. In Lindsay's experience, the actual effect was more one of forced, fake congeniality and awkward invasion of privacy, with no one getting any real work done at all.

This particular space, though, somehow seemed different. There was more color, more individuality than Lindsay was used to. There was artwork everywhere that seemed to have been made by kids of all ages, and even some that could have been made by talented adults. Plants abounded, on desks, by the doorways, even in the middle of the floor. Knick knacks were everywhere, too. Stuffed animals, Lego race cars, fiddle toys. There was a personality to the room that seemed more genuine than Lindsay had expected. It was more like a den in a well-appointed home than the saccharine office spaces Lindsay had worked in before.

"Everyone who isn't directly involved in design, test, or assembly works here," said Mac. "Finance, procurement, HR, legal, PR, marketing, creative. Maggie's desk is over there." He pointed toward the far side of the room. "Mine is next to it, though I never really use it."

"Where did my father work?"

Mac chuckled.

"He used his desk even less than me," Mac said. "He would just carry around an iPad, usually, or sometimes a laptop. Sometimes just his phone. But he always said his real job was making sure everyone else here was happy, feeling fulfilled with their jobs, getting what they needed to do their best work." Mac stuffed his hands in his pockets, his face taking on a wistful look. "He would just wander around all day, checking in with people. He seemed as genuinely interested in what Georgina in facilities was doing with her kids that night as he was with how the new chassis design was performing in the wind tunnel."

Lindsay saw a warm light in Mac's eyes as he talked about her father. Whoever this man had been, he'd been well-liked by Mac. And by Ms. Hayes. Lindsay wondered whether she would have liked him, too, if they'd met under other circumstances. If she hadn't been his abandoned daughter from another continent. If she'd been Georgina in facilities, would Lindsay have loved him, too?

"He was one-of-a-kind, your father," said Mac.

It was a pointless line of thinking, impossible to prove. And what difference would it make now? Maybe Lindsay would have loved her father. Maybe she would have hated him, resented him for turning his back on her and her mother so many years ago. But it was a moot point. Her father was gone, and she felt nothing toward him. No more than she would a stranger on the street.

What remained was the mess he'd left for Lindsay to sort out. And for that, Lindsay wasn't too happy with him at all.

Mac led her down a stairwell at the far side of the floor, one that led to the showroom, near the front door of the building.

"I'd better walk you through the collection here," said Mac, "since it's obvious you have no idea what you've been looking at."

Lindsay ground her teeth, but kept her tongue in check.

"These cars are arranged chronologically," Mac said, "from oldest at this end, near the front door, to newest at the far side."

Indeed, the first car in the row was very old. It looked like a refrigerator box on wheels. Lindsay couldn't imagine anyone racing in that car. They'd be signing their own death warrant.

"It was dangerous, for sure," said Mac in response to Lindsay's comment. "But racing has always been dangerous. Even now, when the cars are the safest they've ever been, when we keep the safety of the driver first and foremost in our minds at all times as we design these cars, there's still a real chance of injury or even death. It's just the nature of racing."

They walked slowly along the line, the cars becoming flatter, sleeker, more experimental in their designs. The tires grew wider and smoother, the chassis more aerodynamic. Fins and wings and air vents appeared in the designs. The body shapes changed from boxes to wedges to thin little tubes that looked like kazoos. Lindsay could see the creativity, could imagine the engineers trying new things, testing new hypotheses, all in search of... what? Speed? Stability? Victory against the competition?

"All of the above," said Mac, shrugging. "Everyone is a little different, motivated by different things. It's always nice to win a race or a championship, but winning isn't everything. Sometimes, just working out a kink in the design or the build, solving some problem that's been eating away at your brain at night is as satisfying as winning a race. For us builders, anyway." He smiled. "If you ask the drivers, they may say different."

"Where are the drivers?" asked Lindsay. "Do they only work during the week, too?"

Mac laughed. "No, they work all the time during the season. Seven days a week. Racing from Thursday to Sunday, then traveling, always analyzing the last race and planning for the next race. They're in Sakhir now with the rest of the race crew. They'll be analyzing the testing results and prepping for this weekend's race."

"Why aren't you with them? Don't you go to the races?"

"Yes," said Mac, his voice taking on a tinge of irritation, "I do. But we've been trying to get ahold of you." He gave her a curt smile. "Not so easy to do, as it turns out."

Lindsay ignored the comment. They continued on.

"All of the cars to this point have been from other manufacturers. Right here," said Mac, pointing to a car-sized hole in the line of vehicles, "is where the Ferrari you drove today will sit." He glowered at Lindsay. "Once it's repaired."

How on earth she could have damaged anything just by driving the stupid car was beyond her. Wasn't that what cars were made to do? Drive? These people were just perfectionists. Probably trying to roll back the odometer or something.

Again she ignored him.

"This here," said Mac, pointing to a sleek, blue-and-purple car with stubby wings on the front and a wide fin on the back, "is the first car your father ever built. Built entirely by hand, all on his own."

Lindsay walked around the car, examining it from every angle. It looked a lot like the newer cars, just more crude. Like a prototype of the newest designs.

"How did he make the..." She waved a finger at the car. "...the outside. Did he do that himself?"

"The chassis?" said Mac. "He took the bodies of existing cars, cut them up, then welded the parts into the shape he wanted. Same with the mechanical parts. A few he bought new, but he didn't have much money back then, so most were taken from existing cars. Some old race cars, some just normal cars from the junkyard."

He walked around to stand beside Lindsay, both of them admiring the vehicle. The movement brought his scent to Lindsay's nose. It was that same spicy, earthy smell she remembered from the garage the day before. Her stomach fluttered and her head felt oddly light. She pushed the feelings from her mind.

"Back then, your father didn't have the means to manufacture anything himself," Mac continued. "He was just a kid. Eighteen years old. But he had some wild ideas." Mac pointed back down the line of cars toward the kazoo-shaped vehicles. "At the time, all of the cars used that more rounded design." He pointed back toward the car before them. "This was a real departure. A wild experiment."

"A wild hair?" said Lindsay.

He grinned at her.

"Turns out your dad got them, too," he said. "A hell of a lot more than me, truth be told."

"So this was the car that changed racing forever or something?" said Lindsay. That's the usual plot of these kind of stories. Boy from nowhere, with nothing but his brains, his determination, and a heart of gold changes the world forever.

"No, this car was a disaster," said Mac, shaking his head. "The aerodynamics were completely wrong. It was more like an airplane than a race car. Way too much lift, not enough downforce. Your dad nearly died the first time he drove it at speed. That's how he tells it, anyway." He swallowed hard. "Told it," he corrected himself.

"Huh," said Lindsay, nodding. The car was an actual experiment, then, not a corporate-sanitized prop to show the greatness and infallibility of the company's history. The first car, but a total failure. And here it was in the showroom of the company's headquarters for everyone to see and discuss.

Lindsay admired that.

Failure was no fun, but it was the only way to success, in her mind. If you weren't failing, you weren't doing something new, you weren't learning, you weren't pushing yourself to explore new ground. Work hard, fail often. That was Lindsay's philosophy.

And her father's philosophy, too, apparently. Celebrate the failures, because trying and failing is a hell of a lot better than not trying at all.

"He iterated from there," said Mac, continuing down the row of cars, "testing his way to a design that worked." He stopped beside another car. It was similar to the first, but the edges were smoother, the lines more refined. "This is the car that brought your father his first podium." He ran his hand along the edge of the fin on the back. "That's a top-three finish," Mac said when he saw Lindsay's questioning look. "You stand on a podium to receive a trophy. Sort of like the Olympics."

They strolled further down the line past more cars, each design a bit different from the one before. Some were a lot different from the ones before. Lindsay could see the innovation, the wild hairs. Some were obviously doomed to failure, even to Lindsay's novice eye, but the next car in line usually incorporated and improved upon some element of the failure before it.

Failing fast, and failing your way to success. Lindsay hadn't achieved the success part yet, but she'd certainly had her share of failures.

They reached the end of the line of cars, by the door that led to the conference rooms, then crossed to the other side. Another row of cars stretched before them, these far more polished and perfect looking.

"This side is all of the Hart Racing cars for the last twenty years," said Mac. "That side," he gestured to the cars they'd just reviewed, "is the history that led to the company. This side is the history of the company itself."

As they looked at the cars, all of them sleek and beautiful, more and more modern as they progressed down the line, Lindsay's mind wandered. She looked out the windows at the lake and the fields beyond. She couldn't quite see the ocean, but knew it wasn't far beyond the line of trees on the horizon. The sun was already dipping in the sky, its light slanting through the windows. Based on the angle, it should have been blinding her. Maybe the windows were photoresponsive somehow, their tint growing stronger in response to the amount of light coming at them. Mac had said Lindsay's father had designed the grounds. Would he have designed the windows, too?

It was clear he was an innovator. A tinkerer and an engineer. Lindsay must have inherited that from him, since her mother was much more of a conventional thinker. Independent and fierce in her defense of that independence, but not someone who thought too far afield. She'd been a gifted investor, paying for her life and Lindsay's life with smart, solid investments, some of which paid off in a big way. Microsoft and Apple and IBM. Her mother had seen the tech boom before anyone else, and it had funded their lives for years afterward before she died. They hadn't had a lavish life, but it had been a comfortable one, based on her mother's smart, conservative, logical thinking and calculated risks.

Lindsay wondered what her father was like. He was clearly smart. Was he conservative like her mother? Was he a logical thinker like her and Lindsay?

"And that's the tour," said Mac.

Was that what had drawn him and Lindsay's mother together in the first place?

"For now, anyway," Mac continued, his voice distant in Lindsay's ears. "You'll want to see the travel setup, too, and meet the team. This is the bones of the operation, the foundation, but that's the beating heart of it. But we'll save that for later."

And what had driven her parents apart? Lindsay had never

thought about it before, never cared. Her mother had never been willing to discuss it beyond a quick dismissal, and Lindsay had trusted that it wasn't important. Now, though, her curiosity was growing.

"Hello?" Mac waved his hands in front of Lindsay's face. "You there? Earth to Barbie. Come in, Barbie."

Lindsay sighed.

"Please don't call me that," she said.

"Lost you for a minute there," said Mac.

"Thank you for the tour," Lindsay said. "I think I'll go home now, come back tomorrow when the finance team is in."

"There's more to see," said Mac. "I haven't shown you the grounds yet. Your father did some groundbreaking stuff there." He grinned. "Pun intended."

Lindsay smiled weakly at him. She hadn't pegged Mac for the dad joke type. "Thanks, but I'm still kind of jetlagged, I think, and I have some other things I need to take care of."

Mac furrowed his brow.

"Right," he said, "okay. I'll just bring the car around."

"I can drive myself home."

Mac snorted. "You've proven that you can't. For the safety of all of England, and Scotland, too, your driving privileges are officially revoked." Before Lindsay could protest, Mac strode away. "I'll get the car," he called over his shoulder. "Just wait out front."

He was gone before Lindsay could mount a protest. This whole hand-holding thing was already getting old. Lindsay needed to find a way to get off on her own so she could poke around and see what this company was really all about.

She needed to find the skeletons, and that wasn't going to happen with Mac hanging around.

A long, sleek black sedan pulled up outside the windows. Lindsay got in, and five minutes later she was at her front door.

Okay, maybe she had had a little trouble with the other car

this morning. It had taken her a lot more than five minutes to get to work.

"Dinner at eight," said Mac, rolling down the window as Lindsay shut the car door.

"No, I'm okay," protested Lindsay. "Thank you, though."

"Maggie will be here to pick you up. Seven forty-five."

He grinned again. Lindsay was momentarily dazzled again by his startlingly perfect teeth. Dental hygiene had really come a long way in the UK, apparently.

"Be ready," Mac said, "and don't let her calm demeanor fool you. Maggie doesn't like to be kept waiting."

He rolled up the window and peeled away.

Lindsay sighed and checked the time on her phone. Three hours until dinner.

Time to do some real work.

9

Lindsay rubbed her face in her hands, her elbows propped against the kitchen table. The jetlag was still kicking her ass. When she had walked in the house and found herself alone, finally, in a quiet space, the fatigue had hit her like a Mack truck.

Or maybe more like a race car?

No. Those little cars wouldn't do nearly the damage she felt. She felt like she'd fallen asleep in the middle of the road and been run over by a steamroller, peeled off the drum, folded like origami, then crushed in one of those car crushing things they have in junkyards.

"You look like Wile E. Coyote at the end of an episode," said Marina on the laptop screen.

"Meep-meep," Lindsay replied with a sigh.

Marina's eyes popped wide, her mouth hanging open.

"Was that a joke?" she said, incredulity in her voice. "In the three years I've known you, I don't think I've ever heard you make a joke."

"Don't be ridiculous. Of course I have."

"Raj?" said Marina. "Can I get a ruling on this one?"

"You," said Raj, moving his hand in circles in front of the

camera, as if he were wiping the lens, "are definitely a joke-free zone, Lins," he said.

Lindsay was too tired to protest.

"Okay, so can we do four weeks, then?" she said.

"Yep, there's the Lindsay we know and love," said Marina. "Not that we mind the jokey Lindsay. She's probably a hoot, too, so if you feel like adding a little more—"

"Marina," said Lindsay, the weight of that fatigue feeling just a little heavier.

"I can do four weeks on my side, but only once Rajanesh," she rolled the 'r' like a snare drum, "does his part."

"Only my mother calls me that," said Raj. "And you are not nearly as hot as her."

"Ew, Raj," said Marina, her face screwing up in disgust. "Are you crushing on your mom right now?"

Raj shrugged. "Beauty is beauty," he said. "I call it like it is. Besides," he gestured to himself, "this perfection had to come from somewhere."

"The real question," said Marina, "is where you get your delusions about reality."

"Raj, can you get the environment online with dummy data in two weeks? That way Marina can get started on her end."

"I'm betting on drugs," said Marina. "Heavy drugs."

"I can have that done in one week, boss," said Raj, "because I love you and I am just that good."

"Wow. *Very* heavy drugs," said Marina. "Lindsay, you should really have him tested."

"You should have your eyesight tested," said Raj.

"Good one," Marina said. "You've really stepped up your game from the 'yo momma' jokes."

Raj shook his head. "You know   "

"Okay," said Lindsay. If she didn't intervene, she knew those two would go on like that for days. "Raj, you'll have the tables set up in a week. Marina will have the UI ready four weeks later."

"And I'll have live data piped through and validated three weeks after I set up the tables," said Raj.

"That'll give Marina one week to test the UI." Lindsay blew out a long breath. "So, five weeks, total."

They'd cut the timeline down from eight weeks to five weeks. A reduction of thirty-seven and a half percent.

Hopefully, that would satisfy the Brinksley VP. She'd pushed back hard on Lindsay's initial estimate. Probably just the usual corporate posturing, something that would let the VP tell her boss that she'd squeezed the most from Lindsay that she could. Still, Lindsay wanted to make her happy.

She needed to make her happy. Lindsay needed the Brinksley account to come through. She didn't have anything else lined up, and it wasn't going to be easy to drum up more work while she was messing around in merry old England.

Eight weeks had been a comfortable timeline, with room to correct if things went wrong, which they inevitably did. Five weeks was bare-bones. No room for error.

Which meant Lindsay should push back on the pricing, too. That old saying about fast, cheap, and good—you can pick two, but you can't have all three—applied here. Lindsay would never compromise on the quality of the work she and her team delivered. It would be good, even if Lindsay had to kill herself to make it so. That meant it could be fast or it could be cheap. Since the Brinksley VP just pushed to make it faster, Lindsay now had to push to make it pricier.

And that made Lindsay feel even more tired. Her skill was in analyzing data, not in negotiating with Type-A corporate executives who cared nothing about the real value of work. They just wanted maximum effort for minimum price. It took all of Lindsay's energy to battle people like that.

Lindsay had full confidence in Raj and Marina, but she had her own job to do on top of the pricing negotiations. And as tired as she was in that moment, she wasn't feeling confident at all.

"Okay, guys," she said. "That's it, then. Thanks. Let's talk in a couple days."

"Good afternight, you two," said Raj with a jaunty salute before dropping from the call.

Lindsay rubbed her face in her hands again. It was seven PM, the daylight fading in the window before her, the sea on the horizon glinting with the last touch of the sun's rays.

Seven PM. That was what, eleven AM in San Francisco? Lindsay's body was exhausted, like it had been up all night. Because that's exactly what had happened. Now, her brain was trying to wake up at the same time that her body was trying to rest, and the stress between the two was sapping Lindsay's energy even more. She needed food and she needed sleep.

And she needed to get some work done.

Lindsay pulled her head out of her hands. Marina's face was still on-screen, watching her.

"You don't look so good," she said.

"Thanks."

"How did you sleep last night?"

"I don't remember," Lindsay said. "Mac says my driver practically carried me to bed."

"Mac?" said Marina, a hint of a smile playing at the corner of her lips.

Lindsay sighed. "Marina..."

"Come on, Lindsay. You're on a nickname basis with England's most eligible bachelor." Her hint of a smile turned into a wicked grin. "Please, just let me live vicariously."

Lindsay was not in the mood for the high school dating game.

"There's nothing to live vicariously for, unless you want a long, boring tour of a race car factory."

"He's already seen you in a towel. When's he going to return the favor? Then maybe you'll both drop the towels and—"

"Not going to happen, Marina," said Lindsay, her voice hard, the fatigue getting the better of her. "I know you think he's hot—"

"I'm not sure that's a strong enough word."

"—and he is... attractive, it's true. Physically."

Marina sat back in her chair, a smug, satisfied look on her face.

Lindsay pointed a warning finger at the camera. "But he's an asshole. Demeaning, misogynistic, disrespectful." She ticked off on her fingers, then sat back in her chair. "I mean, I spent practically the whole day with him and I can't even count the number of times he insulted me. He's arrogant and rude—"

"Okay," said Marina.

"—and he called me Barbie again."

"Oh dear."

"Again! Can you believe that? And he won't even let me drive a car—"

"That's probably wise."

"—as if he gets to tell me how to live my life." Lindsay threw up her hands in frustration, the last of the gleam on the horizon winking out as dusk fell. A blue darkness enveloped the room for a brief moment before lights came on around her. Soft, subtle, gentle light arrayed around the room, suffusing it with a yellow glow that felt to Lindsay like she were sitting in front of a warm fire, the logs crackling and hissing in the fireplace.

Must be on a timer. Or an ambient light sensor.

"Wow," said Marina. "He sounds like a real piece of work." She had an odd expression on her face, one that Lindsay couldn't quite interpret. Not in her jetlagged state, at least. Marina's eyes were twinkling, almost like she were laughing, but her face was neutral, her head nodding like she was really understanding what Lindsay had been saying.

Lindsay didn't know if Marina was being sarcastic or not, but she was too tired to worry. She just took Marina at her word.

"I've never met a man who was such a total asshole in my life," said Lindsay. "And that's saying something, because Silicon Valley is full of them."

"Why don't you just stay away from him then?"

"I can't," said Lindsay. "I tried. I have to put a valuation on this company before I sell it, so I don't get screwed in the deal, and apparently he's the only one who can show me everything I need to know. And I have to wait eight more months before I can get rid of this company and move on with my life."

"That's terrible." Again with that inscrutable expression.

"Believe me," said Lindsay, "as soon as I can be rid of Mac McEwan, I will be. The finance team is back in the office tomorrow. I'll get what I need from them and Mac can go be an asshole to someone else."

Lindsay rubbed her stomach and winced. The muscles were tight, and her stomach felt acidic, like something was burning inside.

Marina's expression darkened as she furrowed her brow. "When's the last time you ate?"

Lindsay's stomach growled, loudly, in response.

"I don't know," she sighed. "It's been a while. I have to go get ready for dinner, actually."

"Get ready? Are you going out to dinner?"

"Yes, with Mac and Ms. Hayes."

Marina got that look on her face again, open and interested, but with that twinkle in her eyes.

"I guess I'll leave you to it, then," she said. "Enjoy your dinner, Lindsay." This time, she grinned. "Tell Mac I said hello."

Lindsay rolled her eyes and hung up without bothering to say goodbye.

She flipped over to her email and composed a quick response to the Brinksley VP. The eight-week timeline could be compressed to as little as five, she wrote, but not without significant effort on the part of the team. Lindsay's fingers hovered over the keys as she thought about the best way to word the next part. "That effort would increase the cost of the project." Too abrupt. "Should this be preferred, it would require an additional investment..." Too weak and corporate. "Faster delivery means higher prices." Too in-your-face.

Lindsay stared at the screen, her mind whirring with phrases, the words sliding past her eyes.

The sound of the doorbell woke Lindsay with a start.

As she lifted her head, the skin of her face peeled away from her laptop keyboard, where her head had fallen. She rubbed her cheek and felt the rough dents of the keys. On her screen was the email she'd been writing. "Faster delivvvvvvverjhjhsyol," it said, followed by four lines of random characters. She checked the clock in the corner of the screen as the doorbell rang once more.

Seven forty-five, on the dot.

Shit.

A surge of adrenaline jolted Lindsay awake and onto her feet. She ran down the hallway to the door.

"Hello, Ms. Rhodes," said Ms. Hayes, smiling on the doorstep. Her smiled faded as she eyed Lindsay from head to toe and back again. "Ready for dinner?" she said, wryly.

"I'm so sorry," said Lindsay, her throat scratchy and dry. "I just need a few minutes to... clean up."

"Not to worry," Ms. Hayes replied, stepping through the doorway. "Take your time. I will make myself at home."

Ten minutes later, after brushing her teeth, pulling a brush through her tangled hair, and doing her best to look somewhat human, Lindsay emerged to find Ms. Hayes nowhere to be found.

"Ms. Hayes?" Lindsay called.

"Down here," came a voice from the end of a hallway.

Lindsay followed the sound into a deep room she hadn't seen before, one lined with tall bookshelves on every wall. A leather couch and several poofy, inviting leather chairs surrounded a low table in the center of the room. Rolling ladders hung from the shelves on each wall. Ms. Hayes stood before one of the shelves, holding a leather-bound book, her hand smoothing the cover.

She'd changed from the pantsuit she'd worn at work that morning into soft grey slacks with boots and a silky button-down blouse that hung untucked under a thick deep-blue sweater. Though the outfit looked very comfortable, it somehow made Ms. Hayes seem even more elegant than her work attire, especially in the dim light of the library. The book in her hand only added to the effect. Lindsay—dressed in the same clothes she'd worn all day—her usual dark jeans, grey t-shirt, black blazer, and Vans—felt like an unsophisticated teenager in comparison.

"Sorry to keep you waiting," she said.

Ms. Hayes smiled faintly at her, a distant smile, as if Ms. Hayes' mind were very far away from that room, from that moment.

"Your father loved these books," she said, her voice small and remote. "He collected them from all over Europe."

In the long pause that followed, Lindsay didn't know what to say in response. "I didn't know he liked to read," was all she could come up with.

"He didn't," said Ms. Hayes. She laughed, a short, sudden note that hung like the chime of a bell in the room. The sound seemed to startle her. She looked up at Lindsay as if realizing for the first time that she was there. "He read," she said, "but he certainly wasn't a bookworm." She slipped the book back onto the shelf. "In fact, it took years for me and my husband to convince your father to start a book club with us. He agreed to join only if Mac agreed, too." Ms. Hayes chuckled. "Mac joined in, he said, just to hear what your father would say about Fifty Shades of Grey."

Ms. Hayes looked up at Lindsay, tilting her head. Lindsay didn't like being looked at, in general, but under Ms. Hayes' gaze she felt a warmth in her chest, a loosening. It felt good to be seen by Ms. Hayes, somehow.

Ms. Hayes trailed her fingers over the leather spines as she walked toward Lindsay. "No, your father wasn't a bookworm, but he loved these books. Loved this room," she said, looking with fondness at the space. "We had a lot of laughter in here." She stood close before Lindsay, leaned in and winked at her. "And not just from Fifty Shades of Grey."

Lindsay followed Ms. Hayes through the house to the front door. She walked without hesitation, with an ease that reminded Lindsay that Ms. Hayes—and Mac, too—had a long history in this house. Even though the house belonged to Lindsay now, its memory belonged to them.

"Do you have everything you need?" Ms. Hayes asked.

"Yes, I think so," said Lindsay. She looked around for her keys by reflex, then realized she didn't have any. She'd left the house completely unlocked this morning.

"I never got any keys," she muttered.

"Not to worry," said Ms. Hayes, opening the front door and shepherding Lindsay to the car with one extended arm. "Your father installed a sensor on his locks that responds to your phone. It locks the house automatically when you leave and unlocks it when you arrive."

"But how does it know my phone?" said Lindsay as she buckled her seat belt.

Ms. Hayes just smiled patiently at her as she settled behind the wheel.

"We set it all up for you, Ms. Rhodes, the night you arrived."

What else had gone on that first night Lindsay had stumbled home, while she was passed out in bed?

"But, even so," continued Ms. Hayes, "this area is quite safe, and we're not going far."

"Where are we going?"

"Mac's house," said Ms. Hayes. "It's just next door."

"Mac lives next door?" Lindsay's blood chilled.

"He and your father were very close."

Lindsay was never going to be rid of this guy. First he wanted to chaperone her everywhere in the company, then he wanted to be the one to drive her wherever she went, and now he lived next door, like an overprotective governess. She sighed, pinching the bridge of her nose under her glasses as the car swung out of the driveway onto the main road.

"Did you enjoy your tour of the facilities today?" Ms. Hayes asked. Lindsay looked over at her, wondering how she knew. "I spoke to Mac a short while ago," Ms. Hayes said in response to Lindsay's look.

"It was..."

Lindsay searched for something she could say about her afternoon. Infuriating? Frustrating? Condescending? Confusing?

She realized these were all words to describe Mac, not the tour itself.

"It was very interesting, actually," said Lindsay. "I had no idea how much care and creativity goes into making race cars."

"Were you expecting otherwise?"

Lindsay shrugged. "I never really thought about it." She looked out the window at the passing trees, darker shadows within the darkening night. "If anything, I guess I figured it was just a bunch of greasy mechanics with corporate logos on their shirts."

Ms. Hayes laughed, the sound making Lindsay smile. "Not too far off, in some ways," Ms. Hayes said. They turned and wound along a curving drive. "But behind the logos and the grease," she said as a beautiful house, lit up in the night, came into view, "I think you'll find there's quite a bit more."

Ms. Hayes parked in a circular drive in front of the house. As Lindsay got out of the car, she looked up at the home towering above her. Her father's home—her home, now—was modern, all cantilevered concrete and weathered wood on the outside. Absolutely gorgeous, massive, but modern, inside and out.

Mac's house was equally gorgeous, equally massive, but much more traditional. It was built of stone and brick, with a cobbled driveway that rounded a small flower garden in front of the house. Several peaked roofs towered above Lindsay's head, all bathed in beautiful soft blue-white lights that dropped from the eaves like a curtain. As she stepped from the car, Lindsay felt she was stepping into a landscape filled with magic.

A fairy tale. That's what it felt like. The cool night air against her cheeks. The smell of the sea. The faint sound of waves breaking on the shore nearby. The magical lighting. The fairy-tale mansion before her. It was impressive and incredible, yet, like in a fairy tale, it was somehow unassuming at the same time. It truly took Lindsay's breath away.

"You're late," came a voice that put that breath right back and made Lindsay want to get in the car again.

10

MAC STOOD ON THE DOORSTEP, door open behind him. "I was starting to wonder if I should inform the police."

"Fifteen minutes is hardly grounds for a missing persons report, Mac," said Ms. Hayes smoothly.

Mac raised his eyebrows, then cast a quick glance at Lindsay. "Right," he said. "My mistake."

A white kitchen towel hung over one shoulder and he wore an apron tied around his waist, the bib hanging down from his hips. He wore jeans and sneakers, with a black t-shirt that clung and bulged in all the right places, showing off those powerful biceps, that strong chest, and a flat stomach that seemed to ripple under his shirt as he moved. Lindsay swallowed hard, suddenly wanting to get back in the car for an entirely different reason.

"Come inside, then," Mac said. "The salmon is dry enough already. Salads are already on the table."

He led them both inside the house through a short entryway to a living room with comfortable couches and chairs arranged in front of a crackling fireplace. Several side tables and a coffee table were interspersed throughout, with books, throws, elegant lamps, and even a few candles for decoration. The ceilings were at least twenty feet high, lending the comfortable space an air of tasteful beauty. Lindsay would not have been the least bit surprised to see this very room in the pages of Architectural Digest or Better Homes and Gardens or some other magazine that showcased beautiful, expensive homes.

She wondered who had decorated it for Mac. There's no way he could have done it himself.

Mac peeled off into the kitchen while Lindsay followed Ms. Hayes into a formal dining room. A long, beautiful wooden table that could have easily seated ten people was set for just the three of them, with full place settings at one end. Plates, chargers, several forks and spoons and glasses and knives and napkins. It was like stepping into a fancy restaurant, but with the casualness and intimacy of a family gathering.

Salads were already set at each place, vibrant mixed greens with bright red strawberries, the dressing glistening in the subtle light from several pendant lamps hanging above the center of the table.

Ms. Hayes sat on one side of the table. Lindsay took the seat opposite, leaving the setting at the head of the table for Mac. He entered the room carrying a bottle of wine and filled Ms. Hayes' glass without asking. She nodded her thanks.

"Wine?" said Mac to Lindsay. "We have Maggie's favorite, this lovely Sauvignon Blanc, which will pair beautifully with the salmon. Or, if you prefer red, we've got Zinfandel or Pinot Noir, Syrah, Cabernet." When Lindsay didn't respond, he continued. "We've also got Riesling, Rosé. Or beer, if you'd rather have that."

Lindsay's brain was having trouble processing what she was seeing. Mac in an apron serving wine. So incongruous with everything she'd learned about him so far. It just didn't fit with her image of the condescending asshole who had locked her out of a building just a few hours earlier. And now he was listing every type of alcohol known to man like his only wish in life was to make her dining experience the most pleasant it could be.

"Or are you more of a cocktail kind of girl, Barbie? Hmm? Malibu Sunrise, maybe? I've been told my Sex on the Beach is incredible." He grinned.

Ms. Hayes just sighed.

Lindsay's face hardened as the world snapped back into place once more. There was the asshole she knew and hated.

"Just water for me, thanks," she said.

It could have been her imagination, but it seemed to Lindsay that Mac's face actually fell when she said it. She was expecting a cutting retort, but Mac just nodded, his face serious, and went to the kitchen. He returned without his apron, carrying a glass of white wine for himself and a silver carafe from which he filled all of their water glasses.

"Please," said Mac, gesturing to the salads as he sat at the head of the table. "Enjoy."

They ate the salad quietly. The greens were fresh, the dressing light but lively on Lindsay's tongue. Lemony and bright. The strawberries were tangy, not overly sweet, but just sweet enough to offset the peppery greens and the bright lemon beautifully. Lindsay wasn't a foodie, but this salad was the best thing she'd eaten in months. Maybe years.

"Bit early in the season for the strawberries," said Mac between mouthfuls, "but it's hard to resist them when they show up at the market."

"It's delicious, Mac," replied Ms. Hayes. "Thank you for having us."

He looked strangely at Ms. Hayes for a moment, furrowing his brow, then glanced at Lindsay. He gave her a tight smile.

"How is your salad, Barbie?" Ms. Hayes cleared her throat. "I mean Lindsay," said Mac quickly. "How's your salad?"

"It's fine," said Lindsay, her voice hard and short.

No. She wasn't going to be like that tonight. Not with Ms. Hayes there. She didn't want to make this dinner uncomfortable for her. Or for herself, for that matter. Regardless of how tired she was, regardless of how much of an asshole Mac was to her, she would hold her head up and take the high ground.

She took a deep breath and let it out.

"It's delicious, actually," she said. "I haven't eaten this well in a long time."

Mac looked askance at her. "Really? It's just a salad."

"It's a really good salad."

"What do you normally eat? You're from California, yeah?" Lindsay nodded. "The produce there must be fantastic."

Lindsay swallowed the bite in her mouth, the food lighting up her senses. She could practically see colors, the flavors were so vivid.

"I eat a lot of take-out," she said. "DoorDash, GrubHub, Uber Eats. Just whatever is convenient."

"Those are delivery services, not types of food," Mac replied. "What do you actually eat?"

Lindsay shrugged. She honestly couldn't remember anything she normally ate. She just didn't think about it much. What was the last thing she had eaten?

"I'm usually working," she mumbled as she thought.

She remembered waking up on the couch with dry chicken and crusty noodles that had fallen on the floor.

"Chinese food," she said. "I eat Chinese food sometimes."

Mac had a forkful of salad halfway to his open mouth. He let his hand fall back to the plate, mouth still open, and stared at her for a long beat. He looked at Ms. Hayes, who just looked back, politely eating her food.

Mac nodded slowly, clearly restraining himself from saying whatever asshole thought was on his mind.

"Well," he said at last, each word stumbling out, haltingly, "I hope you enjoy your dinner." He smiled and tucked the forkful of salad into his mouth.

And Lindsay did enjoy dinner. It was incredible. Shockingly, deliciously good.

The main course was salmon, but unlike any salmon Lindsay had ever had. "Grilled Salmon With Rhubarb Curry and Coconut Cream," Mac announced as he served them. Three rectangles of salmon lay atop a soft red curry, with bits of green leaves arrayed throughout. The salmon had a thick dark crust on the top that crunched when Lindsay bit into it, the texture playing on her tongue with the silkiness of the salmon meat. The skin was smoky and rich, the salmon muted. Both came alive against the curry, a sweet, warm slurry that was as vibrant on her tongue as its soft red color was in her bowl. She actually closed her eyes and moaned when she took her first bite.

Her eyes popped open when she heard herself, steeling for the inevitable comment from Mac. Something about making her moan again in bed, maybe. Or something about her eating habits, how it must feel good to eat actual food for the first time. Or maybe something about needing to loosen up a bit, if eating dinner was enough for her to make that sound.

Instead, he just looked down at his plate, cutting his salmon with a knife, a slight smile on his face.

Lindsay glanced at Ms. Hayes, who was just pulling the fork from her own mouth. Ms. Hayes just smiled and raised her eyebrows at Lindsay, eyes twinkling.

They finished their entrees in silence, too focused on their food to speak. For Lindsay, each bite was like seeing fireworks for the first time. Like seeing an analysis finally come together after weeks of wrangling data. It fed her body and her mind, lit her senses and her imagination.

"Did you really make all of this?" she asked Mac as she set her spoon down in her empty bowl after scooping up the last of the curry. It was all she could do not to lick the remnants still clinging to the china.

"Why so surprised?" asked Mac.

"I don't know," said Lindsay, frowning. Why was she so surprised? He was an asshole, for sure, but even assholes could have skills and talents. In fact, if the reality shows were any indication, being an asshole was almost a requirement to be a great chef. Maybe that was why Mac was so good at it. "I guess I just didn't picture it."

Mac stood and gathered the empty bowls and dirty silverware. "We've only just met," he said. "I may surprise you yet." He winked at her.

It would have been almost sweet, if it weren't for the wink.

The winking was definitely creepy.

Ms. Hayes smiled faintly at Mac as he took the plates into the kitchen. "Dessert coming up in a bit," he called over his shoulder. "First, though, coffee or tea?"

"Herbal for me," said Ms. Hayes.

"Herbal for you," said Mac at the same time.

Ms. Hayes smiled that faint smile again.

Dishes rattled as Mac set them down in the sink. "Lindsay?"

The meal was settling into Lindsay's belly, weighing down eyelids that were already propped on toothpicks. She needed coffee, for sure, if she were going to make it much longer. But she didn't want to drink crappy coffee, especially after such a delicious meal.

"Do you have espresso?" she asked, bracing herself for the inevitably disappointing response.

"I do," said Mac, his low voice close behind her. Its rumble sent warm shivers through her body. Lindsay turned in her seat to see him right behind her chair, leaning against the doorway to the kitchen. "But I'll admit that I'm no expert at the espresso machine," he said. "I prefer the French press, myself."

Lindsay stood from her chair and turned to him. He stood up straight, eyebrows arched in surprise.

"Do you mind if I have a look?" she asked.

Mac turned to the side and extended one arm in invite, giving Ms. Hayes a shocked and amused look.

Stepping into Mac's kitchen was like stepping into a high-end restaurant, but far more nicely appointed. There was a huge refrigerator on the far wall, with four square doors arranged in a 2-by-2 grid. To Lindsay's left, along the wall, was a long row of cabinets on the top and the bottom, with a marble countertop in between that contained a deep sink and a faucet. On Lindsay's right was an island with another sink and faucet, more counter space, and a wooden chopping block with a beautiful dark parquet pattern. A bar and several tall chairs adjoined the island.

But the most impressive part of the kitchen was the island in the center. At least twelve feet long and eight feet wide, one side housed a massive range with ten burners and two ovens, long with several large drawers for storage. The other side had a large grill, a long, smooth griddle, and some kind of appliance that looked like a toaster oven on steroids. A shelf full of pots and pans stood above the island, accessible from both sides, with a huge steel hood fluting from the ceiling above it all. On either end were more storage drawers, more counter space, and another sink and faucet.

"The espresso machine is over here," said Mac, leading Lindsay to a small nook on her left that she hadn't noticed when she'd entered. The nook was bathed in light from two recessed fixtures in the ceiling above, but it might as well have been the light of angels. Lindsay could certainly hear them singing when she laid eyes on the espresso machine that sat so modestly on the countertop.

It was a La Marzocco KB90, Lindsay's dream espresso machine. Two group heads with straight-in portafilters, dual independent brew boilers, and ABR scales to precisely weigh the espresso doses and stop extraction based on the mass of the grind. A Mazzer Robur S grinder stood beside it. Top-of-the-line equipment, all around.

"Do you know how to work it?" asked Mac.

Lindsay had not yet regained the power of speech. She just nodded.

Yes, she knew how to work it. She dreamed of working it at night. She had practically memorized the schematic diagrams on the La Marzocco website. She had fantasies about visiting the headquarters in Florence and taking home her own unit.

But she would never have thirty thousand dollars to blow on an espresso machine.

And yet, here was one in Mac's kitchen. And he said he didn't even like espresso.

"I got it for your father," Mac said softly when Lindsay asked him about it. "He came over for dinner a lot, and he loved to drink espresso." Mac laughed. "But he was such a stickler about it. I originally had one of those automatic espresso machines."

"The Keurig?" said Lindsay, wrinkling her nose.

"Yes," Mac snapped his fingers, "a Keurig. At first. Then the Nespresso. Then a... Jury? Juris?"

"Jura," nodded Lindsay. Those machines ran into the thousands of dollars.

"Right," said Mac. "But he complained every time. Too bitter. Tastes burnt." Mac laughed. "So finally I did some research, flew to Italy, talked to the folks at La Marzocco, and had this machine waiting one year when your father came over for his birthday."

Lindsay raised her eyebrows. "That's some gift."

"Oh, it wasn't for him," said Mac. "I mean, I bought it for him to use, but I kept it here. Wouldn't let him take it home." He grinned. "He was over her for dinner practically every night, anyway." Mac shook his head slowly. "You should have seen his face when he saw this machine for the first time. I could almost hear the heavens open and the harps of the angels play for your father." He smiled, a tight, flat smile, nodding. His eyes shined in the overhead light. "That was a good night."

Lindsay could see in Mac's face how much her father had meant to him. And Ms. Hayes had said it herself several times.

Lindsay couldn't help but wonder who her father had been. What was it about him that inspired such devotion in the people he worked with? The people he employed?

"Has it been used since he died?" asked Lindsay, turning to the espresso machine.

Mac cleared his throat quickly. "Um, no, it hasn't."

Lindsay quickly ran the machine through a cleaning process, then pulled herself a shot. The hum and thump of the machine matched the thump of her heart as the espresso slipped into the cup. She tipped it into her mouth. The taste on her tongue was electric.

"Wow, you really like espresso," muttered Mac. "Your dad used to make that same sound when he drank it."

Lindsay didn't even notice, but she was indeed humming softly as she drank.

She pulled another shot and brought it back to the table to savor more slowly. They sat and sipped their coffee and tea—true to his word, Mac drank coffee from a single-serving French press—and chatted about nothing much for a few minutes while their stomachs settled and the caffeine roused them from their food comas. Mac served dessert, a dark chocolate mousse with Bailey's Irish Cream Liqueur. It was silky and cool from the refrigerator, with a restrained sweetness that was satisfying without being cloying, like most desserts.

Lindsay was starting to think she'd been missing out by focusing so much on her work and so little on her food. San Francisco was supposed to be a culinary city, but the most adventurous she'd ever been with food was to order take-out from the Ethiopian restaurant in SoMa.

Once the mousse was finished, Mac put the dishes in the kitchen and they moved to the living room. Lindsay sank into a deep-cushioned chair in front of the fire. Mac offered her a glass of cognac. She'd never had it before, but it was a night for trying new things, so she accepted. Ms. Hayes demurred, so Mac and

Lindsay drank cognac in front of the fire, the thin glass surprisingly heavy in Lindsay's hand. "Tulip glasses", Mac called them, and they were shaped like their name suggested, with a wide bowl on the bottom that cupped into Lindsay's palm and a curved mouth like pouting lips that brought the rich scent of the drink to Lindsay's nose with every sip.

The cognac burned as it went down, in the best possible way. Filled with Mac's delicious meal, her senses alive from the beautiful espresso, reclining into a comfortable chair by a warm fire, a peace like she hadn't felt in years settled over Lindsay. She turned in the chair and threw her legs over one arm, leaning back against the other, gazing into the fire without while she sipped her drink and felt the fire spread within.

Mac and Ms. Hayes chatted around her, talking about races and travel schedules and people Lindsay hadn't met. Their voices mixed with the crackling of the fire and faded into a sussurating lull that enveloped Lindsay like a warm embrace, rocking her back and forth with its rhythms, that peace spreading through her body, melting her tired muscles, soothing her tense mind, guiding her gently by the hand to a place of warmth, safety, and endless possibility.

11

FOR THE SECOND time in as many days, when Lindsay woke, she found herself in a strange room with no memory of how she had gotten there.

She was fully clothed, save for her shoes, and lay under a heavy fleece blanket on top of a thick comforter on a low queen bed. The blanket smelled faintly of spice and earth, like Mac's cologne. Lindsay pulled in a deep breath through her nose. He may be an asshole, but he was one of those nice-smelling assholes.

The room was dark, but there was light bordering the curtain hanging over a window to her right. Lindsay sat up, too quickly. Her head pounded as gravity pulled the blood away. She sucked in sharply and discovered that the same family of squirrels had somehow found her and again set up camp in her sleeping mouth. She slid her tongue around in her mouth to serve them their eviction notice, but they wouldn't leave.

Lindsay pulled back the curtain and winced, turning her head from the blinding light. Her hair fell over her face, diffusing the bright light. Once her eyes had adjusted, she pushed back her hair and looked out to see a wide wooden deck with metal rails. She must have been near a corner of the house, for Lindsay could see one edge of the deck, while the rest extended out of sight to her right. The ocean crashed on the sand beyond the rail. The sky was blue, the sun bright, but something about the gunmetal color of the waves told her that water would be frigid this time of year.

A flash of movement caught the corner of her eye. She craned her neck and saw a man's arm and leg. The leg was barefoot in fleece joggers, the arm bare and muscular in a t-shirt sleeve. She was starting to recognize the particular curve of that arm. The bulge of that bicep, the veins cording that forearm.

Mac's house.

Had she spent the night at Mac's house?

A chill ran up Lindsay's spine. She wasn't quite sure if it was excitement or revulsion. The fact that she wasn't sure was even more disconcerting.

The arm lifted, then came back down. Mac was drinking something from a mug.

Lindsay had a sudden urge—no, a need—for coffee, strong coffee, something that would take away her headache and send those squirrels packing for good.

She hadn't been drunk last night. At least, she didn't think so. But her memory came back in bits and pieces as if she'd been on a raging bender. Fireplace. Dinner. Cognac. Dessert.

Espresso.

Lindsay pulled on her shoes and headed out of the room, stumbling her way into the kitchen where that beautiful KB90 sat waiting. It hadn't been a dream. Lindsay clapped her hands together in front of her face, barely resisting the urge to squee with delight.

She pulled a shot and let it sit on her tongue, bathing her taste buds, before tilting it down her throat. This time, she did make a sound, a soft, satisfied sound, half-sigh, half-moan.

"Should I get you a bath towel," said Mac's voice behind her, low and growling in a way that reverberated deep within Lindsay's body, like a car drifting off the side of a road onto the rumble strips, "or would you prefer I just leave you two alone?"

Lindsay finished the shot and pulled another, taking her time, then turned to face Mac with the tiny espresso cup cradled in her hands.

"Why is it that you're always here when I wake up?"

"Just lucky, I guess," said Mac with a grin, his coffee cup dangling from his fingers, "only this time, you're the one intruding. This is my house, after all."

"And how is it, again, that I wound up sleeping here?"

Lindsay knew nothing had happened, but she couldn't help the accusatory tone that slipped into her voice. There was just something about Mac that set her on edge.

She was going to have to work on that.

"You fell asleep, Barbie," said Mac, a warning in his voice.

Barbie. Lindsay suddenly remembered what set her on edge. Mac was an asshole.

"All I did was carry you to a guest room so as not to wake you." He furrowed his brow at her. "I am a gentleman, I'll have you know."

Lindsay snorted into her espresso cup.

Mac folded his arms across his chest, making his biceps bulge in a way that made Lindsay's body overheat.

Or maybe it was just the second espresso.

"I was hoping a good night's sleep might improve your mood," said Mac, "but, obviously, I was wrong."

Mac rinsed out his coffee cup and set it in a dishwasher cleverly disguised to look like another cabinet by the sink.

"Do you eat breakfast in the morning," Mac asked, "or don't the Uber drivers deliver that early?"

Too much asshole, too soon after waking. Lindsay just sipped at her espresso.

"I've got oatmeal, cereal. I can make you some eggs, if you like," said Mac, adding soap to the dishwasher and starting it running. "I just had yogurt with more of those strawberries that were on the salad last night. Nice with a bit of local honey drizzled on top. How does that strike you?"

Lindsay wanted to strike Mac, but just sipped her espresso again. She was starting to feel like an asshole herself. Mac was just offering to feed her, after all. To cook for her, no less. But she had just woken up and her coffee hadn't hit her yet.

And he'd called her Barbie. Again.

"Or maybe you'd feel more at home with some overpriced guacamole on a thick slice of wheat toast?" The dishwasher hummed and clicked to life, quiet in the background, as Mac crossed his arms again, he and his biceps staring at her from across the kitchen.

Lindsay tossed back the last of the espresso and walked slowly toward Mac, holding his gaze like a lioness on the prowl. She wasn't sure why she was doing it. It definitely was not something she would normally do. But once she'd started, she couldn't stop.

Electricity coursed through her body. Her eyes were fixed on his. She couldn't look away. Like the paralysis that comes when you grab an ungrounded electrical circuit, as she'd done in her basement once when she was younger. No matter how much she wanted to let go, she couldn't drop the plug. No matter how much she wanted to look away, she couldn't drop her gaze from Mac's eyes. So blue, like the deepest sky, the clearest sea, the truest sapphire all mixed into one.

She walked toward him slowly, slowly, across the kitchen. He stood fixed in place, his arms still folded, his eyes widening slightly. His scent grew stronger. Like the scent of that blanket, but multiplied a hundred times. More vivid. More alive. More present. Lindsay pulled it into her lungs, drawing deep like she'd never draw breath again. She feasted on it, hungered for it.

He stood beside the sink. She drew closer, close enough to feel the heat from the morning sun radiating from his skin, to feel the heat of his core pushing into the air around his body. Like the crashing of the sea she could hear faintly outside, Lindsay felt Mac's heat in waves. Like the waves of the ocean, it pushed her with the impact, then pulled her with the undertow, closer, closer, until she was standing right in front of him, looking up into his eyes. Looking up and falling down, down.

She reached her hand out, never dropping his gaze, setting her espresso cup down in the deep sink. Her forearm brushed his knuckles with the movement, jolting a static shock through her with an audible crack.

They both flinched. He must have felt it too.

But neither of them moved. Neither of them dropped their gaze.

"Aren't you going to rinse that cup?" said Mac, his voice husky. Something stirred in Lindsay at the sound, something low and primal, something that hadn't stirred in a long, long time.

"I'll let you take care of that," whispered Lindsay.

What was she doing? What was she saying? Lindsay felt like she'd lost control of her own body and mouth, that her mind was no longer in control of her actions. Who was this person standing so close to Mac, to that condescending, misogynistic asshole who called her Barbie all the time?

These thoughts ranted and raged in a corner of her mind, in a bubble behind glass, the raging muted and distant. The rest of her mind was focused completely on the heat flowing from Mac's body, the scent suffusing Lindsay's senses. On her mouth suddenly dry, her lips suddenly parched. She ran her tongue over them and felt a switch click below her gut, some setting flipped to a position it had never been in before.

Asshole or not, she wanted Mac. She wanted to trace the cords on his forearms, run her hands over those biceps, pull off that t-shirt and feel the firm muscles of his chest, feel his heart beating hard beneath. She wanted to skim her fingertips over the ridges of his stomach, then lower, slide along the sharp, well-defined angles where his torso joined his hips.

Lindsay felt her face flush hot, felt a hot flush lower, too, one that sent hot shivers through her body. She felt alive, electric. Every hair on her skin stood erect. Every nerve ending humming, singing, aching for stimulation.

She held Mac's eyes, those blue eyes. His brow was furrowed. He swallowed hard. They were so close Lindsay could hear it, could feel his heart thumping under his shirt. His smell, his scent was stronger, hotter, the spice of his cologne mixed now with some kind of musk, something more feral, more primal. She drank it in, her head swimming with it, intoxicating her.

She wanted to slide along those sharp, well-defined angles, slide slowly lower, lower, feel his skin against the smooth of her palm, then down below the waistband, and feel—

The doorbell rang, followed by a sharp knocking.

Like two magnets repelling each other when they get too close, Mac and Lindsay each took a step back, putting feet of distance between them in a heartbeat.

Lindsay stared down at the floor, one steadying hand on the counter. Cold air rushed to fill the empty space between them, to cool whatever fever had overcome her in the last few seconds.

Seconds? Minutes? Hours?

She had no idea how long they had stood there.

And she had no idea what madness had consumed her. If she didn't know better, she'd wonder if Mac had drugged the espresso, somehow laced the beans or doped the water.

She smoothed her hair away from her brow. Her hand came back covered in sweat.

The doorbell rang again, then the front door opened.

"Hello?" Ms. Hayes' voice rang out. "Just me, Mac. I'm coming in."

"It's alright, Maggie," said Mac, clearing his throat. "We're in the kitchen. I'm just trying to convince Barbie here to let me make her some breakfast."

"Oh, I would definitely suggest you let him make you some eggs Benedict," said Ms. Hayes, smiling as she came through the doorway from the main room. She glanced between both Mac and Lindsay, her smile fading. "It's truly something special," she said, her voice trailing off.

An awkward silence fell over the room.

Even the Barbie comment wasn't enough to penetrate the fog of confusion and emotion and odd physical sensations raging through Lindsay's mind and body in that moment. She felt untethered, like an airplane whose engine quits during ascent, drifting silent and uncertain, awaiting the nosedive.

"Apparently they don't eat breakfast in America," muttered Mac, finally.

"I'll be sure to bring my own next time I visit," said Ms. Hayes. "Ms. Rhodes," she said, "I thought I'd bring you in today and introduce you to Mrs. Kintey, our finance director. She can get you the information you've been requesting."

Lindsay looked up at Ms. Hayes, her face giving her a point of reference in the fog, something to center her mind and pull her from the momentary insanity she'd fallen into.

She nodded. "I'll just... get my things," she said, hurrying from the kitchen.

Back in the hallway, she stopped for a moment, hand on her chest, feeling her heart still racing. Whatever that was, whatever had just happened in that kitchen, it was intense. Lindsay's body was a mess. Heart racing, breaking out in a sweat, no control over herself, barely able to think straight.

She closed her eyes and pulled in a few long, deep breaths.

Whatever that was, Lindsay didn't like it.

Whatever that was, she needed to get her shit together so it wouldn't happen again.

She opened her eyes again and walked down the hall to the

spare room, forcing her strides to be long and smooth, forcing her mind to focus, forcing her heart to settle down to a normal rhythm.

Ms. Hayes was here to bring her to the finance team. Lindsay would collect the data she needed and sift through it, figure out what was going on with the company and how much it might be worth.

She got to the bedroom. She didn't actually need anything. When she'd come the previous night, she'd brought nothing with her but her phone, which was already in her pocket. What she needed was a moment alone to come back to her senses.

She combed her fingers through her hair, wiped her brow with her sleeve, and stared out the window at the cool sea extending far to the horizon, grey against a blue sky. She would go with Ms. Hayes, leave Mac behind. She'd meet this Mrs. Kintey person and start actually working, moving toward a goal, instead of just wandering around the building and feeling useless and confused all the time.

With the information Mrs. Kintey would provide, Lindsay could look forward to a day of data analysis. A brand new dataset to explore. It was her favorite thing to do, like going to a movie that you had heard was excellent, but which you knew nothing about. A green field of data to play in for the whole day. Full of unexpected surprises, twists, and turns.

A whole day of just her and the data.

And no Mac.

That was definitely something Lindsay could look forward to.

12

Ms. Hayes offered to bring Lindsay home to freshen up, but Lindsay just shook her head, stopping only long enough to grab her laptop. They rode the short way to the office in silence, Lindsay desperately trying to clear her head and focus. She stared at her hands. She stared at the light on the horizon. She stared at the trees sliding by outside her car window. Anything to try to erase the images in her mind.

Of Mac's arms.

Of Mac's chest.

Of those sharp angles peeking out above the waistband of his joggers.

"You coming?" said Ms. Hayes.

She was leaning in the open door of the car. They'd already arrived and parked, and she'd already gotten out of the car. All while Lindsay was lost in the images she was trying not to get lost in.

Ms. Hayes led Lindsay in the front door and up the staircase, stopping to set her bag on her desk. The office was still mostly empty. It was still early. But there were perhaps two dozen people milling around, fixing tea or coffee and chatting with each other, smiling and laughing.

Ms. Hayes' desk was in the middle of a short row of three cubicles in the corner of the huge open-floor office space occupying the top floor of the building. She pulled two stacks of boxes off the desk beside hers, setting them against the wall.

"You can use this space here, if you like," she said. The desk was bare, the low glass walls of the cubicle empty. No photos, no papers, no toys or trinkets or fidget spinners. No pens or pencils or even a charging cable. Lindsay would have thought the desk was entirely unused, except for a name placard attached to the outside corner of the cubicle wall. "Kellen Hart," it read.

That's all. No mention of his title or his purpose or the fact that he owned the entire company. Just "Kellen Hart".

"That was your father's desk, as you can see," said Ms. Hart. A wry smile quirked the corners of her mouth. "He didn't use it much."

Lindsay just nodded, not sure what to think. The desk was in the far corner of the large, open top floor of the building. It didn't offer much privacy, but there was some granted by being near the corner.

"Let me introduce you to Mrs. Kintey."

Lindsay followed her down the row of cubicles, bristling at the placard on the last cube: "Mac McEwan". She lifted her chin and focused on making smooth strides and following Ms. Hayes, desperately trying to ignore the memory of Mac's scent, the spice and musk, the heat from his body...

"Hello, dear."

The voice reminded Lindsay of Mrs. Doubtfire, a sing-song, grandmotherly hooting. Her eyes focused on a short, round woman that fit the voice well.

"Lindsay Rhodes, this is Mrs. Kintey, our finance director."

"Oh, call me Helen, dear, please," the woman hooted. "Or just call me Gram. That's what most people do."

"They... call you Gram?" said Lindsay, her mind still not quite focused.

Helen shrugged. "I don't mind it," she said. "Most of these kids are young enough to be my grandchildren, anyway, and I think of them that way, more or less." Her smile was wide and kind. It pulled Lindsay in like a life ring thrown from a rescue boat. "Would you like some tea, Lindsay?"

"No, thank you, Gr... Helen," said Lindsay. It just seemed too weird to use the name "Gram" for the director of finance in a company she was valuing for sale.

"Well, I'll leave you to it, then," said Ms. Hayes. "Call me if you need anything."

She and Helen nodded at each other, the look they shared freighted with some meaning Lindsay didn't catch. It put her on guard. Surely they wouldn't try to hide anything from Lindsay. Would they?

It didn't matter. Data didn't lie. That's one thing that Lindsay loved most about it. It didn't lie, didn't get offended or angry. It didn't seek revenge or play power games. It didn't try to seduce you, then punish you for not being seduced.

Data was pure, honest, and good. If you worked hard and thought logically, data would reward you in kind.

Helen pulled over a chair for Lindsay to use. They squeezed into her cubicle together, their shoulders touching.

"What would be the best way I can help you, dear? What is it you'd like to see? Annual reports? Monthly summaries?"

"Actually, is there a way I can access your database directly?"

Helen's face darkened with confusion, her head tilting. "That would be difficult to use," said Helen. "You'd need specific technical knowledge in order to make any sense of it, you see."

"I'm a data scientist," replied Lindsay, trying hard not to sound condescending. "I know how to use a database."

Helen's face brightened at that. Her entire demeanor changed in a heartbeat, from the coddling granny to a sharp, fast-moving executive. "Ho ho," she chortled, "thank goodness. Here I was thinking I'd have to spend all day holding your hand through reams of reports." Her smile was just as wide, just as kind, but now her eyes sparked above it. "Do you understand the rules and practices of financial accounting?"

Lindsay nodded. "I'm no expert, but I know enough. I've got my own data science company, a startup. I work very closely with my accountant."

Her eyes twinkled again. "An entrepreneur like your father," she said. "Apples and trees, dear. Apples and trees." She tapped on her keyboard, screens flashing by on her monitor. "Okay, then. You're all set," she said a few seconds later. "I've created an account for you with full privileges to all our financial data. The account mirrors the privileges your father had."

"Was he a technical person, too?"

"He was an engineer," Helen said, "happiest with a wrench in his hands, I think. Or a drink at a party," she laughed. "He had to give up most of the mechanical work a long time ago. But, he learned what he needed to know to run his company." She smiled to herself. "And he ran it well. Very well."

Lindsay opened her laptop and downloaded the software and user profile she needed to configure her access to the company's financial data. It was an older database, not the kind she would normally use for data science. It was built for well-structured data, the kind often created by finance organizations, who used accounting practices that were well-established and closely regulated. The types of systems her startup built were more free-form and flexible, able to handle just about any kind of data, and in massive quantities. Using the system Helen had provided was like using a slide rule for calculations instead of a computer.

But, it would work just fine.

"Thanks, Helen," said Lindsay, face buried in her laptop, already exploring the table structures in the database schema.

"You let me know if you have any questions, dear."

Lindsay didn't. Not that day or the next or for the rest of the week.

She sat at her father's desk for the rest of that day, long after the sun had set and the light in the office had switched from sunshine through the window-lined walls to the warm glow of the overhead bulbs. Lindsay's mind shifted away from the data long enough to notice that the light wasn't the usual sterile fluorescent light found in every office she'd ever worked in, but was the warm, soft light you were more likely to find in someone's home, emanating from dozens of recessed fixtures set into the ceiling.

For the rest of the week and into the weekend, Lindsay didn't bother to go to the office at all, preferring to access the database from home. Ms. Hayes and Mac would both make appearances from time to time, but quickly shifted from smiling offers to drive her in to the office to concerned questions about her needs—food, questions, recreation, companionship—to silent offerings of meals in glass containers covered with tin foil or plastic wrap. Mac, in particular, fell into a routine of providing three meals a day, either delivered wordlessly from the doorstep in person or, if Lindsay didn't bother to answer the doorbell, set quietly on the counter in the kitchen.

All of these movements swept past Lindsay in a haze, like shadows or dreams. Her reality was on her laptop screen. Queries and data results output to flat files. She used her own library of code to process the files, to summarize the data, define its shape, derive its meaning, and tease apart its insights. She was enrobed in the process she loved, the process at which she excelled: data analysis.

Lindsay was no financial analyst. That was a specialized skill, and one for which Lindsay had a great deal of respect. But she was familiar enough with the basic metrics to get a good sense of the health of the company.

And what she found shocked her.

Not only was the company surprisingly large, both in head-count and in revenue, but it was remarkably profitable. Unlike what she had expected, there was very little debt on the books. What was there were the remnants of notes issued decades earlier and nearly paid off. The cash flow was healthy, the balance sheet even more so. The return on assets and the gross margin were remarkably robust. If this company were publicly traded, it would undoubtedly be a hot stock.

Not only was Lindsay not a financial analyst, she was also not an expert in corporate valuation. But, she did some rough math based on her own common sense, using average annual net profits and growth rates as a guide to estimate what someone might reasonably pay for the company. The number she came up with nearly made her fall off her chair.

Hart Racing, Inc., the company of which Lindsay was now half-owner, was worth two billion British pounds. Nearly two-and-a-half billion US dollars.

Billion.

With a B.

The bank account for Lindsay's data science company had maybe twenty thousand dollars in it, before she paid her payroll and expenses. Her personal bank account had more like two hundred dollars in it.

Her father's company was worth two billion dollars.

No wonder Mac and Ms. Hayes and everyone else were watching her so closely. If some complete stranger suddenly took over something that valuable, Lindsay would want to keep an eye on them, too, if for no other reason than simply to make sure they knew what value they had suddenly obtained and make sure they didn't screw it up.

And now that she knew, Lindsay was a lot more interested

in the details of how this company worked. Now more than ever, she needed to know the intimate details of how this company made money, how it spent money, how it planned to grow for the future. Her valuation was based on the company's worth at that moment in time. But, Lindsay had no idea how a racing company was worth that much in the first place. And she certainly had no idea how to value its future. Was her father planning for rapid growth before he died? If so, the company was surely worth a lot more than two billion dollars. Were the growth years already behind it? It might be worth less.

Lindsay was off to a good start, but she needed to know more. A lot more.

The next day, thankfully, was Monday. She'd spent one solid week immersed in the company's financial data. But now she had questions, and she was glad that Helen would be in the office to answer them.

Lindsay caught a ride with Ms. Hayes, arriving at the office just as Helen was settling in to her desk with a cup of tea. They huddled in her cubicle for hours, Lindsay peppering her with question after question, verifying her own conclusions and clearing up a few uncertainties caused by her lack of expertise in financial analytics. Helen told Lindsay she was impressed with the depth of Lindsay's insights, especially in such a short time-frame. Thanks to Lindsay's data science techniques, Helen said she'd even learned a few things she hadn't already known.

But there was one area that confused Lindsay the most, one category of spending that dwarfed the others, even bigger than the facilities costs: travel. The travel expenses for the company were enormous, far larger as a percentage of total expenses than would be reasonable at most companies.

"It's the race team, dear," said Helen. "It's not cheap to race in a different country every week, you know."

Lindsay looked at her quizzically.

"The race team?" said Helen. "You know, the 'race' part of Hart Racing, Incorporated?"

In all her analysis, in all her review of the cars and the production facility and the history of the company, Lindsay had never stopped to think about the racing part of it all, the actual tires on the road and the crowds and the noise. It just hadn't really occurred to her.

She knew it was there, of course, but hadn't stopped to really think about it.

"Mac will tell you all about it," said Helen, patting Lindsay on the knee.

Lindsay recoiled at the thought. She'd spent a blissful week during which she hadn't had to think about Mac at all, let alone spend actual time with him. She was hoping to continue that pattern for as long as possible.

"No," she said, a little too quickly, "I need to know about the fiscal aspects of the racing, not the racing itself."

"Okay, right," nodded Helen. "Mac's your man."

"No," Lindsay smiled patiently. Helen clearly wasn't under-standing what she needed. "I need someone who understands the numbers, not the cars."

"Right, I see," said Helen, nodding. "Someone well-versed in the balance sheet as it relates to the racing activities."

"Exactly."

"Someone intimately familiar not only with how the racing team operates, from a financial perspective, but how it generates revenue, as well."

"That's what I need," said Lindsay.

"And that's what Mac can tell you," smiled Helen. "Don't be fooled, Lindsay. Mac's not just a pretty face..." her eyes drifted away, unfocused, "...and chest and arms..." She focused on Lindsay again, smiling devilishly. "I may be old, dear, but I'm not dead yet." She turned back to her monitor. "And Mac's as sharp as they come. He knows these numbers backwards and forwards and inside-out. Gets a report on his phone every morning."

Mac knew the numbers? That didn't fit with Lindsay's image of him. Mac was a meathead, asshole, grease-faced mechanic, not some savant business executive. Wasn't he?

"Talk to Mac, dear," said Helen, typing away, eyes on her screen. "Once you've done that, if you still have questions, I'll be happy to answer them for you. But Mac can tell you a lot more than I ever could."

Lindsay thanked Helen and sat down at her own desk, laptop resting on her lap, staring into space.

She sighed.

So much for her blissful time away from Mac McEwan.

13

Lindsay had texted Mac and they'd arranged for him to give her a ride home after work. Once there, he'd made her a quick dinner, remixing the leftovers from the dinners he'd brought her during the week, somehow managing to make them into a dish that tasted incredible, like he'd made it completely from scratch instead of by cobbling together week-old food.

They sat in lounge chairs on the back porch, Lindsay huddled under a blanket she'd pulled off the couch. She nursed an espresso, Mac sipping on a cup of French press coffee. The light from the kitchen coming through the massive window-wall behind them balanced the light from the setting sun tinting the sea and the horizon in front of them.

The air was cool enough for the blanket, but not cold. The sound of the waves crashing on the beach, mingled with the setting sun, the good food, and the blanket warming her outside while the espresso warmed her inside all combined to put Lindsay into a pleasant haze. She felt happy, rested, comfortable.

She couldn't remember the last time she'd felt that way.

She turned her head toward Mac. The fading sunlight tinted his skin gold, the strong lines of his cheekbones practically glowing, his thick, long hair swept back off his face. He looked almost childlike in that pose, in that light. Lindsay could imagine him as a young boy, a teenager. Handsome, popular, a rich man's son, probably beating back the girls, but with a spark in him that most people didn't have.

He was smart. Lindsay could see that now. Behind the asshole behavior, she could see the intelligence, the talent. And most of all, the love for what he did. He loved food, loved cooking, loved cars, loved racing.

And he had clearly loved Lindsay's dad.

"How did you meet my father?" she asked.

Mac turned his head to her, eyebrows raised, then looked out toward the sea again, the setting sun now putting sparkling gems in his blue eyes.

"I grew up in Edinburgh. My family had nothing. Dad drank. Mom... tried to disappear."

He stared hard at the sea for a long moment, his eyes sparkling with more than just the sunlight.

"I lived on the streets from the time I was ten or so, truth be told," he said quietly. No shame in his voice, just quiet.

A pit formed in Lindsay's stomach. That was definitely not the childhood she had imagined for Mac. She murmured something apologetic.

Mac gave her a look Lindsay couldn't quite decipher. It seemed part surprise, part amusement. And part of it, she was sure, was him holding back some asshole comment or another.

But at least he held it back this time.

Mac turned back toward the sea.

"I learned how to boost cars," Mac said. "One of the older kids showed me how on an abandoned junker, then dared me to steal a real car." Mac shrugged. "Turned out I was good at it. I understood the mechanics. Could break in to anything, hot-wire anything. I learned how to override security systems and car alarms." He nodded toward Lindsay. "Mind you, this was well before GPS and those kinds of tracking systems were in every car."

"What did you do with the cars after you stole them?"

"We sold them," Mac said. "That older kid took the money, of course. I think he thought of himself like he was my manager or something. Like I was a musician and he took his cut for finding me the gigs." Mac laughed. "Except his cut was one hundred percent." He swirled his coffee, staring into the cup. To himself, he mused, "I guess he deserved something. He was the one who sold the cars to the chop shops, after all. But, he kept me fed and sheltered, for the most part. That was enough for me."

Lindsay couldn't even imagine that kind of life, for anyone, let alone a ten-year-old kid. Living on the streets, committing crimes every day just to survive. It was so foreign to her, she almost couldn't even imagine it.

"Where did you sleep at night?"

"Wherever," shrugged Mac. "There were plenty of abandoned warehouses in Edinburgh back then. We'd move around so the cops wouldn't catch on to us. We mostly slept during the day, so we'd sleep on the beach once in a while, on sunny days. That was always my favorite place to go."

Lindsay just shook her head, astounded. She couldn't even fathom such a life, growing up that way. And yet, Mac was here, sitting across from her a few hundred yards away from his very expensive home by the sea, living a life so successful that just about everyone in the world would be envious of him.

"So, how did you get from there to here?" She gestured toward their surroundings.

"Your father," Mac smiled.

Lindsay shook her head. "Did he adopt you or something?"

Mac laughed, a staccato run of notes that made Lindsay smile involuntarily.

"He did, after a fashion," said Mac. "I was fifteen. My birthday, actually. I saw this car sitting outside a pub downtown, an

Aston Martin Vanquish. One of the very first ones. Might have been pre-release, even." Mac shook his head slowly at the memory. "It was in the James Bond movie that year," he said, looking to Lindsay for any sign of recognition.

Lindsay had no idea what he was talking about.

"A very fancy, very expensive, very unusual car," explained Mac, "especially for downtown Edinburgh at the time." He shrugged. "So, naturally, I stole it. A birthday present to myself. Wasn't going to tell anyone."

He sat up in his chair, swinging his legs over the side to face Lindsay.

"Only it was your father's car, and he had some crazy security setup in there, something I'd never seen before," Mac said, growing animated with the telling, setting down his coffee cup and using his hands to accompany the story.

Those hands that Lindsay suddenly imagined doing other things.

She pushed the thought away.

"It was an early GPS system, as it turns out. Way ahead of its time. Crude by today's standards, but still effective. Took me a few minutes to figure out how to override it." Mac smiled at the memory. "But your father had some kind of alert system, separate from the GPS, set up to buzz his Blackberry if someone tampered with the car. Really cutting edge stuff back then. This was early days in the internet, even, long before everyone had cell phones with apps and all of that."

"So he caught you stealing his car?"

"Well," Mac laughed, "yes, he did. But he didn't yell at me and call the cops or anything. He just stood there, off to the side in the shadows, watching me hack his system. Took me a lot longer than usual, but keep in mind that I was good." He puffed his chest a little. "I might have been the best in the city. I could walk up to a locked, secured car, break in, disable the security, hotwire the car, and be driving away in less than a minute in those days. So, when I saw it took a long time, I was only fiddling with your father's car for maybe three minutes. Five, at most.

"He just watched me do it. As soon as I started the engine, he hit a kill switch on his Blackberry, locked the doors remotely, and came up to the driver's side window, staring down at me."

"Did he arrest you?"

"No," laughed Mac. "He rolled down the window—remotely, again—and asked me my name. I lied, naturally, gave him a fake name. 'Rolly Fingers'. An American baseballer, I think. Saw the name in a paper one time and it never left me. Took it as my stage name, as it were."

Lindsay smiled at that. "What did my father do then?"

"He said, 'Well, Mr. Fingers, I'm impressed with your abilities. How would you like to come work for me?' I figured he was some crew boss or some kind of kingpin in the city. I was good, but I wasn't stupid. I didn't want to be in gangs forever. So I turned him down.

"He just shrugged and said, 'You can come work for me or you can go to jail. Your choice.' Then he rolled up the window and walked away. Just left me there, locked in his Aston Martin for hours while he went back into the club.

"When he finally came back out, he just opened the door, made me scoot into the passenger seat, and drove us away."

"That's it?"

"That's it," said Mac. "He called me Mr. Fingers for the rest of his life." He laughed.

Lindsay sat back in her chair. That was definitely not the story she'd been expecting. She thought Mac had been a spoiled rich kid and her father some buttoned-up corporate magnate. Instead, Mac was a kid criminal and her father could think far enough outside the box to recognize talent even when it was literally trying to drive away in his car.

She shook her head. Everything she thought she knew was being proven wrong. Her father was not some asshole who abandoned his child and her mother. He'd put Lindsay in his will.

And Mac was not an asshole, either. Well, not a complete asshole. He'd pulled himself up from abject poverty to become a rich, successful man. He was still a dick from time to time, but knowing his story changed Lindsay's impression of him. A lot.

"I know you're trying to figure this business out," said Mac, "but if you really want to understand the ins and out of the business, you've got to come to the races," said Mac. "Helen is right. If the top floor, with all of the finance and admin teams and such, is the head of the business, and building the cars is the heart, the race team is the body. They put everything into action."

Lindsay shook her head. She'd lost enough time on the Brinksley work already. She was sure Marina and Raj had held up their end, though she hadn't even taken the time to check her email to catch up. But now she had work of her own to do. She couldn't afford the disruption of traveling all over the place.

"Melbourne is next weekend," continued Mac. "I've got to be there. I've missed the first two races already. It's not fair of me to make Sam handle everything, my job on top of everything else, all of Sam's regular duties as crew chief." He leaned toward her, his voice earnest and persuasive. "Come out with me. Join up with the race team. It'll all make a lot more sense then. I promise."

"You want me to fly to Australia next weekend?"

"Well, we'd leave on Monday, really. The race is on Sunday, but practice starts on Friday."

"Then why would you leave on Monday?"

Mac grinned. "See, this is why you need to come. It would all make much more sense."

Lindsay snorted. No wonder the travel expenses were so high. If they went on Monday when they only needed to go on Thursday, they were just wasting money on food and accommodations.

"I'm sure I can learn from here," Lindsay said.

Mac just looked at her. She could see that he wanted to object, to say more. Lindsay turned to face the ocean, sipping her espresso. But she could feel the heat of his stare on her cheeks.

Or maybe it was just her blushing.

Thankfully, Mac didn't press the issue, though Lindsay could feel him restraining himself. Instead, he just sat back in his chair. They listened to the waves in silence for a few moments, sipping their drinks.

"Fine," said Mac at last. "But I'm teaching you to drive before I leave."

"I already know how to drive."

Mac barked a short laugh. "You may know how to drive some shitty car in America. A Prius or a Tesla or something."

"Teslas are shitty cars?"

Mac ignored her comment. "But you don't know how to drive anything in your father's garage. I won't allow you to wantonly injure another classic car, but you can't just sit around all the time begging others to drive you places like some teenage girl trapped in her parents' house."

That stung, if only because that was exactly how Lindsay had been feeling lately. And she didn't want to insult the driver —what was his name? Danny?—by forcing him to drive her from home to work and back each day. She was pretty sure she could figure out how to drive three miles round trip each day. If a couple of driving lessons from Mac were the price of that freedom, Lindsay would pay it.

"Good," said Mac. "Time for your first lesson, then."

Lindsay started at Mac's comment. "What? Now? It's getting dark." She wasn't prepared for a driving lesson.

"Not dark yet," said Mac. "Let's go."

He led her into her father's garage and flicked a light switch, turning on the overhead lights, one shining on each vehicle like a spotlight at a car show.

"Do you have any idea what these cars are?" said Mac.

"Should I?" asked Lindsay.

He huffed and put his hands on his hips. "How about this. How much do you think these cars are worth?"

Lindsay sighed. Boys and their toys, always bragging about how valuable they were, trying to convince everyone that because they owned expensive cars, they must be important, themselves.

"I don't know, Mac," she said with a sigh. "A lot, I'm guessing."

Mac pointed to one car halfway up the row, a tiny, shapely red thing. "That's a 1967 Alfa Romeo 33 Stradale," he said. "Only eighteen were built." He glanced at her. "It's worth about three million pounds."

Lindsay's jaw fell. Mac smiled when he saw it.

He pointed to a gaudy black and white car, low and sleek and as ostentatiously ugly as a car could be while still somehow being kind of beautiful. "That's a 2005 Bugatti Veyron Super Sport. Fastest street-legal car in the world. Goes 267.856 miles per hour."

Lindsay rolled her eyes. Why on earth would anyone need to go that fast on a street? And where the hell would they do it?

"About three million for that one, too," said Mac.

He pointed to a third car on the far end. "Lamborghini Veneno. 2013. Four million pounds."

Lindsay was stunned.

He pointed to another. "Porsche 550 Spyder. Six million." Another. "2008 Mercedes Maybach Exelero. Eight million."

Stunned turned to numb. "Now you're just bullshitting me."

Mac shook his head. "I'm not. Hand to God." Another. "1962 Aston Martin DB4 GT Zagato."

Why were the names always so long? The thought wound through her numbed mind, a thin tendril of sanity. The name was longer than the car, a cute little green thing with curved lines and a grill on the front that looked like a grinning mouth. She thought she'd seen those driving around San Francisco before.

"Fourteen point three million pounds for that one," said Mac.

She had definitely not seen one of those driving around San Francisco.

"You want me to drive these?" spluttered Lindsay.

"No," said Mac. "Definitely not. I want you to know what these are so you give them the respect they deserve. Or at least give their value some respect, even if you don't respect the incredible place each of these cars holds in the history of car design and manufacturing."

Lindsay shook her head in disbelief. Not awe. Not respect. Disbelief. She didn't care much about the history of car making or whatever, but she couldn't believe how much money was sitting in the garage in front of her. How much money did her father have? And why would he spend so much of it on cars?

A thought occurred to her.

"How much was that car I drove to the office worth?"

She cringed inside as she thought about the herky-jerky way she'd driven it. The grinding, rattling sounds filled her memory like accusatory fingers. Was that car worth a million pounds, too? No wonder Mac had been mad.

"Your father bought that one for eight hundred thousand pounds," said Mac quietly.

Lindsay released a breath she didn't know she'd been holding. Eight hundred thousand was an astronomical price for a car, but at least she hadn't taken a ten million dollar car and driven it like a toddler on their first bumper car ride.

"He paid that price back in the seventies," continued Mac. "It's gone up in value since then."

Lindsay stomach sank. "How much did it go up?"

Mac nodded silently. "One like it sold at auction last year for forty-five million dollars."

That breath she'd just released flew back into Lindsay's lungs again.

"Your father's car was special, though," continued Mac, "driven by a famous race car driver in the sixties."

Lindsay felt faint.

"That boosts the value, of course."

Faint became sick.

"It's estimated value is around..." Mac tilted his hands back and forth, estimating. "I'd say a hundred million."

"A hundred million dollars?"

"Pounds."

Lindsay's knees wobbled, her head suddenly feeling light. She had to sit down, right there on the floor of the garage, dropping her head between her legs.

Mac just laughed. He squatted down in front of her.

"Don't worry," he said. "Sam and Gerald already checked it out. Minor damage to the transmission. Just a couple of ground gears and a new pad for the parking brake. That's all."

Lindsay looked up at him through a veil of blonde hair that hung down over her face. "That's all? And that's no big deal?"

"No big deal."

"You promise?"

Mac reached forward and parted the veil of hair, tucking one half behind her ear. The gesture was gentle and soft and sweet. "I promise," he said softly.

Lightning bolts coursed through Lindsay's body, every sense coming alive. She could feel the rough skin of his fingers gentle on the cup of her ear. She could smell his spiced musk full in her nostrils, so vivid she could taste it on her tongue.

And he was so close, squatting before her on the garage floor. She could see the hairs of his beard, surrounding his red lips. Those lips looked soft and full and Lindsay wanted nothing more in that moment than to bite them, hard, then press her own lips against them to make it better.

She felt a hot flush deep within her core at the thought.

Her gaze slid slowly from his lips to his eyes, those electric blue eyes. Like his soft touch, there was a softness in those eyes, as well. But it was a sadness, a distance, that made them soft. Like some painful memory. Maybe he was thinking about his childhood, or about his parents.

Lindsay's heart broke for him even as her body yearned to make it better, too.

Mac held out his hand. Lindsay took it.

They stood up together.

The movement helped Lindsay's brain start working again. She looked around the garage, seeing nothing but fancy-looking cars.

"So, which one of these do you want me to drive?" she asked, grateful when the heat of the moment drained away.

Mac laughed. "None of them," he said. "This is your father's collection garage." He led Lindsay to the right, through a door that Lindsay hadn't noticed before. It led to a much smaller space that held only two cars.

"You can drive either one of these," he said. "They're both very nice cars, but they're much less expensive." He pointed to the one on the left. It looked like a fancy off-road kind of car, like a Jeep for rich people. "That's a Mercedes AMG G63," Mac said. "Brand new."

"How much does it cost?" asked Lindsay. "Only two million pounds?"

Mac smiled. "More like two hundred thousand," he said.

That was a ridiculous price to pay for a car, but after the prices from the last garage, Lindsay was relieved.

"And it's an automatic," said Mac. "No stick shift."

That made Lindsay feel even better.

"But, I'm going to teach you how to drive that car." He pointed to the one on the right. It looked much more like a normal car, albeit a very, very nice one. Low and sleek, it had two seats, set far back in the body, with a long hood that was fully half the length of the jet black car. "This is a Jaguar F-Type," said Mac. "About a year old. Costs about two hundred thousand pounds, with the modifications your father made, but it's a manual transmission." He held his hands out, palms up, at Lindsay's pained expression. "You've gotta know how to drive stick if you want to own a racing company. It's heresy, otherwise."

Lindsay wasn't at all sure that she did want to own a race company, but she definitely didn't want to damage any more cars. She figured a few lessons might be a good idea.

She took a deep breath. "When do we start?"

14

THEY STARTED THE NEXT MORNING, early. Mac drove the Jaguar to a short track near the office. It snaked in a narrow paved circle through some trees and around a low building, forming an undulating oval shape like a long rubber band resting slack on a countertop, with one long straightaway on one side. The ground around the track was low and sandy, with tufts of grass interspersed with the occasional copse of low trees.

"This is a little track I use to test my wild hairs when I get them," grinned Mac. "It'll do for your first lessons."

He stopped the car at the start of the straightaway, shut off the engine, and swapped places with Lindsay.

"Why'd you turn the car off?" she asked as she buckled herself into the driver's seat.

"So you can learn how to turn it on."

"I know how to turn on a car," said Lindsay, pushing the button on the dash.

"No, wait—" said Mac.

The car lurched forward and snapped to a halt, both Lindsay and Mac jerking forward and back in their seats.

Lindsay cringed. Damn.

"I forgot to step on the left pedal," said Lindsay.

"The clutch," sighed Mac. "Yes, you did."

Lindsay pressed the clutch down to the floor with her foot and reached for the starter button again. Mac stopped her, holding her hand in his for a long moment, both of their arms extended.

His hand was warm, and it was large. Lindsay's hand fit completely inside it. Mac's rough palm scratched over her skin as he slowly pulled his hand back, sending warm shivers through Lindsay's entire body.

"Not yet," said Mac softly. "First, let's get used to the pedals."

He explained the arrangement of the pedals, what they did, how to use them. Had her practice pushing the clutch down and letting it up, getting used to the tension. Had her practice releasing the clutch while stepping on the accelerator. Had her quickly move her right foot to the brake and stomp both feet down on the clutch and the brake as if she were making a sudden stop.

"Now hold down the clutch and try the gears," Mac said.

Lindsay pushed the shifter through the pattern of gears shown on the shifter handle, struggling to cycle cleanly through them. She kept getting stuck, like bumping into a wall while trying to navigate a series of hallways in the dark.

"There's a natural center point," Mac said, resting his hand atop Lindsay's on the shifter, sending those warm shivers through her body again. She released her grip, holding the shifter handle lightly, letting Mac's hand guide hers from on top as he popped the transmission out of first gear and let it find a natural resting point between third and fourth gear. With each movement, Mac's hand pressed against hers, slid rough and warm along her skin. "You have to let it come to its natural center without fighting it. Otherwise, you'll overshift and go too high or too low."

He moved her hand under his, shifting smoothly through the gears, slow at first, then faster. "You can skip gears, too, if it make sense to do so, based on how fast you're moving," he said, guiding the shifter through the gears in different patterns, every movement smooth and precise, holding her hand all the time. With each movement, with each subtle caress of her hand, Lindsay felt a heat grow in her cheeks.

And in her body.

Mac took his hand from hers. Lindsay may have been imagining it, but it seemed that he moved his hand slower than he needed to, sliding it gently over the back of Lindsay's hand instead of just lifting it off. Lindsay bit her bottom lip as lightning bolts ricocheted through her body.

"Now, you try," Mac said.

His voice sounded lower, thicker than before. But, Lindsay may have been imagining that, too.

She worked through the gears like Mac had shown her, taking care to allow the shifter to push naturally back to its center, being careful not to force it, allowing for the natural movement to do some of the work. The shifting came much more easily once she'd made that adjustment.

"Good," said Mac. "Now try skipping gears."

He made a game out of it, calling out a gear while Lindsay shifted to it as fast and as smoothly as she could.

"Perfect," said Mac, his smile broad. "Well done."

An odd flush of pride went through Lindsay at his words. Even while it did, she felt a strange unease. Why should she care if this man approved of her shifting? And why should she care how well she shifted gears on a parked car, anyway? It wasn't exactly a valuable life skill. Nonetheless, she was happy to be improving from what she now saw was the rough and careless way she'd driven the first time.

"Now," said Mac, "keep your foot down on the clutch and start the car up."

The engine roared to life, a low, loud feline growl that thrummed through Lindsay's body. She hadn't felt it when Mac had driven them to the track, but something about having her hands on the wheel and her feet on the pedals, something about being in control of that thrumming power, thrilled Lindsay.

"Okay," Mac said, "now slowly, gently let up on the clutch while stepping on the accelerator, like you practiced earlier."

Lindsay did so, moving very slowly, very carefully. The engine raced, the car did not move. She let up on the clutch more quickly.

The car jumped forward, slammed to a halt, sputtered. Lindsay shoved her foot down on the clutch and the engine returned to its lion-like growl.

"Well done," shouted Mac.

"What are you talking about?" said Lindsay. "We didn't go anywhere."

"No, but you saved the engine from stalling. You pushed on the clutch before the engine died. That's exactly what you want to do."

Lindsay nodded to herself. She remembered when she had driven the other car, when it had jerked forward and stalled. Mac was right. This was progress.

She tried again, working to balance the movement of her left and right foot. It took many, many more attempts, several more quick rescues to keep the engine from stalling, but finally Lindsay managed to move the car forward slowly, carefully.

"Yes, yes," urged Mac, sending another thrill through Lindsay's body as the car slid down the track. "Good work. Now let off the clutch and keep going on the accelerator."

He talked her through the process as she slowly gained speed down the straightaway. The interplay between the clutch and the gas became much easier now that they had forward momentum to keep the car from stalling. Shifting from second gear to third gear was a lot easier than shifting from first to second.

"Okay, now slow down again," said Mac.

Lindsay stepped on the brake. The engine shuddered once more. She pressed the clutch to save it, returning it to its low growl. The car rolled forward in neutral.

"Okay, so slowing down is the reverse of speeding up," said Mac. "You want to learn to control the car at all times, keeping it in gear as much as possible so you've got the power to do whatever you might need—speed up, slow down, turn to avoid traffic or something in the road, and so on."

He talked her through the downshifting process. It wasn't any more complicated than the acceleration process, but it required Lindsay to adjust her thinking to be constantly ready.

"The car will tell you when it wants you to shift," explained Mac, "either up or down. You can hear it in the engine. You can feel it through the wheel and through your feet."

The way he spoke, it was as if the car were sentient, as if it had its own will, its own desires, and its own ability to communicate.

"When you hear the engine racing like that," he said as Lindsay downshifted too soon, the engine roaring in her ears, "it wants you to either shift to a higher gear or step on the brake to slow down." She slowed down until the engine was guttering, low and halting. "When it does that," Mac explained, "it wants you to either downshift or speed up."

Lindsay quickly reached the end of the straightaway and had to throw steering into the mix. It was overwhelming at first, trying to coordinate both feet—one working the clutch, the other working the brake and gas—and both hands—one on the shifter, the other on the steering wheel—while also worrying about staying on the track without driving through a curve into the sandy ground alongside it.

But Mac guided her through it, carefully and surprisingly attentively. It was as if he could sense her anxiety, her uncertainty, and tailored his instructions to help her focus on what was important. When she was starting from a standstill, he instructed her to keep the accelerator at a fixed point, focusing on keeping the sound of the engine at a stable pitch, so that she could think more clearly about the clutch and where it released enough to start the car moving, what Mac called the "friction point". When she was moving forward and shifting through the gears, he had her focus on the rising and falling pitch of the engine as a clue to when to change gears. When she'd used up the length of the straightaway and had to negotiate the curves of the track, Mac had her keep a constant speed, removing any concerns about shifting or engine sounds so Lindsay could work around the track and back to the straightaway again.

She didn't realize it at the time, but after a while, once she had grown more comfortable and was moving the car around the track with ease, albeit no higher than fourth gear, she recognized the skill and care with which he'd delivered his instruction, controlling as many variables as possible so Lindsay could focus on one thing at a time, thus not only learning more quickly, but controlling the sense of overwhelm that had plagued her the first time she'd tried to drive a stick shift.

"You're a good teacher," said Lindsay after she'd brought the car to a growling stop at the start of the straightway, one foot on the brake, the other holding the clutch to the floor. After their first few meetings, Lindsay definitely would not have pegged Mac as a patient teacher.

Mac nodded his head in quiet thanks.

"I've been taught by a lot of good teachers over the years," he said, "including your father. Especially your father."

Lindsay stared at her hands on the wheel, feeling the life of the engine thrum through them.

"What was he like?" she said, her voice barely a whisper.

Mac didn't respond for a long time, long enough that Lindsay wondered if he'd heard her at all. They just stared forward, Lindsay at her hands, Mac staring down the track.

"It's hard to talk about your father, to be honest," said Mac.

"It's only been a couple months since... he died." His voice hung on that last word, hitched on it, like he still couldn't quite get his mind to accept it as true.

"Was he a good man?" asked Lindsay, her voice sounding thin and high to her own ears, like the voice of a small girl.

"He was." Mac's voice thickened and wavered. "A great man, Lindsay." He turned to look straight at her, his eyes liquid and brimming. "Your father was the best man I've ever known."

Lindsay furrowed her brow, stared back at her hands on the steering wheel. It felt good to know that her father engendered that kind of devotion in the people around him. She'd seen the respect, the love for him that was in the eyes of the people she'd met. Ms. Hayes, Helen, Mac. They all seemed to hold the memory of her father with a sort of reverence.

But if he was such a great man, why hadn't he ever tried to contact his own daughter?

Lindsay didn't feel any sense of loss in her life. Her life with her mother had always felt complete. The two of them against the world. And that had always been enough. Would always be enough.

But now she had discovered this other person, this other resource, someone who could have taught her things her mother hadn't. Could have taught her about cars and business, sure, but also, it seemed, about leadership. About kindness to strangers. Maybe about a different approach to life, one that was more...

She didn't know how to describe it, what word to assign to it. It was a feeling she had, something nagging at the back of her brain, some quality or philosophy of her father's that was emerging from the comments people had made about him and the things she'd observed about the way he built his life, organized his home, ran his business.

Lindsay felt nothing lacking in her life, in herself. But here she had encountered something that she felt could have expanded her life, her worldview. She felt like there was something here she could have learned, something she hadn't come across before.

And it felt right, like she'd been carrying a key on a chain around her neck for her whole life, thinking it was just a pretty necklace, only to find that it opened the doors to a whole new world. A world that she was a part of, naturally. By birth.

But why hadn't her father loved her the way he'd clearly loved all the people she was meeting? Why had he consciously and intentionally shut her and her mother out of his life? It just didn't make sense, didn't fit with what she was learning about her father, as a man. By all accounts, he was kind and compassionate and considerate. He seemed to love people, seemed to have an open heart. He cared for his employees like they were his family.

Why had he never opened his heart to her? She actually was his family. Biologically, at least.

But maybe that wasn't enough. Maybe that wasn't good enough. Maybe she'd done something or represented something that her father just couldn't love, didn't want in his otherwise magical life.

Lindsay swallowed hard. This line of thinking wasn't going to get her anywhere. It wasn't going to help her value this company or find a buyer at a fair price. It wasn't going to help her finish the work that was piling up on the Brinksley job. It wasn't going to help her get home sooner.

"I think I've got it now," she said, her voice a bit hoarse.

"Got what?" said Mac.

Lindsay cleared her throat. "The driving," she replied, willing her voice to be strong and clear. She forced herself to look at Mac, to hold his blue eyes in her stare. "Thanks for the lessons. I think I've got it now."

Mac looked back at her for a long moment, long enough that Lindsay felt uncomfortable, lost her nerve, broke his gaze and looked straight through the windshield, her hands tight, crackling the leather on the steering wheel as she squeezed it.

"Okay," Mac said softly. "But that's just the first lesson—"

"I think I can figure the rest out on my own," replied Lindsay. "Thanks for your help, Mac."

Another long moment, another long stare.

"Why don't you drive us to the office, then?" he said at last, his voice so soft and kind that Lindsay wanted to kick him out of the car. Or, better yet, kick herself out of the car, out of the country, out of this new life.

Or even just kick herself. Period.

Lindsay had no idea how to get to the office from where they were, but she didn't stop to worry about it. She needed to move, to get away from the track, the car. From Mac. From England. From these maddening, useless thoughts swirling a tempest in her mind. She wanted to go back to San Francisco and get on with her life.

She pulled ahead on the straightaway, worked her way around the curves of the track, moving smoothly through the gears, ramping up in speed. She wasn't thinking, was barely even looking at the track or the world around the car. All she heard was the engine, starting in a low growl, then rising up, louder and louder until it was screaming, filling Lindsay's head with its roar, then dropping low again, and rising to a scream once more.

Mac guided her off the track and onto the road, pointing this way and that. Left turn, right turn. He may have been speaking. Lindsay didn't know. She just heard that engine moving from a growl to a scream over and over until the office rose on the horizon in front of her, until she pulled into the parking lot and stopped by the front door.

"Wow," said Mac. "You're a fast learner, Lindsay," he said. Lindsay turned off the car, sat staring straight ahead. Mac got out and shut the door behind him. "I still think you could use a few more lessons, though," he said.

"Thanks, Mac," said Lindsay, her voice faint and distant in her ears. She started the car again. "Maybe I'll take you up on that."

She shifted into gear and drove away, Mac getting smaller in the rear-view mirror, his hands held out to his sides, confusion on his diminishing face.

Lindsay still didn't know where she was going, but she needed to hear that sound in her ears again, that engine cycling between the growl and the scream. She drove and drove, letting that sound fill her mind, push every other thought away, empty it completely.

Until she found a long highway, worked the engine to its highest gear, and heard nothing but that screaming in her ears.

She had no idea where she was or where she was going. She just let the car take her away.

15

Lindsay had driven for hours, driven until she was forced to stop and find a gas station. Petrol station. The maps app on her phone led her back to the house by mid-afternoon.

By then, her mind was clear enough for her to focus on the Brinksley job. She had a handful of emails piled up from the Brinksley VP, but she ignored them. It would be better for Lindsay just to bang out some work, make some progress. Then she could send the VP an update that, even if it was late, would contain good news, news that the work was on schedule. She figured that good news delivered late would be better than bad news delivered on time.

Lindsay could have lied and just told the VP everything was on schedule, but Lindsay didn't stoop to such petty tricks. She did her work, made the best timelines she could, and stuck by them. If shit fell apart, she'd own it.

Lindsay flopped in a chair with her laptop, pulled up Marina's website in progress, connected to Raj's database under construction, and slipped into her code, the familiar functions she had written and optimized over the last five years or so. It was like re-reading a beloved book or slipping into a hot bath. Or both at the same time. Familiar. Safe. Well-understood, yet still welcome and even a little bit exciting, in a controlled way. A controlled dose of familiar excitement.

Lindsay worked at the table in the kitchen, the shadows lengthening around her until the glow from the screen was the only light in the room. Lost in her work, making quick progress, Lindsay barely noticed until the automatic lights kicked on around her, countering the ghoulish blue glow of the screen with a comforting warm yellow light.

Lindsay heard a knock at the door.

She ignored it, focused on her code, where she was just finishing up some custom modifications to one of her analysis libraries. After all these years, she'd distilled her code to cover most data science situations, allowing her to make quick progress with each new job, focusing only on those slight modifications needed to suit a specific client. A lot of work, still, but a lot less than building the code base from scratch each time.

The knock came on the door again. Again, Lindsay ignored it.

Brinksley had requested one analytical tool that would require some custom work. It was undoubtedly a test, since the request was useful, but not essential. It required a relatively advanced understanding of data science techniques, though, and Lindsay was quite sure some clever director of data science at Brinksley had thrown it into the Statement of Work just to test Lindsay's mettle and see if it was worth establishing a deeper relationship with her company, one that would be longer-term and more lucrative for Lindsay and team.

Lindsay could see that test for what it was, as obvious as a light in the darkness. Any test revealed as much about the tester as the person being tested. This test told Lindsay that her client was a few years behind the cutting edge of data science, lacked the understanding and ingenuity needed to push that cutting edge forward, and wasn't smart enough to realize either of those two points.

In other words, this director of data science was a typical Silicon Valley type: probably a man, probably mid-to-late-thirties, probably thinking they were a god because they'd become very rich at a relatively young age, and therefore confused their success with their abilities, completely ignoring the benefits of pure luck. They'd undoubtedly worked hard and had skills, but they were also in the right place at the right time. Good for them, but that didn't make them a genius.

And, from the nature of the test, Lindsay could clearly see that a genius they were not. The test was more work, but nothing that would challenge Lindsay beyond just another long night on her laptop. Too many years in management had left this person spending too much time watching their share price and not enough time keeping up with trends in data science.

"I brought you some food," said Mac.

Lindsay didn't respond, her focus on her laptop. Her mind registered the sound, recognized it as Mac's voice, but quickly stuffed that information into a box and buried it deep in some dark corner of her consciousness. She needed to work. She needed to focus. She needed to forget that Mac and her father and this whole situation even existed.

Lindsay banged out her code, checking box after box on the to-do list in her mind, whizzing through her work. She was damn good at her job. As she worked, she felt her world straighten, tidy itself, like the scene in that Harry Potter movie when the disheveled room, looking like it had been ransacked by a gang of thieves, magically rights itself piece by piece, bits of broken furniture and shards of glass flying through the air to their rightful place, picture frames squaring themselves on the wall, tipped-over decorations standing straight again until the room returned to perfect, beautiful order.

Lindsay needed that order, that feeling of rightness. The past weeks had been chaotic and maddening, one curve after another, never able to see what lay on the road ahead. As she worked, those roads straightened for Lindsay. She could see what she needed to do: do the Brinksley work and secure the bigger contract, then value her father's company and sell it, then get back to San Francisco and grow her own company further.

Even as she thought it, her fingers blurring on the keyboard, making changes she'd made a dozen times with other clients, nagging loose ends needled her mind. Would she want to keep working once she'd sold the company? She'd be rich then. Why would she work?

What about Marina and Raj? Lindsay had given them each a stake in the company to entice them to join, but they wouldn't get anything from the sale of Lindsay's father's company. Would they want to continue at Datasure? Lindsay could buy them out, somehow, and shut the company down. But what if they wanted to continue? Would Lindsay ask Marina and Raj to buy her out so they could keep the company going without her? Would Lindsay stay and keep the company alive for their sakes?

And what about Helen and Ms. Rhodes and all the others working at her father's company? It was clear they all loved working there. By selling her share to another buyer, would Lindsay be betraying them in some way? Did she care about that, given that she'd only just met those people a few weeks ago?

Lindsay heard a clicking sound on her right side. She glanced down and found a plate there, loaded with some kind of round, wrinkly potsticker dappled with sliced circles of green onion. The scent hit her nose in the same moment, ginger and onion and sesame and pork. Lindsay's stomach growled and her mouth filled with so much saliva Lindsay felt like she would drown in it. She hadn't eaten since breakfast.

"I don't mean to disturb you," said Mac quietly, "but you should eat."

And then there was Mac.

Mac was a subject Lindsay would prefer to have ignored

altogether. If she could just avoid him until it was time to head home, she would.

She felt a pang in her chest at that thought.

Probably just her hunger, which was now so strong that it was practically taking control of her limbs, forcing her to save her work, push her laptop aside, and dig in to the food Mac had brought.

"It's called Sheng Jian Bao," Mac said. "Yue Zhou from the data team is from Shanghai. You said you liked Chinese food, so I asked her to make some. Best bao buns in town." Mac held up his own plate. "Mind if I join you?"

Lindsay just nodded, her mouth full of food, the flavors sending warm shivers down her spine. Satisfying ravenous hunger was one thing, but doing it with food as divine as this was practically orgasmic. The tops of the tiny bundles of joy were soft and the bottoms were perfectly crisp. The filling was juicy and savory, with a warm, soupy texture that slid pure sunshine into Lindsay's stomach. Even if her mouth hadn't been full, she would probably have been unable to form words in that moment.

She'd momentarily lost the power of speech.

Mac sat at the table across from her, watching her wolf down her food, a faint smile on his face. His presence made Lindsay conscious of how disgusting she probably looked, ripping into her food like a wolf on the hunt. She forced herself to slow down, to chew and swallow every bite before loading her fork for the next.

"What are you working on?" asked Mac, nodding toward her laptop.

Lady-like to the last, Lindsay wiped the corners of her mouth with the back of her hand, then realized she had smeared sauce all over herself. Mac reached across the table and slid her a napkin that lay hidden under Lindsay's plate. Lindsay could feel her cheeks grow hot as she nodded her thanks and cleaned herself up.

"I have a company back home," she said. "We build data science portals for companies in the Valley, giving them access to automated tools and techniques for analyzing their data without hiring a large team of data scientists to do it."

"Huh," said Mac, a loaded fork paused on its way to his mouth. "So that's what you do for a living? Web design?"

Lindsay bristled at the oversimplification, then cooled herself down with a breath. She realized that she and Mac had never really talked about anything beyond her father and his company. Aside from what he had told her the previous night about his own childhood. Lindsay had never shared anything about herself with him.

She still wasn't really sure she wanted to.

"I own the company," said Lindsay with a curt smile, the effect no doubt diluted by the mouthful of food behind it. She swallowed. "I am a data scientist. I handle all the data science stuff. I have two employees who handle the data engineering and the web development."

Mac nodded while he chewed. "How long have you been doing that?" he asked.

Lindsay filled him in on her education and work history, including her years working for big tech companies and her decision to leave to start her own business. She wanted control of her own destiny, the feeling that her hard work would translate directly into results she could see and feel, instead of all of her work falling into a corporate abyss that padded someone else's pockets, but didn't change her own fortunes at all.

"You wanting control?" said Mac with a chuckle. "There's a shocker."

"What's that supposed to mean?"

Mac looked surprised at the question. "Well, you're a bit of a control freak," he said. His casual tone suggested it were an obvious and accepted fact.

"I am not."

Mac chuckled again. "You drove a hundred million dollar car you don't know how to work just so you didn't have to be at someone else's mercy—"

"That's not a control issue. I just didn't want to have to spend any more time with you."

"—you forced Helen to give you your own access to the database instead of reading the reports she gave you—"

"She thanked me for that, I'll have you know. That saved us both a lot of time."

"—you go around studying everything about the company without speaking to anyone who actually works there and actually knows about it—"

"I need to find unbiased information. Plus," she squirmed in her seat, "I don't want to bother anyone."

"—and you isolate yourself, holing up in your house trying to do everything on your own when you've got an entire company full of people who would love to help you with whatever it is you need doing."

Lindsay opened her mouth to reply to that, but couldn't think of anything to say.

"We're a family here, Lindsay," said Mac. "We lean on each other when we stumble, and we support each other when we see people falling. That's what family is for."

Lindsay furrowed her brow. The world that had just started to come back into some semblance of order in her mind began to scatter again, those shards of glass and bits of furniture breaking apart, picture frames tilting once more on the wall.

Her family had only ever been herself and her mother, the two of them against the world, as her mother had always put it. And she did lean on her mother for support, but her mother was more like a brick wall or a riding crop behind the knees than a grandmotherly hug.

When her mother died, it had been just Lindsay, alone against the world.

She had Marina and Raj, sure, but they were employees. They did what she asked them to do because that was their job. Their loyalties were to their paychecks and the prospects of bigger payouts in the future, not to Lindsay herself.

Lindsay had no family anymore.

And now this man was telling her that she'd suddenly been adopted into a family of hundreds of people, all bequeathed to her from a father she'd never met.

A father who had rejected her.

"Thanks, Mac," said Lindsay, pushing aside her empty plate, "for the food." The last bite had turned acidic in her mouth. She pulled her laptop open and focused on it again, ignoring him.

"That's it?" said Mac. "'Thanks for the food, Mac?' That's all you have to say?"

Lindsay shrugged, doing her best to tune Mac out and focus on her work.

"Lindsay, we're in this together. Whether you like it or not, you have to work with me. You can't go this alone."

Lindsay didn't respond, didn't look up. She was typing, desperately trying to focus, but the code was blurring on the screen in front of her. She didn't even know what it said.

"This family, *our* family, is depending on us to make the right choice, here."

"*Our* family?" said Lindsay, unable to pretend to focus any more. "*My* family was my mother and me. Two of us. And now it's just me."

"It's not just you any more."

"Oh, because my wonderful saint of a father left his family to me in his will? Where was my father when he was alive? Where was he when I was a child?"

Mac's face darkened. Lindsay shook her head, a feeling welling up in her that she had tried for too long to keep under wraps. Her pulse pounded in her ears, louder and louder, like the beat of approaching war drums.

"He ignored me," she said, "rejected me. He turned his back on me and my mother for my entire life. He chose to do that."

The drum beat was now a cacophony, like being at the locus of a massive thunderstorm, thunder and lightning crashing inside her mind. Her vision funneled down to Mac, only Mac, the rest of the world fading away.

Only it wasn't Mac. It was her father sitting there across from her.

She rose to her feet, driven by some power outside her control, chair screeching across the floor as it shoved backward. Lindsay's fingernails dug into her palms.

"Where was he when I needed him?" she hissed. "Where was he when I was young, when he was alive? He was here," she spat the words, "with his new *family*. But he left his real family in the dark to fend for themselves."

Pressed back in his chair, Mac opened his mouth wordlessly, then shut it again.

Lindsay lifted her chin, looking down her nose at Mac. She reined in the wild drum beat, the wild thunder in her mind, controlled it, focused on her truth, her rightness. She channeled that wild energy, and it gave her strength. It gave her power.

It gave her control.

"We didn't need him then," she said, her voice low and as thunderous as the sounds in her mind, "and I don't need him now."

Her breathing was fast. Staring down at Mac, whose face was ashen, she stood for a few moments breathing deep and long, slowing her breath, calming her mind. The pieces that had scattered fell back into place with a solid thunk, fitting together like pieces of a puzzle. Lindsay felt calm and sure again for the first time since she'd left San Francisco.

She sat back down, pulled the laptop in front of her again, and began to clean up the nonsense she'd typed earlier.

"Thank you for the food, Mac," she said, not bothering to look up.

Mac just sat there for a moment in silence, then stood. Lindsay heard the sink running in the background as he cleaned up the dishes, then heard the front door click shut.

She was alone again.

Alone with her work.

16

Mac's text the next day was short and to the point. 'Leaving for Melbourne. Join on the road when you want. Maggie will know where we are.'

Lindsay stood in the kitchen holding her espresso cup, an odd mix of feelings coursing through her. On the one hand, Mac was gone. Far away for a long time. Lindsay had learned that races were held all around the world, usually every other weekend, but sometimes on subsequent weekends. With all the travel and coordination, she wasn't sure if the race team bothered to come all the way back to England between races or just went to the next destination and spent two weeks there. Either way, Mac was on the circuit now, and she felt fairly comfortable that he would be out of her hair, at least until the race in England in July.

That gave Lindsay three months, three blissful Mac-less months in which to get her shit together, put a solid valuation on her father's company, and figure out how to find a buyer.

Three months without Mac.

Without his annoying presence at all hours of the day and night, usually without warning or invitation.

Without his needling, his teasing, his outright rudeness. No more 'Barbie' this or 'Why can't you do' that. No more driving lessons or speeches about how great her father was.

No more delicious meals, delivered piping hot to Lindsay's side just when she needed them most.

No more conversations about his crazy, fascinating, surprising past. No more insights into who her father really was and why he may have made the decisions he made or how he built such a successful company from the ground up.

No more growling voice or rumbling chuckles. Lindsay wondered what Mac's true laugh sounded like, his full, spontaneous laugh. Would it roll across the landscape like thunder or light up the sky like lightning?

No more jawline sharp enough to slice bread. No more broad pectorals or ridged abdominals. No more bulging biceps with veins like licorice twists that she wanted to lick all over.

That wasn't all she wanted to lick.

Lindsay shivered involuntarily.

She tossed back her espresso like it was a shot of tequila.

It was good that Mac would be away. Lindsay really needed to get her shit together.

"All good on my end, boss," said Raj on the video call an hour later.

It was a bright, clear morning and Lindsay sat on the deck in the same lounge chair she'd used when sitting beside Mac a couple nights earlier. She was wrapped in a blanket she'd grabbed off a couch inside. The massive blanket enrobed her entire body, dragging on the floor and slipping underfoot as she had walked outside with her laptop. Now she tucked her bare feet under the thick fleece, soft and warm against her cold feet, but left her face and neck open to the cool breeze sweeping off the sea.

She pulled on a pair of sunglasses to shade her eyes from the sunrise staring her down. She'd found the glasses in a rack in her father's closet, along with at least six other pairs in varying shapes and lens colors. His clothes, shoes, and other items were still in there, presumably just as he'd left them before he died. It was an eerie feeling for Lindsay to walk through such a mundane and intimate space, a private memory of a life she'd never shared of a man she'd never known, but who was nonetheless more important to her, then and now, than any man she had known.

"Looking very chic, Lindsay," said Marina. "The racing life suits you."

Lindsay scoffed. "Hardly," she said. "I'm counting the days until I can get back home, believe me."

Marina scowled into the camera.

"How long are you gonna be across the pond, anyway?" asked Raj. "America misses you."

"I'm hoping to be back by Thanksgiving, but, realistically, it probably won't be until December."

"Thanksgiving? Damn," said Raj, whistling. "Long trip."

"You have no idea."

"Well, England will do its best to show you a good time before then," said Marina, putting on a bright smile. "When are you coming to London, anyway? I've got plans, girl. I'm gonna show you what London is all about. The real London, not that bullshit they show you in Hollywood movies."

"She's gonna feed you bangers and mash, blood sausage, blood pudding, blood... in a glass. Is everyone in England a vampire like you, Marina? Is that why there's so much blood-based food in England?"

"Yes, Raj, but our laws state that we can only use blood from idiot tourists. When are you planning to visit?"

"I'm hoping I'll have more time soon," Lindsay interjected. "Hopefully things will be calmer around here for the next few months."

"Why is that?" said Marina.

"That's good," said Raj at the same time. "We're cranking on this Brinksley thing, but they need a lot of help. Those guys think they're driving Lambos, but they're really rocking a Fred Flintstone."

"Everything okay, Lins?" said Marina.

"You see what I did there," said Raj, "with the car thing?"

"You're a comic genius, Raj," said Marina.

"Yabba dabba doo, Marina," said Raj, deadpan, into the camera. "Yabba. Dabba. Doo."

"Things are fine," said Lindsay. "Mac left for the race circuit, so he won't be bothering me for a while." She sighed. "Now, hopefully, I can get some actual work done."

Marina nodded, a thoughtful expression on her face. "London is ready for you when you are," she said.

Lindsay nodded, suddenly grateful for the dark sunglasses. There was a twist in her stomach that she didn't understand and didn't want to try to explain to Marina if it somehow showed on Lindsay's face. She was probably just tired, tired from all the chaos and from yesterday's histrionics.

Focus. That's what Lindsay needed most of all. Sleep, sure, but mainly focus.

"Database is ready?" she said.

"Check," replied Raj.

"Front end is good?"

"Ready to go," said Marina. "Just waiting on that add-on. How's that coming?"

Lindsay sighed again. She'd made all of the updates to the standard libraries, but hadn't been able to finish the custom work, the so-called test the Brinksley team had given her. "I'll have it done by end-of-day today," she said.

"Okay," replied Marina, "then I'll test it tonight and it'll be good to go by morning."

"Perfect," said Lindsay. "Thanks for all the hard work, you guys. It's looking great."

"We live to serve you, boss," said Raj. He gave a jaunty salute and signed off.

"Mac's gone?" said Marina.

Lindsay sighed once more, a long, deep sigh that seemed to come from her toes. It was early morning. She'd only been awake for an hour, had just had two espressos. And yet, somehow, she felt like she needed to crawl back in bed for another eight hours. At least.

"Yikes," said Marina. "Three sighs in under a minute. What's that all about?"

"Nothing," said Lindsay. "I'm just exhausted. Too much going on, I guess."

Marina looked at her for a long moment. "Give me your address," she said.

"What? Why?"

"I'm coming to get you."

Lindsay had never met Marina in person. Or Raj. She'd hired them via video conference. During the pandemic, that was standard practice, but Lindsay would have done it that way even if there were no pandemic. She didn't see the point in having a physical office. It just added unnecessary overhead, extra costs that served only to stroke the founder's ego. And she didn't believe the bullshit Silicon Valley constantly spewed about "serendipitous hallway meetings" leading to so much innovation and creativity. Lindsay could count on zero fingers the number of useful hallway conversations she'd had at work. They usually involved some asshole hitting on her or some group of people discussing inane celebrity gossip. Remote work was the best model, in her mind, with in-person meetings arranged only when absolutely necessary.

The prospect of an impromptu, in-person meeting with Marina made Lindsay nervous. She wasn't sure why. Lindsay wasn't anti-social. Asocial, maybe. She just didn't feel any driving need for social interaction. Lindsay was perfectly happy to spend days on end in her apartment, absorbed in her work, not seeing anyone or speaking to anyone. But she didn't shy away from social interaction when it was necessary. She'd been interacting with plenty of people since she arrived in England.

But meeting Marina somehow seemed unnerving. Incongruous.

"I really need to get through this custom work, Marina," she said, "but thank you. I'll take a rain check."

Marina gave Lindsay another long look. Marina was a brilliant web developer. She was smart and funny and witty, brash and bold in her appearance and her attitude. She was the opposite of Lindsay in many ways. It was part of the reason she was such a great addition to the team. But she was also eerily perceptive and insightful, at times. And she seemed to read Lindsay like a book.

"It rains a lot in London," she said. "I'll have lots of chances to cash that rain check."

"I don't think that's how rain checks work."

"That's how mine work," Marina smiled. "I'll see you soon, Lindsay."

She signed off and Lindsay closed the laptop, staring at the bright sun slowly rising above the sea. She closed her eyes, seeing the orange glow behind her eyelids, like a fire inside her skull, bathing it, burnishing it. The warmth of the sun on her face, the warmth of the blanket on her body and her bare feet, she drifted through that healing flame as if it were a bank of clouds, letting the flame turn her to wisps of ash on the wind from the sea.

Lindsay woke with a start.

Her laptop had slid to the deck, tilted against one leg of her chair. Her blanket was skewed across her body, half on her, half puddled on the deck, her bare feet uncovered. A thin sheen of sweat clung to her skin, her body muggy and sticky under her clothes, like she'd drunk too much last night and her body was trying to flush the toxins out.

And those squirrels had found her again, moved back into her mouth while she dozed.

That's what she got for sleeping outside.

How long had she been asleep, anyway?

The world around her was dark and shrouded. She pulled off the sunglasses. That helped, but the world was still dim, cloudy and blue. A mist had moved in off the ocean, and the sun was clearly on its way out for the night, already below the roofline of the house at her back.

If the sun was already setting, that meant Lindsay had slept on the porch all damn day.

And she still felt tired. Bone-weary, really, as if her skeleton were suddenly made of tungsten, hard and heavy. She let the quick surge of waking anxiety fade from her bloodstream and settled into the heaviness, just lying there, rumpled on the deck lounger.

She was so tired. So existentially tired.

She was too young to feel this way. This was not how Lindsay Rhodes operated. Lindsay Rhodes worked. Hard. She didn't sleep on decks all day by the English seaside wearing five hundred dollar sunglasses. She might as well have had a stack of bonbons on a gold plate by her side. This was not what Lindsay Rhodes did.

And Lindsay Rhodes definitely did not refer to herself in the third person.

Lindsay groaned out loud. She was losing her mind. And if her mind went, what of Lindsay remained? She was her mind. Her thoughts, her abilities, her intelligence, her determination. That's what defined her. She was smart and she worked hard. That's who she was.

And yet, her mind was logy with sun-drenched sleep, and she couldn't motivate herself to move from her spot. The sound of the waves was so soothing. The feel of the mist, probing her face with tentative, searching tendrils, felt cool and cleansing, dissolving the flop sweat from what heat the day had brought. It was as if her body didn't want to move, as if it were on strike, demanding a day of rest in the sun by the sea.

But Lindsay had so much work to do. She'd already lost a full day when she could have been—should have been—finishing the Brinksley job. She'd promised Marina she'd have it done by now. Even if she leapt up and immediately started working, she wouldn't be done before midnight. The test might be a simple one, but it still required time and effort to complete.

And yet she still couldn't bring herself to move. She'd never had this problem before, never been unable to motivate herself to do the work. That was her true superpower, her simple ability to sit her butt in her chair and focus on the task at hand. When everyone else was off watching Netflix or playing video games or drinking in a bar trying to convince someone to sleep with them, Lindsay was working, getting shit done. That's why she owned her own company now and her former co-workers were still begging their bosses for raises that would beat the rate of inflation.

She had to do something. She couldn't lay here forever.

With the effort of a thousand bodies, Lindsay levered herself up off the deck lounger to a tottering, standing position. She grabbed her laptop in one hand, bunched the edges of her blanket around her throat with the other, and proceeded with shuffling, sliding bare feet across the deck, through the sliding glass door, and back into the house. She set her laptop down on the kitchen table and stared down at it for a long moment.

Of its own volition, outside of Lindsay's voluntary control, her body shuffled on, through the kitchen, down the hallway, her blanket still clutched in one hand by her throat, trailing behind her like the robes of a medieval queen, until her body steered into the bedroom and collapsed on her father's king-sized bed, her robes billowing up and settling over her like the loving hand of a parent tucking in their child.

The king is dead. Long sleep the queen.

17

AND LONG DID SHE SLEEP. It was nearly noon the next day when Lindsay awoke, but when she did her head was finally clear, her body filled with a surge of energy she hadn't felt in a long time. For the first time in Lindsay didn't know how long, her body actually wanted to wake up.

She showered, had coffee, dressed, and—in a burst of productivity that was remarkable, even for Lindsay—finished her work on the Brinksley job before the sun had set that evening. She checked it in to the repository where her team stored their code, triggering notifications to both Raj and Marina that the work was done. Within minutes, she had messages from both with thumbs-up.

Lindsay cleaned up her emails, sending a reply to the Brinksley VP apologizing for the delay in her response, but informing the VP of the good news that the work was in final internal testing and would be ready for client review by the end of the week, on schedule.

Lindsay rode the adrenaline high of getting things done and cleaned up her inbox, deleting spam, scanning newsletters, answering minor client questions, and checking in with her accountant.

One email caught her eye. The subject line read "Proposal for Purchase of Hart Racing, Inc."

Lindsay's throat caught as she scanned the email. It was from some company called Everbright Securities Group, LLP. Lindsay didn't recognize the name, but the company identified itself as an English private equity firm. They'd been interested in purchasing Hart Racing for some time, the email said. With condolences about her father's passing, they were making gentle inquiries into Lindsay's interest in divesting her stake in the firm. Fair market value, considerate continuity of management and strategic direction, maintenance of staff and compensation, etc., etc.

Just like that. Out of the blue, someone who wanted to buy Lindsay's share in the company.

Just like that, all of the adrenaline drained from Lindsay's body. The buzzing, ordered mind she'd enjoyed all day, firing on all cylinders, stalled, lurched, and shuddered to a halt.

This was what she'd been waiting for, someone who could buy her share of the company so she could go home to San Francisco and get on with her life. She'd be rich and she'd be financially free, back home alone in her apartment, able to live whatever life she wanted to live.

But if that's what she'd been wanting this whole time, why did she suddenly feel so tired again? Her limbs felt heavy, her bones tungsten, like they had the day before.

Maybe it was just the constant back and forth, the tug-o-war between the work with her own company and the work with her father's company. Or the mental strain of having a foot on two continents. Or the simple physical dissonance of being in a strange place, with different diurnal rhythms, different climate, different food. Even the different speaking accents might be enough to throw her off on some deep psychological level.

Whatever it was, it took every ounce of energy in Lindsay's body just to power through it all.

And the last ounce had just been used for the day.

Lindsay sent a quick reply to the email, leaving the door open for discussion, but explaining that nothing could be done until the end of the season.

Then, she closed her laptop and dragged herself down the hall to her bedroom, flopped back on the bed, pulled her blanket back over her head, and slept.

～

"Lindsay."

Lindsay rocked back and forth. She was on a boat at sea. It was night, and the sky was dark and misty. The ship was a sailboat, maybe fifty feet long, with one mast in the center towering above, a lone light at the top the only thing cutting through the darkness. The light was like some kind of lighthouse searchlight, circling and sending a beam of silver light slicing through the mist.

Despite the size of the boat, Lindsay was alone, the only person on board. She stood at the wire rail, looking out into the darkness, straining her eyes to see ahead each time the rotating lamplight illuminated the sea before her. Each time failing to see farther than the dark water beside the boat.

The sea was calm, a gentle breeze in her face. But soon the breeze picked up, first tossing Lindsay's hair behind her, then casting light spray into her face. The waves grew larger. The boat began to pitch and roll. Lindsay gripped the rail tight, the wire cutting into her palms.

The waves increased, now tossing the ship high, then dropping it low again, giving Lindsay a sick feeling in the pit of her stomach. The beams from the searchlight above swung crazily in the sky as the light rotated faster and faster.

The waves grew even larger, now crashing over the side of the boat, the spray kicking up into Lindsay's face, into her eyes, the salt stinging, the slithering water pulling at her feet. She held to the rail even more tightly, her hands raw.

Now the wind grew to a moan, then a howl, then an angry bellow in her ears. The searchlight spun faster, crazier, like a disco ball in a washing machine. The boat pitched up almost ninety degrees, straight up the face of a massive wave. Lindsay's feet fell out from under her. She held on to the wire rail, feeling hot blood on her palms, running down her forearms, her feet dangling in mid-air above the inky sea roiling far below.

The boat crested the wave. The deck leveled and Lindsay slammed down against it, her hips and legs blooming with pain. A gush of salt water loosed her grip on the rail, her palms on fire where the blood had been oozing from a long gash down the center, the salt now burning inside the wound.

The boat tipped over the top of the wave and pointed down the back, again nearly vertical, now pointed straight down into the water, into the heart of the sea. Lindsay reached for the wire rail, reached for a grip to hold her in place. But her hand was slick with blood and seawater. The grip was too fleeting, the pain too great. She could not hold herself.

She tried to spin on the deck, to orient her feet downward, but couldn't shift in time. She slid down, head first, down the deck of the boat, down the steep vertical. The rough deck scraped and tore the skin of her hands, forearms, elbows. Her chin banged against the decking, knocking her teeth together, making her see stars.

The bow grew closer and closer. In the canting, spinning disco searchlight, Lindsay held up her hands to break her fall, to maybe grab the rail when she hit the top of the boat.

A shattering sound.

The searchlight went out.

All was darkness and sliding and scraping and howling and stinging and bleeding.

Then a heavy thunk against her head.

And Lindsay was tilting, spinning.

Falling.

Falling in the dark.

Aware of falling only because of her limbs pedaling in air.

Of the sickening drop in her stomach.

Of her body tumbling ass-over-head in darkness.

Then the hard smack of water.

Like being hit by a baseball bat.

Immediate, blinding ache behind her eyes.

Blood pounding in her ears.

And Lindsay was in the water, under the water, shoved and held down by the water.

She could not swim. Could not move.

Could not escape.

She fought the need to breathe.

She knew if she did she'd die.

She'd pull in a lungful of seawater and drown, alone in the dark.

She fought with all her will as she sank deeper into the black sea. Her chest burned. Like it was imploding. Like her rib cage was crushing in on itself.

Her throat was on fire.

Then her mind was on fire. She wanted nothing more than to open her mouth and take a breath. Her body wanted it. Needed it. She'd die if she didn't.

Her mind knew she'd die if she did.

She fought it.

The fire in her mind was all-consuming.

Focus.

It lit her skull with its white-hot light.

Focus.

It burned her brain with its searing heat.

Focus.

The heat seared her chest as she sank ever deeper. Seared her lungs.

Her heart.

Focus. Focus on the pain. Focus on the heat. Focus on the light.

The light.

A light in the distance.

A white pinpoint.

Her throat, like claws against the inside.

The pinpoint became a dot.

Like a clawing beast inside her, desperate to escape.

The dot became a circle.

It would rip her to shreds with its claws.

The circle became a moon.

Its claws would tear her apart.

The moon became a sun.

Its claws would shred her into nothing.

From the sun, a hand emerged, palm up.

She would cease to exist.

Behind the palm, a face.

Her father's face.

"Lindsay," her father said, his voice kind and soft and deep, his eyes smiling and sad. "Lindsay," he repeated.

Lindsay reached out her own hand.

Her fingers were claws.

Her father took Lindsay's clawed hand in his and the world became warmth and light, like Lindsay had entered the sun. She felt like she were a rocket shooting up through the depths of the sea, up, up into the air again, no longer night, but now bright daylight, into puffy white clouds and blue sky, her hand in her father's, trailing him into the brilliant blue.

They slowed, hovered, spun in the air, the sea far below, a field of jewels twinkling in the sun.

Her father took Lindsay's other hand in his. She was facing

the sun. His face was dark, backlit as they spun. He held both her hands, his skin soft and dry. She felt safe. She felt secure. She felt loved.

She felt at home.

"Lindsay," said her father as they spun ever so slowly, high in the air. His voice was deep and soothing, like a blanket tucked around her as she drifted into sleep.

"Lindsay," he said again, his voice now a low growl that sent shivers of warm heat through Lindsay's body, lighting her up from the inside. They spun in the air, the sun moving to the side, half-shadow illuminating her father's face at last.

"Lindsay," he said once more with that low growling voice.

Not her father's face.

Mac's face.

More shivers, like lightning coursing through her, a wild pressure building, building from the inside, from deep in the core of her body. Rising, rising up through her, a pressure so full and so strong and so wild and so electric that Lindsay knew it would break her apart.

"Lindsay," Mac growled again.

She resisted the pressure, held it down. But that only made it stronger, more solid, more wild and electric.

They spun and the sun lit Mac's entire face. His brilliant blue eyes shone in the light, turned the bright blue sky grey around them.

"Lindsay," Mac growled once more, his voice slow and husky and hot.

One final overwhelming primal surge, and Lindsay could resist no more. She let that pressure take her, let it burst her into a million shards of glass, diffracting the sunlight around her like so many diamonds, filling the sky with a light so bright, so hot, so intense that it made the sun pale beside it.

Lindsay cried out with the release, shuddering and shaking, cried out with a scream that carried sadness and joy, suffering and success, loss and love, a scream that shuddered her entire body, bowed her backwards, and brought tears streaming down her face.

"Lindsay," said a voice, urgent and alarmed.

Lindsay lifted her eyelids, slowly, languidly, her pulse still hard and quick in her chest.

A face slowly resolved into view above her. Her mother's face, bearing a crazed, confused expression. "Are you all right?"

Lindsay could not form words. Her body was still quaking, little electric aftershocks sending spasms—intense, pleasurable spasms—coursing through her again and again.

"Mom?" she rasped.

Something hot against her cheeks, she reached up to wipe them. Her fingers came away soaked with glistening tears.

She looked again at the face, at her mother's face. Lindsay's eyes cleared as she blinked away her tears. It was Ms. Hayes' face that hovered above her.

Ms. Hayes released a long breath. "You screamed," she said, fussing with the blankets around Lindsay. "It didn't sound like pain, really. More like..." She lifted her eyebrows, her eyes darting down the length of Lindsay's body for a moment. Her mouth twisted up at one corner. "Well, you seem to be all right, thank goodness." Her face grew serious again. "*Are* you all right, Lindsay?"

Lindsay released a long, shuddering breath. She nodded, then struggled to sit up. Ms. Hayes helped her lean back against the headboard of the bed.

"I had a dream," she said, her voice hoarse.

"A good one?" asked Ms. Hayes without a trace of irony or sarcasm, just sincere concern.

"A... strange one," said Lindsay, gulping as another flurry of electric aftershocks spun through her body. She brought one hand up to wipe away more tears, her hand fluttering as she lifted it.

Ms. Hayes mouth set in a thin, tight line.

"Sit tight, darling," she said. "I'll make us some tea."

They moved to the library, to the comfortable, overstuffed leather chairs there. Lindsay sat with her legs tucked up underneath her, the leather cool against the tops of her bare feet. She'd brought the blanket from the bed, tucked it around her waist, covering her legs as she sipped her tea. The hot drink was sweet and soothing, the milk and sugar caressing her tongue, the heat like a hug from the inside as it slipped down her throat. A few silent sips and the caffeine kicked in, brightening Lindsay's mind and her mood.

Ms. Hayes just sipped in silence from the chair beside her. She'd slipped off her shoes and tucked her own stockinged feet under her on the chair, as well. She looked so much like Lindsay's mother that, if Lindsay let her mind drift for a moment, she could believe that she was there in her father's library with her mother by her side, like a happy family. That her father was just off using the restroom or fixing his own tea in the kitchen, soon to return.

"I don't know what I'm doing here," said Lindsay at last, softly. "It all happened so fast. So much change all at once. So far from home. I can't seem to wrap my head around it all."

Ms. Hayes sipped her tea, silent, patient.

The swirl of thoughts, the chaos of the last few weeks, pressed in against the warm, familial feelings, spearing through them like icicles. Lindsay took another long sip of tea, trying to stave off the chill of those thoughts.

But Lindsay couldn't pretend they weren't there, couldn't pretend they didn't exist. And she couldn't pretend that she was prepared for them. She wasn't. She had been pulled far outside her comfort zone. And she was flailing.

And no matter the feeling, no matter the resemblance, the woman quietly sipping tea in the chair beside her was not her mother. And her father was not in the kitchen, soon to return.

Lindsay's parents were gone. They weren't coming back. All of the talk about her father, the uncanny resemblance of Ms. Hayes to her mother, the dreams and thoughts that arose in Lindsay's mind, these were all just a fantasy. An illusion. A cruel coincidence.

Where once that simple fact may have brought cold clarity to Lindsay's mind, allowing her to focus on the heart of her work, to cut through all the extraneous bullshit and focus on getting the real work done, here in this place, that fact just weakened Lindsay, confused her. Her mind felt clouded and addled.

She'd never felt that way before, and the sensation only amplified her confusion.

Like in her dream, Lindsay felt lost at sea.

"I don't know what I'm supposed to be doing here," she whispered through the steam wafting from the cup held close before her lips.

They sat in silence for a long time, Lindsay swirling deeper into the dark recesses of her confusion.

Finally, Ms. Hayes spoke. "Why did you start your company?"

Lindsay furrowed her brow.

"Your company in San Francisco. Datasure. Why did you start it?"

Lindsay let out a long sigh. She thought back to that time, to that day when she quit her job and set off to start her own venture.

"I was tired of working for a bunch of arrogant men who thought they understood the world simply because they'd gotten rich from a tech IPO at age thirty. They considered themselves enlightened and compassionate, yet they were condescending toward women, while pretending they weren't, and competed with each other to see who could drive the fastest car or overpay the most for expensive houses on the beach, like little rich boys in the schoolyard."

Anger flared up through Lindsay's confusion, like a torch lit in a dark room. "And these are the people moving our society into the future? These are the people with so much control over modern life? Emotionally pre-pubescent, but somehow meant to solve all of the world's problems?" She shook her head. "I couldn't keeping working in that kind of place, letting my future be subject to the whims of those kinds of people. I had to go off and do my own thing, be in control of my own destiny."

Ms. Hayes nodded quietly, then took a slow sip of her tea. "And is it control you sought? Or something else?"

The question clanged off of Lindsay's mind, hitting some kind of barrier that wouldn't let it through. But it came back again and again, clanging each time on the hard shield around Lindsay's mind, demanding entry.

There was that word again. "Control."

Mac had accused her of being a control freak. Raj and Marina had hinted at similar things in the past. Lindsay had never thought of herself in that way. But she did like to be aware of what was happening, to have influence over it. She just wanted to make sure things were done properly, to avoid unnecessary extra work down the road, when things would need to be fixed due to mistakes or poor planning.

And it wasn't that she wanted to control things, per se. She didn't want power over people. Avoiding more work down the road would make things easier for everyone so everyone could have more time to do whatever they wanted to do. Lindsay wanted to finish the project at hand, turn it over to the client, collect their payment, and be done. Be free of the thing, so she could move on to the next thing.

"Freedom," Lindsay whispered. Ms. Hayes raised her eyebrows. "That's what I want, really. I want to be free. Free from the assholes and idiots who want to tell me what to do. Free from the oppressive systems our society has created, systems that create wealth inequality and stoke constant competition with each other over material possessions. I want to be free from constraints on my time and my resources and my imagination."

Something swung loose inside Lindsay. That shield came down or some block fell away or some door swung open. Perhaps some shutter opened on a light inside her. Maybe all of those things. But saying those words out loud was like the searchlight in her dream, cutting through the fog of confusion in her mind. A thin strand of clarity, of strength, of solidity in a mist of doubt.

"Freedom and control are not the same," said Ms. Hayes, "and they often cannot co-exist." She arched an eyebrow at Lindsay. "Which one do you want more?"

A week ago, Lindsay probably would have said she wanted control. A week ago, control was the same as freedom, in her mind. If she controlled everything around her, she was totally free from the influence of others.

But now she saw that total control meant being shackled to a reality that had to be narrow enough for one person to control it all themselves. In order to achieve total control, you had to limit yourself, limit your life, to something small enough to be controlled by one person.

Lindsay didn't want any limits at all. Her whole life, the world had been trying to place limits on her. Because she was a woman, she couldn't be good at math or lead a team of men. Because she wasn't rich, she couldn't go to college or run a company. Because she wasn't glib and giggly, because she didn't wear push-up bras and the latest fashions, she couldn't talk to certain people or go certain places or even sit where she wanted in the lunch room.

But Lindsay wasn't just good at math. She was great at it. And she didn't just go to college. She graduated at the top of her class, with a double major in Computer Science and Applied

Mathematics. And despite her gender and her asocial tendencies, she was a natural leader simply due to her intelligence and her confidence in it.

All of the limitations were bullshit. They were driven by the insecurities of the men who were already in power, or who inherited the mantles of power because of their gender or their skin color or their pedigree. Those men invented the limitations, or the systems that perpetuated them, to keep people from challenging their power. If those men could convince people not to believe they were worthy of their own power, then those men would never have to defend the power they had seized.

That was the insidious part of their method. That was the devious part of their plan, the way that they convinced people that they themselves were inadequate or unworthy. They convinced people to give up on themselves before they'd even tried, all so that those men could use people to enrich themselves. Keep them buying stuff they didn't need. Keep them working in jobs they didn't like. Keep them striving for some ever-changing ideal that no one could possibly ever achieve.

And Lindsay had had quite enough. She would not be held back any longer by the schemes and insecurities of others. Those men were like the Lilliputians who had roped down the giant Gulliver. With enough small ropes and the right application of physics, Gulliver was trapped, stuck to the ground on his back. But he had the power to stand at any time, to shake off those tiny restraints, those tiny creatures, and be free, so long as he could get just a tiny bit of leverage.

"I don't want control," said Lindsay softly. "I want to be free from being controlled by others."

"Then you'll need to relinquish some of the control you have now." Ms. Hayes tilted her head toward Lindsay. "Do you see that?"

Lindsay could feel the truth in what Ms. Hayes said more than she could see it with her conscious mind. It was as if her body, her heart, already knew the truth, but her mind was still catching up to the logic of it. That was a very odd feeling for Lindsay, but one she'd had once or twice already since coming to England.

Lindsay nodded.

"And you'll need to stop thinking about what you're *supposed* to be doing here, and start thinking about what you *want* to be doing here. Do you see the difference?"

Again, there was a disconnect between Lindsay's mind and her heart. Intellectually, she understood the difference. One was focused on following some rule or expectation set by an outside power. The other was focused on following an inner guide, with no concern for outside judgment.

That was what her mind understood.

Her body understood something much more. Exceeding external expectations was something Lindsay had done her whole life. That was how school and corporate life worked. Your teacher or your boss set some expectation, and you worked your ass off to exceed it. That was, to a large extent, how she defined herself, how she built her confidence. She was a person who exceeded expectations. She was a high achiever.

And she felt determined resignation at the thought of doing more of that kind of work. She knew she could do it, and do it well, but she didn't really want to. The rewards no longer justified the sacrifices.

Following an inner guide felt different. Setting her own rules, her own expectations. Following the path that made sense to her and her alone, without any care for how it looked to outsiders. Lindsay felt a flush of excitement at the idea.

But with that excitement came a shroud of cold fear. What if she was foolishly unprepared? What if her ideas were hopelessly naive and ill-informed? What if she failed spectacularly and looked like a complete idiot in front of the entire world? Was freedom really worth that risk?

Was her fear enough to keep her caged in a prison of external expectations for the rest of her life?

Lindsay nodded again. She saw the difference between the two paths Ms. Hayes was proposing.

But she couldn't follow the safe path any longer.

Her heart would not allow it.

"I understand, Ms. Hayes," she said. Her voice was still soft, but there was a steel in it that hadn't been there before. "But can you help me?"

Ms. Hayes gave Lindsay an appraising look, that wry smile twisting the corners of her mouth again.

"It's about time you asked," she grinned. She finished her tea and set the cup and saucer on the tray on the table. "And I'm pretty sure I just saw you orgasm in your sleep," her grin broadened, lighting the whole room, "so call me Maggie, for God's sake."

18

Knowing you wanted to follow your inner guide was one thing. Knowing what to do about it was another thing entirely.

"Just take a few days to get used to the idea," had been the advice Ms. Hayes—Maggie—had given Lindsay. "Watch your mind."

"Sounds like meditation," said Lindsay.

"I suppose it is," Maggie replied. "You'll see a lot of fear and discomfort at first. You'll want to revert to your old habits, doing whatever it is you think you *should* do or are *supposed* to do."

"But don't do those things? Some of them might make sense."

Maggie smiled. "Just be patient. Just wait and watch. You'll know what to do when your body just starts doing it."

That advice had made no sense to Lindsay then, and it still made no sense now, two days later. Two days of sitting around watching her mind. She felt in turns bored, useless, and a total slacker. She fought the urge to pick up her laptop every five minutes just to check her email or fiddle with her code.

She fought every habit she had developed in her adult life. Anything the old Lindsay would have done without thinking, the new Lindsay avoided. She wanted to wipe the slate clean and start fresh, see the world from a whole new perspective.

It didn't work.

All she did was drink way too much espresso, pace around the house for a while, sleep off the caffeine crash, then get up and do it all over again.

For two whole days.

She'd had enough. She had to do something.

An idea came to mind.

More a name than an idea.

Yue Zhou.

Lindsay drove to the office in the Mercedes G-wagon. After a little direction from Helen, she walked to the production center, through a small maze of hallways, and found a door with a plaque beside it that read: "Server room". Beneath that, another plaque: "Yue Zhou".

Lindsay knocked, then pushed open the door.

The room was long and narrow, the concrete floor filled with black metal racks that reached almost to the ceiling, arranged in four rows set close together like the stacks of a library with too many books and not enough floor space. In the racks were dozens of black plastic boxes, rectangular and thin, each with a series of green and red lights blinking on their front and a nest of cables extending from their back. The room was dark, lit only by soft blue lights overhead and the glow from the lights on the server boxes themselves, and it was cold, the drone of whirring fans and the hiss of air conditioning loud in Lindsay's ears.

"Hollo?" Lindsay called, walking down the aisle in front of her. "Yue? Anyone here?"

At the end of the aisle in the distance, a rolling chair zipped backward across the concrete into Lindsay's field of view. A woman about Lindsay's age sat in the chair, a pair of headphones on her head, cocked to uncover one ear. She held a sandwich in one hand and she was chewing.

"Yo," she said around a mouthful of food.

"Are you Yue?" said Lindsay.

"Yep," said Yue.

"I'm Lindsay." Lindsay reached out her hand. "Lindsay Rhodes."

Yue looked at Lindsay's hand like it was an advertisement being offered to her as she walked down a city sidewalk.

"Okay," said Yue, taking another bite of her sandwich.

Looked like peanut butter and jelly, only the jelly was white.

"Fluffernutter," said Yue in response to Lindsay's look.

"Excuse me?" Lindsay had no idea what the hell the woman had just said to her, but it sounded mildly obscene.

"I see you eyeballing my sandwich," said Yue. "It's a fluffernutter."

She took another bite, the white stuff gathering on the corner of her mouth, gooey and sticky. A quick swipe of Yue's tongue brought it into her mouth like a frog casually swallowing a fly that was crawling for its life.

"No one here knows what they are," she said. "Peanut butter and marshmallow fluff. Fluffernutter. It's an American thing."

"I'm American," said Lindsay, "and I don't even know what the hell you just said."

Yue paused her chewing for a beat, then resumed.

"Maybe it's a New York thing, then," she said. "I had them when I was in college."

"Where—"

"Columbia."

"What—"

"Comp Sci."

Lindsay frowned. "Computer Science at Colum—"

"It's a good program, okay?"

Yue took another bite, this time with a sharpness that matched the fire in her eyes, as if she were daring Lindsay to say something about her degree. Columbia was a good school, but Lindsay hadn't ever heard much about its Computer Science program.

But it didn't matter. She shrugged.

"I just wanted to thank you for the bao buns you made the other night. Mac shared them with me." Lindsay's stomach growled at the memory, reminding her that she hadn't eaten lunch yet. "They were... incredible."

Yue sat back in her chair, rolling slowly away from Lindsay with the force. She just chewed her sandwich, giving Lindsay an appraising stare.

"My mother's recipe," said Yue after a pause. "She grew up in Shanghai."

"Well, they were amazing. I'd ask for the recipe, but," she shrugged again, "I can't cook for shit."

Another appraising stare, then Yue shrugged back.

"Doesn't matter," she said. "I wouldn't give you the recipe, anyway."

"Oh," replied Lindsay. Yue had said it without hostility, but Lindsay was unsure how to take it. Was it meant to be an insult?

"Nothing personal," Yue clarified. "I don't give it to anyone. Family secret."

"Got it." Lindsay looked around. Yue had a small desk in the back corner of the server room. It had a monitor and a whole mess of hardware in various states of disrepair. A phone screen in an aluminum harness, without the rest of the device. A server without its enclosure, showing the circuit boards and wires inside. A pile of cables and wires nearly as high as the monitor that sat on her desk.

"I like to tinker," she said, following Lindsay's gaze.

"What is it you do here, anyway?" asked Lindsay. "Are you the network engineer?"

"I'm a data engineer," she said. "I deal with databases. Oracle. Teradata. Hadoop. I told them that when they hired me."

"Okay," said Lindsay. "So, you're the data engineer?"

"You'd think so," said Yue, "but no. When I said 'data' in my interview, they heard 'everything computer-wise that we don't want to think about'. That's why I'm in here," she gestured toward the servers, "maintaining the servers."

"Huh," said Lindsay. Didn't sound like Mac—or her father—to blindly force someone to do a job they weren't hired for, just out of convenience to themselves. "Do you do any actual data engineering?"

"Yes," said Yue, "God, yes. I do all the data engineering. I built every database and schema they use. But I'm also the network engineer, the database admin, the fix-it guy, and the in-house data scientist. They've got front-end people, thank God. If I had to write CSS code, I'd have fucking quit on Day 2. But everything else that's not on the travel team?" She slapped her chest with one hand. "Me. All fucking me."

"You're joking," said Lindsay. Even a small company should have a good-sized team to deal with their data and the systems that support it. Data is blood these days, and the server room is the heart. If the data systems fail, most companies are dead in the water.

She looked around at the servers, counted maybe forty boxes. "What do you have here, maybe twenty terabytes, with failovers? Not very big. You guys using AWS?"

Yue tilted her head. "You a computer nerd?"

"Data science," said Lindsay. "I'm from San Francisco."

"I won't hold it against you." She popped the last bite of sandwich into her mouth. "Thirty TB, no AWS, and I'm constantly having to deal with a whole bunch of shit, trying to aggregate data down to free up space for the next week's input."

"Why don't you tell them you need more capacity?"

"You think I haven't?" said Yue. "Why the fuck do you think I make my mother's Sheng Jian Bao for Mac? It ain't because he's hot."

Lindsay arched an eyebrow.

"Okay, maybe a little because he's fucking hot," said Yue, "and fucking cool as shit, but I'm also trying to butter him up to get some changes around here."

Lindsay nodded. "You mentioned the travel team? What do they have to do with it?"

Yue snorted. "They're the golden children around here. They've got everything they want. Top-of-the-line shit. They've got their own data team. They do use AWS. Can't haul a room's worth of server boxes around the world with them. But they've got their own network engineers, their own data engineers, data scientists, everything. And most of the UI work is focused on their stuff."

"What do they do with it?"

"They analyze it, real-time during the races. Trying to figure out what's happening with the car, the driver, the track, the weather, the other cars, the other drivers... everything."

That was impressive. Lindsay hadn't even thought about that part of things.

"Do you have access to their data?"

"The real-time data? Sure. I'm the one who has to try to aggregate it and fit it onto these boxes," she jerked her head toward the servers, "for long-term storage. I end up dumping ninety-nine percent of it because I don't have enough room to store it all, but I aggregate the important stuff. Or what they tell me is important."

"And what's that?"

"Lap times, weather conditions, car telemetry. Stuff that they can use to tweak the cars between races, stuff they can use to improve designs between seasons, that kind of thing."

"So they don't do any long-term studies of the detailed data from each race?"

Yue shrugged.

"As far as I know, they don't look back at the second-by-second stuff. Once the race is over, they move on. They'll review the aggregated data from past races as part of their prep for this year's race, but that's it."

"What about AWS? How much is stored there?"

"I don't know. All of it, I guess. I set up their Hadoop environment for them, but that's about all I paid attention to." She squinted at Lindsay. "Why do you care about all of this? Did they hire you to do data science? Because, if so, I've got a shitload of network admin I need you to do for me."

Lindsay grinned. "Let's just say I'm here to help." She folded her arms across her chest. "But I need you to get me access to that Hadoop environment."

Turned out the Hadoop environment stored in AWS, Amazon's cloud storage system, contained all of the data for every single race so far. A massive amount of information, but a drop in the bucket compared to what the environment could hold, and a grain of sand compared to the size of data Lindsay was used to dealing with.

And the system was a mess. The framework was solid—Yue knew her stuff—but there was no aggregation, no analysis. It was like someone had a party in their house, people used the cups and plates and drank the liquor and ate food, then they pushed all the trash off to the side of the room and held another party over the top of it the next week, repeating that process over and over. Every race was another party, but they never bothered to clean up the data from the previous race.

Or to analyze it.

And Lindsay hated to see a good dataset go to waste. That night, back at home, she flopped on the couch under a blanket and dug into the data using the access credentials Yue had created for her. She started by scanning through the schema, familiarizing herself with the different data tables, just getting a sense for what kind of information was in the database, and what structures were used to organize it. Then she dug into the data itself, looking to see what form it was stored in.

Everyone thinks differently, and that includes software developers. Everyone has a mental model that they use to organize and store information in their own brain. Without realizing it, developers often mimic that model, to one degree or another, when they write their own code.

In a typical company in Silicon Valley, a data architect would establish guidelines for everyone to use. Naming conventions, organization principles for the data schema, that sort of thing. Without a coherent architecture for the system—one which likely mirrors the mental model of the architect—you can end up with as many different data models as you have software developers working on the code.

Unfortunately, that seemed to be the case here. She could tell which tables were created by the same developer. There seemed to be eight or nine different coders who had worked on the system, all of them using slightly different terminology for the same fundamental piece of data. For example, one developer identified the cars using a field labelled 'car_id' while another did the same thing, but called it 'auto_id'. A third used the term 'autoID', without the underscore, while a fourth developer, thinking himself clever, called it 'speed_racer_id'.

Not a huge problem, on the surface. Developers could name things whatever they wanted and the code would run just fine. But when you wanted to take a piece of information from one table and combine it with a piece of information from another table, you needed a way to tell the system that they belonged together. In this case, you needed to tell the systems that the two pieces of information described something about the same car. When the labels used for 'car' were different in every table, that created a real pain in the ass for the data scientist.

Lindsay sighed.

Ms. Hayes—Maggie—came to mind, her voice in Lindsay's ears. *Freedom and control are not the same... you'll need to relinquish some of the control you have now.*

In other words, Lindsay needed to start asking for help. And this was a perfect time to start.

"You sure it's okay that we gain access to this data?" said Raj through his video feed. "Do we even have a contract with Hart Racing?"

"Good point," said Lindsay. She didn't know what the rules were when you owned two companies and had them start working together, but she figured she should keep it as separate as possible, as if she were contracting with Hart Racing, Inc. like any other company. "There will be a contract signed by the end of the day tomorrow."

"And they already have a front-end?" said Marina.

"Yes, but it's only used by the race team," replied Lindsay, then cringed, "and I don't have access to it yet."

"What about the Brinksley job?" said Raj.

"That's in UAT right now," said Lindsay, "and so far they haven't reported any issues. I'm sure there'll be something, but we'll work it in when it comes up."

Lindsay knew from past experience that Raj didn't like curve balls. Not in his work, at least. He liked it when he knew the schedule and the plan and everything proceeded accordingly. Lindsay was much the same way. But life loves to throw the curve. Raj would adjust.

"I'll build my own UI," said Marina. "It'll be fun to compare what I come up with to what they're using now. Maybe we can borrow from both designs to create something even better."

"Great," said Lindsay. "Raj, what do you think about the schema?"

"The schema is clean, but the naming conventions are a mess and the data is all over the place. There's a ton of room for optimization here. Amazon is making a fortune off these guys."

"Can you fix it?"

Raj scoffed. "Come on, Lindsay. Remember who you're talking to here."

"Rajanesh Gupta, the Raja of Data," said Marina with mock solemnity.

"Marina," said Raj, imitating the hiss and suck of Darth Vader's breathing, "I am your raja."

"You wish," Marina replied.

"Yes," said Raj, still using his Darth Vader voice, "yes, I do."

"Well, Darth Raja," said Lindsay, "there's one other thing I need you to do."

"*Another* Lindsay joke?" said Marina. "That's two this year."

"Records are shattering left and right," said Raj.

Lindsay just smiled at the camera until Raj and Marina fell silent, waiting.

"Something I need you both to do, actually," she continued when she had their attention. "I need you both to come here. To Skipsea. In person."

19

Maggie and Lindsay arranged the contract in short order the next day, with Maggie signing as a representative of Hart Racing, just to avoid any appearance of impropriety that might arise from having Lindsay's signature on both sides of the contract. And Lindsay had Raj on a plane the next day.

Danny picked both Raj and Marina up in London and brought them to Skipsea. Lindsay had found him in one of the many garages, polishing and maintaining one of the vehicles he drove. She'd brought him a batch of cookies—biscuits—from a bakery in town, one that Maggie told her was Danny's favorite. He must have been a regular there, because when she happened to mention his name to the person behind the counter, they knew just what cookies to give to Lindsay.

"I work for you, Ms. Rhodes," Danny had said in his warm, thick accent. "You don't need to bribe me to do my job."

"I know that, Danny, and thank you," Lindsay had replied. "But I never took the chance to talk with you in the car when you picked me up from the airport, and I never thanked you for your kindness that night when I passed out and you helped me into the house. These cookies are just a way to say I'm sorry and

214

thank you and I look forward to getting to know you and your family more."

Danny had actually blushed when she said it. Lindsay's heart melted for the man in that moment. She pictured him at home with a loving wife and two or three kids running around laughing and playing. That might just have been a scene from A Christmas Carol, playing in Lindsay's memory, but the sentiment seemed fitting, nonetheless.

"That's very kind of you, Ms. Rhodes," Danny replied.

"You're welcome, Danny," said Lindsay. "And please," she smiled, "call me Lindsay."

Lindsay spent the rest of the day in an emotional state that could only be called a tizzy. Her heart pounded in her chest and she would alternately break out in cold sweats and hot flashes. She'd spent three years talking to Marina and Raj through the window of a laptop screen, never seeing more than their heads and shoulders. And in about six hours they'd be here in front of her in person.

To distract herself, Lindsay was working with Yue on setting up the systems so that Marina and Raj could get to work right away. Accounts, access privileges, scratch space in the database, everything would be ready for them to hit the ground running as soon as they arrived.

"How much room in the scratch space, again?" said Lindsay, sitting down on top of an old server box that had been turned on its side beside Yue's desk to act as a makeshift stool.

"Still five hundred gig," said Yue, "just like the last time you asked."

"Okay," said Lindsay. "Okay, good." She stood up, crossed her arms and paced back and forth behind Yue's chair. "And did you get us access to the race team's portal?"

"Yep," said Yue, deadpan.

"Great, great." Lindsay's muscles felt like they were moving of their own accord, twitching under her skin. When she sat, they twitched her to her feet. When she paced, they pulled her back down.

She sat down on the server again. Her knee started to bounce.

"Fucking hell, Lindsay," said Yue, "if you don't calm down I'm gonna fucking quit and let you and your crew of superstars work through this pile of dogshit on your own. That'll get your knee to stop twitching."

"Sorry," said Lindsay, "I don't know what my problem is."

Yue just raised an eyebrow. She was definitely not the warm and fuzzy, shoulder-to-cry-on type.

Lindsay pulled in a deep breath and let it out. "Sorry," she said, forcing her knee to stop bouncing.

"Accounts are ready," said Yue, ticking off on her fingers as she spoke, "access is ready, scratch space is ready. AWS, local data, race portal. They even have admin privileges on every-thing, so you really can take over when I quit. And I've sent credentials and login info to the email addresses you gave me. They have everything they need to get up and running."

Lindsay nodded, staring into space, trying to focus on what Yue had told her, willing herself to stop worrying about meeting her coworkers.

"You have all of that, too," said Yue, pointedly. "*Maybe* you should go through it all and make sure it's working for you."

Yue arched an eyebrow again.

With a grateful sigh, Lindsay nodded. Yue had given her exactly what she needed: something to do to keep her mind occupied.

She spent the next few hours on her laptop, crowded beside Yue in the server room. Lindsay already had access to the data, but she occupied her time in gaining access to the race portal and reviewing every nook and cranny of the interface, as well as the data it presented, digging into the database behind it to see where the numbers were coming from. The user interface was workable, but Lindsay knew Marina would improve it a hundredfold.

Lost in her work, Lindsay's muscles finally settled and the time slid by. She didn't look up until she heard a soft knock on the door and the sound of women's heels tapping on the concrete floor.

"Danny just left your house, Lindsay," said Maggie. "Hello, Yue. Good to see you again."

Yue nodded a greeting, and Lindsay's heart pounded in her chest again. She closed her laptop, stood slowly, and willed her body to obey her mind, calmly and smoothly.

Lindsay and Maggie wound their way through the production facility, up the hill, and through the main building, arriving at the front door just as Danny pulled up in the sleek, black Mercedes he'd used to pick her up at the airport in London. How long ago had that been? It felt like years, but was only a couple of months.

Lindsay clasped her hands in front of her waist to keep them from shaking. Even in the cool afternoon air, her sweat made it hard to maintain a grip. How would meeting in person change her relationship with Raj? With Marina? Maybe, in person, they'd lose respect for Lindsay somehow. Maybe she wouldn't meet their expectations, wouldn't fulfill their mental image of her. Maybe she smelled bad or spoke too loud or had bad breath. As she waited for the car to come to a full stop, all of these thoughts crowded through her mind, competing to cause Lindsay the most mental anguish.

At last, the tires stopped rolling. Lindsay heard the clicks of three car doors opening. Raj was on the near side. He was large, much larger than he seemed on camera, a big, bearded bear of a man, easily four inches taller than Lindsay's already tall frame. He didn't say a word, just covered the ten feet between Lindsay and the car in two huge steps and engulfed Lindsay in a massive embrace. At first, Lindsay was taken aback, but she couldn't resist the pure, honest joy of the hug. By the time Raj released her, Lindsay was laughing out loud.

Still, Raj said nothing. Just held Lindsay with one huge hand on each shoulder, arms extended, and regarded her like a proud father seeing his little girl graduate from sixth grade.

No, not like a father. Like a friend. A good friend.

Raj stepped aside and revealed a tiny woman standing behind him. She had a hoop through one side of her nose and a piercing through her lower lip. Lindsay noticed a stud in her nose, opposite the hoop. Her hair was jet black, shoulder length, shaved on one side and streaked with red, white, and blue on the other. The streaks were tastefully interwoven among the black.

"You know Americans," said Marina, noticing Lindsay staring at her hair. She gestured toward it. "If you don't make a big deal about them when they visit, they get all moody and shit."

"You added a nose piercing," said Lindsay.

Marina shrugged. "Special occasion."

From nowhere, or maybe from some dark place deep within Lindsay, tears swelled, pressed against the back of her eyes, flushed the skin of her face. She opened her eyes wider, hoping the cool air would dry the tears before they could spill.

Marina, studying Lindsay's face, as always, furrowed her brow, opened her arms, and stepped to Lindsay. She was at least six inches shorter than Lindsay, maybe more, but her hug was even more fierce, somehow even more enveloping than Raj's had been. For such a small woman, Marina carried outsized dignity and a heart bigger than anyone Lindsay had ever met.

Lindsay could not hold back the tears, then. They flowed in unbroken streams down her face and into Marina's hair. Lindsay's chest hitched once or twice. After a moment, Raj came in, too, wrapping both Lindsay and Marina in his giant bear arms. He brought his warmth and joy with him. Where Marina's presence had helped Lindsay release her pain, Raj's presence helped her heal it. By the time they all stepped away, Lindsay was smiling again.

"You're taller than I expected," said Marina.

"You're shorter than I expected," replied Lindsay.

"I knew you'd both be shorter than me," said Raj, "though I didn't know Marina was snack-sized." He lifted his eyebrows and ogled Marina. "Tasty snack-sized."

"A little goes a long way," Marina retorted, eyeing Raj right back.

"Prove it," said Raj, with something more than just friendly banter in his eyes.

"We'll see," said Marina with a sly smile, then looked to Lindsay. "Isn't there something you brought us here to do?"

Lindsay grinned and led them both inside.

As Lindsay had expected, Yue meshed with Raj and Marina almost immediately, joining the ranks of Lindsay's team as if she'd been there from the start—though she would never have said that to Yue, who was her usual cantankerous self. But every so often Lindsay would see her looking at Marina and smiling, or humming softly to herself as she worked. She even watched Raj take a bite from her fluffernutter—without asking—and didn't tear his head off for it.

Lindsay had brought the team in for a systems and UI review, looking for suggestions and solutions to bring Hart Racing's data capabilities up to the standards of the current decade. Regardless of whether she was selling her share in the company or not, Lindsay would not be associated with a firm using outdated tech, especially on the data side. It was practically a moral obligation for her to upgrade Hart Racing to something more respectable.

Yue had done her best to apply some data science rigor to the data, but it was clear that her skills lay elsewhere. And the data scientists on the race team had done some good work, but like most of the tech bros in Silicon Valley, it wasn't cutting edge and, to be frank, it lacked imagination.

Lindsay couldn't help herself. She set to work to make it better.

They worked non-stop for weeks, with Marina and Raj staying at Lindsay's house at night, each in one of the many spare rooms. Lindsay discovered with a pleasant shock that the two employees she'd hired via video conference years ago had actually become great friends. They'd work all day, take turns making dinner while the others continued working at the house, then they'd eat and talk all night. Marina and Raj would often stay up talking even after Lindsay had flopped into her bed, overcome with sleep.

Yue would join them, too. At first, it was once a week, then twice, then three times. Eventually, she slipped into the dinner rotation, cooking up traditional Chinese meals that made Lindsay's mouth water for days afterward, just from the memory. None of the four of them were master chefs, nothing like Mac, but between Raj's home-cooked Indian dishes and Yue's Chinese food, they ate well.

Marina, like Lindsay, couldn't cook to save her life. Eventually, their two cooking assignments were condensed to one. Yue and Raj refused to subject themselves to more, they said. So Lindsay and Marina would work in the kitchen together, cobbling from various online recipes and YouTube videos a meal that they hoped was edible.

Sometimes, it actually was.

Raj worked closely with Yue on the data engineering, optimizing their system and determining the ideal setup for their servers and server space. Marina developed a brilliant user interface, putting the existing race portal to shame. After a few weeks, they all cut over to this new setup, dogfooding it to make sure it was robust and useful.

Lindsay focused on the data science. She ported over her standard code library, naturally, but found so much interesting data in the real-time feeds that she found herself writing thousands of lines of custom code just to parse it all and make sense of it. The data was so fine-grained and so disparate, coming from so many sources that were related in such complex ways, that she became totally absorbed, almost obsessed by it. Weather information, track conditions, detailed data on every system in the car itself. Information about the driver and their vital signs before, during, and after the race. Then there was the layout of the tracks and the lines the drivers were taking through it, the actions of the race team and the information and instructions they relayed to the drivers. And finally, there was all of the same information about every single car in the race, or as much as Hart Racing was allowed to access, anyway. It was an incredible trove of rich data that Lindsay could use to rebuild the race from start to finish, painting a detailed rendering of the race, after the fact.

At first, Lindsay focused on pulling everything together into that coherent picture. She worked with Marina to find ways to visualize it, building an animated recreation of the race in Marina's user interface, with TV-quality detail.

Then, as she watched these replays, Lindsay found herself looking for ways to improve performance. Not the performance of the database or the web portal, though she and the team were constantly looking for improvements there. Instead, Lindsay was surprised to find herself interested in improving the performance of the drivers, of the cars, of the race team.

They weren't winning. Not even close.

She wanted to help change that.

She wrote more algorithms, setting the system to test thousands of variables in billions of permutations that took days to compute. She would identify the factors that seemed to make a difference to the outcome of the race, discarding those that were irrelevant or were so highly correlated to other factors that she didn't need both. Then, she'd feed those factors into various types of data science models to figure out which ones had the greatest impact on the outcome of the race. She did this with the full slate of tracks in the schedule, with each track run under a variety of race conditions. In the end, she was hoping she'd find the optimal setup and strategy for each driver on each track under any weather situation against any field of competition.

It was a lot to ask, and a lot of factors to sort through. Frankly, Lindsay didn't yet understand racing well enough to tweak the algorithms to find quick results. It would take months, maybe years, to develop such a system. But she did see some opportunities for improvement right off the bat.

"Who's Marcus Leygren?" Lindsay asked Yue one day while they were working in the server room. Yue and Raj were doing something amid the server racks while Marina and Lindsay crouched over their laptops on Yue's desk.

Yue snorted. "Since you have a vagina, I'm going to assume you've never been within five hundred meters of Marcus Leygren. Otherwise, he would have slithered over and introduced himself to you." She looked at Lindsay. "Marcus Leygren is the former boy wonder of the Formula One circuit. Now, he's a has-been who isn't ready to give up the spotlight." She turned back to whatever she and Raj were tinkering with. "He joined our team two years ago. English hero come home for his final act. Women all over the UK shuddered and locked their doors at the news."

"Bit of a playboy, is he?" said Raj.

"Notorious skank is a better description," Marina chipped in without looking up from her monitor, where she was updating the animations on her race re-creations. "Got three or four kids with three or four different women."

"That he knows about," said Yue.

"Okay, got it," said Lindsay. "Asshole. Understood. But what about his driving?"

"Like I said," said Yue, "he was incredible once. A phenom. Won two driver's championships in a row when he was twenty years old or something. Youngest ever at the time." She turned back to her work. "Then he got more interested in getting wasted, crashing expensive cars, and fucking any woman he could find than he was in his career. Google it. You'll find tons of shit."

"If all he does is chase women, why did we hire him for the team?" asked Lindsay.

Marina pulled up an article on the monitor in front of them and pointed it out to Lindsay. "Like Yue said, he's a hometown hero. And he's still competitive. All that natural talent doesn't just disappear."

The article was about the announcement that Leygren was joining Hart Racing. He had once driven for Mercedes, where he won his four championships, including the famous two-in-a-row, then Ferrari, where he won one more. But that was five years ago. And now he was coming back to England with the welcome of a former champion, but the record of a has-been.

"How do I get his email address, Yue?" asked Lindsay.

"You can't possibly be that desperate," Yue retorted without looking up from the server she was working on. "I mean, true, you look nerdy as fuck, but that's kind of in these days. Hang out at any bar long enough and someone will take you home. You don't need to stoop to Marcus Leygren."

"Thanks for the feedback, Yue," said Lindsay. "Now where can I get his email?"

Yue sighed and came over to pull up the company directory, which had the contact information for everyone on staff. Lindsay saw Helen's name and Maggie's. Her heart skipped a beat when Mac's name went by. She'd been so busy, she had gone almost two or three hours now without thinking about him.

Almost.

Yue found Marcus Leygren's name and address and Lindsay typed out a quick email to him. She decided to go with the short and sweet approach. "Marcus," the email began, "I'm a data scientist back at headquarters and I found some information that may be of use." Hopefully that would get his attention.

She went on with details about the recommendation—to throttle back in every left turn at the upcoming race in Azerbaijan, only pushing the throttle again when he was at least three-quarters of the way through the turn—and extensive documentation to support her conclusion, including data tables, statistical analysis, and output from Marina's user interface. Marcus had developed an odd tendency to rush the exit from his left turns. Lindsay had no idea why, but she hoped this advice would get him to hold back and wait just a bit longer, giving him acceleration along a straighter vector coming out of the curve.

The first practice rounds for the race began in two days. Hopefully, he'd absorb the information in time to apply it by then.

❦

Time went on in similar fashion, with the four becoming closer than ever, working harder, longer hours than before, but somehow enjoying it. In fact, despite the hard work and little sleep, Lindsay felt more alive than she had since she'd arrived.

More alive than she had in years, really.

She checked the practice results from Azerbaijan. Leygren's performance was no better than usual. She reviewed the detailed data and saw that he hadn't implemented her suggestions, even though she could see that he'd read her email. She sent him another message, summarizing her findings even more simply, adding in the new data from the first two practice sessions.

She checked the results again the next day. Still no improvement, still no sign that he'd applied her suggestions in the third practice session or the qualifying. As a result, he'd qualified well back in the pack. Lindsay sent another email, with even clearer language and a thinly-veiled insult or two. Hey, the man was supposed to be a professional. He should be able to handle it.

The next day, she checked the results of the final race.

He'd put her suggestions to work about halfway through the race. According to the recordings of the race chatter with the team in the pits, he'd been so far out of contention by then that he basically said "fuck it" and gave it a shot.

In fact, he had uttered the words "fuck it" under his breath in the recordings.

But, Lindsay didn't care. He gained five places from that point, a massive improvement, and just barely missed tenth place, where he would have earned his first points of the entire season.

He'd taken her suggestions, and they'd worked.

She sent him an email pointing that out, then offering her suggestions for the next race, in Canada.

"Damn," said Yue when Lindsay reviewed these findings with her, Raj, and Marina. "This shit actually works."

They doubled down on their efforts.

Lindsay added a tip to Marcus about his execution in overtaking, especially on the straights. She found that drivers who waited until closer to the turns to overtake tended to hold onto their position for longer. Passing in a straightaway made them too vulnerable to drag, probably. She passed this observation to Marcus.

That weekend, Marcus qualified in seventh position, his highest qualifying spot in three seasons. His fifth-place finish in the race was his highest all year by a wide margin.

Of course this shit really worked.

Lindsay had already prepared emails for Marcus for the next five races. She would update each missive with any new insight from the fresh data that had come in, but had the bulk of each email ready to go.

The following race was back home in England the weekend after next at Silverstone Circuit, about two hours northwest of London and three hours southwest from Hart Racing headquarters in Skipsea. Before the end of the race day in Canada, she had sent Marcus an invitation to meet with her and her team at Hart HQ to review their findings more extensively in person, to address any questions he had, and to show him the new race portal. She hoped that he would find it useful and serve as an ambassador to the rest of the team, which would probably be reluctant to try anything new. Most employees in most companies were resistant to change, even if the change would make their lives easier. People just really hate change.

The race team would be traveling on Monday, so she'd set the meeting for Tuesday afternoon. On Monday evening, she and the team were at the house, prepping and reviewing the presentation for Marcus. Music was playing softly in the background, some kind of punk rock that Yue had picked out and Lindsay had forced her to turn down to at least a level that let them hear each other without shouting. It was Raj's turn in the kitchen, and the smells of coriander and cardamom filled the air, lighting up Lindsay's senses and making her stomach growl.

"What the fuck do you think you're doing?" came a different sort of growl that made Lindsay's heart leap out of her throat.

She turned to see Mac standing in the hallway, his suitcase still in one hand. His hair was disheveled, his beard unkempt. His eyes had the wild, red-rimmed, sunken look of someone who had been unable to sleep for far too long. He wore a blue, button-down shirt, the top several buttons undone. A bag slung over his shoulder and across his body pulled his shirt to one side, revealing enough of his smooth muscular chest to make more than just Lindsay's blood heat up.

Mac dropped his suitcase to the tile floor with a hard thump and stepped closer to Lindsay. The wildness in his eyes was almost feral. His scent washed over Lindsay, carried by his movement. She pulled in a deep breath of it, closing her eyes, nearly fainting with relief, relief that she could finally smell that heady scent in her nostrils again, instead of just in her memories.

Lindsay opened her eyes. Mac stepped closer. She fell into the brilliant blue depths she found there. In that moment, she didn't care if she ever came out again.

"Lindsay," said Mac, his voice still a growl, but deeper now, with some kind of undertone Lindsay couldn't quite place, but which set her already racing pulse to double-time. Mac stepped even closer, now close enough that she could feel the heat from his body. If Lindsay rocked forward on her toes, she could rest her head against his muscular chest.

For a moment, Mac's eyes softened, seemed to lose focus. Lindsay could feel herself tilting forward, toward Mac, could swear that he was tilting forward, too, as if some magnetic force were pulling them together.

"Hey, man," said Raj, emerging from the kitchen wearing an

apron, wiping his hands on a towel. "I'm Raj. You staying for dinner? We've got plenty."

Mac looked up at Raj, startled. He looked around the room at Marina and Yue as if noticing for the first time that there were other people present.

When he looked back at Lindsay, that wild, feral look was back in his eyes, even more intense than before.

"Who the fuck are these people," he growled, "and why the fuck are you meeting with Marcus Leygren?"

20

Lindsay didn't know what had come over her. Mac had appeared, as if from her dreams, materialized right in front of her, looking wild and wanton, smelling incredible, his clothes askew, the hot skin of his chest taunting Lindsay. Her hands itched to undo the buttons of his shirt even more. Her hands ached to touch that hot skin. Her lips begged to work across that expanse of muscle, across and down, down...

And then he'd spoken to her in that tone, that asshole, alpha-male tone, like this house was his property. Like she was his property, demanding to know who were these strangers who were setting eyes on her without his express advance approval.

"These are my guests," said Lindsay, taking a much-needed step back, letting some air circulate between Mac's body and hers. "I've invited them." She put a hand on one hip. "The real questions is what the fuck are *you* doing inside *my* house?"

The feral look in Mac's eyes grew wilder, more intense for a fraction of a moment, and Lindsay felt something swing loose inside her, something that hung now by only a thread, a thin thread of self-control. She knew that if he touched her right then, she'd explode. Whether in rage or... something else, she didn't know. But she knew that she would lose her mind. She would have no control over herself any longer.

A part of her wanted that.

Desperately.

Another part absolutely did not, especially in front of her friends.

The look in Mac's eyes cooled, the wildness receding, leaving behind the usual spark of humor, like he was quietly enjoying some joke only he understood. He smirked and raised his hands in a placating gesture.

"I'm sorry," he said. "I swore I wouldn't barge in like this anymore. Please, forgive me." He put one hand over his heart.

Over that hot, bare skin.

Lindsay swallowed hard.

Then rolled her eyes.

What was it about this asshole that got her so worked up?

"You already know Yue," said Lindsay.

"Welcome back, Mac," said Yue, sitting on the back of the couch, her legs draped over the side, munching from a bag of chips in her hand. She had a very odd expression on her face. Mac gave her a half-wave.

"This is Raj," said Lindsay, "our chef for this evening."

"Pleasure to meet you, my friend," said Raj, approaching Mac. Mac held out his hand for a shake, but Raj kept coming, came all the way in to wrap Mac in a huge bear hug. As large as Mac was, Raj made him disappear. All Lindsay could see was his face, eyes wide with alarm over Raj's shoulder as Raj squeezed him tight. "Food's up in ten," said Raj, releasing Mac and heading back to the kitchen.

"And this," said Lindsay once Mac had had a chance to right himself after Raj's hug, "is Marina."

She gestured to the table behind her, where Marina was seated, one arm slung casually over the back of her chair.

Marina just nodded slowly, her eyes moving back and forth between Mac and Lindsay.

"I'm gonna give you a pass on not calling me," she said to Mac at last, "because I know how Lindsay is. I tell her to give you my number, she forgets before the conversation's even over."

Mac grinned. "Sorry about that," he said. "Truly."

Lindsay felt something cold spike through her body.

"You can make it up to me," said Marina.

"How's that?" Mac replied.

Marina shrugged. "I'll think of something."

"Oh, I like her," he said to no one in particular.

The cold spike turned to flame inside Lindsay.

Mac glanced at Lindsay. His eyes widened for a half-second, then he grinned even wider. "I like her a lot," he said slowly, tilting his head and watching Lindsay with intent.

Lindsay forced herself to hold his gaze, willing her face to be neutral while she pulled in a slow, very slow breath, then let it out.

"Good," she said, her smile and her voice dripping with sugar. "I'm glad." She dropped the smile and let her voice ice over. "Now why the hell did you break into my house again?"

Mac's eyes narrowed, his grin slipping just a fraction. Then his face popped into an expression of friendly animation.

"I couldn't resist that smell," he said, then moved quickly past Lindsay toward the kitchen. "Is that garam masala?"

"You betcha, buddy," said Raj brightly from in front of the stove. "Wanna taste?"

Dinner was a simple vegetable curry with cauliflower, potatoes, and carrots over rice, served with homemade naan, but Raj elevated it to incredible heights, somehow infusing the dish with flavors beyond its ingredients. Even Mac was moaning with pleasure with each mouthful, grilling Raj for information about how he'd prepared the dish.

Afterward, they showed Mac the new race portal and data

system, and discussed Yue's challenges that had led Lindsay to bring Raj and Marina into town. Mac admitted that data and tech systems had never been his strength, or Lindsay's father's. They'd hired people to the race team to monitor the data from the cars and the track and whatever else was necessary to run a race properly in this modern age, but had never given any real thought to technology at the company as a whole.

Lindsay vowed to correct that oversight.

Mac whistled with appreciation as he watched the simulation of the last race over Marina's shoulder. "This is fantastic, guys," he said. "Even better than being there." He gave a few suggestions to Marina for enhancements. Additional angles, additional information, additional views of the data that would be useful. Marina nodded and took notes.

Despite numerous cups of espresso, Lindsay was yawning by the time she walked Mac to the front door.

"You've got a great crew here, Lindsay," he said. "I'm glad you brought them on board."

"They're not 'on board'," she bristled. She wasn't sure why she was taking such a nasty tone. Maybe she was just tired. "They're under contract. My company is under contract."

Mac released a breath, staring at Lindsay, then nodded.

"Well, I'm glad you brought them under contract, then," he said softly. He opened the door, then stopped halfway out. "We never talked about Marcus."

"What about him?"

"You don't know what he's like, Lindsay," Mac said. "He's..."

He ran a hand through his already tousled hair, his brow furrowed. Something twinged deep within Lindsay. She felt a wild urge to dig both hands deep into that hair herself, to pull Mac's head down to hers, then down farther.

"Dangerous," said Mac.

Lindsay swallowed hard, her mouth suddenly dry. "What?" Her voice quavered.

"He doesn't treat women well."

He was talking about Marcus. Lindsay breathed a silent sigh of relief.

And, hidden behind the relief, disappointment.

"Does he break into their houses?"

Mac rolled his eyes.

"Does he yell at them when he first meets them?"

He shoved both hands deep into his pockets, looked down at the floor, and nodded, enduring Lindsay's barbs.

"Does he abandon them for weeks at a time without even a text or an email?"

Mac's eyes darted up to Lindsay's.

With a start, Lindsay realized what she'd just said, but moved on quickly, hoping Mac wouldn't notice.

"I'm sure I can handle him," she said, pushing Mac's shoulder to turn him, then shoving him in the back, out the door. "Good night, Mac. I'll see you tomorrow."

She shut the door behind him and leaned her head against it, breathing hard, listening to his footfalls recede, his car roaring to life and pulling away. Lindsay's heart beat hard in her ears long after the sound of the engine had faded in the distance.

"Smooth," said Marina from behind Lindsay.

Lindsay spun. Marina, Raj, and Yue were all standing in the hallway, watching. Raj was grinning, Yue looked bored, and Marina had her arms crossed over her chest.

"You guys will have hot babies," said Raj.

"'Hot babies'?" said Marina. "Ew."

"What? Their kids will be gorgeous."

"Yeah, but 'hot babies'?"

"What's wrong with that?"

"Yue?" said Marina.

"It's gross, dude," replied Yue.

Lindsay shook her head, but couldn't shake the fatigue and

confusion that weighed her down. She said goodnight and went to bed, alone and exhausted.

She didn't sleep for hours.

～

Lindsay had trouble getting out of bed the next morning. She taken so long to fall asleep the night before, and had woken so many times in fits and starts, that she wasn't sure what was reality and what was a dream. She moved as if she were merely an observer in her own life, watching it play out around her, dispassionate, feeling neither responsibility nor care for what happened.

Marina had come in first with the maternal approach, gently waking her by squeezing her shoulder and whispering, "Lindsay" again and again. Lindsay had cracked her eyes, nodded and stirred enough to get Marina to leave the bedroom, then fallen asleep again.

Raj had tried next, coming in loud, his disposition sunnier than the light streaming in through the curtains he threw back, trying to wake her with the pure joyful energy of his personality. He pulled the blankets off of Lindsay, pulled her to her feet, and danced—actually danced—with her, Lindsay's arms flopping like slack wires in his hands, until he felt confident she was awake.

He was wrong.

As soon as he left the room, Lindsay collapsed back onto the bed, pulling the covers over her head inch by inch until they blocked the sunlight completely and darkness surrounded her once more.

It was Yue who finally got her up.

In her unreality, half-dream world, half-real world—though which was which, she couldn't say—Lindsay felt a niggling in the corner of her mind. Some kind of irregularity.

234

An aberrant energy, like the wavy vision when you squat down in a parking lot on a scorching hot day and look up, the heat rising from the pavement warping your view of whatever lies in the distance.

That warped feeling, plus an odd crunching noise, like a soldier marching through crusted snow. These incongruous sensations niggled at Lindsay's mind, pulling her up from the depths of her stuporous half-sleep until she opened her eyes.

And saw Yue.

Sitting on the side of her bed.

Watching her.

Munching on jicama sticks, a clear plastic tub of them in her hand.

Yue watched Lindsay like that for a long moment, finishing the jicama stick in her mouth, then munching another, watching in silence.

Yue swallowed.

And watched.

Lindsay watched back.

"Get up," said Yue at last. She wasn't loud. She didn't shout or exhort or urge. She merely said the words, matter-of-fact, then put another jicama stick in her mouth and crunched down on it.

Lindsay pulled in a deep breath, let it out with a heavy sigh, then nodded.

Yue didn't move an inch, just munched away, watching Lindsay.

Lindsay sighed again, threw back the covers, and got up. She looked at the clock. It was already quarter to one in the afternoon.

Her heart spiked with adrenaline.

Fuck. The meeting with Marcus was in fifteen minutes.

Seeing the expression on Lindsay's face, Yue nodded and turned to the door, jicama sticks in hand.

"Why didn't you tell me we were late?" cried Lindsay.

In the doorway, Yue shrugged. "You didn't listen to Marina or Raj. I figured you needed to figure it out for yourself."

Lindsay, Raj, Marina, and Yue finally entered the conference room ten minutes late for the meeting. Marcus was already there, standing at the window, looking out at the lake and the trees in the distance, the light from the high sun bathing his face in a warm glow.

"I forget how beautiful it is here," he mused.

He turned toward them.

Marcus was slim, with muscular limbs and a powerful build. His black hair swept high off a broad forehead. An aquiline nose shadowed full, sculpted lips and a chiseled jaw with a fashionable few days' stubble on it. A fan of lines at the edges of his dark eyes were the only hints of age on his otherwise smooth and unwrinkled skin.

"Which of you beauties is Lindsay?" he said. He pointed at Raj. "I'm going to assume it's not you."

"I'm deeply offended, sir," said Raj, a coquettish hand to his breast. He grinned and held out his hand. "Raj Gupta. Data plumber extraordinaire."

Marcus smiled back and shook Raj's hand. "That leaves the three of you," he said. He took Marina's hand in his, smoothing his other hand over the top like he was going to read her fortune. He arched a questioning eyebrow at her.

"Marina," she said, her face expressionless.

"Marina," Marcus repeated, purring her name, then bending down to kiss her hand. Marina winced and pulled her hand back from Marcus' grip. Marcus turned toward Yue without losing his smile.

"And you, my dear?" he said.

"Yue." Yue looked bored to tears, her eyes dull, eyelids half-shut, as if enduring a long lecture from her parents, counting the minutes until she could leave. She stood with her hands in her pockets, turning a piece of gum over and over in her mouth.

"Yue?" said Marcus, bowing slightly and reaching out for Yue's hand. "That's a beautiful name."

Yue didn't offer her hand, didn't move at all, just let Marcus stand there, his hand awkwardly outstretched, his back bowed.

"We've met," said Yue. "Like, five times. I've worked here for years."

Marcus' smile grew wider and somehow even more charming. Even through the undeniable ooze of a predator, which Marcus emanated in spades, that charm came through, both attracting and repelling at once, though in not quite equal measure. When he was younger, perhaps before his reputation had come to define him, Lindsay could see how Marcus would have been a real shark. But now, his spiel seemed a little tired.

"I'm sure I would have remembered meeting such a beautiful woman," oozed Marcus to Yue.

"Yeah?" she replied. "Well, either I'm not beautiful enough for you or you've got a shitty memory." She folded her arms. "We've met. Like, five times." She said it slowly and clearly.

Marcus' smile faltered then, but only a touch. He reeled in his hand, straightened his back, and turned his attention to Lindsay.

She felt his gaze like a spotlight on a stage, felt immediately nervous, naked and exposed. Philanderer or not, the guy had some serious charisma. For another kind of woman, that sort of attention, that feeling of being the only person in the world other than Marcus, would probably be enough to get her into bed. Some women—some people—just feel so unseen, so invisible in the world, that any attention at all, let alone attention with the firepower that Marcus had, would feel like the light of heaven and the song of angels.

But, Lindsay was not that kind of woman.

She took one step toward Marcus, took his hand, and shook it firmly. Standing in front of him, Lindsay was mildly surprised to discover that she was taller than him by at least an inch or two. Marcus' personality, his unwavering confidence, somehow made him seem larger than he was.

"I'm Lindsay Rhodes," she said, dropping his hand just as he bent to kiss it. Lindsay wasn't interested in any of that faux courtship bullshit. She was here to help Marcus win more races. If he just wanted to get her into bed, this would be a short meeting. If he wanted to win, they could get some real work done.

They all scattered to take seats around the conference table. Whether on purpose or by instinct, the three women sat on the opposite side of the table from Marcus. Raj took a seat beside him, either oblivious to or unperturbed by Marcus. Most likely oblivious.

Lindsay plugged her laptop into a cable that led to a television on one wall of the conference room. "Your last race was a dramatic improvement," she said as she opened her presentation and displayed it on the screen. "You took my advice."

Marcus grinned. "If I'd known how beautiful you were, I'd have taken it sooner."

Marina groaned softly.

Lindsay stared at Marcus, saying nothing, keeping her face deliberately neutral, her eyes as cold as she could manage. Marcus' smile eventually faded. He swallowed and nodded.

"Yes," he said, clearing this throat and shifting in his chair. "Thank you for sending it to me." He looked down at his hands in his lap. "I guess, over the years, my technique has gotten... sloppy."

A bit of humility. Could be progress, or could just be a shift in tactics from a man who knew how to charm people, especially women. Lindsay didn't want to assume anything, didn't want to prejudge the man. His reputation had her on guard from the start, but a race didn't care about reputations, and data didn't lie. If Marcus was willing to learn, Lindsay would keep an open mind.

"We've got some ideas that could help with that," said

Lindsay.

The door swung open behind her.

"Sorry I'm late." Mac entered and sat at the end of the table, beside Lindsay. He was immaculately dressed in casual business attire, dark suit pants and a pure white button down shirt, open at the top two buttons. "Somehow, the meeting invite didn't show up on my calendar," he said.

Lindsay sighed, deliberately avoiding even a glance at the skin exposed on Mac's chest. She kept her eyes fixed on his. "I wonder how that could have happened," she said.

"Happens all the time," Mac said. "Computers." He shrugged. "I hope I didn't miss anything important."

"Lindsay here was about to show me everything I'm doing wrong," said Marcus with that charming grin again.

Mac frowned. "I thought this meeting was only an hour long," he said. "Now I'll have to clear my whole afternoon." He laughed and winked at Marcus, whose answering grin faded too quickly and didn't meet his eyes.

Lindsay didn't know if there was bad blood between those two, but the feeling in the air had changed when Mac had entered, and it was clear from their exchange that Mac held the power in that relationship. How and why, Lindsay didn't know. Was it simply because Marcus was the driver and Mac was the team lead, let alone part-owner of the company, or was there some deeper story there?

She filed the question away in a corner of her mind and moved on with her presentation.

Marcus kept up appearances, smiling and nodding and making engaged noises in all the right places during Lindsay's presentation, but it was clear that he wasn't overly interested in the data, the data science, or even the mechanics of the race portal itself. He seemed bored by anything that required mental work on his part, even if that work would ultimately help him with his racing. He didn't sit up and show any real interest until

Marina took over, opened the portal, and ran her re-creation of the last race.

They had tweaked the re-creation to show not only the race that Marcus had actually run, where he came in fifth, but also what would have happened had he implemented their current suggestions. They layered the suggestions one by one, each one shaving a fraction of a second off Marcus' time. In the simulation, they showed his actual race in full color and a greyed-out ghost of a car superimposed on top, showing the race he would have run with their suggestions. The ghost car moved slightly ahead of the actual car, with the gap growing larger and larger as they layered on each new suggestion.

The race had been a close one, with only a half-second or so separating second place from fifth place. The simulation showed that Marcus would have come in second—or, at worst, a close third—if he'd implemented all of their suggestions.

That really made Marcus sit up and pay attention, as Lindsay figured it would. Marcus hadn't finished in the top three in a long, long time. She knew he'd do just about anything to stand on the podium again.

Even Mac had straightened in his chair. Marina had added the simulation late last night, after Mac had left the house, so he hadn't seen it yet.

The discussion became animated, with everyone now focused on the data, the improvements, the gains in lap times. All thought of reputations and charisma were forgotten while they worked. Hours passed in the blink of an eye, the sunlight outside growing more and more angular as the sun dropped in the sky.

Lindsay realized that Marcus was interested in learning, was interested in the data. He just wasn't a numbers person or even an analytical person. He was a visual person and a tactile person. He learned with his eyes and his hands.

Which may explain the womanizing.

When the information was conveyed in a visual form, Marcus became immediately engaged, offering ideas and suggestions of his own. If Lindsay could somehow combine the visual with the tactile, they could really make some progress.

When the photo-sensitive switch automatically kicked on the overhead lights, Marcus looked up like a man waking from a dream. "This is incredible, Lindsay," he said, all trace of arrogance or manipulation gone from his voice.

This was not Marcus Leygren, skirt-chasing C-list celebrity. This was Marcus Leygren, Formula One race car driver. Still hungry, still looking for victory. Lindsay could feel his hunger in her bones. He just needed someone to help him figure out how to find it, how to feed it.

"Thank you," Marcus continued, then gestured to Marina, Raj, and Yue, "thank all of you for working on this."

Marcus stood, and they all followed suit. He went around the table shaking everyone's hand. No kissing or bowing, just gratitude that seemed sincere.

"Amazing stuff, guys," said Mac, nodding. "Even better than I realized when you showed it to me yesterday."

Lindsay had felt good when Marcus had finally realized the value of what they were showing him. But Mac's words sent a pleasant shiver of heat from her scalp to her toes.

"This is what we do," Lindsay said quietly.

Mac arched an eyebrow at her, a faint smile on his lips. "You do it very, very well," he said.

"You're goddamn right she does," said Marina, throwing an arm over Lindsay's shoulder. She had to stand on her tip-toes to do it.

"Lindsay is the best," agreed Raj, throwing an arm over Lindsay's shoulders from the other side.

Mac grinned at the three of them, then looked at Yue, standing to one side.

Yue shrugged. "She's good."

They all laughed and broke apart, collecting their belongings.

"Lindsay," said Marcus, coming to Lindsay's side as she unplugged her laptop and slid it into her bag, "may I ask you something?"

Lindsay looked up at him. He seemed almost nervous. Again, Lindsay didn't know if it was a clever act or if it was genuine. She had no idea what would make an inveterate player like Marcus feel nervous.

"There's a formal affair on Thursday evening," he said, "after the first practice rounds. It happens every year. Hart Racing hosts all of the teams and their significant others at a venue here in Skipsea for a night of bonhomie before the competition begins." He smiled and ran a hand through his thick hair, making it stand even higher on his head. "It's a little awkward, to be honest. A bit tense. But it's usually good for a laugh. For a few hours, anyway."

Lindsay heard Mac grumble quietly behind her. She ignored it.

"I can understand if you don't want to, given my... reputation," said Marcus. Lindsay could have sworn she saw pink on his cheeks, but he had ducked his head so she couldn't see it clearly. From the corner of her eye, she saw Mac move around behind Marcus. "But I'd be honored if you would accompany me."

Lindsay stood up straight, taken aback by the offer. Marcus Leygren wanted to take her to a formal event? In public? He was a handsome celebrity. A bad boy, sure, but still a celebrity. His face had been on magazine covers, not to mention tabloids. And not that long ago. And he wanted to be seen in public with her, a nobody who didn't even own a dress?

Marcus' head lifted, his eyes wide, at her reaction. "Not a date, not a date," he said, holding his palms out toward Lindsay. "Purely platonic, I assure you. Just a way for me to say thank you and to perhaps get to know you a bit better. As... friends." He furrowed his brow, eyes a bit distant, as if the concept of only wanting to be friends with a woman felt wrong to him.

She was flattered by the offer, surprisingly so. The room had grown silent, everyone listening while pretending they weren't, and Marcus seemed shockingly vulnerable in that moment, asking her in front of everyone, seeming to suddenly become aware that Lindsay might not say yes. Again, Lindsay wasn't sure if the vulnerability was an act or not, but if it was, Marcus was one hell of an actor.

Still, formal events were not exactly Lindsay's kind of thing.

"Thank you, Marcus," said Lindsay, "that's very kind of you, but..."

Lindsay looked over Marcus' shoulder at Mac, glaring at her. Again with that asshole, alpha-male attitude, as if he owned her. It was as if he were commanding her with his eyes not to agree to go anywhere with Marcus, who 'doesn't treat women well'.

Lindsay had known plenty of men in Silicon Valley who 'didn't treat women well'. Marcus didn't seem to Lindsay like a violent man, merely manipulative. And Lindsay could handle her own emotions well enough. She didn't need an alpha telling her how to feel, what to do, or who to do it with.

"But?" asked Marcus.

"No but," said Lindsay, staring at Mac. She shifted her eyes to Marcus and forced herself to smile. "I'd be happy to go with you, Marcus," she said, then looked back at Mac again. "Thank you for asking me."

Marcus' face brightened at the same time that Mac's darkened. It was as if a thundercloud had moved across the sky from Marcus' face to Mac's. Lindsay lifted her chin and stared at Mac.

Mac, glowering, muttered something to himself and stormed out of the room.

Lindsay smiled to herself.

Who's the alpha now?

21

AFTER DISCUSSING her thoughts with the team, Yue mentioned that Hart Racing had a simulator, a sophisticated rig in a dedicated room. There was a driver, one who wasn't quite good enough to make the race teams, but was very close, who was hired full-time to drive on the simulator. They used that process to test new design ideas before committing resources to actually build them. The simulator was as close as you could come to being in a Formula One car without actually strapping on a helmet and rolling onto a track.

The simulator was sophisticated enough to model every course and every weather condition that the drivers would ever face during the course of the year. And every car configuration was loaded into the system, including the configuration currently in use in the live races.

That gave Lindsay the perfect way to combine the visual and the tactile for Marcus.

After some wangling and coordination, they secured time in the simulator the next afternoon. Lindsay, Raj, Marina, and Yue crowded into a control room behind the simulator, while Marcus sat in the driver's seat.

The driver's seat was a literal driver's seat, a perfect replica of the steering wheel, seat, and body position used in an actual Formula One car, but without the chassis around it. Directly in front of that was a wall with a massive curved screen on which was projected an ultra-high-definition rendering of a simulated track and its environs. Sitting in the driver's seat, the curve of the screen enveloped the driver's vision from side to side and top to bottom. The simulation projected on the screen was vivid and detailed enough to make anyone believe they were really there.

Through a large picture window along one wall of the control room, Lindsay and team could watch Marcus from behind, seeing what he could see on the screen, as well as Marcus' physical reactions, while also monitoring a raft of metrics via a bank of computer monitors arrayed in a console in front of them. Just as in a real race, they could monitor Marcus' vitals, the condition of the simulated car and track, the other racers simulated on the screen, and more. Cameras showed Marcus' face and body from the front, as well, so they could monitor his mental and physical state via observation.

They had loaded up the simulation for the Silverstone Circuit, the track on which Marcus would be racing in just a few days.

"Ready, Marcus?" asked Lindsay through a microphone that fed into an earpiece Marcus wore.

Marcus gave a thumbs up.

"We'll start with just a baseline. Three laps. Take it as you normally would."

Lindsay heard the door to the control room click open and shut behind her. She didn't have to look to know that Mac had just entered. She could feel the change in the air. It became more charged, more electric. She could feel it prickle the skin of her arms.

The alpha returns, again uninvited. Lindsay just ground her teeth and stared ahead through the picture window.

"Okay, Marcus," she said into the microphone, her voice cool, smooth, professional. "Here we go."

They spent that afternoon and much of the evening in the simulator, running scenario after scenario, adding suggestion after suggestion from their analyses, letting Marcus get the feel of them into his body. His lap times improved with each iteration. Lindsay could feel the energy, the excitement growing in Marcus and in the team around her. Even Mac was leaning in to the console, staring hard at the simulator screen and the metrics readouts on the console, looking for lap times and improvement deltas.

They came back the next day, too, and ran from sunup to well after sundown before calling it a night so Marcus could get some sleep before the practice rounds on the real track the next day.

That night, at home, Lindsay, Raj, Marina, and Yue celebrated with a bottle of champagne Lindsay found in a very well-stocked wine cellar she'd only just discovered. She wasn't much of a drinker, but her father had apparently had a taste for fine wine. Or, perhaps, he'd just been a collector. Either way, there was plenty of champagne to choose from. With no idea what she was looking at, Lindsay had chosen a bottle at random and put it on ice to chill.

After an incredible dinner courtesy of Yue, Lindsay popped the cork and filled four crystal champagne flutes. They stood in a close circle beside the kitchen table with their drinks.

"To data science," said Lindsay.

"To data science," the others shouted, raising their glasses.

"To England," said Raj.

"To England," came the response, champagne flutes lifted.

"To the miracle of Marcus Leygren actually learning something," said Marina.

The others repeated the phrase in a jumbled, uncoordinated mess of words, followed by laughter.

They all looked to Yue, who stared down at the floor, shifting from foot to foot.

"To you three," she said in a small, quiet voice.

Lindsay had never seen her so diminished, had never see her as anything other than blustering, cynical, and confident. The Yue in front of her now was like a young girl, a child, uncertain and embarrassed.

"To you three," Yue said again, her voice a little louder, a little braver, "the best friends I've found since... ever." She held her glass out before her, into the center of their circle, looking each of them in the eye in turn. When she looked at Lindsay, Lindsay could see her eyes shining and knew it wasn't just the light.

Saying nothing, just staring at each other, they all touched their glasses together in the center of the circle, then took a long drink from the flutes.

"Group hug," shouted Raj, wrapping his massive arms around them all and pulling them together into a squishy mass. Champagne sloshed over clothes and onto the floor, but no one cared. Everyone just laughed and hugged each other.

When they separated, Raj grabbed Yue around the shoulders and gave her an extra hug. Lindsay could tell he was resisting the urge to put her in a headlock and give her a noogy on the head. Warm feelings or not, Yue would not have liked that. But he razzed her in a brotherly way for her comment.

"We're kind of like a family now, aren't we?" said Marina to Lindsay, both of them watching Raj and Yue.

"Better than that," said Lindsay. She looked at Marina and smiled. "We're friends."

～

Lindsay was the first one up the next morning. It was still very early, the sun barely over the horizon, caressing the couches and chairs through the huge glass window of the kitchen with broad, gentle, warming strokes before piercing them with the sharp needles of morning.

She'd been unable to sleep. The first practice round began at two in the afternoon, with the second round starting at five. They would know then how well their efforts of the last few days had paid off. Until then, all Lindsay could do was wait.

And she was not very good at waiting.

She sipped her coffee, watching out the window as the sea softened with the rising sun from grey to gunmetal to green, when she heard a knock on the front door.

"Hello, Lindsay," said Maggie when Lindsay opened the door. "I've come to whisk you away."

"To where?" said Lindsay.

Maggie eyed Lindsay from head to foot, a dubious expression on her face.

"I don't criticize your choice of wardrobe, my dear," she said. "Not at all."

Lindsay looked down at herself. She was wearing what she wore literally every day. Dark grey jeans, light grey t-shirt, black blazer or sweater—depending on the weather—and Vans. That was her outfit. She ascribed to the Steve Jobs philosophy: find a comfortable outfit that you like, buy several of each item, then never waste time or mental effort thinking about what to wear again.

"To each their own," continued Maggie, "and you wear this very well. You really do."

She reached up, tucked a strand of hair behind Lindsay's ear, and cupped her hand along Lindsay's cheek. Her hand was as warm as her gaze. Lindsay felt a tear welling unbidden in her eyes as a warmth flowed from Maggie's hand through Lindsay's entire body. Maggie looked just like Lindsay's late mother, and now she felt like a mother to Lindsay, too, with her loving touch and her compassionate gaze. It felt like forever since Lindsay had felt that way.

"But," Maggie said, "you can't wear jeans and sneakers to a formal ball."

The warmth coursing through Lindsay's body immediately turned to ice.

She'd completely forgotten about the stupid dance she'd agreed to attend with Marcus.

"That's tonight?" Lindsay said, gulping audibly.

"That's tonight," nodded Maggie, then gestured from Lindsay's feet to her head, "and we've got work to do."

Maggie drove them to Kingston, where she said there was a boutique that she frequented called Bella Potenza. They specialized more in business wear than in formal wear, but they did have a small collection of formal attire, as well. Maggie had called ahead, asking them to set some pieces aside for Lindsay to consider.

Situated on the second floor above a small antiquarian bookstore, the boutique was tiny, but incredibly elegant. The floor was covered in a sumptuous carpet of pure white, and several tufted white leather benches were scattered around the room amidst an audience of headless, armless mannequin torsos, each wearing a different evening gown for Lindsay's perusal. The room was so white, Lindsay felt like she'd climbed the stairs and stepped inside a cloud.

They spent about two hours there, trying on outfit after outfit, looking for something that Lindsay felt comfortable in. Dresses and shoes and things to stick in her hair to give her an idea of what the gowns would look like with various hairstyles. It was a whirlwind of satin and sequins and lace and chiffon, with enough spaghetti straps to feed all of Italy.

Lindsay begged Maggie to just pick something for her. She knew she would never feel comfortable in anything they found, no matter how beautiful or well-tailored it was. Lindsay simply was not an evening gown kind of person. She'd never worn one in her life. She'd skipped the proms in her high school. They were just rights of passage that seemed to her to end less often in cherished memories and more often in drunken regrets, at least for the girls. There had been no formal dances to speak of at her college, and certainly not in her work life. Silicon Valley's idea of formal attire was a brand-new hoodie.

But Maggie refused to impose something upon Lindsay. She just pressed on. Each time Lindsay expressed discomfort with an outfit, Maggie would kindly and quietly signal to the store clerk to bring out another option. Even when Lindsay did her best to pretend that she liked something, Maggie seemed to be able to see right through her act.

In the end, they found nothing suitable there, though Lindsay had spotted a range of pantsuits and business attire in a second room of the shop that looked intriguing. She could see where Maggie got her clothes from. This really must have been a favorite boutique of hers. Lindsay felt a little ashamed that she couldn't find anything there that she liked among their selection of evening gowns.

Maggie waved her off in the car when Lindsay mentioned as much. "Never, ever apologize for being true to yourself, Lindsay. As long as you're not being deliberately hurtful in the way you communicate your feelings to others, you have no need to be ashamed for pursuing what you want." She patted Lindsay lightly on one knee. "I know a few more places to try." She winked at Lindsay. "We're just getting started, my dear. Why do you think I picked you up so early?"

Lindsay groaned, and Maggie laughed out loud.

They spent three hours in two shops in York, then another hour in a shop in Leeds, all to no avail. Lindsay felt certain they'd need to drive another two hours to London to find anything, at which point it would become too late to get back in time for the event. That was just fine with Lindsay. With each passing hour, with each tick of the clock, the time of the event drew nearer, and her regret at agreeing to attend grew stronger.

By the time they came to the next shop in Leeds, it was nearly three in the afternoon. With a ninety minute drive back to Lindsay's house and the party set to begin at seven, they were cutting things close. This would have to be the last stop, successful or not. Worst case, Lindsay figured, she'd just go to the party in her usual clothes. Who cared what other people thought?

Lindsay's mouth had gone dry.

She cared, apparently.

The last shop was a low building with an arched brick entryway covered in vines and flowers just beginning to bloom. The entryway led to a small courtyard with bricks widely spaced in the dirt floor and a couple of wrought iron tables and chairs scattered haphazardly around the space. The courtyard overflowed with a riot of plants and flowers, either in pots or attached to the brick walls. Creeping ivy clung to the brick and seemed to sprout from the mortar. Bright pink and white flowers spilled from wide flower boxes hung from nails set into the brick. There was even some kind of moss growing along the ground between the bricks, with tiny green droplets for leaves. Lindsay had the feeling she'd stumbled into the secret garden from the books she'd read as a young girl. It was utter chaos. Living, breathing, beautiful, vivid chaos.

An old woman emerged from the door to the building. The wrinkles on her face were like canyons, etching lines around her mouth and eyes and across her nose and forehead as if she were a character in a comic book, with the artist drawing lines to show that she was surprised or scared.

But it was clear from the way she moved that this woman was neither of those things. Despite her obvious age, she moved with the fluidity and grace of a dancer, and a much younger one, at that. Maggie hugged her warmly. The woman only came up to Maggie's chest and was as wide as she was tall, but there was a presence to her that filled the courtyard, seemed to rise up and fill the air above it, as well.

She released Maggie and turned her gaze to Lindsay. The smile immediately fell from her face.

"Oh dear," she said, casting a sidelong glance at Maggie. "You've brought me a day-old loaf this time, haven't you, Margaret?"

Maggie looked down and shuffled her feet, but Lindsay could still see the smile she was trying to hide.

The woman approached Lindsay, slowly circling her, appraising her from head to foot, clearly finding much to be desired.

When she arrived back at Lindsay's front, she was standing startlingly close, staring up at Lindsay. Her eyes were deep, dark brown and magnetic. They pulled Lindsay down, physically down, bending her at the waist. The woman placed a hand on either side of Lindsay's head, her fingers wrapped around the back of Lindsay's neck. She turned Lindsay's head from side to side, inspecting her eyes, her ears, her skin. She even used her thumbs to pull Lindsay's lips back into a rictus, inspecting her teeth like she was a horse being traded.

Once she had finished her inspection, the woman stared long at Lindsay's eyes, long enough for Lindsay to cycle through surprise, mild alarm, and slightly less mild annoyance into resignation and, finally, curiosity. Who was this woman and why was she taking so much time to look at Lindsay's face? None of the other shopkeepers had even spared Lindsay a glance. Maggie had been their customer, clearly, and Lindsay was just an object to be dressed to Maggie's liking.

But this woman seemed to want more than just to dress Lindsay. She seemed to want to understand her. Or to dominate her, to cow her into submission. Maybe that was her sales tactic, to intimidate her customers into buying whatever overpriced merchandise the woman needed to get rid of.

The woman grunted and released Lindsay's face.

"Okay, day-old," she said, turning back toward the door of the building and waving for Lindsay to follow. "Come inside. Let's see if we can make you fresh again."

Lindsay followed the woman as she shuffled past Maggie, who was still stifling a laugh, and through the door.

The inside of the shop was even more chaotic than the courtyard had been, only instead of plants, there was a riot of color and creation. Half-finished dresses, jackets, blouses, and skirts were hung and draped over every imaginable surface. Bolts of fabric stood on wooden poles along one wall, fabrics of every color, material, pattern, and sheen. Bright blue satin gleamed beside red sequins that twinkled in the pale yellow light from the aged sconces on the wall. Rough lace-textured green rubbed against a matte black so dark it seemed to suck the light into itself.

Everywhere, with no rhyme or reason that Lindsay could detect, were tailor's dummies, with fabrics draped over them, pinned or partially sewn together, measuring tapes hanging from shoulders and across torsos. In the center of the room was a long, wide table that was strewn with more fabric, thread, scissors, tape, small ceramic pots filled with pins and needles.

And above it all, hanging from the exposed beams of the low ceiling, was more ivy, creeping along above their heads like a storm cloud gathering. Lindsay had to duck to avoid the odd leaf or offshoot that hung down too far. She felt like the vines were grasping at her hair, teasing it and tickling it and pulling it loose. The feeling made her skin crawl and her scalp itch, as if she, herself, were coming loose from the inside out.

Lindsay looked over her shoulder at Maggie. She couldn't imagine a woman with Maggie's poise and elegance frequenting a shop in such disarray. There weren't even any actual clothes anywhere that Lindsay could see. No finished outfits, no dresses or blouses or blazers to buy. Just a bunch of fabric and half-finished work. The promise of potential and the chaos of creation.

And yet Maggie seemed perfectly at ease as she followed Lindsay and the woman through the mess, a faint smile still playing at the corners of her lips.

The woman led Lindsay through the room and through another doorway into a tiny closet, barely big enough for the three of them to stand, dimly lit by a single lamp in the corner. The closet was taken up by the classic tailor's stage, a small raised platform with three angled mirrors in front of it. Unlike others Lindsay had seen, this stage also had mirrors behind, forming a broken circle of six angled mirrors that reflected each other.

"Strip down and stand up there," said the woman to Lindsay.

"I'm... what?" said Lindsay.

"Take your clothes off, girl," said the woman, reaching up to pull the blazer from Lindsay's shoulders. "Get down to your skin. We can't dress you properly if you're already dressed, can we?"

Lindsay glanced at Maggie, who nodded reassuringly.

"I can send Margaret away if you're too Puritan to be seen in your nudes," said the woman. "I know you Americans prefer to be naked in your text messages on the internet, not in the real world."

"It's fine," said Lindsay, stripping down in a daze. She'd certainly never gotten naked in a seamstress shop before. Though, to be fair, she'd never been to a seamstress shop before. But she didn't think this was a standard practice.

Still, Lindsay trusted Maggie, and Maggie seemed unperturbed. She undressed down to her bra and panties.

"Skivvies, too," said the woman.

Lindsay hesitated.

"Nothing there we ladies don't know about, I suspect," said the woman. "Let's go." She motioned for Lindsay to get on with it.

Lindsay removed her underwear, dropping them on top of the pile of her clothes on the ground, and stood with her arms crossed over her chest.

"Up on the stage now," said the woman.

Lindsay climbed up and stood shivering on the platform. The woman flicked a switch on the wall. Lightbulbs running across the top of the mirrors bloomed into life, filling the room with an ethereal white glow. The bulbs emitted a heat, as well, that soon stopped Lindsay's shivering.

Lindsay could see the light reflected in her eyes as she looked at herself in the mirror. She could see her front and both sides at once in the three angled mirrors before her. But in the reflection of the mirrors behind her, she could also see her backside at the same time. And those reflections reflected in the front mirrors, which reflected in the back mirrors, creating the effect of Lindsay, in a three hundred sixty degree view, reflected over and over, extending back as if through a tunnel in time.

Combined with the white glow from the lights, the effect was mesmerizing. Lindsay felt her breath hitch in her chest. All thoughts of self-consciousness in her nudity disappeared, swallowed by the expanse of that time tunnel. In fact, all thoughts of Lindsay herself, her anxiety, her insecurity, her petty fears and worries of the moment, fell away through the enormity of that tunnel.

It was like some kind of witch's spell, like the old woman had waved her hand and wiped Lindsay's mind clean. But only the momentary disturbances, not the bedrock at the bottom of her mind. Not the frame and foundation of Lindsay, just the cracked and crumbling siding that hung from it.

"I see you now, child," said the woman, hidden in the darkness behind the mirrors. "Do you see what I see?"

Lindsay nodded.

"Tell me what you see."

Lindsay regarded herself in the circle of mirrors. She focused on the image in the center, the Lindsay of this time, this place, ignoring for the moment the lines of past and future Lindsays extending out into the distance.

She saw the thin frame, the scraggly blond hair, the pale skin. She pushed these things from her mind. These were surface things. Siding, changing with the days, like weather.

She looked into the eyes of the woman in the mirrors. Brown with a hint of orange. Odd eyes. Unusual eyes. Eyes that had embarrassed her in the past, when she was younger, when she wanted to fit in, be accepted by her peers.

Which meant being exactly the same as her peers.

Lindsay had never been the same as her peers.

She looked deeper. The eyes were clear, with a depth to them, like looking into a shallow stream of clear water on a bright day, seeing the rocks and lichen on the bottom, greys and blacks and oranges and greens, magnified by the running water. Those eyes brought clarity, to Lindsay and to the world around her.

Lindsay considered the body in the mirror before her. She had always thought of it as wiry and thin. It was hunched slightly at the shoulders now, bowed at the middle of the back, the jaw jutting forward, as if her body were trying to minimize itself, to shrink away, to be hidden. Lindsay stood straight, pulling back her shoulders, lifting her chest, tucking her chin. She pulled taut the muscles of her abdomen and stood straight, tall. Her breasts pushed forward and separated, no longer swallowed by the curl of her shoulders. It felt brazen, exposed.

It also felt powerful and confident.

It felt good.

More important, it felt right.

An energy moved through Lindsay, like that clear stream had been undammed, the piled, roiling waters behind the obstruction now stretching and moving, elongating like muscles in use, finding their strength again.

Lindsay appraised her body from toe to head. Tall, straight, strong, poised. Her eyes narrowed as she gazed at them again in the mirror. She stepped closer.

The line of Lindsays in time and space moved around her in a ripple. Delayed, not simultaneous. Lindsay noticed that each image was slightly different from the one before it and behind it, as if Lindsay weren't seeing reflections of herself, but the evolution of herself through time.

What kind of mirror was this? What kind of place? What kind of woman was the owner?

And what kind of woman was the woman in the mirror?

Lindsay looked closer at her own eyes in the mirror, at that limpid stream.

She fell into it.

The water was warm against her bare skin, the current strong, but gentle. Swiftly she drifted forward, downstream. The colors of the rocks and lichen blurred into streaks in the clear water below her. Above her, she saw blue sky, white clouds. Beyond, she could see into the dark pointillism of space, dotted by stars.

She could see sky and space at once. Infinity.

She looked to her side. Along the sloping banks of the stream, extending into the distance to her left and right, she saw trees and grass and people and buildings and cars and animals. Natural and artificial, born and man-made. All creation, all creativity, all blending into a single, variegated expression of the energy of life, of exploration, of curiosity, of play.

Sights and sounds and smells and textures and tastes blended together. The rough-edged rasp of a bow across cello strings blended with the close, sweaty scent of a subway station as a train rattled through, blended with the texture of rough paper tugging at the tips of her fingers and the rich, spicy sting of Mac's curry on her tongue. All intermingled, streams and eddies of energy. No judgement or values imposed on them, no good or bad. Just sensation. Observation. Stimulus and receptor. The experience and the experiencer.

Mac.

She saw a swirl of energy on the bank beside the stream, a concentration of light that formed a shape, a familiar shape.

The shape of Mac's body.

Beside and behind him, the shape of Maggie's body, and Marina's and Raj's and Yue's. Of her mother and, less defined but no less discernible, her father.

What was happening? Had the old woman somehow drugged her, put something in the air to make her hallucinate these things?

She shook her head. She knew that was impossible. Or unlikely, at least. And Maggie wouldn't subject Lindsay to that sort of thing.

What, then? What was causing these strange thoughts, these odd visions? The logical part of Lindsay's mind screamed at the strangeness of it all.

But something deeper, something wiser, brought Lindsay a feeling of calm, of strength. She looked at herself in the mirror again, the infinite lines of Lindsays extending, evolving, from her past toward her future. She stood tall and straight and strong. She looked at her nakedness, open-eyed and unashamed. She didn't shrink from it or judge it or try to hide from it. She looked at it. And she saw it for what it was.

Her self.

"What do you see, child?" whispered the woman from behind Lindsay.

"I see... me," said Lindsay.

The old woman stepped forward, emerging from the darkness so that her face was half-lit by the lights above the mirrors. The shine of the lights reflected in her eyes like the sparks of stars.

She stared at Lindsay's eyes in the mirror. Lindsay stared back.

The woman nodded.

"Now we can begin," she said.

22

BY THE TIME they'd finished at the old woman's shop, another hour had passed. Lindsay and Maggie had had to rush to get back to Skipsea. Maggie had been on the phone the whole way, arranging for a hair stylist and a makeup artist to meet at her house. Lindsay had texted Marcus to let him know she'd be running late and would meet him at the venue.

By the time they got to Maggie's house—a home that matched her personality perfectly: elegant and refined without being the least bit ostentatious—they had only an hour before the event was scheduled to begin.

The next ninety minutes were a blur for Lindsay, a blur of blow dryers and makeup brushes and bobby pins. The hair stylist and the makeup artist were both clearly very competent, experienced professionals. They worked on Lindsay and Maggie in parallel, doing their work quickly and efficiently.

Maggie's husband whistled when they both descended the stairs. He watched his wife with a gleam in his eye that set even Lindsay's heart racing. If she ever did marry, she hoped her husband would look at her that way after decades together.

Maggie and her husband embraced at the bottom of the stairs. Maggie introduced Lindsay to her husband, Don, who admired and complimented Lindsay as if he were a proud father.

A limousine waiting outside brought them all to the event. Lindsay glanced at the driver as she stepped into the back seat.

"Danny?" she said.

The driver turned his head toward her.

"Hello, Miss," he said in his warm accent. He smiled at her. "Lovely to see you again."

"You, too, Danny," said Lindsay. "How is Sarah?"

Lindsay had looked up Danny's personnel file, wanting to know a bit more about him. The file was digitized, but part of it was a scan of the original paper file. It was filled with hand-written notes.

Her father's handwriting, she'd been told.

Scrawled beside the typical typed information with Danny's name, address and so on, her father had written in more personal notes, including the names and birthdays of Danny, his wife, Sarah, and their five children, ranging in ages now from thirteen to twenty-two.

"She's just fine, miss," said Danny, a hint of surprise in his voice. "Thank you for asking."

"Call me Lindsay, please. And the kids? How's Deirdre finding life after college?"

Danny chuckled. "Taking London by storm, she is, as expected. She's a firecracker, that one, no mistake."

Lindsay smiled.

"Glad to hear it," she said. "Her degree was in computers, right?"

"Software development, miss," nodded Danny.

"Not exactly my field, but I know a lot of developers in California. Please let me know if I can help her in any way."

Danny's eyebrows shot up. "That's very kind of you, miss. Er... Lindsay." He gave her a sheepish look. "Most kind of you."

The event was at a seaside venue on the opposite side of

Skipsea from Hart Racing's headquarters. The venue was a wide, two-story building made of stone and brick accented by thick columns of rich wood. It reminded Lindsay of the Craftsman-style homes she had seen in California.

The limousine pulled up to the front of the building, where Lindsay was shocked to see a red carpet and a gaggle of photographers kept behind two black velvet ropes on either side of the walkway.

"What are they all doing here?" she asked Maggie.

"Racing is a big deal," she replied, "and the paparazzi love to see rich, famous people getting dressed up." She shrugged. "We just get caught up in the fuss. No big deal."

Marcus was standing at the curb as the limousine pulled up.

"Well," said Maggie, grinning at Lindsay, "maybe a slightly bigger deal if you're with him."

Marcus looked suave and handsome in a black suit with a black necktie and white shirt. His hair was coiffed up and away from his face, his rugged chin fashionably dappled with stubble. He looked more like a movie star than a race car driver, and this event felt more like the Oscars than a simple gathering of race crews.

Marcus opened the limo door and held out his hand for Lindsay as she climbed out of the car. She took his hand with a smile of thanks as she carefully set one foot outside the car, exposing a lot more leg than she intended. The flashbulbs from the photographers popped in her eyes, momentarily blinding her.

This was the first time Lindsay had ever worn heels, and these were four-inch black stilettos. Lindsay had been wearing Vans sneakers for most of her life. Having her heel four inches off the ground felt decidedly unnatural, but she'd practiced at Maggie's house and had the hang of it. Mostly. Still, she was grateful to have Marcus there to support her as she levered herself up to a standing position.

The clatter of camera shutters continued, like a chorus of castanets or the applause of a thousand crabs as they walked slowly down the carpet, Lindsay's arm tucked under Marcus'. Lindsay focused her eyes straight ahead, doing her best to balance on her heels without wobbling, leaning too heavily on Marcus, or spraining an ankle.

"You look absolutely stunning, Lindsay," said Marcus, leaning in to whisper in Lindsay's ear.

Lindsay's gown was of black satin, smooth and cool, but didn't shine in the light. It was a matte fabric that pulled the light in rather than reflecting it. Lindsay had never seen anything like it.

The gown sat low across her chest in an off-the-shoulder style, leaving her shoulders and her arms bare save for two thin loops of satin around each bicep. The rouching on her waist and sleeves hugged the curves of her chest and hips before allowing the gown to fall to an elegant pile at her feet. A long slit along her right leg came halfway up her thigh, exposing the length of her long leg with each step, her calf muscles accentuated by the stilettos.

Lindsay wore no bra and no panties. The sheer fabric wouldn't allow it, would show the lines of the undergarments too clearly. She'd tried wearing a thong—another thing she'd never done in her life—but it felt too weird to her. After a few minutes, she pulled the thong off and decided to just go commando.

Now, with each movement, the slick, cool satin caressed her skin. With each step, the cool sea air slipped along her exposed leg and under her gown. The sensuality of the gown, the slow seduction with each movement through the night, was exciting and overwhelming. Lindsay had never worn a formal gown before, but if they all felt like this one, she could definitely see the appeal.

Her blond hair had been straightened, side-swept and

twisted to set back off one ear and hang long over the opposite shoulder and down over her chest. The effect was elegant and startling, even to Lindsay. She had never seen herself that way, in her mirror or in her mind.

"You clean up pretty good yourself," she said.

Marcus leaned away, regarding Lindsay for a moment. She looked at him and raised a questioning eyebrow. Marcus smiled a broad, gleaming smile and chuckled, a deep, melodious sound.

Lindsay could see why women fell for him. Marcus was charming and handsome with blue eyes so pale they were almost grey, and he had a boyish innocence that played just beneath the surface, peeking through from time to time. It was infectious, filling Lindsay with her own sense of wonder and excitement. Even though she had no romantic interest in Marcus, she could see how attractive that feeling was. But she knew that once Marcus set that hook, the innocent boy would step aside and the philandering man would land his fish.

As if he were listening to her thoughts, Marcus transferred Lindsay's left hand from his right forearm to his left hand, then slid his freed right arm around her waist. In the process, he brushed his hand quite a bit lower than Lindsay would have liked.

Still keeping a smile on her face as they strolled down the red carpet, Lindsay pulled his right hand off of her hip, swung it behind her back again and returned them to the position they'd been in a moment before, with Lindsay's left arm tucked under Marcus' right arm, her hand wrapped over his right forearm.

"I'm here as your friend and co-worker," she said through smiling teeth. "But if you pull any bullshit like that again, I'll be sure your face is in all the papers tomorrow. For all the wrong reasons. Understood?" She turned her head and smiled at him, hoping that the look in her eyes was enough to convince him of her seriousness.

Judging by the way he gulped, his eyes widened, and he started nodding quickly, she figured he got the point.

They entered the venue through two wide double doors held open by doormen dressed in black tuxes and tails, white shirts, white bow ties, and white gloves. Very posh, very British. Through an opulent lobby carpeted in thick pile that nearly sent Lindsay and her heels for a tumble, then another set of double doors with two more posh doormen, Lindsay and Marcus emerged at the top of a set of wide wooden stairs that led down to a patio area overlooking the beach, lit by electric lanterns, heat towers, and dim overhead lights.

Several dozen very well-dressed men and women milled around a series of tall tables arranged around an open space in the center where a few couples were dancing. A bar stood on the left side of the patio, a buffet on the side straight ahead of them. On the right side was a jazz quartet laying a soft bed of background music that floated just above the murmur of the chatter from the guests and the gentle swell and shush of the waves breaking on the shore.

The men all wore dark suits or tuxedos. The women were resplendent in a dazzling array of plumage, from long, flowing gowns to puffy-sleeved statement pieces with odd designs, to simple, sleek outfits like Lindsay's. The whole crowd oozed wealth and privilege. It was simultaneously exciting and repulsive to Lindsay. All this wealth and influence, and they spent their time doing nothing but trying to impress each other.

Lindsay and Marcus stood at the top of the stairs for a long moment, every head in the crowd turned toward them, the new arrivals. The breeze from the ocean stirred, tousling the drape of Lindsay's gown back off of her bare leg. Where she once might have shied away from the weight of so much attention in such a setting, here she pulled herself taller, straighter. She stood as she had stood in the mirror hours earlier, tilted her chin higher, and stepped her bare leg slightly forward, exposing it even more.

If they wanted to look, let them see her.

She surveyed the upturned faces, staring at them one by one. She didn't feel competitive or afraid or jealous or eager for their approval. She didn't care one bit about their approval. She didn't even know most of the people there. But she did feel a sense of freedom that she hadn't felt before, and that sense of freedom gave her a feeling of power.

She didn't know where the feeling was coming from or why, but she was grateful for it. She could tell from a distance that the gathering below her was a tank full of sharks. Without that feeling of power and freedom, she would be nothing more than a bucket of chum. Instead, she was a shark, too.

No. She laughed to herself. She was the woman in the boat floating above them all, the marine biologist researching the behavior of the sharks swimming below.

"Shall we?" said Marcus, leading Lindsay gently forward.

As they descended the stairs, Lindsay spotted a familiar face, one that stopped her heart, made her hesitate mid-step. If it weren't for Marcus' reflexes, stopping and steadying her, she might have tumbled down the long staircase.

That face. It had always looked gorgeous, but now it looked otherworldly. He was standing in a group, talking with two women and another man, but his eyes were watching Lindsay descend the stairs.

Even from a distance, she could feel the intensity of those brilliant blue eyes, could feel an animal heat from them. She could feel them devouring her body, could feel her body react to their touch.

She slowed her descent, accentuated each movement. With each shift of weight in her hips, the satin of her gown slid slowly over her skin. With each step, she extended her bare leg farther, felt the gown fall from it, felt the breeze taste her skin, left it exposed for a fraction longer than necessary before stepping down again.

His eyes seemed to glow, no longer even pretending to attend to the conversation he was having. They stared at her, and she could feel the hunger in them. She felt her breasts tighten, her nipples peaking. A flush of heat swept down her body, swelling her core. With each step forward, the cool air swept under her gown, swept over that heat, made it ache and swell even more.

He leaned in to the tall woman standing beside him, rested his hand on the small of her back and whispered in her ear.

Lindsay felt a hot flash of anger.

"Who's that woman with Mac?" said Lindsay, her throat dry, her voice rasping.

Marcus scanned the crowd. "That's Sam," he said. "Chief mechanic."

"That's Sam?"

Sam, Mac's chief-of-staff, his main confidant, the one he relied on whenever anything important needed doing, the one he spent months and months on the road with during race season. Sam, Mac's right-hand man... was a woman?

And a gorgeous bombshell, at that. Tall, slim, with dark eyes that flashed in the lantern light. Smooth, clear brown skin, and long dark hair set into dreadlocks that somehow didn't look dirty and gross at all, but looked sexy and incredible, long dreadlocks that draped casually over her huge tits and curvy hips and voluptuous butt.

She had tattoos up and down her muscular bare arms, but they were tattoos that didn't look like stupid, drunken mistakes, but like cool, intentional, creative expressions of the profound depths of her soul and the arch wit of her mind.

And, on top of all of that, she was a master mechanic who could fix any mechanical problem and could probably drink all the boys under the table, too. Sam, Mac's right-hand man, was a wonder woman, the manic pixie dream girl made real.

Fuck.

Mac met them both at the bottom of the stairs.

"Marcus," he nodded. "Congratulations on the practice rounds today," he said with a thin smile.

In all the rush to find a dress and get ready, Lindsay had completely forgotten about the practice rounds. Apparently Marcus had done well.

"I owe it all to Lindsay," Marcus said with a grin, squeezing his arm over hers and tugging her gently against his side.

Mac's smile faded into a scowl.

"Looks like your work is paying off," he said to Lindsay.

Lindsay would have to ask Marcus what had happened on the track earlier in the day, but for now, she didn't want to let on that she didn't know. Something about Mac's attitude was rubbing her the wrong way.

As usual.

"So far, so good," said Lindsay, keeping her face neutral, "but the real test is on Sunday."

Mac nodded slowly, staring at her with those deep, blue eyes. He opened his mouth to speak.

"You must be Lindsay," said a deep, sultry voice. "I've heard a lot about you."

Sam sidled up to the group, a half-empty champagne flute balanced nonchalantly in one hand. She held out the other to Lindsay.

Lindsay slid her eyes from Mac to Sam and shook Sam's hand.

"Sam Callin," she said. "I'm a mechanic on the race team."

"Lindsay Rhodes. Data scientist."

"And half-owner of the company," said Mac, furrowing his brow. "Don't forget that part."

Lindsay said nothing, just gave a curt smile.

"Sorry to steal Mac away from you for so long," Sam said.

She slid her arm around Mac's waist. Lindsay felt that hot flash of anger grow cold in her belly, like frost spreading over a windowpane.

"Tough to be on the road without him," Sam continued. "Our team needs its captain."

"It's alright," said Lindsay through gritted teeth. She stared hard at Mac. "You can have him."

Lindsay didn't know why she said it, but when a dark scowl came over Mac's face again, the frost in Lindsay's belly spread a little more, satisfied with his response.

Maybe that's why she said it.

"Come on, Marcus," said Lindsay, pulling on Marcus' arm. "Let's get some of that champagne." She pulled Marcus away toward the floor. She didn't know where she was going, really, but she just wanted to get away from Mac. "Nice to meet you..." she glared at Mac over her shoulder, "...Sam."

Lindsay dragged them away. "They'll come around with the champagne, Lindsay," said Marcus, stumbling forward with a soft laugh. "You don't need to pull my arm out of the socket."

Lindsay looked over her shoulder again and couldn't see Mac or Sam through the crowd. She released a heavy breath she didn't know she'd been holding and stopped, letting go of Marcus' arm.

"Sorry," said Lindsay, "just didn't feel like chatting, I guess."

"Well," said Marcus, looking around at where they were, "I hope you feel like dancing, then."

Lindsay looked around and realized she'd stopped right in the middle of the dance floor. The band launched into a peppy old-school jazz number.

"Oh, no, I don't   "

"Here we go," laughed Marcus, taking Lindsay by one hand, his other on her waist, and leading her into some kind of waltz or something. "You know how to foxtrot, don't you?" he said.

"I really don't—" said Lindsay, then laughed, surprising herself, as Marcus led her around the dance floor, a wide boyish grin on his face. She let go of her anger, let the frost in her belly melt, forced herself to forget all about Mac and Sam, and just let Marcus lead her through a few dances.

He was an excellent dancer and a gentle partner. He never tried anything too complicated, and he made sure to keep his hands well above Lindsay's hips. Lindsay seemed to have made her point well on that score. She was able to relax and genuinely enjoy her time with him.

After a while, they stopped to catch their breath and have a drink. Lindsay opted for plain cranberry juice, passing on the alcohol.

"A real heavy drinker," teased Marcus as he collected his whiskey and handed her the juice.

As they stood and sipped, Marcus was constantly waving or saying quick hellos to people as they stopped to shake his hand or clasp him on the shoulder. He seemed to know everyone there. And despite his reputation, everyone seemed to like him.

"You two seem to be having fun," said Don as he and Maggie emerged from the crowd. "Reminds me of when Maggie and I were younger."

"Lindsay is a wonderful dance partner," said Marcus graciously.

"For someone who has no idea how to dance," Lindsay laughed, sipping from her drink. "Marcus is a good teacher."

"I ran into Mac a while ago," said Maggie, pulling Lindsay to the side as Don and Marcus joked about something. "He said he needed to speak with you. It sounded important."

Lindsay gritted her teeth, that frost creeping back into her belly.

"I'll talk to him later," she said, a sharp edge to her voice. She forced a smile to her face, forced a lightness back into her voice. "Tomorrow," she said. "We're meant to be having fun tonight, right? Not talking about work."

Maggie nodded slowly and said nothing.

"Marcus," said Lindsay brightly, interrupting Marcus mid-sentence, "why don't you introduce me to some of these people you keep saying hello to?" Marcus' face clouded with puzzlement, but he just nodded and offered Lindsay his arm. They nodded goodbye to Maggie and Don and moved off into the crowd.

They spent the rest of the evening chatting and dancing. Lindsay met dozens of people and found most of them to be warm, personable, and fascinating. Not sharks at all. Just people who loved what they did and wanted to be the best in the world at it. She met drivers and mechanics and team owners and team leads and even a couple of data scientists. She had more fun talking to total strangers than she'd ever had in her life.

All the while, Lindsay carefully and studiously avoided Mac. When she saw him approaching, she'd pull Marcus in the other direction or pull him onto the dance floor. As she and Marcus stepped and spun, she could see Mac in the shadows to the side of the floor, scowling and brooding.

Good. Let him brood. Lindsay didn't owe him anything.

And he didn't owe her anything, either. They were both adults, and nothing had happened between them. Not a thing. If he wanted to screw his chief mechanic and Sam was okay with it, good for them. Lindsay couldn't care less.

"Come on, Marcus," she said after one dance, when they had been dancing a little too close to Mac for her taste. "I think maybe I need a stronger drink, after all."

Before Lindsay knew it, Maggie and Don were saying their goodbyes and other couples were drifting up the stairs and out the door. Lindsay had thoroughly enjoyed the dancing and the conversation. And, after their initial misunderstanding, Marcus had proved to be an entertaining and interesting companion.

She told him as much in the limo ride home. He smiled and

patted her hand in thanks, but there was a wistful look in his eyes. He turned without saying anything and stared out the window into the passing darkness.

Lindsay stumbled through the front door, her stilettos dangling from her hand, fatigue suddenly overcoming her.

"Damn, girl, look at you," said Raj from the couch where he, Marina, and Yue were watching a movie. "You look like a damn movie star or a Victoria's Secret model or something."

"Don't be an asshole, Raj," said Marina, "and close your mouth. You're drooling all over everything."

"Don't be jealous, lady," said Raj to Marina. "You haven't put a ring on this finger yet."

"Yet?" scoffed Marina. "What'd you put in those brownies you made us? You must be hallucinating."

"You can try it," said Raj, "but you can't deny it. What we've got is unstoppable."

Yue, munching on a bag of popcorn on the couch, made barfing noises into the bag.

"How was the event, Lindsay?" asked Marina, rolling her eyes, but smiling slightly, too.

What had Lindsay missed while she'd been away?

"It was goo—" Lindsay began.

There was a pounding on the front door, slow, deep, loud, and insistent. The door rattled in its sturdy frame.

Lindsay opened the door to find Mac standing on the porch. His hair was wild. His bow tie was undone, hanging loose around his collar. His shirt hung open at the first few buttons. It lay askew on his chest, like he'd been tugging at it. He looked sweaty and disheveled and thoroughly discombobulated.

From the corner of her eye, Lindsay had seen Mac and Sam leave the venue about half an hour before her. Lindsay didn't want to think what they may have been doing to make Mac look like he did. But why the hell was he here now instead of in bed with Sam?

"Took you long enough to come home," said Mac, his voice a low growl. He peeked over Lindsay's shoulder into the house. "Marcus in there?"

Goddamn alpha again. Sleeping with one girl and trying to keep another one at home in the wolf den for when he got bored? Fuck that.

Lindsay stepped out onto the porch and closed the front door behind her. There was no way she was letting Mac inside.

Mac refused to move backward. Fucking alpha. Lindsay didn't care. She was an alpha, too. She stood almost toe to toe with him. He was taller than her, but only by a couple of inches, even without her heels. She stood close enough to feel his heat in the cool air sweeping off the ocean, to smell the mix of spice and sweat emanating from Mac's body.

In the back of her mind, something triggered from that smell, something hot and feral and deep within her. Her skin suddenly felt the caress of her dress again. Her feet felt the cool of the concrete porch against the heat of her body. Her nipples peaked and ached in the night air, pressing forward against the satin dress, sending electric shivers through Lindsay's body with each subtle movement.

But Lindsay wasn't thinking about any of that. She was too hot with her own anger.

"Fuck you, Mac," she said, poking one hard index finger into the center of his chest. His shirt was open to that point. She could feel the slick heat of his skin under her finger. That slick heat was echoed in her own body. "Who the fuck are you to tell me when I can come home or who I can come home with? You're not my father."

The wildness crept into Mac's eyes again, like she'd seen a few nights earlier. Only this time, she matched it with her own ferocity. She would not be bullied by this man or any man, ever.

"Marcus is not a good man," Mac said, his voice low and full of warning. Whether that warning was about Marcus or about himself, Lindsay couldn't tell.

"Fuck you, Mac," Lindsay said again. "I can take care of myself. And I decide who I spend my time with. I don't need your fucking approval." She poked his chest once more, poking him in the pectoral. It was like stabbing a brick wall.

Mac moved even closer. She could feel his breath against her face, hot and smelling faintly of whiskey.

"You don't know what you're getting involved with, Lindsay."

The way he said her name sent a hot spike of longing straight to her core. Lindsay lifted her chin higher, looked hard at his eyes. Her body arced toward him. They were so close that she had to arch slightly backward to see his face clearly. Doing so pushed her hips forward. She could feel his body grazing her hipbones ever so slightly through her dress. Her body ached and stiffened, as if reaching out for him.

"And you're going to teach me? You're going to rescue me? Protect me?"

Lindsay could feel her body reacting to Mac, to his closeness. She didn't want to focus on it. She wanted to focus on her anger, on that feeling of power it gave her. But she couldn't force the sensations of her body down any longer. The anger and the arousal both surged in her, making her mind toss and turn like the sea in a storm.

"Yes," growled Mac. "I will."

He stepped forward further. His hips pressed against Lindsay's hips. She could feel him, hard and bulging, through the sheer fabric of her dress. Her body exploded with that touch, a wash of heat and slickness burning between her legs.

Her body wanted him. Badly.

Her mind refused.

She stepped backward, her back against the front door, putting only an inch or so between them. She put both hands on his chest, against his pectorals. The feeling of those hard muscles against the palms of her hands sent hot shivers through her arms, straight to that fire at her center, stoking it even further.

"I'm not a damsel in distress, Mac."

She pushed as hard as she could with both arms, sending Mac backward a step. He came right back, even closer. Lindsay put her hands on his chest again, again felt those shivers, like shovels full of coal being thrown into the furnace of a steam train chugging for a steep downslope.

"I'm not a fucking princess in a tower."

She pushed again, levering her arms straight, her back flat against the front door behind her. Mac again fell back a step, again came forward once more, now bracing himself with his arms on either side of Lindsay's head, leaning his hips against hers, pushing them into her, pressing, insistent. She could feel the coolness of the door against her ass through the thin fabric of the dress. It made the heat on the other side feel even more intense.

She put her hands out again, but he was too close for her to put them on his chest. She could only put them against his stomach. She felt his rock-hard abs through his thin shirt, felt the heat coming from him burning against her palms. She looked up at him, at those brilliant blue eyes, now smoldering with an intensity she hadn't seen before. The wildness was still there, but joined now by a need, a determination, a barely restrained primal desire that she could feel echoed in her bones, in her body, even in the back of her mind.

"I don't need saving," she whispered, falling into those eyes.

Mac swallowed hard. His eyes roamed over her face, searching. Back and forth over her eyes, her nose, her cheeks, her mouth, centering on her mouth.

"I do," he whispered back, his voice hoarse and shaking.

His mouth met hers, soft and warm and insistent, hungry. Her mouth responded in kind, opening to let him in. At that movement, Mac whimpered and pressed against her, hard, pressed his mouth into her, pressed his hips into her, lifted her off her feet slightly, pressed up against the front door.

Lindsay pressed back with her mouth and her hips, arched her back, wrapped her arms around his torso. She wanted to feel his muscles, his chest, not through the shirt, but pressed against her skin. She tugged his shirt out of his pants and slid her hands under, slid them along the smooth, hot skin of his back, feeling the deep trough above his spine, digging the tips of the fingers on both hands into that trough and pulling, pulling him against her body. She wanted to feel him against her, in her. She wanted him closer. She wanted to absorb him.

Mac groaned, his tongue greedily exploring her mouth, searching and sucking and teasing. His lips were full and soft. The heat of his body matched Lindsay's own. That heat washed up and over her, her body finally winning its battle against her mind.

Winning the battle, but not the war.

Something nagged at Lindsay's mind, even as she let her hands roam up and down Mac's wide, strong back, across the muscles of his broad shoulders. Something persistent, but quickly fading. The heat of her body, the need of her body was pushing that nagging thought further and further away.

Mac ran his hands along Lindsay's side. Each place his hands touched through the thin satin sparked like lightning against her skin. While his tongue explored her mouth, his hands slowly explored her body, down her side, then cupping her ass and pulling, pulling her up off her bare feet, pulling her hips hard into his, grinding his immense swelling against her, sending a flood of desire, of need through her. She moaned, the sound low with need, wanting release more than anything she'd even wanted.

Still, that nagging thought, fading now like a drowned woman sinking in a deep sea, reaching for the surface. Still reaching for rescue, for recognition.

It came back to her in a rush.

Sam.

He still had Sam, probably waiting naked in his bed at his house.

The fucking man-whore.

Lindsay didn't care how much she wanted him—and she did want him, she couldn't deny it—she would not be with a cheater.

Lindsay struggled to get her hands in front of Mac's body, but her struggles only made him pull her tighter against him. She couldn't make any room between them, so she did the only thing she could think of.

She bit him.

As he kissed her, she bit down on his lip and his tongue.

Hard.

He yelped in pain and backed off, holding one hand to his mouth, blood welling on his lower lip.

That gave Lindsay enough room to put both hands on his chest and push as hard as she could, using the door again for leverage.

She managed to push him back a step, then hauled off and slapped him across his face as hard as she could. The contact was solid. It stung her palm and her fingers, snapped his head to one side. She could see a red mark already blooming on his cheek.

"Fuck you, you fuck-boy, you player."

Mac's eyes were wide, his expression wounded.

Good.

Lindsay opened the door behind her and stepped inside, not taking her eyes from Mac's face.

"Get the fuck off my porch," she said, and slammed the door in his face.

Lindsay closed her eyes and fell back against the inside of the door. She struggled to catch her breath as her heart pounded in her heaving chest. She felt a sharp ache low between her legs. Must be what blue balls feel like.

She heard Mac's howl of frustration fade into the distance on the other side of the door.

Must be.

God, it hurt like a bitch. She'd never wanted someone so badly in her life, and now her body, ready and aching and wound tight as a guitar string, was demanding release. Lindsay put a hand on her stomach to settle her breathing. Even that touch, through the satin fabric of her dress, sent lightning bolts through her.

"Wow," said Raj's voice.

Lindsay's eyes fluttered open.

Raj, Marina, and Yue were all standing in the hallway, watching her. Marina stood in front of Raj. Beside them, Yue slowly moved small handfuls of popcorn from the bag to her mouth.

"Sounds like you had a fun night," said Marina.

Yue spoke through a mouthful of popcorn. "Sounds like it was almost a whole lot better."

Lindsay closed her eyes, blew out a breath that didn't even come close to expressing or relieving her frustration, and stalked to her bedroom without a word.

That night, she tossed and turned in bed. When she finally did fall into a haze of half-sleep, she dreamt of smoldering blue eyes and tight-wound springs and things pulling, pulling against each other, like two winches winding in opposite directions on the same cable. Pulling tighter and tighter, winding and wind-ing, the winches drawing closer and closer to each other, the tension between them mounting until she was sure the cable would break and send both winches flying apart, shattered.

When her hand in the night grazed the apex of her bare thigh under her pajama shorts, she woke instantly with a throaty gasp. She kept her hand moving and shattered herself.

It didn't help.

23

THE NEXT MORNING, all the espresso in the world couldn't help Lindsay's surly mood. The others in the house wisely kept a wide berth, each one offering a version of a cheerful "good morning" before seeing the look on Lindsay's face and retreating to go about their own business in silence.

Lindsay and her team monitored that day's practice session and the qualifying session from Lindsay's house, tapping into the real-time data used by the race team at the track. Marcus was on his game that day, focused and employing all of their data-driven suggestions to perfection. He qualified with the fifth-best time, giving him his best starting position all season.

Marcus came by the house that evening on his way home from the track, stopping by to thank Lindsay and the others, and to share a celebratory drink with them. Marcus didn't want to jinx anything by having alcohol on the night before a race, so he'd brought along sparkling apple cider for everyone to share.

They laughed and shook hands and slapped backs and grinned at each other while downing the apple soda, then huddled together around Lindsay's laptop to review the practice round and the qualifying session, looking for optimizations. Yue spotted one, Marina another, and even Marcus saw something in the simulation that led to an idea for improvement.

Lindsay nodded and smiled to herself. She didn't know what Marcus had actually been like before she'd started sending him emails a few months earlier. She had heard the horror stories about a washed-up prima donna who cared more about chasing skirts than chasing the leaderboard. She didn't know if those rumors were true or not.

But the Marcus she saw then, staring at the laptop screen, rewinding and replaying the simulation in slow motion, even frame by frame, studying it for any advantage, was not that man. This Marcus was focused and driven and had the energy of a rookie getting his first taste of success.

He reminded Lindsay, in a way, of herself when she had first started flexing her muscles as a data scientist, focusing on the data and the code rather than the reactions of her male counterparts who made jokes about her blonde hair and asked her to "be a doll" and "fetch me some coffee", somehow managing to call her a Barbie and a dog at the same time. It was real Don Draper shit in the middle of Silicon Valley during the #MeToo movement.

But those assholes were clueless. They were rich, and they thought they were woke. They drank their LaCroix seltzer, practiced TM every morning, kept their Teslas between 20% and 80% battery, and composted in their kitchens. By all appearances, they were perfect. They only showed their true selves to those they felt were beneath contempt.

Like Lindsay.

So she'd left. And made them all look like the fools they were.

And now, she was going to help Marcus do the same. She was going to help him leave his old self behind and show the naysayers, the ones who said he was washed up, what Marcus Leygren was really made of.

They huddled and strategized for a bit longer. Marcus even wanted to take a late-night spin in the simulator, but they talked him out of it, arguing that a good night's sleep and vivid dreams about the race and the new ideas would help more than an all-nighter in the sim. He went home full of energy and ideas.

The next morning, Lindsay and the others were all up early, buzzing with excitement. Lindsay called Maggie and arranged crew passes for the four of them so they could drive down to Silverstone and watch the race as it happened from among the crew.

Lindsay hadn't really thought about it, but if she had, she would have expected the crew pits to be a loud, smelly, messy group of loud, smelly, messy men screaming to be heard over the noise of the car engines, coughing amid clouds of exhaust as they shooed the drivers onto the track.

Instead, the pits were not smelly at all, but fresh and well-ventilated. They were not messy, but meticulously clean and orderly, with every tool in its place, every drop of oil swiftly wiped away, and every member of the race crew focused on their task.

They were, in fact, very loud. Her assumption was spot-on there. But every crew member wore a headset with thick noise-cancelling ear cups that dampened the sounds to acceptable levels and a microphone that allowed them to communicate clearly with anyone and everyone else on the team at the press of a button on a controller clipped to the belt of their jumpsuit. It was a civilized, efficient, and very well-oiled machine.

The pit itself was a deep, wide room with Marcus' blue and purple car in the center, surrounded by banks of monitors and computers, rolling chests full of tools, and the same gleaming floor that Lindsay had seen in the maintenance bay back at headquarters on her very first day. One wall was open. Through it, Lindsay could see the river of pavement that was pit row, the narrow road that led from the track into the pits and out again.

The sun was bright, filling the pit with light, gleaming off the tools, the floor, the car.

As Lindsay and the others pulled on the headsets they were given, Lindsay scanned the race crew. She saw Mac seated in a row of chairs facing a bank of monitors, his back to pit row. He was conferring closely with his team, his brow furrowed in concentration.

Lindsay quickly looked away, but spotted a mane of dark dreadlocks tied up like a bundle of sticks on the head of a tall woman in a dark jumpsuit. Sam was pointing and issuing calm orders to a never-ending stream of race team members. They'd approach her and ask a question. She'd look at the paper or screen they held out to her, think for a quick moment, then issue an order or make a decision. The team member would scurry off to carry out Sam's bidding, only to be replaced a fraction of a second later by another team member with another issue.

Yet, through it all, Sam never seemed to raise her voice, never seemed to lose her cool, and never seemed at a loss for an answer. Her team approached her without hesitation, and left to do her bidding the same way. She was the undisputed leader. That much was clear just from a minute of Lindsay observing. Whatever the hell she was doing with Mac, she was a bad-ass at her job. Lindsay had nothing but respect for that.

She saw Marcus come from a room in the back, his face relaxed, his grey eyes focused, his movements fluid. He spotted her from across the bay and nodded, a quick, serious motion, then returned his gaze to the track.

Mac stepped around the corner, locking eyes with Lindsay for a fraction of a second. She saw his eyes widen, then refocus on the task at hand.

Like Sam, Mac was a pro.

He shook Marcus' hand and clapped him on the shoulder, giving him a searching look. Marcus nodded solemnly. They discussed something briefly and Marcus moved toward the car, climbing into the cockpit, his tall body somehow disappearing into that tiny car as he wedged himself in.

Lindsay suddenly realized how dangerous this sport was. Marcus would be traveling at two hundred miles per hour, his body inches above a hard, concrete surface, encased in a metal tube, surrounded by nineteen other drivers in the same situation, maneuvering their tubes around countless curves and chicanes, jockeying for position, their tires millimeters from each other or from the wall. A tiny miscalculation at any moment could send their car spinning across the track or against a wall or pinwheeling end over end through the air.

These people were crazy.

"Lindsay," said Mac beside her.

Lindsay shook herself from her reverie and met Mac's eyes. She could see pain in them, but it was pushed back behind a steely focus. She forced herself to find that same focus, to push back her own pain and confusion from the night before and focus on the race. Mac, Sam, Marcus, and all of these other crew members were there to do a job, and they were excited. She could feel it in the air, the thrumming of hope and possibility. She wouldn't do anything that might jeopardize that.

"Mac," she replied. "How can we help?"

Mac hesitated for only a fraction of a second, then nodded. He showed Raj and Yue to where the telemetry data and other information fed into the room so they could help monitor the data pipelines. He showed Marina to a cluster of monitors displaying her new race interface, which Mac had pushed out to the race crew this week, so she could monitor its usage and provide any tips that might help.

"Lindsay," said Mac, "you'll be over here with me."

Lindsay raised an eyebrow, but Mac's face showed no hint of trickery or taking advantage.

"This is where the leads monitor the race and communicate with the drivers," he said, showing her to the row of seats he'd been occupying when she'd entered. He made introductions to the others seated beside them, introducing her as "our newest data scientist". That introduction made Lindsay vaguely uncomfortable.

Lindsay took her seat beside Mac and acquainted herself with the displays. A series of monitors showed the status of the cars, the vitals of the drivers, and the weather forecast. Another bank of monitors showed split-screen views of every inch of the track, as well as a monitor showing the current race standings and some information about the other cars.

"Why are we out here?" said Lindsay, her voice tinny in her headset, "instead of inside in a control room or something?"

"From here, in two steps we can be right by the cars in the pits." He gestured to one side where Marcus sat in his car, waiting while a sea of mechanics scurried like ants over the chassis, making last-minute preparations. Then he gestured to the other side, where the team's second driver, Timothy, sat waiting in his own car, another team of mechanics prepping him and his car for the race.

"We can watch the pit stops from here," Mac continued, "to see how they're going and be first-hand witnesses to any issues. And if we lean back," they both leaned back, craning their necks first to one side, then the other, "we can look up and down pit row to see how the other teams are getting on."

Something flashed down the row, catching Lindsay's eye. She leaned back a little bit farther and nearly fell over backwards. Her feet kicked and her arms pinwheeled as she tried to regain her balance. Mac reached one arm around her shoulder and pulled her back into a seated position.

Lindsay could feel his bicep flexing behind her shoulder, could feel the warmth of his arm through her t-shirt. He was staring at her with those big, blue eyes. She could see the hurt in them, the pain. She felt a flush all over her body again, wanted to lean into him, into his soft, full lips...

Lindsay cleared her throat and sat back, rubbing her suddenly clammy hands on the legs of her jeans. She darted a quick glance from left to right to see if anyone had noticed. No one had. They were all absorbed in their pre-race work.

"Plus," Mac cleared his own throat, "it's a convenient place to be if we need to confer with race officials or anything like that."

"Right," said Lindsay, nodding her head perhaps more vigorously than needed, "that makes sense."

And it did make sense to Lindsay now, even if the feeling of having her back to the track did feel pretty weird to her. It just seemed odd to have so much noise, so much potential danger happening behind her. And it wasn't like it was fifty yards behind her, either. She was close enough to feel the wind as the cars drove down pit row. It was an odd, exposed feeling, like wearing one of those hospital gowns with the backs wide open, showing your bare ass to the world.

Lindsay settled into her seat and studied the monitors before her. She was proud to see Marina's interface being used just about everywhere except for the live race feeds. The only place they weren't being used was on a screen that was currently blank, just a shell of the interface with a grey box in the center.

"What's supposed to be on this screen?" she asked.

"Once the race starts," Mac explained, "that will fill with a projection of where the race would end under the conditions of the moment. It's kind of a prototype. Not super useful, but we have it up just to try it out."

Lindsay made a note to watch for that screen once it populated. She was curious to see how accurate it was and how it might be making its projections.

Things moved very quickly from there. The engines of both cars started. Lindsay had thought it was loud before. Now, it was deafening. After a fraction of a second, the noise-cancelling feature of her headphones increased, blocking out the increased volume of the engines, but Lindsay knew that if she took those headphones off, her ears would be ringing for a week.

Crew members stood in pit lane to direct traffic while the cars pulled out of the garages. A long line of race cars drifted past as the drivers made their way onto the track for the first time. The sound of the cars was like a nest of angry hornets as the drivers took a few laps to check out the track and warm up themselves and their cars.

Lindsay watched on her monitor as they took one more slow lap, then lined up according to their qualifying order in a formation determined by little square brackets painted on the track at the starting position. Staggered two by two, with one car of each pair slightly ahead of the other, they waited while a series of five pairs of vertically-stacked red lights came on one by one in a horizontal array that hung over the track where it could be seen by all the drivers.

The lights came on in one-second intervals, then hung there, fully lit, for a long moment. Everyone around Lindsay, seemingly everyone in the entire track complex, was holding their breath, waiting in a moment of mental free-fall for the race to begin.

At last, the five lights went dark. A scream like a thousand angry banshees reverberated through the entire place, shaking Lindsay's seat, as all twenty drivers floored their engines, speeding away from their starting position and immediately maneuvering for advantage against fellow drivers who may not have been as quick off their starting lines.

The next hour was a ballet of danger and precision, both on the track and off. Lindsay had never witnessed so many professionals with so much determination, focus, and common purpose working so closely and so in concert with one another.

When Marcus or Timothy came in for a pit stop, a swarm of at least twenty crew members would sprint to surround the car. Each person had a role. Some would lift the on jacks from the front and back, others would stabilize it with jacks on the sides. One person on each tire would remove the lug nuts, another would remove the tire, a third would put on a new tire, and a fourth would bolt it down. That happened simultaneously on each tire. Then the jacking teams would lower the car back down and send it on its way. The entire procedure took place in less than three seconds.

Lindsay had heard of pit stops in races before, but had never witnessed one via video or in person. She was stunned by the speed, precision, and professionalism of the pit stop crew. And as soon as they had completed the pit stop, they immediately huddled to debrief, discussing what went well and what could have been better.

The division of labor among the rest of the pit crew was extensive and exacting. There were teams of people devoted to analyzing telemetry data from the car, others focusing on track data, weather data, the data systems themselves to make sure the information was flowing properly. Systems engineers monitored computers and networks. Other people were focused on the competitors, analyzing race strategy. And one manager was assigned to communicate with each driver, serving as the single point of contact for that driver.

It was incredibly impressive, and every member of the team, even the pit crews when they were waiting between pit stops, were focused completely on the race, watching the progress on screens and monitors throughout the pit bay, cheering each advance in position, wearing determined expressions—but never complaining—with each retreat.

These roles were doubled, one set of crew for Marcus' car, another for Timothy's. Mac and Sam served as leaders for both teams, doubling their responsibility, doubling their burden. Sam was constantly moving back and forth between pit bays, stopping often in-between to confer with Mac.

Mac tended to stay in his seat, monitoring the race on the

screens before him. The driver managers sat beside him, allowing him to monitor their communication, keeping him informed of the condition of the drivers and their assessment of the track and the car.

Lindsay kept her mouth shut and merely observed. For the first full hour of the race, she didn't say a thing, just watched and learned and looked for ways she could contribute, while making sure that she did nothing to disrupt the workings of this well-oiled machine.

Marcus was racing well. He had started in fifth position, quickly moved to fourth before the first turn. A well-timed and brilliantly executed pit stop gained him a position against his closest competitor, moving him into third place by the midpoint of the race.

The monitor before her, the one showing the prediction of the race ending, lit up after a few minutes. She figured it took that long for the program to have enough race data to feed its algorithms. It was claiming that the race would end the way it was currently running, with Marcus in third place.

After about ten minutes of observation, Lindsay could see that the program was using a fairly simple extrapolation of up-to-the-second race trends to make its predictions. If a certain driver had held his position for the whole race, the algorithm would assume he would continue to hold it at his current speed and lap time. If another driver had gained ground, the algorithm assumed he would continue to gain ground at his new speed and lap time. It was pretty basic. Lindsay wasn't sure why they were using it, but, as Mac had said, it was just a prototype. Maybe the more robust version was still under development. Lindsay made a mental note to check into it later.

Clouds slowly gathered overhead as the race progressed, changing the day from bright and sunny to dark and overcast. It would almost certainly rain before the end of the day, but

Lindsay felt sure it would hold off until well after the race ended.

When the crew started chattering about changing the type of tires on the cars, she asked Mac what was going on.

"Even though it's not going to rain during the race," he said, "the cloud cover is cooling off the track. A cold track has different grip than a hot track, so we change to a different tire setup to accommodate."

Not only was the coordination among the team members astounding, there was science behind the race strategy, as well. Lindsay had severely underestimated what was involved in these race teams. They were far more than sweaty, greasy men. These were artists and scientists and competitors, all pulling for one outcome: victory on the track.

Lindsay bent her own mind to that purpose, studying the screens all around her, trying to understand what they were telling her and how it all fit together. She fell back into a familiar and comfortable state of mind. Data analysis. The various data feeds swirled in her brain, fitting together like Lego bricks. Sometimes data made an undiscernible mass of bricks, nothing useful or interesting. Sometimes the data made beautiful and surprising structures.

That was the case now.

Maybe it was because she'd been so steeped in the data while working with Marcus over the last few weeks, but the data she was seeing on the screens made intuitive sense to her, fit together naturally into one coherent image in her mind.

She saw an opportunity, a path that might make victory more likely. But she needed to test it.

"Mac, can I control one of these screens? Get to a network terminal somehow?"

Mac shrugged, but said something into his headset. A worker who Mac introduced as Sara appeared by Lindsay's side and showed her how to flip one of the screens from a view of the track weather into a computer terminal. Lindsay now had access to the company intranet and cloud storage system, just as if she'd brought her laptop along with her.

She navigated through the file system to where she kept her own code and applied it to the real-time race data feed, adjusting several parameters to speed up the process based on what she'd been observing. She pressed a button and set her algorithm to working.

Marcus' car flew into the pit behind her, the swarm of crew members swapping his warm-weather tires for the cold-weather tires in the blink of an eye, then sending him flying back out onto the track. Thanks to their skill and execution, Marcus didn't lose position at all.

Lindsay waited, drumming her fingers on her chair as the code cranked through the data, precious seconds of race time slipping by. She'd never felt impatient waiting for results to return in the past, but now she felt each moment like a hammer blow. Speed and efficiency in the code were as essential as speed and efficiency on the track. Lindsay could see that now. She could feel it in the beating of her heart, which grew louder with each minute that elapsed with no results.

She heard a cheer from the crew in the pit bay and peered around the corner. They were all sitting in folding chairs, in full jumpsuits and helmets, ready to leap to their jobs at a moment's notice. They were looking up, watching the race on television screens above them. Lindsay checked her own view on the banks of screens in front of her.

Marcus had gained another position. He was now in second place.

The weather had taken a turn for the worse, the clouds overhead growing darker, a cool wind picking up. As a result, Lindsay saw that the temperature had dropped five degrees in the last couple of minutes. The switch to cold-weather tires had been a gamble, but a brilliant one, and it had paid off against their more cautious competitors.

Finally, after what seemed like forever, Lindsay's algorithm returned with its results.

Her intuition was confirmed.

"Mac, can I talk to Marcus?"

Mac furrowed his brow.

"Only Trevor here talks to Marcus during a race," he said, nodding toward the man seated on the other side of Lindsay.

Lindsay turned to him.

"Trevor, I need you to tell Marcus something."

"Roger that, ma'am," said Trevor in a smooth, professional radio voice. Lindsay felt calmer just listening to him. No wonder Trevor was tasked with talking to Marcus during the race.

"Tell Marcus that Lindsay has found a way for him to win."

24

LINDSAY FELT Mac's stare as she said the words. Mac was a competitor, one who wanted to win. Win fairly, but at any reasonable cost. When she said she had found a way to do just that, she knew she would have his attention.

What she didn't expect was the tingle, the shower of sparks washing down her spine at just the feel of his gaze upon her.

She wasn't even looking at Mac. She was looking at Trevor as he relayed information to Marcus while Lindsay explained what she'd discovered. And yet she could feel Mac beside her as if she were standing in his embrace.

Was it only Mac that was giving her that feeling, or was she starting to feel the thrill of winning, too? The thrill of working hard, studying a problem, implementing the solution, then practicing until it paid off?

"You'll only get one chance to use this, though, Marcus," Lindsay relayed through Trevor. "The Mercedes team is too smart to let you get away with it twice."

"Roger that," said Marcus, his voice clipped, cool, and completely confident.

"You sure this will work?" asked Mac once Trevor had

switched off the speaker and Lindsay had settled back in her chair.

Lindsay shrugged and leaned forward, drumming her fingers nervously on the console before her. Time was running out. There were only ten laps left, and in order for her plan to work, Marcus needed to close a two-second gap against the first place car, a Mercedes.

"His average lap times are consistently faster now," she said. "The Mercedes is still on the warm-weather tires and won't have time to change them, at this point. If Marcus can maintain his speed, he should have time to catch up before the last turn."

Mac nodded, then reached forward and put one hand on top of Lindsay's, stopping her fingers from drumming. His hand was warm and dry, his skin rough against hers. That shower of sparks became a torrent of lightning bolts.

Lindsay may be starting to feel the thrill of the race, but most of the excitement she felt was still coming from Mac.

"Try to relax, Lindsay," Mac said softly. "Tapping your fingers won't help you any. It'll just drive the rest of us crazy."

He moved her hand off the console and set it in her lap, his hand still on hers. The feeling of his hand in her lap sent more than just lightning bolts surging through Lindsay's body. A wave of heat flowed straight to her core at his touch, the ache from the other night returning from the shadows.

Sam came around the corner behind Mac. Lindsay jerked her hand from Mac's. His brows furrowed and hurt flashed in his eyes. Lindsay ran her hand through her hair, trying to play off the jerky movement. It was a weak attempt.

"Mac, Tim's coming in," said Sam.

Lindsay could tell from the look in Mac's eyes that she hadn't played the movement off at all. But he didn't look ashamed or contrite or even self-conscious at Sam's appearance. He didn't seem to care at all that Sam was there, or that she might have seen Mac holding her hand.

Was Mac really that much of a player? Or did he and Sam have an open relationship? Or maybe they were just using each other for sex?

Either way, Lindsay wasn't interested. She didn't need that kind of noise in her life.

Mac stared at her for a long second, then turned his attention to Sam. Lindsay stared straight ahead at her monitors, doing her best to seem busy while really just trying to settle herself down.

"What happened?" she heard Mac ask Sam.

"Lost power," said Sam. "Might be something with the fuel system."

Mac nodded grimly.

"Any issues with Marcus?"

"No," replied Sam, "he's still green all around."

"Okay, let's get Tim's car into the workshop for a tear down tonight."

Sam nodded and left. Lindsay felt Mac's stare on her face once more, but kept her gaze forward toward the monitors.

Toward the race, where Marcus was closing the gap.

With eight laps to go now, he had closed to within a second and a half of the leader. Lindsay tuned in to the channel where Marcus was conversing with Trevor. She couldn't speak on the channel, but she could listen.

"How's it looking behind?" Marcus asked.

"All clear behind, Marcus," said Trevor in his cool, calm voice. "Two-point-five seconds ahead of Bennett. You're looking good."

Trevor's soothing voice actually helped Lindsay to calm herself down. She wished he would just keep talking for a while. Didn't matter what he said. Just read a technical manual or something.

Lindsay switched off the audio feed and examined the

prediction algorithm on the screen in front of her. It claimed that Marcus would lose by a fraction of a second.

It would be wrong. Lindsay could feel it.

And then she'd rewrite that damn program to be more intelligent about its predictions.

Two more laps went by, then another. Marcus closed to within one second, his progress steady, but agonizingly slow. The driver of the Mercedes car was Tomas Heingren, a five-time world champion who had won two of the last three championships and was at the top of his game. He knew how to hold off someone challenging from behind, and Lindsay had no doubt he knew that Marcus was threatening.

But Marcus was no rookie. When Heingren had won his first championship years ago, Marcus had been the reigning champ.

The laps spun by in a blur.

Four laps remaining.

Three laps remaining.

Marcus was within half a second of Heingren.

Two laps remaining.

And then they were on the last lap. The front wing of Marcus' car was practically rubbing against Heingren's back tires. Lindsay leaned forward in her chair and realized that everyone else was doing the same thing.

She peeked around the corner to look into the bays. Everyone in both Timothy's bay—including Timothy—and in Marcus' bay was staring intently at a screen, watching the last lap unfold.

On the screen before her, Lindsay watched Marcus and Heingren move around the track, accelerating through the straightaways, slowing to nearly a crawl through the tight curves. As she watched, she could hear the roar of the engines from the track behind her, could smell the odors of fuel fumes and hot tires, could hear the screams and cheers of the crowd.

Marcus was right on Heingren's tail. Through each turn, he

would nose Heingren's tires. On each straight, he would draft in Heingren's wind shadow for a moment, then use the momentum to swing around to one side or the other, trying to get ahead, edging for an opening, for any advantage.

But Heingren was cagey, skilled, as Lindsay figured he would be. She didn't know much about car racing, but you didn't get to the top of your field in anything—sports, arts, science—by making basic mistakes. Heingren would know how to fend off Marcus.

Lindsay had expected Heingren to be cagey.

But science was science, and data didn't lie.

Lindsay expected Heingren's skill. She now hoped her idea would work. Science or not, the real world sometimes had a mind of its own.

The last section of the track was a sequence of two turns of practically ninety-degrees each—first a left, then a right—followed by another right-hand turn that was a little shallower and had a gentler approach. In most turns, drivers would start wide on the outside of the curve, then come to the inside at the apex of the turn, then swing wide again as they exited the curve. This was the ideal line, preserving optimal speed through the curve.

With this sequence, however, that optimal line wasn't possible. In order to prepare for the rapid sequence of turns, drivers would tend to stay on the inside after the first turn so that they would be in the best position for the second and third turns and on into the final straightway that led to the finish line. They would sacrifice speed in the first turn, which demanded a lot of braking, anyway, so that they could preserve it through the remainder of the sequence.

That gave Marcus an opportunity.

If he took a slightly more aggressive line in the first turn, kept a touch more speed than normal, and if he was already close enough to Heingren when they arrived at the first turn, he might be able to edge Heingren into second place.

It was risky. Marcus would be carrying more speed than he was used to, more speed than he would normally want. And Heingren might be forced toward the outside of the track. But there was a wall where the turn began. If Heingren refused to budge before that wall came, Marcus would be forced to back off to avoid a crash.

There were rules about who should back off in certain situations, but what happened on the track was what really mattered. Nothing Lindsay had suggested was illegal, by racing rules.

But it was certainly aggressive.

Marcus and Heingren were approaching the first curve. They would know before the curve even began whether or not the plan would work.

Marcus tucked his car in behind Heingren on the straight leading to the turn, following him like a shadow as Heingren set up for the typical line into the curve.

They approached the sharp left-hand turn. Marcus braked hard, early, allowing Heingren's car to slip slightly ahead.

When Heingren's brake lights came on a fraction of a second later, Marcus whipped his steering wheel to the left, swinging around Heingren's car, then accelerated hard, flying around Heingren toward the inside of the curve.

This was the moment of truth. Would Heingren back off? Would he force Marcus off the track or cause an accident?

Marcus was alongside Heingren now, his nose slightly ahead of the Mercedes.

The pit bays around Lindsay were dead silent. Every single pair of eyes bore into a screen, watching the drama unfold on the track. Every breath was held.

Marcus had to brake soon, had to trim some of the extra speed he was carrying. Otherwise, he wouldn't be able to turn fast enough and would run straight into the wall ahead of him.

But he needed to wait for Heingren to cede the front position first.

It was a game of chicken at a hundred miles an hour in fifteen-million-dollar cars in front of millions of fans.

Lindsay's fingers drummed on the console.

Mac's hand reached over to still them.

Neither looked at the other. They just held each other's hand, staring at the screens in front of them.

Waiting.

Waiting to see what Heingren would do.

Brake lights came on behind the Mercedes.

A fraction of a second later, Marcus braked, as well.

The Mercedes fell in behind Marcus' car. Because of the added speed and the delayed braking, Marcus had to take a slightly more awkward line through the next curve, but there was no way for Heingren to capitalize on the inefficiency.

Marcus had overtaken the Mercedes.

As the two cars came through the last curve and sped down the final straightaway, Marcus' car pulled away slightly, increasing his lead over Heingren as Marcus flew under the checkered flag and across the finish line.

In first place.

The pit bays erupted in screams and shouts of joy, a sound that washed over Lindsay like a tidal wave of elation. In it, she could feel the years of pent-up frustration, the countless hours of work and study and striving to find an edge, to find a way to do what Marcus had just done.

Win.

The tidal wave of joy lifted Lindsay and Mac and Trevor and everyone else off their chairs and onto their feet. It lifted Lindsay into Mac's arms. They hugged each other tightly, overcome with shock, surprise, excitement, and pride.

After a moment, they both felt something more.

Lindsay pulled back slightly, looked up into Mac's face. In

his eyes, she saw that hunger she'd seen the other night. She felt that same hunger responding in herself, a low, feral growl from some deep, primal place within her.

Lindsay swallowed hard, screwed her eyes tight, and pushed Mac away, gently but firmly.

It nearly killed her to do it.

But she would be second to no one. Not even to someone as amazing as Sam.

Lindsay turned away without looking at Mac and gave Trevor a hug. Sam raced by from Marcus' bay, passed in front of Lindsay. Lindsay heard her squeal as she no doubt threw herself around Mac in an embrace that would be more than just professional excitement. Lindsay didn't bother turning to watch.

She pushed through the clusters and crowds of celebration in the pit bay to find her own crew. Raj and Marina were locked in a long hug, with Raj swinging Marina back and forth, her feet swaying like a pendulum about a foot above the floor. Yue was doing a kind of hopping, pointing dance of celebration beside them.

"Lindsaaaay," Yue called out when she saw Lindsay coming toward them.

Raj and Marina opened their embrace and welcomed Lindsay and Yue into it. They formed a small, hugging ring, bouncing and rotating like drunken fans after a wild soccer match.

A surge of collective movement pulled everyone out of the pit bay and onto the track. Lindsay had no idea where they were going, but no one around them looked worried. On the contrary, everyone looked positively ecstatic.

When the sound of approaching engines reached her ears, Lindsay realized what was happening. The racers were pulling up. Marcus was coming in, and the entire crew was pushing out onto the track to greet the winner.

The crew formed a horseshoe, allowing room for Marcus to

pull his car in amongst them. Photographers and race officials joined the throng, and fans cheered from the stands above.

Several crew members stepped forward to help Marcus from his car. When he freed his arms from the cockpit and pressed himself up and out of the car, he stood on his seat, one foot on the rim of the cockpit, and raised both hands in triumph, his head held high toward the stands. The crowd and the crew all responded with raucous cheers.

Marcus pulled off his helmet and held his arms up again for another round of cheers. Mac, clapping, came to the side of the car and reached up to shake Marcus' hand vigorously. Both men grinned at each other as the photographers' cameras clicked and whirred.

Marcus scanned the crowd, occasionally pointing and giving a thumbs up, but clearly looking for someone in particular.

Then his eyes settled on Lindsay.

"Lindsay Rhodes!" he screamed from his perch atop the car.

Everyone turned to look at Lindsay. Marcus leapt off the car and the sea of crew members parted to open a clear passage between them.

Lindsay couldn't help but laugh at how surreal it all was. She was a data scientist from San Francisco. A few months ago, she was helping an office supply firm optimize their catalog mailings. Now, she was standing on a famous English racetrack amid a crowd of Formula One race professionals, with screaming fans and journalists all around her.

Marcus strode to her, held her at arm's length. His grin looked like it would wrap around his head, if it could, and his boyish face looked so goofy with unadulterated six-year-old joy that Lindsay couldn't help but laugh again.

Marcus pulled her into a giant bear hug, bent backward to lift her off her feet, and spun her in a slow circle while she laughed and threw her arms around him to keep from falling.

As he turned her, Lindsay glimpsed Mac, standing in the

crowd with his arms folded, his face as dark and glowering as she'd ever seen it.

And that was saying something.

Marcus set her back down and planted a big wet kiss on each cheek before tucking her under one arm and facing the crowd.

"Lindsay Rhodes!" he called again, this time toward the crowd. He pointed one finger at Lindsay. "She's a fucking racing genius!"

Lindsay, still a little dizzy from the spin, laughed and laughed and leaned against Marcus for support as the cameras clicked and whirred.

Mac looked like he was going to punch someone. He spun and stalked off, pushing his way through the crowd.

Totally surreal.

25

Equally surreal were the tabloid headlines the next day, though not nearly as fun to experience.

Lindsay's face was on the front page of every single one of them.

In some cases, it was Lindsay on the track, usually during the moment when Marcus' lips were planted on her cheek.

In other cases, it was Lindsay in her evening gown, striding arm and arm down the red carpet with Marcus.

Some issues had the evening gown on the cover, the race track on Page Two. Others had it the other way around. But in every single case, the gist of the headlines was the same.

According to the British tabloid press, Lindsay Rhodes was Marcus Leygren's new arm candy.

Lindsay sipped her espresso and pushed aside a curtain, peering into the driveway. The crowd of photographers had grown even larger. Balding men with rounded bellies laden with camera gear over both shoulders and around their necks milled about in front of her house, craning their necks to peer through windows or wandering from side to side, looking for a way around the house.

It was incredibly intrusive.

And incredibly annoying.

"Who the fuck are all those people?" said Marina as she stumbled, bleary-eyed, into the kitchen. Uncharacteristically, Raj walked in behind her and moved straight to the espresso machine without so much as a grunt in Lindsay's direction.

"Paparazzi?" said Lindsay with a sheepish shrug.

Marina stood beside Lindsay and looked out the window.

"Somehow I always thought it would feel cooler to have paparazzi outside the door," she grumbled.

Lindsay had never felt that way. Ever.

She and Marina walked back to the kitchen. Raj handed Marina a cup of cappuccino and sipped his own.

Lindsay looked at the two of them, standing side by side, sipping their coffee.

She blinked.

Raj was wearing pajama bottoms, his chest bare.

Lindsay had never seen him bare-chested before. It made him seem at once both more imposing and more cuddly. His broad chest had just a touch of fuzzy black hair over his sternum. His belly was smooth and just barely rounded.

He had the quintessential dad bod.

But that wasn't what caught Lindsay's attention.

Raj wasn't wearing his pajama shirt.

But Marina was. With nothing on underneath it.

Lindsay raised her eyebrows.

Raj grinned like a cat who'd just caught a hummingbird.

"Let's not make a big deal about it, okay?" grumbled Marina, sipping her coffee.

Raj's grin grew even wider as he put his arm around Marina and squeezed her to his side.

She didn't object. Not even a snide comment.

And though Marina quickly covered her mouth with her cup, sipping the last of her cappuccino, Lindsay was sure she had seen just a hint of a smile at the corners of Marina's mouth.

Raj and Marina.

The thought made Lindsay immeasurably happy.

Lindsay returned Raj's grin, then reeled it back in and just nodded.

"Okay," Lindsay said, with as much nonchalance as she could muster. "No big deal."

Lindsay half-expected Mac to pull up and rescue her and the others from the paparazzi, but he didn't show. Instead, she piled into the Mercedes G-wagon in the garage with Raj, Marina, and Yue and crept through the crowd of photographers, cameras snapping away toward the tinted windows, until they could accelerate out of the driveway and make their way to work.

Raj, Marina, and Yue broke off, headed for Yue's server room —which had become the crew's de-facto headquarters—while Lindsay went in the main building.

She had made some excuse about wanting to talk to Maggie about something, but she was really just wandering around.

Okay, she was looking for Mac.

She checked the conference rooms, but they were empty. Only Gerald was in the garage, and he hadn't seen Mac that day. But he said Mac would most likely be somewhere at the office for at least a few hours before leaving for the next race in Austria.

Lindsay wandered up to the office floor. The room was buzzing with energy and excitement. When Lindsay came up the stairs, someone let out a wild cheer and the whole floor stood from their desks and gave her an ovation. Lindsay felt her cheeks redden and grow hot as she walked the length of the room to her desk, wishing she'd thought to come up the stairs on the other side.

She nodded shyly, shook the occasional hand, and even gave

a quick hug or two. By the time she got to her desk, she was laughing at all the sincerity and exuberance. These office workers who were usually so quiet and intense were practically bouncing off the walls.

Helen threw her arms around Lindsay with a great, matronly hug and put her hands on Lindsay's cheeks.

"Well done, dear," she said. "Well done. You've only been here a few months and look at what you've accomplished already." She winked at Lindsay. "Your father was a wily old fox, but he had a great head on his shoulders. It was no mistake him bringing you into this family."

That word, family, hung in the air. It rung in Lindsay's ears as she smiled and thanked Helen and moved on toward her desk. She turned and looked back over the room, at the workers laughing and teasing each other or, for the few able to focus on their actual work, asking each other questions or seeking opinions.

It was a typical office environment, with its cubicles and rolling chairs, but the feeling in the room was unlike any office environment she'd ever been in. There was no cold, awkward professionalism. No sanitized hiding of real human beliefs and dreams to fit into the corporate mold. The corporation didn't dictate the humanity of the workers. In this company, the workers determined the humanity of the corporation. The corporation truly was the reflection of the accumulated person-alities, ideas, hopes, dreams, and hard work of the people within it.

Lindsay had never seen a corporation like that before.

In truth, she'd never seen a family like that before, either.

Even her own family had never been that way.

She and her mother had been very close. Lindsay owed everything she was today to her mother's guidance and encour-agement.

But it had never felt like a partnership. In corporate terms, it had been a traditional employer-employee relationship. Her mother set the task—whether that was washing the dishes or graduating college—and Lindsay found a way to accomplish it.

Here, at her father's company, things felt different. Here, the employees, from top to bottom, shared a common goal: winning races. There were a lot of moving parts that came together toward that end, with accounting and design and engineering and the race teams and so on. But everyone was united around that single purpose.

And now that that purpose had been achieved, at least for this one race, everyone was excited. Not just Marcus, but Timothy, the other driver, too, even though he hadn't won, hadn't even finished the race. Not just the pit crews and the race team, who had been in the pit bays when Marcus crossed the finish line, but the office workers in the cubicles in front of Lindsay, who had probably watched on television from home or seen it in YouTube clips later that night. Lindsay had no doubt that even the cleaning crews were thrilled by Marcus' victory.

It really was a family, but not by the definition that Lindsay had always known. It was a different kind of family.

A bigger one.

A healthier one.

A happier one.

One that Lindsay was proud to be a part of.

"Ah, Lindsay," said Maggie as she came up the stairs behind Lindsay. "Wonderful to see you, dear. And congratulations on the race. Your work with Marcus has done wonders. It's been years since I've seen him so..." She searched for the word for a moment. "...unadulterated."

She grinned and winked at Lindsay.

Lindsay knew exactly what Maggie meant.

"How are you holding up?" Maggie asked. "With the press? I know the tabloids can be difficult."

Lindsay shrugged.

"I'm okay," she said. "I mean, no one actually believes that stuff, right?"

Maggie shrugged.

"You'd be surprised," she said. "In Britain, the red tops are outlandish, to be sure, but they occasionally scoop the quality papers simply by being so damn persistent. Most people don't take The Sun at face value the way they would The Times, but they still pay attention."

"But the stories aren't true," said Lindsay.

"The truth has never stood in the way of a good story for The Sun or The Mirror or any of the others," said Maggie. "Ask Mac about that. He can tell you his share of stories."

Lindsay felt a pit open in her chest at the mention of Mac's name.

"Oh, don't worry," said Maggie, a concerned look on her face. She touched Lindsay's arm. "I'm sure they'll get bored soon enough. Marcus will be in Austria this evening. Out of sight, out of mind. And you're not exactly a public figure. They'll find something more easily photographed to put on their covers."

Lindsay nodded and gave Maggie a weak smile.

"Have you seen him yet today?" Lindsay asked. "Mac, I mean?"

"He was here this morning, but he's gone to the airport now, I believe." Maggie frowned. "Didn't he say goodbye to you?"

Lindsay bit her lower lip and shook her head. She hadn't seen him at all since they'd left the race track.

She shook her head again, this time to clear it. What the hell was she so obsessed about, anyway? Mac was with Sam. Yes, he had shown interest in Lindsay. Strong interest, it had to be said. But that just proved him to be the asshole Lindsay had suspected he was from the beginning.

And yes, Lindsay had been attracted to Mac. Strongly attracted. That also had to be said.

But that was in the past. Lindsay had no interest in being the other woman, and she had no interest in breaking up a strong couple. Lindsay didn't know Sam well, but from what she did know, Sam was an incredible woman. She respected Sam and hoped that once they got to know one another, they could be friends.

And women needed to stick together, support each other. Lindsay would not be one of those women who would tear down another woman just to get a man.

That's exactly what men wanted. To keep women fighting amongst themselves so they'd be too busy to recognize their own power.

Fuck that.

Those kind of men weren't worth fighting for. And the men who were worth fighting for would never ask two women to fight in the first place.

"I'm sure you can still call him before his flight leaves," said Maggie, checking her watch.

Lindsay shook her head again.

"No, that's okay. I don't need to speak with him." She smiled, more broadly than she felt. But the smile itself helped to lift her spirits. She raised her chin. "I'm fine," she nodded.

Maggie tilted her head and gave Lindsay an appraising stare. She blinked slowly, that typical hint of a smile playing at the corners of her lips.

The woman had X-ray vision. Lindsay felt like she was peering directly into her soul, reading her heart like the pages of a fucking book.

Well, let her read. Lindsay didn't need Mac or any other man. Yes, she was hurting, but she would rather hurt and move on than get sucked in with some man-whore who was playing her against another strong, independent woman.

"Yes," murmured Maggie, "I think perhaps you are."

Lindsay felt a warmth expand from the center of her chest,

flowing outward into her extremities. She felt lighter, stronger, just from Maggie's words.

"I hope so, anyway," continued Maggie, "because we have some things to discuss. I've received some papers that I need you to review with me."

Lindsay squared her shoulders. Mac didn't matter. Lindsay owned a racing company now, a company with a storied past and a bright future. It was her father's legacy, and she now had the chance to move it forward, to shape it to her own vision.

"They're from a private equity firm called Everbright Securities Group, LLP," continued Maggie.

Lindsay's heart sank.

"They said you'd agreed to sell your share of the company to them." Maggie looked Lindsay square in the eye, her gaze unflinching.

This time, there was no hint of a smile on her lips at all.

26

THE NEXT FEW months passed in a blur. The heat of summer reached its apex in all its sweaty, sticky, humid English coastal glory, then ceded control to the cool breezes and colorful leaves of autumn.

Where Lindsay had been pushing up the sleeves of her grey t-shirts, dark sweat stains embarrassingly visible in ways she'd never had to deal with in San Francisco, she was now pulling her black wool blazer around her shoulders more tightly to stave off the cool wind coming off the ocean as she stood alone on her back porch, sipping coffee and staring at the empty chairs sitting side by side on the deck.

Hart Racing was in the headlines more and more, though the circus surrounding Lindsay's fictitious relationship with Marcus had, mercifully, been very short-lived. Maggie was right. It must have been too hard for the tabloids to get new photographs. And a certain British politician had been caught on video doing some decidedly impolitic things in a well-known local house of ill repute. That scandal had proven to have very long legs, pushing Lindsay out of the minds of the scandal-sheet editors for good.

Marcus had not stopped providing news for the legitimate

papers, though. He and the team had continued to optimize and find advantages, and Marcus' confidence on the track reached levels that exceeded even his performance in his younger days.

The pool of Formula One drivers was graced this season with incredible talent. It made for thrilling races for the fans and a tightly packed leaderboard for the Drivers Championship. No one driver had established a commanding lead prior to Silverstone.

Each year, a tally of points was kept based on the finishes of the two drivers on each team. The tally was used to award a winner in what was called the Constructors Championship, where the teams competed against one another for the highest aggregate score.

But, there was also a second tally that tracked the performance of each individual driver. This tally determined the winner of the Drivers Championship, awarded to the individual driver with the best aggregated performance across all of the season's races.

Marcus had been well back in the pack in the standings for the Drivers Championship prior to his win at Silverstone. But in the eight races since his victory in England, he'd had five more wins, two second-place finishes, and one third-place finish.

It was an unprecedented comeback. And it had catapulted Marcus to third place in the Drivers Championship. If his streak of wins continued, he had a real chance of winning his first Drivers Championship in seven years, and the first for a Hart Racing driver in more than a decade.

The entire company was practically levitating with excitement. Every Monday, the energy at headquarters would ratchet up another notch, with everyone chattering about Marcus' performance the day before. No one was catching replays on YouTube or reading about the results in the papers anymore. Even with races halfway around the world in Singapore, Japan, and the US, every single employee was staying up into the wee hours of the morning to watch the races live.

Including Lindsay and her crew.

They were working around the clock, improving their systems, their data aggregation, the speed of their real-time data processing. Marina had already iterated her race interface three more times, adding so many improvements that it was unrecognizable from the version they'd used at Silverstone. It was so good that some of the pit crew had admitted to using only Marina's interface, watching it instead of the live video from the actual race.

And Lindsay had been furiously iterating on her analytical algorithms, testing literally millions of parameters and configurations and combinations of features, looking for a process that would yield consistent, actionable, proven insights that Marcus could use to his advantage on the track.

She'd extended the same tools and insights to the second driver, Timothy, too. He didn't have a chance of winning the Drivers Championship, but his finishes had improved dramatically. Hart Racing was now in a competitive position for the Constructors Championship, too, though the two drivers would have to perform extremely well in the last three races for the company to win that trophy.

All of this work had occupied all of Lindsay's time and energy, but it didn't feel tiresome. The energy of the entire company was swelling, pushing everyone to levels of effort they didn't know they could achieve. Lindsay would work from the moment she woke to the moment she passed out on her bed, laptop open on her lap. She would dream of more improvements while she slept, then wake up and code them in.

It was all-consuming, and Lindsay loved it.

Plus, it kept her mind off of Mac.

He hadn't called, hadn't texted, hadn't even emailed since the day Marcus won at Silverstone.

That was fine with Lindsay.

Good, even.

That meant he'd finally realized what an asshole he was being.

He'd finally realized what an incredible woman he already had in Sam.

He'd chosen her, committed to her, and was building a life with her.

Lindsay was happy for them both.

Truly.

Still, she felt a twinge—just a twinge—of pain when the wedding invitations arrived.

She didn't even bother to open hers. She heard the others talking about it.

Mac's and Sam's wedding.

Everyone in the company had been invited, of course. The wedding would be held in Skipsea in six weeks, early December. Two weeks after the last race in Abu Dhabi.

The invitations were tasteful and elegant, with just a hint of panache in the choice of font to show some of Sam's character. It wasn't the curlicue calligraphy that many wedding invitations used. Instead it was a bit chunkier, a bit more industrial, while still exuding class.

It was, in short, beautiful.

From the outside, at least. Lindsay had no intention of actually opening the envelope.

She'd attend the wedding, of course. She'd be there to support both Sam and Mac, and to sincerely wish them a long and happy marriage.

But she didn't want to think about it any more than she had to.

And she really didn't have to at all. There were more important things to think about.

She dove even deeper into her work, constantly running

simulations and analyzing the results, then tweaking her algorithms and running the sims again. On the days when they weren't on the track racing, Lindsay video-called and texted and emailed Marcus and Timothy all day. On track days, she did the same all night, depending on the time zone, analyzing that day's racing.

The race team had traveled south from Austin, Texas to Mexico City for the next race. After that, São Paolo, Brazil. Then the final race of the season in Abu Dhabi.

Three more races.

And a lot of ground still to make up if they were to win a championship.

27

THE POP of the champagne cork rang like a shot in Lindsay's ear. The cheers of the crowd around her were like the crackling of flames.

People were bubbling over with energy and excitement, and they had good reason to celebrate. Marcus had won the last two races in Mexico and Brazil, bringing him into a tie for first place atop the Drivers Championship leaderboard.

And what's more, Timothy had finished second in both races, giving Hart Racing a real chance at winning the Constructors Championship. If Marcus and Timothy finished first and second in Abu Dhabi, like they'd just done in South America, Marcus Leygren and Hart Racing would go down in the history books with the greatest mid-season comeback in the history of Formula One racing.

It was all anyone could talk about, in the press and in the company.

No matter what happened with the last race, what Hart Racing had achieved in the last few months was a monumental feat, never before seen in Formula One history and unlikely to ever be repeated.

So, the people around Lindsay on the first floor of the main headquarters building, surrounded by the historic vehicles that Lindsay's father had built, the cars that had made Hart Racing what it was today, had every right to celebrate.

But Lindsay didn't want to celebrate.

She wanted to win.

She didn't want a tie for first place or a remarkable comeback. She wanted to keep working until the last car was over the line in Abu Dhabi. Until the last fan had left the stands.

If they won, fantastic. If they lost, so be it. The outcome was out of her control.

But Lindsay could control her own efforts. And she would not stop working until the season was over.

She didn't want to let her foot off the gas.

Pun intended.

So she smiled and laughed and stayed at the party as long as she felt was required for her to make an appearance and not raise any eyebrows by her absence. But then she slipped quietly out the door and down the hill to the manufacturing building and into Yue's server room, where she knew she could work uninterrupted for as long as she wanted.

Lindsay walked down between the rows of servers to the end, where she'd met Yue months ago.

Felt like years ago. Not in a bad way, but so much had changed since then.

Yue's desk was much the same as it had always been, but now there were three more makeshift desks where Marina, Raj, and Lindsay worked. Marina had a cardboard box for a desk and a torn stool for a seat. Raj had formed a kind of beanbag chair out of packing materials, where he sat cross-legged, laptop balanced on his thighs, when he worked. A huge man folded impossibly into a small seat on the floor, sometimes for hours on end. But, he said he was happy there.

Lindsay's spot had an overturned bucket for a seat and a teetering stack of empty server enclosures for a desk. Lindsay had to hold the stack of enclosures between her knees in order for it to support her laptop without falling over while she typed.

It wasn't perfect, but it was hers. And she loved it. Every time she sat there, she thought to herself that she should improve it, make it more stable or bring in a proper desk. And then, every time, she would get lost in her work and not look up until hours later.

Not perfect, but it seemed to be perfect for Lindsay.

And now, with the others still over at the celebration, Lindsay could sit in silence and lose herself in her work once more. She set her laptop on the rickety stack and opened it.

Abu Dhabi was in two weeks. That's how long they had to figure out how to beat Heingren and Bennett and all the other top drivers one more time.

The other teams were undoubtedly scrambling to figure out what Hart Racing had been doing to effect such a remarkable turnaround. Lindsay didn't think they would stoop so low as to try to hack their systems, though Raj and Yue had already taken precautions to monitor and repel such attacks. But they would certainly be talking to Hart's race team, trying to get them to divulge something, anything that could tip them off to Hart Racing's secret. And the Mercedes team had made some changes to their tactics in Brazil that suggested to Lindsay that they may be pushing their own data scientists to up their game.

Lindsay didn't care about that. Within a year or two, every race team would have sophisticated data science teams working for them. There was too much money in racing, too much notoriety, too much testosterone for the other teams not to eventually figure all of this out and look for their own way to level up their analytical capabilities.

And when that happened, Formula One would become as much a race in the stack as it was on the track. The quality of a team's data stack—including the data coming from the cars and the race conditions and the drivers, the way it was stored and aggregated, the speed and accuracy with which it was moved through the data pipelines, the ingenuity and vision with which it was used for analysis, and the vividness and usefulness of the visualizations, the screens that the race team looked at all day long—all of that would be a competitive advantage for any team that built them well and kept improving them. That was Hart Racing's advantage now, and Lindsay was sure that Mercedes and Red Bull and McLaren and all the others would have something of their own in place within a season or two.

Lindsay welcomed that change. Data science was useful, and it made her happy to see it used. She wanted the whole world to use data science. If everyone acted more logically, if everyone could synthesize all the complexity of the various data that the human body received just by walking around and being alive, take that complexity and form sound judgments from it, judgments based in data and reality, then the world would be a better place.

No, Lindsay wasn't afraid of having her technology stolen. Her approaches weren't state secrets. They were commonly used analytical techniques, available to anyone with the intelligence and determination to figure out how to use them.

The difference was that Lindsay used them better than just about anyone.

And that particular advantage could not be stolen.

"Snuck out?"

Lindsay turned to see Yue standing behind her, munching on a celery stalk, a bundle of celery and carrot sticks clutched in one hand.

"Me, too," she said. She held up the bundle in her hand. "Good snacks though."

Yue was wearing maroon overalls over a white t-shirt, one overall strap hanging loose. Lindsay noticed that the front pockets of the overalls were bulging with rolls and various party snacks that had been wrapped into cocktail napkins.

Yue followed Lindsay's eyes.

"Got cheese," she said, peering into one pocket, then another, stretching them open with her thumb, "some grapes, some of whatever those tasty little stick things were. You want some?"

Lindsay smiled and shook her head, turning back to her laptop.

The door burst open.

"Fancy meeting you two here," bellowed Raj as he and Marina stormed down the aisle between the server racks. "Ooh, are those the pesto straws," he said to Yue, helping himself to one out of her pocket. "Good snag, girl."

"You should not be calling women 'girl'," said Marina. "How would you like it if we called you 'boy'?"

"Not the same thing," protested Raj around a mouthful of pesto straws. "Not even close."

"Oh really?" said Marina.

Lindsay ground her teeth, sighed, and closed her laptop.

"You leaving?" said Raj as Lindsay squeezed past them and walked down the aisle. "We just got here. The party's just getting started."

Raj held his arms up and bumped Marina's hip with his own. Marina pushed him away.

"Where are you going?" Marina asked.

"Nowhere," muttered Lindsay over her shoulder. "I'm just tired. Think I'll go lie down for a bit."

"Lindsay," called Marina. "You feeling okay?"

Lindsay waved her hand without looking back.

She loved her friends. Loved the fact that she could even say that word, friends, and mean it. Marina, Raj, and Yue were the best friends she'd ever had. Maybe even the only friends she'd ever had.

Even more. They were her family now.

But in the last couple of days, Lindsay's patience had been wearing thin. She'd been snappy with them, which was unlike her. She'd been noticing a flash of irritation when they'd enter a room where she'd been working, like just now. It had been happening more and more.

More and more, Lindsay just wanted to be alone. To focus on her work. To lose herself in her code and her algorithms, to dive deep into the problems she was trying to solve. Problems that never lied to her, never changed their nature or shifted their position. Problems that weren't blown by the winds of passion or emotion.

Problems that may be difficult, but that she could trust. If she worked hard and worked steadily, she would eventually solve any problem. It was a straightforward agreement between Lindsay and the work, one that had never been broken.

People... were a whole different kind of problem.

Right now, Lindsay didn't need that kind of problem.

She got in her car and drove home, then idled in the driveway. She knew that Yue, Raj, and Marina would be back soon. Might be ten minutes, might be two hours, but they'd be home soon. Lindsay needed somewhere more private, somewhere she could work without having to worry about being interrupted.

She turned the car around and drove, her hands leading her without conscious thought, pulling the car into Mac's driveway next door.

Mac was with the race team in Abu Dhabi. He'd been gone for weeks, his house locked up.

Lindsay had no idea why she was sitting in his driveway.

She had no idea why she was walking to his front door. There was no one home to answer if she knocked.

She had no idea why she didn't even bother knocking, just tried the doorknob.

She had no idea why the front door to Mac's massive house was unlocked for anyone to enter.

And she had no idea why she did just that.

~

Mac's house was cool and quiet. The shades were half-drawn, slanting the low November light into soft silver shafts from the overcast sky. Lindsay felt her stress slough off, like a snake shedding her skin, the stillness and solitude of that space finally allowing her to relax.

She set her laptop on a side table and wandered slowly through the house. She wasn't looking at anything in particular, wasn't even thinking anything in particular. She was just... sensing. Feeling the space.

She pulled in a long, slow, deep breath.

A flame ignited in her core, like a basement boiler lighting after months lying cold.

She could smell him.

He'd been gone for weeks, but she could still smell him there. That spicy, earthy scent that was unmistakably Mac. It lit chemical receptors in Lindsay's brain like they'd been planted there from birth, waiting for this specific scent to bring them to life, to push some cog that would set some machine in motion, some machinery of fate that had lain dormant for twenty-six years.

Lindsay laughed softly as she continued wandering. She would let herself indulge this fantasy, just this once. In this place she shouldn't be, would never admit to having been. She would let herself have this silly, childish moment. Just this once.

She trailed a hand softly over the surfaces she passed, needing that sensation, that feeling in her body. The cool marble of the countertop in the kitchen, the wood backs of the chairs in the dining room, the subtle texture of the walls in the hallway.

And then she stood in his bedroom.

Mac's bedroom.

She'd never seen it before.

Spacious.

Unadorned.

Dark wooden platform bed, king size, beside a floor-to-ceiling window overlooking the sea. A glass door led to a small deck Lindsay could see through the drawn curtains.

Large soft rug covering a slate-tile floor.

Across the room, a leather armchair beside a lamp and a small side table piled with books.

Lindsay perused the titles, almost as a reflex.

They were books about analytics and data science.

A door led to an adjoining bath.

Soft white lights came on automatically when she entered.

Same slate tile on the floor, echoed on the walls.

Cool. Quiet.

Large doorless shower with a bench seat.

Deep, free-standing soaking tub.

Double sinks and a wide wooden vanity beneath a mirror that rose to the ceiling.

Clean. Neat.

Lindsay lifted a bottle of cologne from a small wooden shelf, closed her eyes and took a deep breath.

She saw colors behind her eyes. Blues and reds and purples, like fireworks. Her skin felt electric, like she, herself, would light the sky.

The flame in the basement boiler set fire to the first floor.

Lindsay sprayed the cologne on her wrist, rubbed her wrists together, crossed her arms like an X over her chest, her wrists up beside her neck, and breathed deep the intoxicating cloud of scent.

She could feel his hands on her arms.

She could feel his lips on her lips.

She could feel his hips hard against hers.

The flame engulfed the entire house. Lindsay moaned and shuddered.

Then stopped.

The sound of her moans echoed around the room.

She opened her eyes wide, saw herself in the long mirror.

A woman.

Alone in an empty house.

Someone else's house.

Owned by someone else's fiancé.

Lindsay slowly uncrossed the X of her arms from over her chest.

She was careful not to breathe deeply as she rinsed her wrists under hot water in the sink.

She dried her arms on a towel, smoothed her hair as she stared into her own eyes in the mirror.

She was better than this.

She did not need to sink into fantasies.

She could make a reality that would be better than fantasy.

Lindsay smoothed her hands over her hair, down the front of her shirt, pulled taut the lapels of her blazer.

She lifted her chin at her reflection in the mirror.

She was Lindsay Rhodes.

And she was better than this.

28

LINDSAY STILL COULDN'T FIND a quiet place to work undisturbed, and her irritation with the disturbances was not lessening.

She tried the office, but couldn't stand the background movement and hubbub of the workplace.

The server room was too prone to interruption from her friends, as was the kitchen at her house.

Even when she told Marina, Raj, and Yue that she needed to be left alone, when she went to her father's study for that purpose and put white noise on her headphones, still her friends could only manage to give her an hour or two before interrupting.

They had good intentions. Even through her annoyance, she could see that. They were worried about her.

But Lindsay didn't need someone to worry about her. She needed to work.

She considered renting a space in town but didn't want to waste time arranging it. She tried conference rooms at the office, squatting in empty cubicles in the production centre, even squatting at a side table in Mac's test garage at the office. Someone would always come along to interrupt, and, in the

325

garage, Gerald was nearly as irritable at having Lindsay there as Lindsay was at being distracted by Gerald's movements.

Lindsay had never had this problem before. She'd always prided herself on her ability to focus and produce high-quality work in any conditions. It was one of the many things that set her apart from the tech bros in Silicon Valley, who seemed to a man to be unable to produce without a specific brand and scent of incense burning in just the right incense holder, the programmable wifi-connected lighting set to just the right temperature and intensity, the ergonomics of their workstation dialed in by an expert, and so on.

Lindsay, by contrast, had written production-level code in the back of an Uber, during an all-hands meeting at work, even while sitting on the toilet in a restaurant during a work function. She could work anywhere, anytime.

Except, apparently, anywhere right now.

The only place she could find that set her mind at ease, that stopped her teeth from grinding, was Mac's house.

And so she'd broken in—even though the front door was unlocked, it was still unlawful entry—every day for nearly two weeks and worked for hours in the living room as the light through the windows faded from grey to black. She didn't eat. Didn't rest. Just worked.

And worked.

And avoided Mac's bedroom at all costs.

She was in constant contact with Marcus and Timothy, and the pressure was mounting. On the first day of practice sessions, they had immediately noticed a change in the tactics employed by their two closest competitors, Mercedes and Red Bull. Instead of using the sessions to practice and ingrain a pre-ordained strategy, as they usually did, both competitors were testing scenarios and variations instead, collecting and analyzing data between practice sessions, then making adjustments in the second round of practice.

They were iterating and analyzing, employing a data science approach.

They were gaining ground even faster than Lindsay had expected.

Worse, they were succeeding.

In recent races, even in the practice sessions, Marcus and Timothy had both shown a clear command of the track and the conditions, foreshadowing the outcome of the race itself days before it was run.

This time, Mercedes and Red Bull showed equal command.

The outcome of the race was no longer so certain.

Abu Dhabi was only a few hours ahead of London's time zone, so Lindsay woke early and worked in real-time with the race team. She was chatting with Raj, Yue, and Marina, as well, determinedly ignoring their questions about where she was sitting. When the race team signed off for the night, Lindsay kept working, analyzing and iterating and reprocessing the data, looking for any edge that would ensure victory.

On the second day, in qualifying, Lindsay's fears were confirmed.

Marcus, who had qualified in first place for the last eight races, came in second place, behind Tomas Heingren.

Timothy came in fifth, behind Heingren, Marcus, and the two Red Bull cars.

Lindsay, watching these results via video as they happened, jerked out of her seat. She ran her hands through her hair, pulling at the roots as if trying to pull ideas up from her brain, ideas that would guarantee a victory for Hart Racing.

She wandered through the house, her brain overclocking, reviewing every detail of the qualifying laps in her mind, looking for an answer.

She'd never thought of herself as a competitive person, preferring instead to think of herself as above the fray, not deigning to sink into the muck of competition, with its silly comparisons amongst competitors. Life was not a zero-sum game, after all.

But racing was.

If someone else won, Hart Racing lost.

Sure, it was all just a game.

But for some reason, Lindsay wanted to win it.

This time. Right now.

She wanted to win.

But how? What had given Heingren the edge in qualifying? How could Marcus and Timothy counter in the race? Starting even just one position behind could be a huge disadvantage, especially on a tight track like the one in Abu Dhabi.

And now they had to overcome that disadvantage, as well as the disadvantage of not knowing what their competitors had discovered, what tools they were using, what insights they had gleaned.

To make things worse, they wouldn't have the advantage of observing those changes over several races, then adjusting to what they learned.

No, they had only one race to figure it out.

Fifty-eight laps to analyze their opponents' strategies, identify a counter-strategy, and implement it successfully.

Lindsay wandered through the darkened halls, her mind as tangled as the hair she was pulling, unaware of where her feet were even taking her.

Until she looked up.

At herself in the mirror.

In Mac's bathroom.

Before she could even think, she pulled in a deep breath.

His scent was still there. The air was saturated with it.

Every nerve ending in Lindsay's body quivered as the scent filled her lungs.

She closed her eyes and saw the colors, saw the fireworks, felt the heat of the flames deep within her core.

Her phone rang in her pocket. She nearly leapt from her skin.

Frazzled as she was, she didn't even bother to see who was calling, just stared at herself, a ghost hovering in a soft white light in the mirror, as she brought the phone to her ear.

"Hello." Her voice was like a saw blade, torn and rasping.

"Lindsay."

Lindsay's breath caught.

Her heart stopped.

It was Mac.

Mac's voice was deep.

Raw.

Pained.

It opened a need within Lindsay that nearly brought her to her knees. A need that clawed at her skin from the inside. A need that hollowed her fiery core, ached and screamed with the emptiness.

"I need you here, Lindsay," whispered Mac.

Lindsay closed her eyes and swallowed hard.

"You do?"

"Will you come?" he asked. "Tonight?"

Lindsay opened her eyes and started. In the mirror, reflecting the soft light, streaks of tears striped her cheeks in silver.

"Yes," she whispered.

Mac was silent for a long moment.

"Good," he said, finally. "Thank you."

Lindsay felt like she were dreaming. Not the warm glow of wish fulfillment, but the off-kilter confusion, the sense of oddness that dreams can bring. Standing here, alone, in Mac's bathroom, floating in the soft light in his mirror, his voice in her head.

"I'll have Maggie prep the jet," said Mac. "You won't have time for a commercial flight. You can sleep on the plane and be here in time for the race."

The race.

He needed her for the race.

Lindsay's dream state snapped shut like a book, dropping her back into reality.

Standing in the bathroom of a house she had broken into.

"I'll bring Marina and the others," said Lindsay, her voice clipped and strong.

"Good," said Mac. Then, after a moment, he added, "Hurry."

29

It was two in the morning in England when they boarded the corporate jet from a small private airfield near the office. Marina, Raj, and Yue were all buzzing with the excitement of riding a private jet for the first time, but Lindsay didn't care about that. She went straight to the stateroom in the back of the plane and collapsed into the queen size bed there.

She was awakened hours later by a flight attendant, politely informing her that they would be landing in an hour. The flight attendant very diplomatically pointed out the private restroom and mentioned that it contained a full-size shower.

Lindsay took the hint. She hadn't showered in days.

By the time they had landed, she was refreshed and focused and ready to work.

And to win.

She'd never been to Abu Dhabi and was unprepared for the blast of dry heat she felt as she stepped off the plane onto the top of the staircase leading to the tarmac. It was like standing in front of a bread oven at full blast. The heat literally took her breath away.

She was hustled down the steps and into a waiting car,

where the air conditioning was already running at full blast. Within minutes, Lindsay was shivering.

Marina had slid into the seat beside Lindsay, with Yue and Raj traveling in an identical car behind them.

Thankfully, Marina kept silent, though Lindsay could feel Marina's eyes searching her face for any hints of her mood.

Lindsay kept her face as neutral as possible. She opened her laptop and set to work. Marina didn't press the issue, just opened her own laptop and followed Lindsay's lead.

It was already after noon. The race was at five PM.

Time was running out.

At the track, the pit crews were in full race mode. The air hung heavy with purposeful tension, every crew member focused on their task, every crew member aware of just what was at stake.

Marina, Yue, and Raj went to their places as they entered the pit bay. Lindsay strode to the front, where she knew she would find Mac.

He wore a white button-down shirt, black slacks, and black leather shoes. His outfit was business casual, but his face showed his strain. Deep worry lines arced across his forehead. They dug deep furrows between his eyes. His cheeks were hollow, like he hadn't slept or eaten in days.

From the way those lines deepened when he looked at Lindsay, he knew she looked the same to him.

"Thank you for coming," he said when she approached.

His voice was stern and professional. Strong.

In his brilliant blue eyes, Lindsay thought she could still see pain, hurt. She still didn't understand why. If anyone should be hurt, it was Lindsay.

Lindsay was the one who had been played.

Lindsay was the one who was left alone.

And yet, she could feel his pain. Even though he tried to ignore it, tried to stay focused on the race, Lindsay could feel Mac's hurt coming off of him in waves.

But on his face, at least, it was well hidden behind a wall of determination.

Whatever his personal feelings, Mac meant business today. He wanted to win as much as Lindsay did.

They all wanted to win. Lindsay had never felt such a collective force of will as she had felt when they walked into that pit bay. Even Raj, who had been joking and riffing with excitement about their plane ride, the late-night departure, the mystery and glamour of it all, fell immediately into a focused quiet, ready to work.

Lindsay pulled on her headset and adjusted the microphone in front of her lips.

"What have I missed?"

Over the next hour, Mac brought Lindsay up to speed on the events of the morning. The biggest surprise was the weather, unseasonably warm, even for Abu Dhabi. In November, temperatures were usually in the mid-eighties. But today, it was nearing a hundred degrees, making for unexpected track conditions. Teams were scrambling to adapt. They'd brought up the hot-weather tires and were adjusting the setup of the cars accordingly. They'd brought in fans and even liquid nitrogen to cool the drivers.

The heat would definitely impact their race strategy. Abu Dhabi's Yas Marina circuit had a mix of long straightaways and tight, technical corners. The high ambient temperature would soften even the hot-weather tires, providing better grip and allowing for more aggressive maneuvers on the tight curves, while the hot air would increase the risk of the engines—Mac called them "power units"—failing if they ran the cars too wide open on the long straights.

As with everything in Formula One, the conditions gave rise

to strategic tradeoffs and risks. That was what made it so interesting from a data science perspective and so exciting from a pure racing perspective. It came down to the choices the various teams made, to how they chose to respond to the conditions facing them.

And that was Lindsay's job: to figure out the best way to respond.

She sat down and got to work.

The hours passed in a blink as Lindsay updated her prediction models and flew through scenario after scenario, testing various permutations, looking for the optimal set of responses to the variety of strategies their competitors could employ against them. Before she knew it, the race crews had fallen still as first Timothy, then Marcus emerged from their prep rooms and approached their cars.

Lindsay shook Timothy's hand. He was a young driver, in just his second year, but he already had the overconfident swagger that seemed to be necessary to even contemplate racing around these tracks with nineteen other cars at two hundred miles per hour. Fortunately for Timothy, he coupled it with a keen intelligence, a thoughtful nature, and a kindness for others that helped him to see the bigger picture at all times. He was a genuinely good person, with loads of talent. Lindsay wished him luck as he clambered into his cockpit.

She walked around the corner to Marcus' bay, where he was standing beside his car, pulling on his gloves.

"You ready, boss?" he asked. His voice was light and cheerful, but the levity did not reach his eyes. Those pale blue eyes were deadly steel, focused, and hard as night.

Lindsay held those eyes, held that steely gaze with her own, and nodded.

The cars spilled from pit row, spun around the track and took their starting positions. Marcus was in the first row of the staggered two-by-two starting configuration, but sat in second place behind Heingren. Timothy was two rows back in fifth place.

The starting lights came on, five pairs of red eyes burning in the heat, hung for that interminable pause, then went dark. The whine of the engines crescendoed to a deafening roar as the racers exploded from the starting blocks.

Three cars crashed in the first turn, their drivers too aggressive, too unyielding in jockeying for position. They spun into the walls and off the track in a cloud of gravel, smoking rubber, and flying debris.

Fortunately, no one was hurt, and Marcus and Timothy had already cleared the corner before the pile-up. They sped onward, settling into a rhythm with the lead group of cars bunched tightly together, weaving through the chicanes, around the corners, and down the straights. The movement of the cars was tight, precise, at once both smooth and convulsive, like a hummingbird around a feeder, carrying the sense of both mastery and surprise needed to succeed in a Formula One race.

Lindsay and the others settled into their own routines, working through their assigned tasks, analyzing, anticipating, communicating with the drivers and each other. The work was mesmerizing, all-encompassing. Lindsay lost all sense of her surroundings, focusing so intently that all she could see in her mind was the track ahead of Marcus, overlaid with the thousands of possible futures, the permutations that each potential decision could bring.

The race was marred with accidents and malfunctions, the unexpected heat playing havoc with the field. By Lap 20, eight cars had withdrawn from the race, including the three that crashed at the start and the second driver on the Mercedes team. The red flag had already been waved several times, indicating dangerous debris on the track, calling the cars back into the pits until the track could be cleared. Once cleared, the cars re-emerged from the pits in the exact order they'd been on the track when the red flag was raised, led by a pace car. The racers weaved back and forth behind the pace car like a snake slithering along the track, warming up their tires, waiting like rabid dogs on chains, chomping and slathering, waiting for the chains to slip from their owners' hands so they could attack.

On top of that, several laps had already been run under the frozen-in-time molasses of a caution flag, where the cars crept through sections of the track where less catastrophic accidents had occurred, forbidden from changing their position in the ranking until they'd exited the section or the debris had been cleared and the green flag waved, indicating that it was safe to resume normal racing.

With the heat, the innumerable accidents and interruptions, and the tension of the standings, the afternoon quickly took on a dreamlike atmosphere. Lindsay felt like she were floating outside of her body, floating above Marcus' car as he weaved around the track. She could feel the hot breeze cooling the sweat standing on her brow as her disembodied ghost flew. The sun glared in her eyes. The dry, oppressive heat squeezed her chest like a boa constrictor. The interminable start-stop of the action heightened the tension that had them all strung tight like garrottes.

In Lap 31, one of the Red Bull cars burst into flame on the back straight, its power unit igniting as it tried to overtake Marcus. Giles Weaver, the Red Bull driver, performed gallantly in keeping his car from taking out Marcus as it snaked and juked and ultimately darted from the track into a grassy area in great brown plumes of soft sand and soil. Crews quickly extinguished the car and Weaver escaped unharmed, but the sight rattled Lindsay, reminding her of what could happen if she or the others forgot the dangers of the heat and grew too arrogant or narrow-minded in their focus on first place.

By Lap 40, with only eighteen laps remaining, the field of twenty racers had been whittled down to just nine. Heingren of Mercedes had held his lead throughout, with Marcus a close second. Thanks to Weaver's fiery exit, the second Red Bull driver, Alex Bennett, a two-time world champion himself, was in third place, followed closely by Timothy. The rest of the pack was well behind, battling for valuable points, but out of contention for the podium and the championships.

Of the three teams—Red Bull, Mercedes, and Hart Racing—vying for the Constructors Championship, only Hart Racing still had both drivers in the race. If one of them finished first, the other could place as low as third and still deliver the championship. Nothing less would suffice. They both had to be on the podium.

And one of them had to win.

"Trevor, we've got vibration in the left rear."

It was Lap 46. Twelve laps remaining.

Marcus voice was calm and strong, but Lindsay could feel the dread creep like a cloud over the pit bay. If it couldn't be easily fixed, a mechanical problem could mean the end of the race for Marcus.

Despite fierce battles to overtake, the running order remained unchanged. Timothy, in fourth place, was running less than one second behind Heingren, the leader. The combined space between the four cars was so small that a fifth car would not have fit into it. Marcus' car in second place was practically scraping Heingren's back tires, with Timothy just as close to Bennett.

"Roger that, Marcus," replied Trevor with his usual optimistic professionalism. "Let us take a look."

Sam flew around the corner from Timothy's pit bay. She stood behind Trevor, her hand on the back of his chair. Mac stood beside her, quickly joined by a small mob of engineers.

Lindsay swallowed hard and looked away when she saw Mac lay his hand casually on the small of Sam's back.

Trevor pulled up a series of telemetry screens. He and Sam and Trevor and the engineers pointed at trend lines and jabbered about heat stress and metallic expansion and bolts working loose. They ran through various scenarios. Could they run the rest of the race this way? How bad would the vibration get? How would it impact speed and handling? Could they afford to pit and change tires?

Lindsay focused on her own screens. Her fingers flew over the keyboard, entering and adjusting parameters in her predictive models as she listened, trying her best to model every scenario they discussed and give them additional points of input to consider.

"If we pit now, we can still win," said Lindsay when her rough estimates had come back. The others turned to look at her, their chatter falling dead silent. Lindsay stared right back at them, in turn. First Trevor, then Sam.

She swallowed hard, then looked at Mac.

"But we have to do it now," she whispered, her throat suddenly dry, "or it'll be too late. We'll have no chance to make up the time."

Mac stared back at her, his clear blue eyes liquid and wavering.

Or maybe it was Lindsay's eyes making them waver. Maybe it was her eyes becoming liquid.

Mac looked at Sam, raising his eyebrows.

Sam glanced at Mac, then stared long and hard at Lindsay.

Lindsay looked back calmly. She had nothing but admiration for Sam. Though the pain was like a knife in her gut every time she thought about it, Lindsay wished Sam and Mac nothing but the best.

Sam nodded slowly, a slight smile playing at the corners of her lips.

"Do it," she said.

"Bring him in, Trevor," said Mac.

Sam clapped her hands and called out to Marcus' pit bay.

"Marcus, coming in for tires," she said. "This is it, people. Make it count."

On her video feed, Lindsay watched as Marcus didn't slow down one bit, riding Heingren's rear wing until the moment he darted down pit lane, slamming on the brakes to slow to just under the speed limit, established at each track for the safety of the drivers and their crews in pit lane.

Lindsay watched as the pit crew stood poised and at the ready, tires and tools in hand, their muscles bunched and waiting, their breathing controlled, as Marcus rolled into position and jerked to a stop. What followed was a blur, so fast and so precise that Lindsay wasn't sure it had actually happened.

Car jacked and stabilized on four sides. Four tires removed. Four new tires mounted and bolted tight. Jacks removed and car dropped. Marcus accelerating back onto the track again.

Once Marcus was away, everyone in the pit stood stunned in place for a moment, then turned to a small screen in the corner that automatically measured the length of the pit stop down to a hundredth of a second.

The average Formula One pit stop lasts between 2 and 2.5 seconds. The fastest recorded pit stop was 1.82 seconds, performed by the Red Bull team at Brazil in 2019.

This pit stop came in at 1.76 seconds.

No one in the pit cheered.

There were no fist pumps or high fives.

Everyone just nodded at each other, acknowledging a job well done, then got back to business.

Silent, rock-solid determination.

Everyone knew the goal.

The goal was not to have the fastest pit stop.

The goal was to win.

30

With the speed of the pit stop, Marcus had only dropped two spots, roaring out of the pits in fourth place, ahead of the pack and right behind Timothy.

Lindsay knew it would be no cakewalk for Marcus to retake Bennett, even working together with Timothy. There were only twelve laps to go.

But she also knew that if anyone could pull it off, Marcus could.

He had the car and the skill.

And the determination.

Over the next ten laps, Marcus and Timothy worked perfectly as a team, using aerodynamics and physics to maximize their speed while putting constant pressure on Bennett, doing their best to wear him down mentally and emotionally.

No easy task. Bennett was a proven champion.

For his part, Bennett tried to take advantage of his new-found second place position by pressuring Heingren. The two competitors waged a cat and mouse battle around the track, with Marcus and Timothy nipping at their heels.

The four cars were so close together, they seemed like one vehicle.

A single misstep by any one of the drivers—a wide corner, a missed acceleration point, a stutter in the power unit—would cost them their position.

And at two hundred miles per hour, a single errant maneuver could crash all four of them in the blink of an eye.

Marcus and Timothy wore Bennett down, millimeter by millimeter, fraction of a second by fraction of a second.

Marcus had the advantage of new tires and a talented teammate, and he used both with mastery.

Halfway through the second-to-last lap, they found their moment. Timothy had pulled even enough with Bennett to force him to compromise his line around a tight sequence of corners, allowing Marcus, with his newer tires and better grip, to pass both of them, skirting aggressively around the outside and overtaking second place once more.

As often happens, when one domino falls, the others fall with it. After Marcus' maneuver, Timothy was also able to overtake Bennett, moving into third place, with Bennett tight on his heels.

Now the two Hart Racing teammates could set their sights and their strategy squarely on the leader, Heingren.

Timothy would hold off Bennett, freeing Marcus to focus entirely on the leader.

But time was running out.

There was only one lap left.

Mac turned to Lindsay.

So did Trevor and Sam and the others sitting or standing around them.

"What's the plan, Lindsay?" said Mac softly.

Lindsay pressed her lips together and exhaled slowly through her nose.

A part of her wanted to protest, to throw her hands up and ask why everyone was looking at her for answers. She was new here. She didn't know a thing about racing.

But Lindsay pushed away that thought. That was just her fear talking.

Lindsay knew this moment would come. She'd been expecting it for fifty-seven laps.

In a way, she'd been training for it for twenty-six years.

Logic over emotion.

Control over chaos.

Data over feeling.

Analysis over gut instincts.

And yet, with all of her logic, with all the control she exerted in her models over the parameters and the possibilities, with all the reams of data and sophisticated analysis she'd employed, there was no clear answer.

There were two options. Either one could work.

Neither one was certain.

One relied on Marcus. Just as at Silverstone months ago, there was a final sequence of turns that Marcus could leverage, using his newer tires to power around Heingren, just as he'd done before.

If it worked, it would bring Marcus across the line in first place, Heingren second. Timothy would come in third.

They would lose the Constructors Championship, but Marcus would win the Driver's Championship.

An incredible, historic outcome.

But there was another option.

It was riskier.

It had more moving parts, relied on more variables.

Not all of which could be controlled.

She needed more than just pure logic to make this decision.

She needed to trust her instincts.

Lindsay looked at Mac, stared hard at those electric blue eyes.

His eyes widened slightly.

She could see the pain there. She still didn't understand it.

But she could also see the determination.

He was desperate to win.

Just like Lindsay.

Would she rather play the percentages, do the logical thing, and settle for, at best, a good outcome?

Or would she rather take the riskier route and gamble for glory?

If they failed, they'd have nothing but a great season that almost was.

But if they succeeded, it would be a season that could change all of their lives forever.

A year ago, there would have been no question in her mind. She would have gone for the safe bet, the sure thing.

The logical choice.

But it had been a crazy year.

Lindsay quickly explained her recommendation to the group.

After a quick back-and-forth, Mac gave her the green light, and the decision was communicated to both drivers.

They were already halfway through the final lap.

Win or lose, succeed or fail, they would know the outcome in less than one minute.

Yas Marina Circuit can be thought of in four segments of roughly equal length.

The first segment is composed of one sharp turn and one long, arcing curve. Not overly technical, but not overly speedy, either.

The second segment is pure straightaway, a flat-out, full-throttle race.

The third segment is similar, another straight that lets the drivers throw their throttles wide open.

But the two straightaways are connected by a quick chicane, a tight left turn followed by a tight right turn. From the first straightaway, the drivers have to slam on their brakes to make it through the chicane, then accelerate as fast as they can into the second straightaway.

The last segment is a series of strategic, technical corners. They entice the foolhardy or risk-seeking driver into maintaining the speed of the straightaway, but the corners are deceptive, lulling the drivers with a few gentle turns followed by sharp, ninety-degree corners.

The risk-reward ratio is high. If a driver can pull off the impossible, carry a ton of speed into those corners and make it through without crashing, they can gain a quick advantage.

But if they can't, they'll almost certainly hit the wall and end their race, and possibly the races of the drivers around them.

Heingren, Marcus, and Timothy were barreling through the second segment of the track, down the first straightaway. All three cars, with Bennett right behind in fourth place, were wide open, driving at max speed.

Two hundred twenty miles per hour.

Headed straight for the chicane.

Time to put Lindsay's strategy to the test.

Lindsay leaned forward in her seat, her eyes glued to the video monitor.

No one in either pit bay moved a muscle, all eyes fixed on one screen or another.

Marcus, with his faster, newer tires, again ran his car just millimeters from Heingren's rear wing, gaining ground ever so slightly.

As they approached the chicane, in the fraction of a second when Heingren started braking and Marcus would have followed suit, Marcus instead swung to the inside, trying to carry just a bit more speed into the turn, gaining an edge on Heingren.

It was the same maneuver that had won him the race in Silverstone. The same trick that had caught Heingren by surprise four months earlier.

This time, Heingren was ready.

Heingren kept just enough speed, ran just enough of a risk into the corner to force Marcus to back off at the last second, slamming on his brakes to avoid ramming Heingren and driving them both into the wall.

Marcus slid back behind Heingren.

The maneuver had failed.

Just like Lindsay wanted.

~

The cars flew through the third segment of the circuit, the second straightaway, throttles open wide, engines screaming in the baking sun.

At the end of this straightaway was a long, sweeping left-hand curve, followed by two gentle right-hand arcs that led to a sharp, ninety-degree right.

As they sped around the left-hand curve, Marcus, with his faster tires, moved to Heingren's right side, trying to overtake him by brute force, simply by running faster around the longer line on the outside of the curve.

Marcus gained ground on Heingren, his front tires coming about halfway up Heingren's chassis, even with the cockpit.

But Heingren was a cagey veteran. He knew the optimal race line and he knew what the rules allowed when it came to defending his lead. He angled Marcus farther and farther off-line, pushing him toward the wall, forcing Marcus to decide whether to back off or risk hitting the wall at over two hundred miles per hour.

Marcus backed off, then pressed forward again for the right-hand curves, trying the same tactic. He again came around Heingren's outside, now on the left of Heingren's car, and tried again to outrace him around the curves.

As before, Heingren forced Marcus toward the wall. This time, Marcus held on a bit longer, encouraged Heingren to maintain his speed a touch longer, before Marcus backed off and the two cars braked hard and worked through the sharp ninety-degree right-hand turn.

There were only four turns left on the track, two hard lefts, a slightly softer right, and one final turn, a right-hand turn of more than ninety-degrees, that led to the finish line.

Time was running out.

Lindsay could do nothing but sit and watch, just like everyone else. Her fingers itched to type something, anything. To put in parameters, to write some code, to run her models to predict the most likely outcomes.

But the race would be over before she even finished typing.

She ignored the prediction algorithm on the screen in her peripheral vision. It predicted a victory for Heingren.

It was wrong.

Or so Lindsay hoped.

She blocked out the screen and blocked out the thought, leaning in and focusing one hundred percent of her attention on the video feed of what was happening on the track in real-time.

Four turns to go.

As before, Marcus carried more speed into the sharp left

turns than he normally would, pushing himself and his car to the limits while trying to squeeze ahead of Heingren.

And just as before, Heingren was ready, maintaining his own speed just enough to keep Marcus at bay.

In the next curve, Marcus pushed even more, holding a bit more speed than the last time, forcing Heingren to push his own car past his comfort zone.

Two curves left, the softer right and the sharp final curve.

Marcus drove his car to its limits, and then some. He again swung to the outside, trying once again to outrace Heingren around the softer right-hand curve.

Once again, Heingren fended him off, boosting his own speed even more to do so.

As a result, both Marcus and Heingren were carrying a lot of speed into the last turn.

Far more speed than was prudent.

Far more speed than either driver would normally carry.

Still Marcus pushed even harder, diving toward the right side of the track, racing for the inside line, delaying his braking even more than he had in the previous turns, even more than he had in previous races.

He delayed his braking longer than any driver would ever recommend.

Lindsay could feel the tension all around her. Every crew member, every mechanic and engineer, every analyst and liaison was dead silent, focused, wound so tight Lindsay could practically hear the tension thrumming in the air.

They knew Marcus was laying it all on the line.

Trusting in his newer tires.

Trusting in his own abilities.

Trusting in Lindsay's strategy.

Whether religious or not, everyone was praying that fate would keep Marcus' car off the wall, would keep his tires on the track, would keep his car from touching Heingren's and crashing both cars mere feet from the end of the race.

All anyone could do was watch.

Lindsay wasn't praying, but she looked like she was. Her hands were clenched together, held up over her mouth, her eyes wide and staring at the screen in front of her, watching the action taking place on the track just a few hundred yards behind her.

Marcus and Heingren were entering the final turn, a sharp right, engines screaming.

Once through this curve, the finish line was mere yards away.

Marcus was on the inside, employing the same tactic he'd used for the last several turns.

Only this time, the curve was even sharper, more than ninety-degrees.

This time, Marcus was carrying even more speed.

Heingren matched his speed, the two cars moving side by side, their tires practically rubbing together.

Neither driver touched the brake as the curve approached.

Neither driver gave up a single inch.

Each waited for the other to yield.

Each held on, millisecond by millisecond.

Daring the other.

Playing with fate.

Holding on.

Holding.

Finally, long after common sense and sheer self-preservation would dictate, both men braked.

Hard.

Heingren, on the outside, with a longer line, cracked first, braked mere milliseconds before Marcus.

At those speeds, the cars moved more than three hundred feet in one second.

A difference of one millisecond equated to a difference of four inches.

With that tiny difference, a difference of inches, Heingren, against the wall, fell behind Marcus.

But both men had braked far too late to maintain their speed or their lines.

Both men overshot the curve, lost their lines, had to over-correct.

And Timothy, who had stayed close behind both cars throughout the entire battle, waiting, watching, shot by both men on the inside.

Into the lead.

~

Men are simple creatures.

Smart, but simple.

Especially when their egos are involved.

And if there was one thing Lindsay had noticed about Formula One, it was the sheer amount of male ego swirling around the paddock.

Lindsay's strategy had been for Marcus to lull Heingren into a one-on-one battle. To lull him into thinking only about Marcus.

And to make Heingren think he knew what Marcus' strategy would be, how Marcus would try to win the race.

She wanted Heingren to believe that Marcus was using the same tactics that had brought him to victory in Silverstone.

Ego or not, Heingren and the men on the Mercedes team were smart.

They learned fast, and they didn't forget.

But on top of that, the Mercedes team had a bunch of new

data scientists, recently hired to try to counter what Lindsay and her team were doing at Hart Racing.

Their mistake was in hiring all men, men who were eager to prove their intelligence to their new bosses.

Men with giant egos.

Lindsay hadn't met the new analysts in person yet, but they had been hired from Silicon Valley. She knew them, recognized their names. She'd either observed them from a distance or, in one case, worked for them in the past.

They were arrogant as hell.

They would assume they knew everything, that their ideas were brilliant and innovative. They would assume without even meeting anyone that they were the smartest people on the track.

Lindsay had been counting on it.

She had Marcus play into that arrogance. She had him feed those assumptions by employing techniques and strategies that she'd used in the past.

She hoped the men would assume Lindsay could think of nothing new, that she was just recycling the same old ideas, hoping they'd work again.

In their arrogance, that's exactly what they did.

Lindsay was willing to bet it had never crossed their minds that Marcus might not be trying to win the race at all.

Inflamed male egos couldn't conceive of that possibility.

They couldn't conceive of the possibility that Marcus might be trying to help his teammate win, instead.

They couldn't conceive of it, so that's exactly what Lindsay did.

Timothy sped by Marcus and Heingren on the inside.

Marcus braked hard to avoid the wall, then darted forward again, racing for the finish.

Marcus was ahead of Heingren. Only by a few inches, but a few inches might as well be a mile in the final yards of a race. He had the advantage and the angle. Heingren could do nothing but tuck in behind Marcus.

So far, everything had gone according to Lindsay's strategy. The only question, the only uncertainty in her plan, was Bennett.

Timothy was now in first place, but Bennett had been hot on his heels.

A first-second or first-third finish would win the Constructors Championship for Hart Racing. It didn't matter which driver came in first, as long as one of them did.

But Marcus had to finish ahead of both Heingren and Bennett in order to win the Drivers Championship. If Timothy came in first, then Marcus had to finish second.

Marcus had known that. Lindsay had made it clear when she communicated the strategy to him. She'd given him the choice to play for the individual victory or the team victory.

Marcus hadn't hesitated. He had chosen to employ the strategy that would deliver victory for the team, even if it meant sacrificing victory for himself.

But there was still a chance for him.

He was ahead of Heingren. If he could come off the wall and stay ahead of Bennett, Hart Racing would win the Constructors and Marcus would win the Drivers Championship.

It was a dicey thing. Marcus had compromised his speed and his line to fend off Heingren and open a space for Timothy.

Now he had to recover that speed and regain that line before Bennett drove into the same gap Timothy had seized.

Marcus came off the wall, Heingren behind him, and started back to the inside of the track, desperately trying to regain the optimal race line before Bennett got there.

Marcus' reaction time was lightning-fast. He'd been off the wall and accelerating in fractions of a second.

But Bennett was too quick, too experienced.

He'd already filled the space Marcus wanted.

Marcus couldn't take it without crashing both cars.

Timothy was on the inside, Bennett right behind him. Marcus was beside Bennett, tire for tire, running along the wall.

They came around the curve, nothing but straight track between them and the finish line.

The checkered flag was waving.

Just a few hundred yards to the end of the race, the end of the season.

All Lindsay could do was watch.

All Marcus could do was race.

Straight ahead. Wide open to the finish.

May the fastest car win.

Lindsay squeezed her hands together in front of her face, the knuckles turning white with the pressure as she stared at her video monitor.

Timothy held the clear lead, running down the inside of the track, headed for the finish with no one to stop him.

Marcus and Bennett were in a dogfight, side-by-side just behind Timothy, in a sprint to the finish line.

Marcus had faster tires, but he was forced to run beside the wall. The line along the wall was rough with tiny bits of rubber that had fallen from the tires over the course of the race. The rubber came off during cornering, the natural side effect of speed and pressure, and came to rest in piles off the racing line. The drivers called them marbles, because when you drove over them, the car had a tendency to lose grip, as if you were driving over a pile of glass marbles.

Marbles were a natural part of every race, but they always fell outside the optimal racing line. Because they got between the tires and the track and disrupted the traction, reducing speed and handling, the drivers never wanted to have to drive through them.

Marcus had to drive through them now.

On her monitor, Lindsay could see the car jumping and jittering, uncertain on the marbles beneath it, the tires searching for solid purchase on the asphalt.

Bennett drove alongside, unyielding. The consummate professional.

He was pulling ahead.

Marcus was falling behind.

Lindsay watched, helpless.

Her strategy had failed.

Failed Marcus, at least.

He'd sacrificed his own personal achievement to deliver a team victory, but Lindsay had hoped her strategy would deliver both.

Marcus had earned it, and Lindsay wanted to help him win it.

But that part of her strategy was outside of her control.

She couldn't control Bennett, couldn't guarantee that he would be far enough behind Timothy to allow Marcus to take second place.

She'd gambled on that aspect of the strategy.

And she'd failed.

Marcus was running in the marbles, running just a hair behind Bennett.

Timothy would come in first, Bennett second.

And Marcus would come in third.

Lindsay fell back in her chair, releasing a long, defeated sigh.

And then she saw brake lights on her screen.

Brake lights on Timothy's car.

Just a touch.

Just a tap on the brakes, a blink of red on the back of Timothy's vehicle.

But it was enough to force Bennett to do the same, to tap his own brakes.

Enough to let Marcus, on the outside of the track, fly by them both.

Into the lead.

Marcus had sacrificed his own victory to let the team win.

And now, in a heartbeat, in the blink of an eye, Timothy had returned the favor, putting Marcus into the lead, with Timothy in second place.

They crossed the finish line that way, a one-two finish, the checkered flag waving madly over their heads.

31

THE CROWD ROARED SO LOUD, Lindsay could hear it through the noise cancellation of her headphones, could feel the vibration through her chair.

The pit bay erupted. People leapt from their seats, leapt into each other's arms. They shook hands and slapped each other's backs and hugged each other fiercely. People were laughing, even crying. They stared incredulously into space, hands on their heads, disbelief on their faces.

It was bedlam.

And sheer, unadulterated joy.

For her part, Lindsay just sat in stunned silence, people cheering all around her, staring at the video screen.

Her mind, normally quick as lightning, was struggling to process what had just happened.

In the space of less than one second, her strategy had succeeded, then it had failed, and then it had succeeded again in the most unexpected way.

A way she had not predicted.

A way she had not controlled.

And now, sitting there, her own dream—her newfound dream, a dream she hadn't even known she wanted, a dream that had fallen into her lap eight months earlier, unbidden, unforeseen, unanticipated—had come true.

She stood in a daze and turned toward the crowd behind her.

Marina, Raj, and Yue raced around the corner, screaming like their heads were on fire.

Marina threw herself at Lindsay, hugging her so tight Lindsay lost her breath.

Yue, normally so stoic, was screaming like a schoolgirl, holding Lindsay's shoulders and bouncing up and down.

Raj swept them all into a massive bear hug and picked them up off their feet, bellowing at the top of his lungs with joy.

The shock finally fell from Lindsay's mind and she screamed, too. It was a tepid, quiet squeak at first, but then it swelled, grew of its own will into a primal roar that seemed to pucker Lindsay's toes from the inside.

She threw her head back and roared at the ceiling, at the sky.

She roared for the joy of winning, of working so long and so hard toward this goal and having it finally, fully, completely come true.

She roared for the joy of her friends, holding her.

She roared for the joy of her mother, who, despite all her shortcomings, had always loved Lindsay and wanted nothing but success for her.

She roared for the joy of her father, a man Lindsay had never known in person, but one she felt she knew now, in that moment, in that place, with all of those people, his people, around her.

His dream.

Now her dream, too.

His life.

Now her life, too.

His family.

Lindsay swallowed hard, cutting her scream short, her cheeks suddenly wet and stinging.

His family.

Now her family, too.

Raj finally lowered them all.

Lindsay held her friends.

Her family.

After one last group hug, Lindsay turned in a circle, looking around her.

Looking for Mac.

As tall as she was, looking across a sea of heads, across a storm of celebrations, she couldn't see him.

He was probably with Sam.

Lindsay sighed.

Just as well.

She looked for Sam's dark dreadlocks in the crowd, thought she caught a glimpse of them hugging someone, but it looked like she was hugging a woman, not Mac.

Before Lindsay could look any longer, the crowd surged out toward the track to greet the drivers, pulling her along with it.

On the track, Marcus and Timothy hoisted themselves out of their cockpits and stood on their chassis, holding their arms up toward the fans going mad in the stands above them. Marcus leapt from his car and ran back to Timothy, lifting him down off of his car and sitting him on one of Marcus' shoulders for a moment, pointing at Timothy and shaking a triumphant fist toward the crowd before letting Timothy drop down into Marcus' warm embrace.

And then Lindsay saw him, Mac, there with the drivers.

Her heart climbed into her throat.

Mac was greeting Marcus and Timothy, hugging them, beaming and cheering for the crowd and the cameras.

In the crowd, champagne appeared like magic, a seemingly endless supply, corks popping and champagne spraying everywhere, stinging Lindsay's eyes and leaving her skin sticky and sweet. She laughed with the others more corks popped and the spray became a shower, then a downpour, dripping from her hair and her eyelashes, her shirt already soaking through.

Lindsay pushed through the crowd, trying to reach Mac.

What she would do when she found him, she didn't know.

She didn't want to think about it.

She just knew she wanted to see him.

To stand with him.

To feel his heat.

To feel his arms around her.

To feel his hands on her body.

Lindsay shuddered involuntarily as a wash of heat swept through her.

She pushed through the press of the celebrations, finally breaking through to where the cars were stopped.

She caught a glimpse of the back of Mac's white shirt disappearing back into the crowd, moved to follow.

"Lindsay Rhodes!"

Marcus wrapped her in a huge hug.

"Lindsay!" called Timothy, wrapping his arms around her, too.

They spun her to face the stands, Lindsay standing between the two drivers, their arms over her shoulders. The fans cheered as Timothy and Marcus pumped their fists.

They turned in a slow circle, first toward the press, cameras snapping madly, then toward the crew, who cheered anew and sprayed more champagne. It sprayed in Lindsay's face, flew into her mouth. She coughed and swallowed and laughed and cheered with everyone else.

Even as she did, her eyes swept the crowd.

Mac had disappeared again.

~

By the time things had settled down and Lindsay had found Sam, she told Lindsay that Mac had already left. Caught an early flight home. Had to take care of some things, Sam said, shrugging, relaying the vague reason Mac had given her.

She seemed as puzzled as Lindsay as to why Mac would leave his team—and his fiancé—so soon after such a huge victory. He should be celebrating until the wee hours of the morning.

Lindsay and her crew did their celebrating in the air. The flight back on the private jet was boisterous and loud, the plane already stocked with champagne chilling on ice.

Lindsay drank more than she normally would. She wasn't wasted, but it was enough for her to pass out on the bed from a mix of alcohol, dehydration, and sheer fatigue.

When they landed, it was, indeed, the wee hours of the morning, and everyone was exhausted. They piled into a waiting car, got out at Lindsay's house, and flopped into their beds with barely a word to each other.

Thankfully, miraculously, Lindsay didn't have a hangover the next morning.

Must have been good champagne.

As she sipped her first espresso, she heard a knock and rushed to the front door, hoping to see Mac standing on the doorstep.

A memory of their last meeting on the doorstep flashed through her mind.

And her body.

She felt her cheeks flush, then chided herself for fantasizing about a man who would be married to someone else in just two weeks.

She took a deep breath, smoothed her hair, and pulled open the door.

"Hello, Lindsay," said Maggie, "and congratulations."

Maggie stood in a cream pantsuit with matching heels, her hair done in a stylish curl. Even at seven-thirty in the morning, she was the epitome of professionalism and class.

As happy as Lindsay was to see Maggie, her heart fell once she realized it wasn't Mac.

"What a performance yesterday," Maggie said. "Absolutely thrilling to watch. And from what I've been told, you were the mastermind behind that brilliant strategy in the last lap. Well done, my dear. Very well done."

Lindsay thanked her and invited Maggie in. She pulled a shot of espresso for her and a second shot for herself.

"I'm not here for a social call, unfortunately," said Maggie.

Lindsay set their drinks down and sat beside Maggie at the kitchen table. The sunlight was bright through the windows, gilding Maggie's profile like she were an angel glowing with the beatific power of the heavens.

Maggie lifted her satchel and pulled a sheaf of papers from it. "And I'm afraid you'll need to hurry to get ready. You have an important meeting to attend this morning."

"A meeting with who?"

"With the principals of Everbright Securities Group, LLP." Maggie tapped the papers on the table to tidy the stack, then set them down and turned them so Lindsay could see.

It was a sales contract.

For the sale of Hart Racing, Inc.

For the sum of five billion British pounds.

In cash.

Five.

Billion.

Pounds.

Nearly six billion US dollars.

The number took Lindsay's breath away.

She had read that phrase a thousand times in books, always thinking it was a literary flourish, a poetic metaphor.

Now she knew it wasn't. She literally could not pull breath into her lungs for a long moment. Her chest was tight, the muscles frozen, an odd panic creeping up the skin of her throat.

"I... I don't understand, Maggie." Lindsay shook her head, once she'd regained the ability to breathe. "I thought we'd already discussed this. I'm not interested in selling my share of the company."

"Yes, I know," nodded Maggie slowly.

She turned the pages over one by one, setting them upside down in a neat pile as she did so.

She came to a signature page at the end of the pile and pointed, tapping a line at the bottom.

Lindsay looked at the signature there.

"Cormac McEwan", it read.

Mac's signature was large and flowing, a beautiful mix of sweeping curves and bold angles. His signature reminded Lindsay of the man himself. She ran her fingers over the page. It felt like it had been so long since she'd seen him, she just wanted to stare at his signature for a while.

But not on this document.

"Mac wants to sell?" Lindsay whispered. Her mouth felt like it were stuffed with cotton balls.

"He signed the agreement," said Maggie.

"He's selling his share?"

"No," said Maggie. She touched Lindsay's arm. Lindsay looked up from the page, from her swirling, confused thoughts, and focused on Maggie's pointed stare. "He signed an agreement to sell the whole company."

Lindsay furrowed her brow and shook her head. Maggie was trying to tell her something, but Lindsay wasn't quite getting it.

"The agreement requires your signature, too."

Lindsay sat back in her chair.

Mac was giving her an out.

Her comments when she'd first come to England. Her comments during the event at Silverstone. She hadn't spoken to him about selling the company in months. As far as he knew, that was still what she wanted.

And he was willing to give it to her.

Why?

"Even if he thought I still wanted to sell my share, why would he sell his share, too?"

Maggie smiled kindly, like a patient teacher explaining a basic concept to a struggling student for the hundredth time.

"Hart Racing is the last Formula One team that is family-owned," she said. "I don't think Mac could stand it if this place became like all the other corporations out there. And that's what a private equity firm would do."

"But they couldn't make any changes without Mac's approval. The ownership share is fifty-fifty."

Again, Maggie gave Lindsay that patient smile.

"And how long would you last against constant pressure to change?" she said. "Especially if you were on the road most of the year and your partners were staying behind, free to make whatever changes they felt necessary?" She tilted her head. "And even if you could withstand the pressure, would you want to? Year after year?"

Lindsay tried to imagine it. For her, the corporatization of Hart Racing would be a gut punch. It would drain the life out of her, like all the corporations she'd ever worked for had in the past. It would grind her down, little by little, sucking the life from her, sucking the joy and the energy from her until she was just a shell who would go along with anything the corporation asked.

She couldn't imagine Mac working like that.

She couldn't imagine him living like that.

She didn't want to imagine him that way.

Maggie set one hand on top of Lindsay's.

"Everbright has lawyers," she said. "Good ones." She sat back in her chair. "Believe me, I know. I trained one or two of them at my firm. They would find a way—a legal way—to do whatever it is they wanted to do." She tilted her head down, staring hard at Lindsay. "And it would not be motivated by a sense of family."

"And Mac wouldn't want to stay here and watch his family fall apart around him," muttered Lindsay.

Maggie nodded.

There were a thousand thoughts swirling through Lindsay's head in that moment, a jumble of feelings and ideas.

But they all centered around one thing.

Lindsay knew exactly what she needed to do.

"What time is the meeting?" she asked.

"Ten o'clock," said Maggie. She checked her watch. "Two hours from now. In the Alfa conference room."

Lindsay started. "That's the room where you first read my father's will to me and Mac."

Maggie shrugged, that hinting smile tugging at the corners of her mouth.

"It seemed fitting," she said.

Lindsay nodded slowly. This woman, Maggie. A shrewd businesswoman. A brilliant lawyer. A kind and warm mother figure.

And smart as a fucking cattle prod.

Two hours.

Lindsay needed to get ready.

32

LINDSAY UNZIPPED the new pantsuit from its garment bag. Dark wool, a charcoal grey that was nearly black, with a white muslin wrap-top double-gauze blouse that tied just above the waist. A professional look. With a sexy, modern twist.

And when you added in the reddish-brown herringbone-patterned heeled boots Lindsay wore with the suit: bad-ass.

"Damn," said Marina as she wandered into Lindsay's bedroom. "What corporate boardroom are you about to take over?"

"My own," said Lindsay, smiling.

As Lindsay brushed out her hair, she told Marina about Everbright Securities, about the offer they'd made, how they'd been ramping up the purchase price with each attempt, with each new **success** for Hart Racing on the track.

She told Marina what Mac had done.

And what Lindsay was about to do.

Lindsay gave a wry smile. "Call it an early wedding present."

Marina frowned.

"For who?"

"For Mac. Who else?" Lindsay shrugged. "Well, for Sam, too, I suppose."

Marina shook her head, confused.

"Wait. Who do you think is getting married?"

Lindsay turned to Marina and released a long sigh.

"How do I look?"

"Like a bad-ass business beeyotch," said Marina, nodding.

Lindsay smiled and strode from the room. She stopped in the kitchen to gather her things. Laptop, car keys, her copy of the purchase contract.

Marina followed her.

"Is Mac going to be there?" Marina said. "In the meeting?"

Lindsay shrugged.

"I don't know for sure. I imagine so." She sighed again. "I hope so."

She wanted him to see her face, to see her eyes.

She wanted to see his, too.

"You should open this," said Marina, handing Lindsay an envelope. "And read it."

Lindsay looked at what Marina was holding. It was Sam's wedding invitation.

"I know what it says."

"I don't think you do," said Marina.

Lindsay shoved everything into her bag and slung it over her shoulder.

"Later, then," said Lindsay. "I'm a little busy at the moment."

Marina pulled at Lindsay's bag, opening it, and stuffed the invitation inside.

"Promise me you'll read it. Before the meeting."

"Bye, Marina." Lindsay headed for the garage. "I'll be back in a few hours."

"Promise me," called Marina down the hallway.

Lindsay waved one hand without looking back.

∽

When Lindsay pulled up to Hart Racing's main headquarters, her heart nearly stopped.

Mac was standing out front, waiting with Maggie. He was wearing a tailored grey suit, white button-down, and a dark grey tie.

Even from a distance, he looked hot. Just watching his profile, standing with his feet apart, his hands in his pockets, his head tilted down toward the sidewalk, Lindsay could feel her mouth water.

Among other things.

Lindsay had been practicing her driving. She wheeled the Jaguar smoothly through the parking lot, downshifting perfectly, letting the engine help slow the car just like Mac had taught her. She steered it into the parking spot right in front of Mac and switched the car off like a pro.

"You look wonderful, my dear," said Maggie as Lindsay approached, admiring Lindsay's outfit from head to toe. "Bella Potenza?"

Lindsay nodded and thanked her, explaining that she'd placed an order for several new pantsuits at Maggie's favorite boutique just a few weeks after the formal event at Silverstone.

Lindsay beamed at Mac. His outfit was immaculate, but he looked miserable, like he hadn't slept in days and had eaten nothing but lemons and hot sauce. Permanent indigestion.

"Hello, Mac," said Lindsay.

He didn't respond, wouldn't even make eye contact. He just stared at the ground. His pockets bulged, his hands curled into fists inside.

Lindsay gestured toward the car. "I drove the Jag. Stick shift. Learned from the best."

Mac nodded slowly, his face grim. He looked at the car, but still wouldn't look at Lindsay. Instead, he turned and walked into the building.

Lindsay felt like she was going to throw up, her insides

suddenly hollow and cold. She didn't know what she had done to make Mac so angry with her.

But he certainly didn't look like a man who was getting married in two weeks. If she had somehow upset him so much that it impacted his wedding to Sam, Lindsay would never forgive herself.

"Come, my dear," said Maggie. "Let's get this over with."

The sale.

Of course. That had to be it.

Mac was devastated about selling the company.

Lindsay would be, too.

But she was about to make Mac a very happy man.

Mac held the conference room door open for Maggie, who walked in first. Lindsay could hear her greeting the people inside as she approached the doorway.

Mac held the door for Lindsay, too, a gentleman to the last, but still would not make eye contact with her.

As Lindsay came close to him, she could smell his scent, that mix of spice and musk. She saw fireworks, pops of blue and purple behind her eyes. Her skin felt electric, just like it had, alone in his bathroom that day.

That day, the sensation had been powerful. Now, with the source of the scent himself standing right beside her, his heat washing over her, it was overwhelming.

Lindsay's knees nearly gave out. She staggered against the doorjamb.

Mac's hand shot forward, gripping Lindsay's elbow to steady her.

At his touch, lightning shot through her like fire. From where his hand touched her, it coursed through her entire body. Her breath caught and her eyes whipped to his.

He looked back.

Finally, he looked back at her, his brilliant blue eyes wide and blazing.

His gaze was like a spark to tinder. It set a fire alight inside her.

She could see it burning in him, too. She could see it in his eyes, could feel it through his touch.

The fire grew higher, hotter.

In a moment, it would leap across the inches between them, set them both ablaze.

Mac dropped his hand from her elbow.

His eyes went cold again.

Cold and dead.

He looked away, stepped past her into the conference room.

Lindsay hesitated for a moment, leaning against the doorway, her mind reeling once more. Her heart pounded in her chest, like it would break through her rib cage at any moment and leap to an anguished death, bursting apart on the floor.

She took a deep, long breath to steady herself, to collect herself.

To remember what she needed to do.

Lindsay stood tall and straight, and strode into the room.

Soft morning light streamed through the wall of windows that looked out over the lake and the trees beyond. The sun was already coming through the breaking clouds, warming the chill December air. Great swaths of blue filled the sky beyond.

It was going to be a beautiful day.

There were three representatives from Everbright Securities standing beside the conference table, shaking hands with Maggie and Mac. One older gentleman, slim and greying, wearing a very expensive suit, was clearly the principal. He introduced himself as John Everbright.

The founder of the company.

He introduced the others as his children: his son, Thomas

Everbright, and his daughter, Amelia Everbright. Both were about Lindsay's age. Professional, confident. Judging by their clothes and briefcases, clearly wealthy, like their father.

They'd brought the big guns to close the deal.

Lindsay was honored, oddly enough. It was thoughtful and considerate of them to show such respect to Hart Racing. Apparently, five billion pounds was as big a number to Everbright Securities as it was to Lindsay.

Lindsay shook their hands, thanked them for coming, and asked everyone to be seated.

She remained standing while they sat.

This was her meeting.

She didn't call it, but she sure as hell was going to run it.

"I've reviewed your offer," Lindsay began. "The terms seem fair and equitable. The purchase price is reasonable."

The older gentleman, John, leaning back in his chair, his hands steepled before him, raised his eyebrows at that, but said nothing. The pleasant expression on his face never wavered for a moment.

His children darted glances at him, then at each other.

Lindsay clocked the subtle movements all at once, processed them in a flash.

The older man, John, was in charge. Lindsay could focus on him.

"Before I sign this document, though," Lindsay continued, "I have a few questions for you." Lindsay stared directly at John.

"Our intentions are honest and honorable, Ms. Rhodes," said John, spreading his hands wide, his smile broadening. "We have nothing to hide here. Please ask us anything you like."

"What is your definition of family?" asked Lindsay.

John's eyebrows shot up at that, the smiling façade on his face cracking just a bit.

Good. Lindsay wanted to get past the corporate bullshit and get to some real truth.

To his credit, John didn't ask for clarification or mutter some stupid filler phrase to stall for time, as most corporate blowhards would. The question had surprised him, but the words were clear enough. After a moment of shock, he considered his response.

"For me," he said, "my family is my wife and our two children." He gestured to Thomas and Amelia.

"That's who your family is, but what does family mean to you?"

"Ms. Rhodes," began Thomas, "I don't see how this is relevant—"

His father held up a hand, silencing him.

"It's alright, Thomas," he said quietly. He turned back to Lindsay. "For me, my family is my legacy."

"Is that all?" said Lindsay.

"No." John smiled, a bit sadly. "It's also my responsibility. To raise my children. To educate them. To provide for them." His brow furrowed. "To protect them and my wife as best I can."

Lindsay nodded, encouraging him to continue.

"They're also the source of my strength," he said softly. He chuckled. "What strength I have, anyway."

The two children squirmed a bit in their seats. They clearly weren't expecting a business meeting to delve into such personal territory.

But that's exactly where Lindsay wanted to go.

"You love your family." Lindsay didn't say it as a question. It was clear that John Everbright was a family man.

His expression proved it. Fierce and determined. This was a man who would give up anything and everything, without hesitation, to save his family.

"With every fiber of my being," he said, his voice low and serious.

His children's heads whipped to stare at him at the words, their faces open and astonished.

They covered the expressions quickly, returning them to professional neutrality. They were good. Well-trained in business dealings, where it's best to hold your emotions close to your vest.

But Lindsay had seen their initial reactions.

John Everbright loved his family more than his own life, but his kids didn't necessarily realize that fact.

Lindsay knew the feeling.

"Kellen Hart, my father, started this company." Lindsay smiled, pacing slowly at the head of the conference table. "Started it when he was thirty years old." She looked at John. "I never met my father. Never even spoke to him."

John glanced at his children, a guilty, furtive glance.

Lindsay looked at Thomas and Amelia. "My mother and I lived in America. She told me my father didn't want anything to do with us."

Thomas looked down at his hands, seeming uncomfortable. But Amelia held Lindsay's gaze, her brown eyes clear, interested. Maybe even calculating. She glanced casually at her brother's movements, then back at Lindsay.

The Everbrights had their own family drama. That much was clear.

"I don't know why my mother said that," Lindsay continued, "but it wasn't true. When he died, my father left half of his company to me."

Lindsay looked up at the ceiling, around the room, out the broad windows that overlooked the lake. It still astounded her that her father had built this magnificent company. Even more so that he had left half of it to her.

"At first, I didn't care. I had my own company back in San Francisco, a startup that I was working to build. I hoped to come to England, sell everything off, and get back home within a week."

She laughed.

"I never met my father, but somehow I think he knew me, anyway." She glanced at Mac, who was staring out the window. Was that a glistening in the corner of his eye? Or was it just the light playing tricks? "He set some provisions in his will to make sure I couldn't sell the company so impulsively." She shrugged. "If he'd died sooner, or if Maggie had been able to contact me earlier, things might have been different."

"Ms. Rhodes," said Thomas, clearing his throat, "as interesting as this is, perhaps we can catch up on family history after we've signed the paperwork?"

John glowered at his son. Amelia watched her brother with that same clear-eyed stare, detached and observant. Thomas shrugged at his father, palms up, mouthed the word "What?"

Lindsay just smiled.

"Forgive me," she said. " You're right. I'll get to the point."

Lindsay picked up the purchase agreement lying before her on the table, flipped through the pages, then pulled the last sheet, the signature sheet, from the stack.

She stared down at it. John Everbright's signature was there, sharp and short and confident. The signature of a man who signed a lot of documents.

Maggie's neat, curling signature was there as a witness.

And Mac's signature.

Lindsay stared at it for a moment.

What had he been thinking when he signed? Was he distraught? Angry? Was he relieved to be done with it? With Lindsay?

It couldn't be about the money for Mac. He was already a wealthy man.

If Lindsay signed, she would be wealthy, too. One of the wealthiest people in the world. She would never have to work again. She could spend the rest of her life experimenting, funding moonshot ideas and research proposals, stepping off of the bleeding edge of data science into the unknown that lay even in front of that. She would be a pioneer. She would break new ground, cut the paths that people would follow for generations. It would be a dream come true.

Lindsay held the paper up in front of her and tore it in half, slowly.

The sound filled the room like she were tearing the air itself, tearing the earth in two.

Thomas gasped and Amelia stared, open-mouthed in astonishment.

Maggie just watched, that maddening smile on the corners of her lips.

John, too, seemed to smile to himself as he leaned back in his chair and regarded Lindsay.

Mac's head whipped away from the window, eyes wide.

Lindsay stared at Mac as she tore the rest of the paper, the sound rising and quickening like the crack of a whip.

Mac's surprised eyes watched, then clouded. He scowled and looked back out the window.

Lindsay started at that, but covered it well.

"I won't sell my father's company, Mr. Everbright." Lindsay lay the torn halves of paper on the table. "Do you see why?"

John smiled at Lindsay, but his smiled faded to a look of wistful sadness. He looked out the window for a long moment, then looked back at Lindsay.

He nodded. "I do, Ms. Rhodes." He glanced at his children. "Hart Racing is your family now."

"Hart Racing is my father's family," said Lindsay softly. "And I'm finally a part of it, too."

Emotion surged in her. Her mouth worked as she struggled to hold it back, but her eyes welled and her face suddenly felt thick and hot. She shuffled the papers on the table, squaring the stack, fighting back the tears, but they still came. She leaned forward, both hands on the conference table, staring down at the stack of contract papers, at the torn sheet, trying to hide her face from the others.

She felt Maggie's hand on hers, warm and dry, soft and comforting.

A mother's touch.

Lindsay squeezed Maggie's hand, held tight for a long second, took a deep breath and let it out slowly.

"I've learned more about my father in the last eight months than I had in twenty-six years," she said, her voice shaking. "I owe it to him to keep his company alive." She looked at John. "But I owe it to myself, too." She stood tall, and a feeling of peace swept over her. "I want to know my father," she said, "and I'll never leave my family again."

Lindsay didn't know what kind of response she had expected. Yelling, threats of litigation, maybe attempts to sweeten the deal or make some other kinds of concessions to convince her to sign. Thomas looked like he wanted to do all of those things, especially the yelling.

But, to his credit, John just stood, buttoned his suit coat, and turned to shake Mac's hand.

Thomas seemed startled by his father's reaction. He stood and gathered his things quickly. He gave Lindsay a perfunctory handshake and rushed into the hallway, looking like a spoiled teenager who didn't get his way.

Amelia came behind him, slinging her leather bag over her shoulder. "Please excuse my brother," she said. "This deal was his idea. His first big acquisition target. He's upset that it isn't going through." She glanced at her father, shaking Maggie's hand behind her. "I appreciate what you said about your father."

Lindsay glanced at John, then looked back into Amelia's eyes. "I don't know him at all, obviously, but your father seems like a good man."

Amelia sighed. "I don't know him at all, either. But, maybe I'll try to get to know him. While I can."

"I have a feeling he'd like that." Lindsay squeezed Amelia's hand.

Amelia nodded. "Good luck, Ms. Rhodes. And..." Her smile wrinkled the corners of her eyes. "Thanks for putting my brother in his place. He could use a little more disappointment in his life."

Lindsay laughed. "They say it builds character."

"Yeah, well, he's starting from ground zero." Amelia smiled again and walked out of the room.

John approached Lindsay, shook her hand, a warm, professional handshake.

"Congratulations, Ms. Rhodes, on your recent success," he said, "and on this decision. Not an easy one to make, I'm sure."

Lindsay shrugged. "I guess it's true what they say. You can't put a price on family."

"Hmm," said John. "You know, I met your father." Lindsay's eyebrows shot up. "Once or twice, at functions. I wouldn't say I knew him. Not in any meaningful way. But anyone who met him could see, instantly, what kind of man he was."

"And what kind was that?"

"Brilliant. Incisive. Driven." John's eyes grew distant, a slight smile on his lips. "But different from the rest of us. Like he knew something we didn't. Some grand inside joke."

Lindsay shook her head, confused.

"That was what I felt at the time. But, looking back on it now, I think your father just viewed the world in a different way. The rest of us all scrapping around, trying to get rich or powerful or whatever it might be." He looked at Lindsay. "I think your father knew that, while those things were useful, there were other treasures in life that were far more important." He tilted his head, giving Lindsay an appraising look. "I see the same qualities in you." He dipped his chin, held her gaze. "I think you truly are your father's daughter."

Lindsay lost her professional demeanor. Tears flooded

forward again. A tingling started at the tip of her nose, spread backward over her face. She could feel the hot sting in her eyes.

"Thank you, Mr. Everbright," she whispered.

A look came over his face.

A parental look.

A fatherly concern.

He put one hand on each of Lindsay's shoulders, held them lightly but firmly.

"Please," he said, "call me John."

Lindsay smiled and nodded, wiping away a tear that had spilled onto her cheek.

"Good luck to you, Ms. Rhodes."

"Lindsay," she whispered.

"Good luck, Lindsay," John said softly. "We'll all be cheering for you."

33

Everyone moved into the hallway, Mac, Maggie, Lindsay, and the Everbrights.

Maggie left to show the Everbrights to the front door. Lindsay turned to Mac, expecting him to be smiling, exultant, maybe even grateful.

Instead, she saw his back, walking away down the hallway.

No questions. No thank you. Not even a handshake.

What the hell was his problem?

Lindsay had just given him exactly what he wanted. Hart Racing was still his. His family was intact.

What more did he want?

Did he want Lindsay to sell her share to him, too? He could fuck himself if that's what he wanted.

Lindsay didn't know what his problem was, but she'd had enough of the mystery.

"Hey, Mac," she yelled.

He didn't turn.

"Mac!"

At the end of the hallway, he pushed through the double-doors into his garage.

Lindsay stomped after him, her shoulder bag banging

against her hip, the heels of her boots clacking against the slate tile floors like the smack of a teacher's ruler or the ticking of a grandfather clock.

How dare he walk away without even a word after what she'd just done. She didn't expect him to fall all over her in gratitude, but she deserved at least some acknowledgement. Not everyone would turn down five billion pounds.

She threw open the double doors. They banged against the walls with a loud smack.

"Goddamn it, Mac," she shouted, "what the hell is your problem?"

"Excuse me?"

A very tall, very slender black woman stood in the center of the garage. She wore white sneakers, torn skinny jeans, and a baggy blue sweater slung low over one shoulder. Her shoulder-length hair was dyed blonde. It flipped to one side of her face as she put her hands on her hips, staring at Lindsay with fire in her dark eyes, like Lindsay had just kicked her dog.

"I don't have a problem," said the woman, "but you will if you talk to me that way again."

Sam came up behind the woman, dressed in her blue-and-purple Hart Racing jumpsuit, wiping some kind of a wrench on a stained shop rag.

"Lindsay," said Sam, "meet Mackensie Thomas." She slid her arm around the woman's waist and pulled her close. "My fiancé."

Lindsay startled like she'd just hit her forehead on an invisible brick wall. She nearly fell backward from her surprise.

"Your... what?"

Sam frowned. "My fiancé." Her eyes shot wide and her mouth fell open. "Oh, shit. You did get a wedding invitation, didn't you? I swear your name was on the list."

Lindsay couldn't speak for a moment. Her mouth was open, but all that came out were little scraping noises.

Her brain wasn't doing much better.

Sam's fiancé wasn't Mac?

It was this Mackensie person?

Mackensie.

Mac.

The gears in her brain slowly started to grind.

And Mackensie was a woman?

Sam was a lesbian?

The gears moved a bit faster.

The power of speech came back online.

"No, I..." Lindsay reached into her bag and pulled out the wedding invitation Marina had shoved in there that morning.

Marina.

Gears moving faster.

Marina had been trying to tell her.

Lindsay ripped open the invitation.

"Well, I'm glad to see you were so excited to be invited," said the woman, Mackensie.

Lindsay pulled out the invite.

A beautifully calligraphed card on heavy card stock. "Happy to announce" etc., etc., "cordially invited" etc., etc., "wedding of..."

"Samantha Jane Callin and Mackensie Philhomena Thomas," Lindsay murmured.

The gears got stuck again.

"Philhom—"

"Do not say a fucking word about my middle name," said Mackensie, holding up one very long, very stern finger.

Lindsay clamped her mouth shut.

The gears turned once more.

Finally, her mind wrapped itself around this new information.

Mac wasn't getting married.

Sam was marrying this woman. Mackensie.

"I... I'm sorry, Mackensie," stammered Lindsay.

"Everyone calls her Max," said Sam.

"You can call me Mackensie, I think."

"I'm sorry, M... Mackensie," said Lindsay. "I didn't mean to seem rude. I wasn't speaking to you when I came in."

"Damn right you weren't."

Sam laughed.

"Okay, Max," she said. "You've already torn Lindsay's head off. You don't need to kick it across the room."

"Lindsay?" said Mackensie. "You're Lindsay Rhodes? The savior of Hart Racing?" She looked at Sam. "The one that Mac is so—"

"Yes, that's the one," interrupted Sam.

"Ohhh." Mackensie folded her arms across her chest and nodded knowingly at Lindsay. "Okay, you can call me Max."

"Um... okay," said Lindsay.

She didn't know quite what to say at that point. Her head was still reeling. She looked around the garage. Gerald was in the back, head inside the engine of a car.

"Um... congratulations on your—"

"Mac went that way," said Sam, gesturing with the wrench toward the back door.

"Thank you," said Lindsay with a sigh of relief. She hustled toward the back of the garage. "Nice to meet you, Max," she called over her shoulder.

"Don't let him give you any bullshit," said Max. "That man's full of it."

Lindsay turned, walking backwards, and grinned at her.

Lindsay suddenly knew that she and Max would get along just fine.

Lindsay burst out the back door of the building into the bright sunlight. She jogged to the top of the small rise between the main building and the production centre, hoping to see Mac walking down the pathway.

There was no one in sight.

Maybe she'd missed him. Maybe he'd been walking fast and had gone inside while she was talking to Sam and Max.

She heard the squeal of tires from the parking lot to her left, ran to the side to get a look and saw Mac's Mercedes racing down the row of cars toward the exit.

Son of a bitch.

Lindsay gritted her teeth.

She wasn't going to let him get away that easy.

She tucked her bag under her arm and raced to her Jaguar, boots clomping on the sidewalk. She threw her bag into the passenger seat and started the engine. It roared as she darted back in reverse, then gunned the engine out of the parking lot, tires squealing.

She caught up to Mac as he was pulling out of the Hart Racing complex onto the main road. Just when she got close, his Mercedes shot forward with a burst of speed.

Fucking asshole.

That's how he was going to play this? Like a fucking teenager making his getaway? Like he'd just stolen the Maybach and the owner had caught up to him from behind?

Fuck that.

Lindsay downshifted and stomped on the accelerator.

If any police officers had happened to be sitting on the side of the road over the next five minutes, they would have gotten two juicy speeding tickets for their trouble.

Lindsay and Mac weaved and careened down the roads at over one hundred miles per hour. Lindsay wasn't even conscious of it until later, but she drove like she was a Formula One driver, not a team owner. She and Mac were bumper to bumper down the straights, slamming on their brakes, tires squealing as they ran stop signs and fishtailed around tight corners, finally coming to a jerking stop in Mac's driveway just a few short minutes later.

They both leapt from their cars at the same moment. But even after that chase, Mac didn't come after Lindsay. Didn't even turn to look at her. He just stomped to his front door.

"Mac!"

Lindsay stomped after him.

"Hey, asshole!"

Mac stopped before the three steps up to the front porch, wheeled around.

"What the fuck were you thinking?" he said, pointing back toward the road. "You could have killed us both, driving like a fucking maniac."

He turned and stomped up the steps.

"You're one to talk," shouted Lindsay. "I was following you. You were the one running away. Like you always do. Like a fucking asshole."

Mac was on the porch, pulling his keys from his pocket. He spun and stomped back down the steps.

"I'm running away? *I'm* running away? That's rich coming from you."

He turned and stomped up the steps again.

"What the fuck is that supposed to mean?"

"You know what that means," said Mac over his shoulder while he pulled his keys from his pocket and searched through them.

Lindsay strode to the bottom of the stairs and stood with her arms at her sides, hands alternately forming and releasing fists.

"No, please, enlighten me. You're the great teacher, after all."

Mac spun and stepped to the edge of the porch, now towering over Lindsay, looking down at her.

He stabbed the air with his finger with each statement. "I try to involve you in the business, and you go off on your own. I try to bring you on the road, and you stay behind." He stabbed in the air toward the Jag. "Hell, I even teach you how to drive, and then you drive away from me."

Lindsay had never seen such fire in Mac's brilliant blue eyes.

"You're constantly running, Lindsay, running from anything that threatens your precious control over everything. You're a fucking control freak."

"I'm a control freak?"

"Yes, you are."

Lindsay wanted to deny it, wanted desperately to throw it back in Mac's face, to show evidence to the contrary.

But she couldn't. He was right. She was a control freak. Or had been. She knew that now. She'd come to see that all too clearly over the last few months.

But Mac wasn't perfect, either.

"Well, that may be—" she said.

"It is."

"—but at least I'm not afraid to talk about my feelings—"

"What the fuck is that supposed to mean?"

"—like some scared little boy."

"I'm not afraid—"

"You want me to travel with you." Lindsay stepped onto the first step leading to the porch. "But say it's all about business."

"It was."

"Then you crawl up my ass because I'm emailing Marcus."

"That... was a misunderstanding."

"And say it's just to protect me."

"I didn't want him to hurt you."

Lindsay climbed to the second step.

"You practically stalk me during the whole fucking formal event, threatening me with that death stare of yours."

"Okay, I may have acted... Wait. Death stare? What death stare?"

Mac took a step back, away from the edge of the porch.

Lindsay climbed to the third step.

"Then you fucking ignore me for weeks, even when I'm standing right next to you."

Mac waved his hands toward her dismissively, shook his head. "I don't know what you're talking about." He turned back to the front door, fiddling with his keys in the lock.

Lindsay took the last step onto the porch, now on even footing with Mac.

"And then, at the very end..."

She stepped toward Mac.

"...when there's five billion pounds on the table—five *billion*, with a B—and I turn it down..."

She stepped closer.

"...rip the offer to shreds and throw it into the bin, even then..."

One final step. Mac's back was still toward her as the lock on the door slid open, but she was close enough now to reach out and touch his shoulder.

"...even when I tell you, *show* you, how much I've come to love this company, to love..."

Her voice hitched.

Hot tears again welled in her eyes.

Goddamn it. Not now.

Mac stopped, hand on the door handle, his head turned toward his shoulder, looking down at the porch.

Lindsay's cheeks flushed. Her nose tingled.

Not now.

Lindsay took a deep breath, forced her emotions to work with her, not against her. She poured that emotion into her breath, into her voice, into what she was saying.

"...how much I've come to love the people here," she said, her voice quiet, but even and sure.

Mac turned where he stood, his back against the front door.

Lindsay's entire body lit up when she looked into his eyes, when a wave of air from his turning washed his scent over her.

Blue and purple fireworks in her mind.

Spice and musk and the scent of passion.

The heat coming off of him would melt any furnace.

And the electricity, the lightning sparking between them, running through Lindsay's entire body, would power a city the size of London for a decade.

It practically lifted Lindsay off of her feet, pulled her toward him like a magnet.

Without even being aware that she was moving, she found herself just inches from him.

"What people?" said Mac, his voice husky and ragged. The sound tore something free in Lindsay, like a gate torn off its hinges by a great, powerful beast.

"What?" said Lindsay, moving even closer. The only thing separating them now was a thin layer of air, air thrumming with electric heat.

"What people do you love?" asked Mac, his breath hot against Lindsay's cheek, his voice a low, thready growl. In it, Lindsay could hear need, could hear pain, could hear hope.

"I..." Her voice barely a whisper.

The thin air between them became superheated, burning Lindsay's skin, searing it with a heat that she never wanted to cool.

"I love..." Her voice barely a breath.

She held her hands hovering over his chest, hands already shaped to the contour of his muscles. Anticipating their touch.

Craving it.

Aching for it.

"I love..." Her voice barely a thought.

She laid her hands on his chest, and the feeling that swept through her defied description.

It lifted her, shot her into the sun, melted her body into his, his body into hers.

She heard herself cry out, but from a distance, a distant gasp from a physical body that no longer had any meaning, any weight in this weightless world of souls intertwined.

His eyes were wide, startled. She fell into the clear blue of those eyes, like falling into the sky.

"...you."

And then his lips were on hers, hot and eager and searching. Lindsay pressed forward, backing Mac against the front door, grinding her hips into his, feeling his swell against her center.

She burst with a fire beyond heat, beyond light. An all-consuming flame that pulled their bodies even closer.

His arms were around her, his biceps hard against her sides. His hands under her jacket, his fingers roaming up and down the valley of her spine, stiff and pressing against her muslin shirt.

Her mouth devouring his, she tugged his shirt up out of his pants, fumbled hastily with the buttons, wishing she could rip them open, hear the buttons bouncing on the wood slats of the porch.

Finally, the shirt was open, his chest bare. Lindsay slid her hands along Mac's steaming sides. He gasped at her touch, arched into it, and Lindsay felt the heat in her core become a flush.

He was hot as a sun. His skin burned under her palms like a steaming bath, the burn sharp, exquisite. She ran her hands over the hard ridges of his stomach, slid them up to his chest, then around his sides to his back, finding the furrow there and slipping her fingers inside, running them up to the top of his spine, then slowly back down, down, tugging him harder and harder against her, pulling his hips against her own.

He moaned softly, and his own hands untied her blouse at the front and slid beneath the fabric. The touch of his hands against her bare skin sent sparks shooting through her entire body, like his fingertips were electric leads, each one sending a jolt of pleasure coursing through her.

When his hands roamed lower, slid over the curve of her ass and pulled it tight against him, against his bulge, now massive, swollen, and rock-hard, the flush in Lindsay's core became a flood.

She wanted him.

Needed him.

Right then.

Right there.

Anywhere.

Everywhere.

She pushed forward with a primal strength, unaware, instinctive. She was thinking of nothing but having him inside of her.

She pushed forward like she could make their clothes tear away if she pressed hard enough.

She pushed him back against the door. His ass pressed against the door handle. It bent down and the door swung inward. They tumbled onto the slate tile floor inside, Lindsay landing on top of Mac with a force that slammed their bodies together in all the right ways.

Lindsay straddled him, pressed her hands on his bare chest and pushed herself up. She took off her blazer and threw it to the side. Pulled her blouse off, too.

Mac slid backwards along the floor, Lindsay riding him along the tile far enough that Mac could kick the front door shut behind them.

Lindsay leaned forward, pressing her body against him, feeling the heat of his bare chest against her skin. She kissed him, gently, slowly. Nibbled his lower lip softly, then one quick sharp bite that made Mac gasp and buck his hips.

Lindsay moaned at the motion.

She kissed his neck, then worked her way down. Worked her lips into the swale of his clavicle, down over the rise of his pecs.

She licked and sucked one nipple, then gave it a soft nip that earned her another moan, another thrust of his hips against her.

Down she moved, running the tip of her tongue down the center line of his abdomen, circling his bellybutton. She sat up, tugged loose his belt and slid it from his pants.

Mac rose up on his elbows, his deep blue eyes burning, lids hooded with a desire that she could feel like a hand pulling her down to him.

She could not resist him.

She didn't want to.

She unzipped and tugged down his pants, and gasped out loud at what greeted her.

One long, engorged vein curled lazily along the throbbing length of his board-stiff shaft. She could feel its heat even before she bent to take him between her lips. His hips rose as she did, thrusting himself into her mouth, his moans ragged and wild, losing control.

She slid her hands under his bare ass as he bucked, felt his ass cheeks tighten with each thrust.

His moans became louder, echoing through the living room, until finally Mac lifted her. With his impossibly strong arms he lifted her in one swift motion and flipped them both around, laying Lindsay on her back, Mac now straddling her.

The look in Mac's eyes was feral, primal. Something deep within Lindsay responded, just as primal, just as fierce.

He took his time.

Slowly, maddeningly, Mac removed what remained of Lindsay's clothing piece by tantalizing piece, exploring each newly exposed area thoroughly with his lips and his tongue.

The cool tile against Lindsay's skin only made the heat rising within her even more intense.

Mac worked his way from her bra, licking and nipping her erect and aching nipples, to her pants, sliding them slowly down, lightly kissing, licking, caressing first her thighs, then her calves, her feet.

Then he slid his hands slowly, softly up along the length of her legs, along the soft skin on the insides of her thighs, up to her panties.

He slipped them off inch by inch.

His kisses were harder, first following her panties down her legs, then coming back up again, ever so slowly up again toward the apex of her thighs, kissing and licking and nipping until Lindsay was lifting her hips, trying to push them, will them, down to his lips.

Just when he was nearly there, his breath hot on the hollow where her leg joined her abdomen, when her anticipation of release was driving her mad, her need for his mouth on her center was more than she could bear, he flipped her onto her stomach and began again.

He slid his fingers and his mouth lightly, softly over her back, the back of her legs, his touch against her hyper-sensitized skin driving her insane.

Lindsay had lost control long ago. Now she nearly lost her mind altogether.

One cheek rested against the hard, cold tile. Held between the heat of his mouth on her back and the cold bite of the tile on her cheek, her nipples, her stomach, her thighs, her body writhed like a snake with every touch of his rough hands, of his soft lips.

When his fingers and his mouth worked their way down to kiss and caress the cheeks of her ass, she raised her hips against him, pushing toward him, urging him toward her core.

He obliged, running one hand down over her ass cheek and up her inner thigh. Lindsay cried out as his fingers scooped her wetness and spread it over her clitoris. He stayed there, teasing her with feathery strokes and circles.

Lindsay lifted her ass even higher, pushing farther back

toward him. Mac responded with firmer strokes, his other hand caressing and squeezing her ass cheeks.

His strokes became faster, his circles tighter, centered on her clitoris. Lindsay rose up on all fours, thrusting her ass back and forth, grinding herself against Mac's hand. He held it in place, let Lindsay control the speed, the force, the movement. She looked back over her shoulder and saw him watching, saw the raw desire thick in his eyes and moaned at the sight, her heat rising.

She closed her eyes and let herself go, let herself fall into the feeling growing low within her. She felt the first tightening thread of release, tugged on it, pulled it closer. She moved her hips back and forth against Mac's fingers, now slick with her pleasure, moved her hips side to side, pressing down against his hand. Slow, tantalizing slow at first, then faster, harder, until she was grinding, grinding, the heat rising, that thread pulling tighter, tighter, tighter, bringing her release closer, until with a cry that echoed long and loud through the room, she shattered, a million pieces of her exploding in white bursts of glittering glass, shattering in exquisite slow motion, then slowly drifting down, making soft, gentle tinkling sounds as they landed on the tile around her.

Lindsay stayed there on all fours, her body spent, her mind slowly reforming. She felt Mac's hands on her hips, felt him rise up behind her, felt the burning tip of his probing shaft along her wetness from behind.

"No," she said.

She stood and turned to him, biting her lower lip.

With Mac on his knees, Lindsay standing before him, his head came up to her stomach.

That put his mouth in just the right spot.

It wasn't what Lindsay had had in mind, but when Mac ran his tongue along her swollen, throbbing core, his breath hot against her, when the need that had just been satiated instantly flared to life again, she didn't object.

He worked his fingers against her clit while his tongue explored her, licked and kissed and sucked her, then slid inside her. Head rolling back against her neck, hands in Mac's thick, dark hair, Lindsay arched up onto her tiptoes, bent her legs wide, and rode him, fucked his searching tongue, grinding down on it, on his face, pulling his tongue deeper and deeper inside her.

The feeling was unlike any she'd ever felt. After the release a moment ago, this felt like a completely new experience. Where that had been soft and slow, this came up on her fast and hard. She lost all awareness of her body, of her mind, of space or time. She felt only his tongue, his hands, his hot breath, and her center, the intensity rising, the pressure growing, rushing, racing.

Then she broke open. She heard her own ragged screams like they were from someone else, distant behind the white light that filled her eyes, the waves of pleasure that swept her from head to toe and back, over and over again.

She held Mac's head against her stomach while her body came back to Earth. She lowered down from her tiptoes, her toes stiff, her legs quivering. Slowly, the world around her returned. Her feet cool against the tile. Mac's soft hair under her fingers. His face warm, his beard rough against her belly.

She took his face in both hands, turned it up toward hers, bent down and kissed him, slow and long, thrusting her tongue deep into his mouth, taking her time, exploring him, tasting him. Then, she pushed him onto his back, first with her hand, then, gently, with her foot until she towered above him, one foot on his chest, like a hunter above her conquest.

Mac lay on the ground, his eyes devouring Lindsay's naked body as she slowly moved to straddle him, to stand above his shaft, rising tall and stiff into the air.

Her eyes never left his as she slowly, slowly lowered herself down, down, until she felt his swollen, burning tip against her wetness, saw Mac close his eyes, heard a soft moan slip past his full lips. He bucked his hips up toward her, but she rose with him, keeping his tip just barely against her core. She rocked her hips back and forth, painting him with her wetness, feeling his tip grow slick and smooth, hearing his moans and watching his face work with the exquisite pain of pleasure.

He opened his eyes again, hooded with longing. He slicked his lips with his tongue, a movement that sent a spear of need through Lindsay. She wanted him inside her, wanted all of him inside her.

From the pleading in his eyes, the way he clenched his jaw, released it with a moan when she rocked her hips, then clenched them again, she could see that he wanted it, too.

So Lindsay moved even slower.

Rocked her hips back.

And forth.

Smoothing his tip, kissing it with her sex.

Then dipping down, quickly down, just an inch, and just as quickly back up.

They both gasped.

Mac clenched his stomach, pulling his head and shoulders up off the ground, eyes wide.

They both looked at each other for a long moment, panting.

Then he relaxed, lay back down, and Lindsay began again.

Rocking back.

And forth.

Back.

And forth.

Then dipping down, and quickly back up.

Lindsay bit her lip hard to keep from screaming. Mac moaned loudly, his head rolling.

She dipped down again.

Slower.

Farther, feeling the contours of his shaft and his tip inside her.

And back up.

Then again.

Then again.

Finally, with her hands on his stomach, his skin burning against her palms, his muscles alive beneath her touch, she took him inside her.

Slowly.

Ever so slowly.

She locked her eyes on his.

Inch by inch.

Their breathing quickened.

She felt her own chest heaving, felt his doing the same beneath her hands. Felt each of his panting breaths inside of her.

Inch by inch.

Their heads rolled back, their eyes clouded as desire and need and pleasure rushed in.

Slowly, slowly, inch by incredible, never-ending inch, she took him inside of her until, when she thought she would break in two—from him or from pleasure—she had all of him, all of him inside her, his hips tight beneath her straddled knees, his shaft deep and hot and rock-hard within her.

And she began to move.

Rocking her hips back and forth, slowly, then faster. Faster.

Then lifting her hips as she rocked, riding up and down his shaft.

His strong, rough hands scraped down over her breasts, her stomach, around to her back. They gripped her hips, lifted her along his length, following and helping her movements. His hips bucked and writhed beneath her.

Each movement sent bolts of pleasure throughout Lindsay's

body. Where her last two orgasms had been explosions of light and heat, this felt like tectonic motion, like the earth itself was shifting beneath her.

Lindsay stopped, leaned forward, over his chest. Her breasts pressed against his chest, her elbows rested on the floor above his shoulders. She nestled her clitoris tight against the base of his shaft, pressed against the hard shelf of his pelvic bone. His hands slid down to cup her ass.

And they moved.

They moved together, their eyes locked. Two bodies in perfect rhythm, the impossible length of him moving inside her, her swollen clitoris grinding exquisitely against him.

They moved faster, one body connected. They kissed, deep and hard and wet.

They moved faster, two souls entwined, their moans the backdrop to the white light that surrounded them, faded the world to a gauzy dream.

Faster.

One soul.

Their bodies gone.

The world gone.

The world nothing but the indescribable ecstasy they felt, rising, white-hot and all-encompassing.

It lifted them, pulled them together.

Faster, faster.

Then a flash of heat and bright light, and everything fell away.

No sound.

No body.

No mind.

No world.

Only pure bliss.

If heaven existed, it was surely a hell compared to this feeling.

Lindsay felt like she were floating in a warm, white space. She could sense Mac with her, entwined with her.

No fear. No anxiety. No pain. No anger. No worry.

Nothing existed in that place but unadulterated love.

Slowly, slowly, that place faded around her.

Faded to darkness.

She heard cries, screams, growing louder, realized it was her voice, and Mac's voice, screaming.

She felt waves of intense pleasure, like she'd never felt before, rocking her body, washing over and through her again and again, her body shaking with the intensity.

She felt Mac's body inside her, beneath her, bucking and quivering.

The dark became grey, then white.

Then she opened her eyes.

Lindsay lay against Mac's chest, both of them slick with sweat, their chests heaving against one another.

She rolled off of him, felt a pang of pleasure and regret as he slid out of her. She lay with her sweaty back against the cool tile, staring up at the ceiling, feeling Mac's body move with his ragged breaths, listening to the sound of her pounding heart gradually slow in her ears.

After a few minutes, they both rolled onto their sides, facing each other, staring into each other's eyes. Mac pushed a strand of hair behind her ear.

Lindsay could not think of words to say to him, could not translate into words the enormity of what she felt in that moment. All she could do was try to convey that feeling through her eyes, through her touch as she ran her fingers lightly along his arm.

She sensed him, sensed his feelings somehow through her touch, through his gaze, sensed that they had shared that incredible experience, that it had been as intense and other-worldly for him as it had been for her.

She sensed something else, something against her leg.

Eyes locked on his, she ran her fingers lightly down his arm, over his hand, onto his thigh.

Then down between his legs.

A slight smile twisted the corners of Mac's mouth.

And Lindsay knew they were going to share that incredible experience again.

And again.

And again.

34

SAM AND MAX'S wedding was held outside behind Hart Racing's main building. The lake was calm, ruffled only occasionally by a breeze sweeping inland from off the sea. The sky was blue, dotted with clouds like cotton balls. The grass still held its green color, remarkable for this late in the season. Between the blue of the lake and the sky, the white of the clouds, the green of the grass, and the unseasonable warmth of the December sun, the setting was idyllic.

Rows of white wooden folding chairs for the guests were bisected by a wide aisle that led to a white wooden archway beside the lake. Embracing the wedding altar, the archway was festooned in lavender and hothouse bluebells, the vibrant purple and blue colors befitting the livery of the Hart Racing team. The occasional cool breeze brought the sweet intermingled scent of the flowers wafting over the congregated guests.

They said their vows just before noon beneath a crisp blue sky. The clouds and the sun were reflected in the still water of the lake and the mirrored glass of the building, creating an effect of infinite reflection that brought to Lindsay an image of Sam and Max moving backward and forward throughout time, forever. As if they had always been and always would be together.

A beautiful metaphor for their union, and a beautiful backdrop for the ceremony.

Both brides were radiant in their wedding dresses. Max wore a white faille gown with a simple, elegant silhouette that left her shoulders bare and hugged her gorgeous curves down to her knees, then flared to a cone like an upside-down calla lily in bloom. Her blonde hair was swept up off of her long neck and tied in an elegant knot, interwoven with blue and purple flowers.

Sam's gown curled down around her neck like a halter top, baring her beautiful, muscular arms and shoulders, curving down to a tight damask bodice, then flaring from there to the floor in a brilliant white satin, underlaid with an intricate embroidered design, ending in a short, flared train. Her dark dreadlocks hung down in splayed glory, a bold addition to the elegance both of Sam's dress and her regal bearing as she walked down the aisle, Mac on her arm.

"Not to give me away," Sam said at the reception after, a defiant flare in her eye. "I'm no man's to give."

Lindsay, Mac, Sam, and Max stood in a small circle beside a tall table set into the grass on the lawn by the lake, champagne flutes in their hands. The folding chairs and wedding altar had been removed, replaced by at least two dozen similar tables arrayed around them. The wedding arch, with its white wood and blue and purple flowers, remained by the lake, like a gateway to hope and happiness.

Sam and Max had invited every employee of Hart Racing, plus some other friends and family, and everyone was enjoying the sunshine, the unexpectedly pleasant temperature, and the endless procession of delicious food and drink.

"I would never give you away, even if I could," said Mac to Sam.

"Aw," Sam cooed. She gave him a loving look, squeezed his arm in hers. "That's so misogynistic and sweet."

Lindsay laughed into her champagne while Mac rolled his eyes.

"Mac is my best friend in the whole world," Sam said. "I asked him to walk me down the aisle just to support me."

Mac put his arm around her, held her tightly, kissed her forehead.

"Whenever you need me," he said softly.

"You're a lucky woman, Lindsay Rhodes," said Max, leaning into her and clinking Lindsay's glass with hers.

"I'm the lucky one, Max," said Mac.

"I think you're both lucky just to be standing," said Marina as she, Raj, and Yue walked up to the group.

All three were dressed beautifully, Raj in a tailored blue suit, Marina and Yue in lovely, simple dresses.

Raj and Marina carried champagne flutes. Yue was stuffing a tuna tartar cone into her mouth, three others held in her fist.

"Every time we came to the front door of Mac's house for the last two weeks," said Marina, "just to make sure you all were alive, we heard nothing but screaming."

"Sounded like you were being slaughtered by an axe murderer," said Yue around a mouthful of tuna.

Lindsay felt her cheeks flush red. She looked across at Mac, who was trying to stifle his laughter.

"Wait. You went to check on them," said Max, "thought they were being murdered in the house, and then what? You just left?"

"Hey, they were already gone," said Raj. "No sense in the rest of us going down with them."

Marina jabbed Raj with her elbow.

"Really, Raj?" she said. "Going down?'"

Everyone groaned.

"That was unintentional, I admit," said Raj. "But I can't stop the humor, babe. It just flows from me. Like water."

"More like verbal diarrhea," said Yue.

"Wow," said Sam. "You three show up and suddenly it's nothing but axe murderers and diarrhea."

"I told you we should have been more careful with our guest list," said Max.

"Too bad, Maxine," said Marina. Max gave her a dirty stare at the name. "We're part of the family now."

"I thought I had veto power," said Max, giving Sam a sharp look. "You said marriage would grant me veto power over the family."

Sam shrugged, tossed back the last of her champagne, set the empty glass on the table, and hooked her arm inside her bride's.

"It's complicated, babe," she said, pulling Max away and toward the other guests waiting for a few moments of their time. "Let's talk about it tonight."

"In bed?"

"Yeah, in bed."

"I wasn't planning on doing much talking in bed tonight."

Sam grinned over her shoulder at Lindsay and the others.

"I think we're going to have a long and happy marriage," she said to Max.

"I think so, too," whispered Lindsay to herself, grinning as they walked away.

The five of them just stood there for a long moment, watching the newlyweds walk over the grass, their wedding gowns flowing behind them like two angels about to rise into the blue sky and take flight.

"To Sam and Max," said Raj, lifting his glass.

"To Sam and Max," echoed the others, lifting their own glasses. Or, in Yue's case, a tuna tartar cone.

"And to the new CEO and CTO of Datasure, Incorporated," said Mac, lifting his glass toward Marina and Raj.

"Don't forget board members," said Marina.

"I hear the chair of the board is a real piece of work," said Raj, grinning at Lindsay.

"Just don't fuck up my company," Lindsay grinned back, "and we'll be just fine."

"Yue," said Raj, "don't forget what we talked about. I still need someone to manage our data stack. I'll make it worth your while."

"Raj," said Lindsay, "are you really going to poach my VP of data engineering while I'm standing right here?"

"It's a dog-eat-dog world, Linds," Raj said. "If you ain't got teeth, git out the kennel."

"Is that how you treat your only client?" said Mac. "Lindsay, maybe we should reconsider our data analysis vendor."

"Funny you should mention that, Mac," said Marina. "Hart Racing is a pretty solid first client, and," she shot Raj a mean stare, "they're gonna stay that way, but I want to shop the UI around, see if the other race teams would buy in."

"I can get you their contact info," nodded Mac. "After what we did this season, I'm sure they'll be interested." He twisted his mouth in a devious smile. "You can set your price to be anything you want." He lifted his glass. "Set it high."

"To price gouging our Formula One competitors," said Raj.

They all laughed and drank to that.

As the champagne flowed into her, Lindsay felt a peace follow it, settling over her like a warm shawl. The looked at the bright sun glittering off the lake and the windows of the building.

The building her father had built to house the company that had become Lindsay's life.

The company that had become her family.

She heard laughter, saw Sam and Max with Maggie and

her husband at a table nearby, throwing their heads back and laughing at some comment or other. She saw Danny and what must have been his wife, Sarah, at another table, talking with a group. Others were milling about in groups, talking and laughing, taking pictures under the wedding arch or by the main building. Kids ranging from toddlers to teenagers played in the grass or explored in the trees or just hung out by the lake.

Peace.

Joy.

And family.

"When are you two gonna make it official?" asked Raj, waggling his eyebrows at Mac and Lindsay.

Lindsay looked at Mac. His eyes flashed, but he just looked back at her, his eyebrows raised in question.

She felt herself flush deep within her. She could barely look at that man without feeling that way.

She wondered if that feeling would ever change.

She hoped not.

She smiled coyly back at Mac, sipping from her champagne.

"What about you?" said Lindsay back to Raj, ignoring his question. "You gonna make an honest woman out of Marina?"

"Are you kidding me?" said Marina. "If anyone's proposing here, it's gonna be me."

"Marina Alana del Carmen," said Raj. "Did you just ask me to marry you?"

"You wish," said Marina, then pulled Raj into a hug. Her head only came up to his chest, but her hug was strong. "But you just keep doing what you're doing, and we'll see."

"Really? What am I doing?"

"You just keep being you, honey."

"Well, hell," Raj grinned up at Lindsay and Mac. "That's my specialty."

He bent down and gave Marina a deep, passionate kiss.

"I think I'm gonna be sick," said Yue, rolling her eyes. "I'm gonna get something to eat."

She walked away toward the buffet tables in the distance, waving back at Lindsay and Mac.

Raj pulled Marina off of her feet in a bear hug. She squealed and threw her arms around his neck.

"Wait a minute, Yue," said Raj, running after her with Marina in his arms. "You can eat some of this." He gave Marina a wet, smacking kiss. "Or how about this?" Another kiss. His voice grew fainter in the distance as he chased after Yue. "Or maybe this?" Another kiss. "That one's delicious. I might have two of those." Another kiss.

And then they were gone, out of earshot.

Leaving Lindsay alone with Mac.

They just looked at each other, a long moment of silence, then couldn't restrain their laughter any longer.

When they finally settled down, Lindsay nestled her head against Mac's shoulder, his arm around her back. They stood like that, looking out over the crowd.

Marina. Raj. Yue.

Maggie.

Sam and Max.

Danny and his family.

All the others, people Lindsay was still getting to know. People she saw in the hallways and the offices and the conference rooms and the garages. People she saw in the pits and on the track.

So many good people. So many friends.

This was her family now.

Her father's family.

His dying gift to her.

And what a priceless gift it was.

The gift of purpose.

The gift of friendship.

She turned, took Mac's face in her hands, stared deep into those brilliant blue eyes.

The gift of love.

She kissed Mac, softly at first, then deeper. He pulled her into his embrace and the world fell away.

Nothing existed in that moment but Lindsay and Mac.

And their love.

A gift Lindsay would treasure forever.

ACKNOWLEDGMENTS

Great thanks to Kim for her help in editing this novel. The collective groans of a thousand readers have been averted by your keen eyes.

As always, my love and thanks to Holly. Without your support, my love, none of this would be possible.

ABOUT THE AUTHOR

Kevin Robert Aldrich lives in California and is the author of several romance novels:

If you love heart-pounding romantic suspense, you'll love Bare Trap and Flames of Freedom.

If you like vampires, witches, and forbidden love, get a copy of Spellbound now.

And if you love powerful contemporary romance, try Racing Hearts today.

MORE FROM THE AUTHOR

To learn more about Kevin Robert Aldrich and stay up-to-date with all of his stories and novels, please visit his website:

www.kevinrobertaldrich.com

To be automatically notified of every new release, join the Kevin Robert Aldrich mailing list at the website above.